A NOTE ON THE AUTHOR

Wendela Lumley, the daughter of a Chilean descended
from a long line of South American artists and writers,
and a Canadian International concert pianist and
academic, was born in London and educated in
England. She read Law at King's College, London, and
went on to study Fine and Decorative Arts at the V&A.
After meeting her English husband, they lived for
many years in Chile with their five children. From
1999 she worked in shantytowns helping women
develop themselves and their communities until her
departure in 2004, when the family returned to
England and settled near Newbury in Berkshire.

For Sascha

VERMILION SKIES

with love

WENDELA LUMLEY

Wendela

Matador
9 Priory Business Park
Kibworth Beauchamp
Leicestershire LE8 0RX, UK
Tel: (+44) 116 279 2299
Email: books@troubador.co.uk
Web: www.troubador.co.uk/matador

ISBN 978 1784622 947

British Library Cataloguing in Publication Data.
A catalogue record for this book is available from the British Library.

Printed and bound by CPI Group (UK) Ltd, Croydon, CR0 4YY
Typeset in Aldine401 BT Roman by Troubador Publishing Ltd

Matador is an imprint of Troubador Publishing Ltd

For our children,
Saskia, Cosima (the instigator), Damian, Natasha and Alexia,
my best teachers, my challenge, my inspiration.

For Christopher, thank you.

PART 1

Chapter One

September brought with it the first glimmer of summer. The snows in the mountains had begun to melt and the rivers to swell. With the warm air, the winter smog that hung over the city of Santiago began to thin and the sky, freed of its veil of winter pollution, took on a new brilliance. Everywhere little paper flags with the five-pointed white star fluttered in readiness for the Independence Day fiestas of September 18th and street vendors displayed sashes and *huaso* hats with bands in the Chilean colours of red, white and blue.

Milana sat on the banks of the Mapocho River gazing at the mountains silhouetted against the phosphorescent dawn, relishing the freedom of the early hour. A gentle breeze skipped over her bare legs, lifting eddies of dust and whispering through the eucalyptus trees as it danced its way downstream. Between her fingers she rolled a fragment of broken porcelain that she had dug up from the earth. A few feet away, her younger brothers picked out rocks from the river bed while the freezing mountain waters swirled about their ankles.

'There's a dead dog here,' shouted Juanito, the youngest, rousing her out of her day dream. Milana tossed the fragment to the ground where the spoils of earthquakes and ancient garbage lay impacted between the layers of earth, and joined him. They stood staring at the mangy creature lying between two sun-bleached pieces of driftwood, its threadbare fur barely stretching over its bony carcass. She leant over and touched the still soft body. A cluster of flies rose from around its staring eyes. Beyond the eucalyptus trees in the shadow of the hills a vulture hovered. Juanito shivered.

'I hate them birds.' Milana glanced up, her gaze remained momentarily transfixed by its hunched predatory form as it settled on a high branch.

'Thanks for coming with us, Mila.' Juanito hugged her gratefully. 'I'd never have come down here without you,' he admitted in a whisper. Ricci, their middle brother, approached, triumphantly lifting a grubby plastic bag.

'Got the best rocks yet, in here! Race you back home,' he shouted to Juanito. The boys set off scrambling over boulders to paint the rocks they had collected. Milana crouched down again by the dead dog and stared into its glassy eyes. Flies hovered impatiently about her suntanned skin. She rose, stepped back and watched the flies take possession of their prize. At the top of the bank she turned to look back at the river; a solitary figure, accustomed to this forgotten wasteland, communing with the whisperings of the waking day.

Others didn't venture to this part of the river. They were afraid of *El Cuco* who might lure them to his fearful lair. Mothers would nurture these folk tales and threaten unruly children with abandonment on the riverbank for *El Cuco* to find them. As they grew, some children dared laugh in the face of these old myths, but older ones told stories about the mysterious man who lived beyond the bend of the river and roamed the banks on lonely nights. They spoke of the graves of his victims and the souls of the murdered that rose with the mist over the river.

For Milana these ancient legends merely served to enhance the enchantment of the wasteland where she would sit for hours digging her fingers into the damp earth by the water's edge. During the winter rains, the river swelled flooding the banks and coaxing all manner of debris, buried for years, to the surface. In the spring Milana would find new treasures delivered up by the flood water; remnants of porcelain or glass. Milana collected these coloured fragments whose edges had been worn smooth by time. With some she made mosaics in the earth, others she took home with her to turn into rudimentary pendants. In the dry season when the water ran so shallow she could easily pick her way across the rocks, she would sit resting against a piece of driftwood and spend time reading the books that were passed on to her in charity bags from the parish. But in the heat of summer, when the wealthy repaired to their holiday villas and charity ran thin, she would lie on the hot, cracked earth dreaming under a cobalt sky. The rushing river, the blazing sunsets and the colossal mountains brought beauty into her dingy life and no grim warning could prevail.

Now, as she gazed up at the great Andean heights, there was a hint of defiance about Milana; something steadfast and determined, almost regal in her stance that set her apart from her peers. Far above her two condors circled. As she watched them, the first rays of the morning sun touched their wings. They soared higher as if they alone, with their majestic ritual, drew the sun over the mountains to where the waking population below could gaze upon another dawn. Milana shook her hair back, closed her eyes and let the first rays penetrate her skin while, somewhere deep within, inexpressible yearnings played out a melancholy symphony.

At five foot eight inches, Milana was the tallest girl in her class. But then the boys and girls of the 52nd Lyceo School were not noted for their height. This was partly due to their poor diet and partly to their genetic build. Many had Mapuche Indian blood. Some were descended from the Auraucanian Indians of the south – eyes set wide apart and melancholy, dark hair and olive skin was typical of these people. But every now and again, one came out different, like Milana, a throwback to a John Smith, fair skinned and in search of adventure, who had chanced upon his Pocahontas on these far-flung shores.

A handsome new bridge linked the 52nd Lyceo on the left bank of the River Mapocho to Avenida Kennedy, the major uptown auto route. When the rain cleared away every last vestige of smog and the sun reflected off the impressive snow-covered peaks, Avenida Kennedy, with its monumental palm trees and breathtaking views of the Andes, became one of the most spectacular avenues in the world: a six-lane 'highway to the Gods'. It began in the wake of the Grand Hyatt hotel and stretched up through residential Vitacura all the way to Lo Barnechea where, in the shadow of the mountains, it suddenly petered out into a little plaza and slipped away over an old bridge. At strategic places along the river, elegant new bridges had been built to link the smart, new residential developments of Santa Maria Manquehue and La Dehesa to the older, elegant uptown districts of Santiago. Newly constructed villas perched smugly in the foothills of the mountains while down in the valley, caught in the shadow of these bridges like a bad smell, lay the shantytown of San Damian.

Milana lived in the second alley down from the baker's shop. The homes on Oleander Alley were rough wooden constructions with sheets of corrugated metal held together by a few nails. Letty, Milana's mother, boasted that theirs was held together by a prayer. The floor was, for the most part, the dark, damp earth of the riverbank. The rough, inside walls were decorated with old supermarket posters and discarded wrapping-paper. There were two rooms: the front room with a plastic table, two wooden stools and an old cane sofa, where Milana and her younger brothers, Ricci, Juanito, and Letty, ate their meals, and the back room, where they all slept on a mattress raised off the floor by a variety of discarded apple crates. On this particular morning, Letty had been peeling pumpkins since before dawn and preparing the dough for her *sopaipillas*. These were the pumpkin pastry rings which she fried and served with the local *pebre* sauce of onions, tomatoes and coriander, and sold from her white metal kiosk on wheels. Usually her clients were hungry bus drivers and construction workers on a meal break, but today she would join the other vendors in the market square for the craft fair that took place every year on the first Sunday of September.

Church bells rang for early Mass. Letty paused, saucepan in hand, to stare out at the women straggling past on their way to beg or sell their paperclips and sticking-plasters on the steps of the church. Today, in addition to their usual wares they carried paper flags clenched like posies of flowers in their gnarled fists. The more flamboyant among them had crammed piles of flimsy plastic *huaso* hats on their heads, in the hope of attracting extra sales. Letty stretched, her limbs still slim and lithe, and pressed her hand into the small of her back; today, at least, she wouldn't have to push her cart up that hill. The shanty shuddered suddenly as someone came racing in. A second later, Milana appeared from behind the plastic shower curtain that separated the eating and sleeping spaces. She observed her mother momentarily with a troubled expression.

'I saw Ana!' she exclaimed breathlessly. Milana's usually melodious voice sounded tense and accusatory. 'She had Oscar pulling that big old cart they're going to use as a stall, all by himself, like he was a donkey and what's more he had another black eye.'

'Oscar's a big boy, he can take care of himself,' retorted Letty turning back to the task in hand. She hummed as she wielded her old saucepan as a hammer, tacking down some plastic sheeting, for want of windowpanes, which had come away from the wooden frame. Milana flung herself down on the makeshift bed and watched her mother's slender fingers tugging at the plastic, pulling it into place.

'Can't Ana stop his dad doing that to him?' She thought of Ana's matronly figure, her large bust and smooth wide face that seemed at odds with her dark sunken eyes. 'She's not afraid of Chevo. Why doesn't she say something to him?'

'Chevo doesn't mean anything by it. He's a good dad, Milana, leave Ana be.'

Chevo, Ana's husband, was one of the big cheeses in the busdrivers' syndicate. He was a burly man with a full mane of stiff hair and a heavy jaw. He had a voice like a rumbling engine and great spatulate hands that he used to knock their three sons about. Oscar, the eldest, was slow witted and excessive bullying had riddled him with ticks and stammers. Only in Milana's company did his speech and manner mysteriously improve leading him to the conclusion that Milana was the answer to his shortcomings. To him she was the embodiment of an angel and his expression usually took on a look of pious adoration in her presence.

Milana's bright eyes flamed with outrage.

'Just because El Chevo is one of the bus drivers who eat your *sopaipillas* he can do no wrong in your eyes. I think he's a lazy thug. I don't like any of those men you hang out with up that hill for that matter.'

'Where are the boys?' asked Letty lightly, she knew it best not to engage when Milana was on one of her crusades. She pushed a strand of dyed red hair off her face, leaving a streak of white flour across her cheek.

'Out back! Doing something to rocks to turn them into doorstops.'

Letty laughed. 'Doorstops? What do we need with those? There's enough cracks in the doors to keep the place well ventilated, never mind these holes which make believe they're windows.'

The sound of the saucepan banging in nails punctuated the ensuing silence. Letty could feel her daughter's dark eyes on her. It made her uncomfortable. Milana was her inspiration and her hope; she'd been told how clever she was by the school principal himself. They had high expectations for her but recently Letty had felt her brooding and distant or restless, like a creature that senses it's trapped.

Eventually Letty straightened and, sweeping the hair off her face again, she met her daughter's quiet scrutiny:

'I don't know what's got into you, girl, but you're up to something *Chica*,' she ventured.

'Everyone's up to something, Mum.' Milana gave her a wry look. It occurred to Letty in that moment that had she opened her heart to Milana and told her the truth about her past, she would have found a strong and intelligent listener in her child. Instead she had chosen to hide it away. Milana, grown up as she was, perceived this concealment and not knowing the reason for it or its nature interpreted it, instinctively, as a breach of trust between them and had become secretive herself.

'What? What are you looking at, Mum?'

'Can't I look at my own flesh and blood? That's something I've done right at least.'

'Don't go laying that kind of responsibility on me Mum,' Milana turned on her stomach and laid her cheek on the bed, feeling the soft plush of the thin bedspread.

'You don't know what my life will be.' In that same instant a sudden noise filled the air like a heavy lorry passing, only no lorry could fit down narrow Oleander Alley.

Milana sat suddenly bolt upright. Letty steadied herself. Around them the room shook, the boards creaked and the furniture shuffled to the vibrations of the earth. The light bulb in the centre of the ceiling swayed back and forth as though some invisible elf were playing there. A fallen mug rolled over the floor and loose bricks clattered over corrugated roofs. In the distance car alarms started wailing. They stared at each other in anticipation of the worst. But just as suddenly as it began, the rumbling of the earth, the groaning of the shanty, the noise and the shaking died. The convulsion passed and nature's fit was over. Only the still swaying bulb testified to the earth tremor that had for a moment threatened to escalate. Letty's murmured prayer died on her lips as the dread of what might have been, subsided; that this would be a big one, like the 1960's earthquake that tore through the earth's crust swallowing whole houses in its wake. Letty moved over to where Milana sat on the edge of the bed and, touched by relief and gratefulness, she stooped down to kiss her daughter. Milana stayed quite still, shocked into silence while Letty smoothed her hair. Then, taking a brush from the upturned crate that was their bedside table, Letty started to brush it gently

'I thought you were busy, Mum.' Milana relished the pull of the brush against her scalp and the gentle stroke of her mother's hand.

'And so I am.'

'I wish you never had to work on the hill among all them bus drivers.'

'*Those* bus drivers,' Letty corrected. 'You may be the only one to talk right round here, but one day it may help you. Besides,

Chiquita, those bus drivers eat my *sopaipillas.* I feed them, they feed us with the money they pay, it's an honest living. And I like it up on that hill,' Letty mused. 'Watching the houses being built and the palm trees being planted, great avenues of them. I can see for miles up there, I can see the mountains circling the city like I was on a level with them and at night the city lights twinkle below like the sky had turned upside down and was laid at my feet. You should see it, *Chiquita.'* There was a quality about the way Letty spoke at times; her voice became more lyrical, just as her wild red hair and brash manner belied a finer beauty that few who knew her had the aesthetic appreciation to perceive. The delicacy of her face and hands, the smallness of her wrists or the turn of her fine ankles were lost on the uncultivated eye of the shantytown folk. They accepted Letty unquestioningly as one of their own kind and never noted the significance of what set her apart from them.

Letty went on brushing Milana's thick mane of hair in long even strokes – soothing and hypnotic.

'We used to be friends remember, *Chica*? You told me about the wasteland and the treasures you collected there. You used to tell me stories you made up. I love the world inside your head. Let me in again, girl, don't block me out. It makes me sad.' She spoke as though she were weaving her insinuations through each glossy lock.

Milana stared ahead unblinkingly to stop herself revealing a single tell-tale response. Suddenly Letty prodded her playfully:

'Hey, don't play deaf, *Chica*! Doris saw you.'

A sudden wave of heat coursed through Milana.

'Mum, Doris dishes out school dinners, she sees me every day,' she responded quick-thinkingly.

'Well, you weren't eating school dinners when you knocked on the door of some fancy house in Vitacura last week.'

Milana wheeled round eyes ablaze to check the degree of information that might have been imparted.

'Got you there, girl!' Letty grinned.

'What was Doris doing in Vitacura anyway?'

'Following you *Chiquita.'*

Milana shrugged affecting indifference.

'They wanted a part time maid,' she lied.

'You're fourteen! You're too young for that. Try again.'

'Doris should mind her own business.'

'You were in there for an hour. Doris worries about you.'

Doris had no cause to worry, with no husband or children to fuss over, only her cakes which everyone agreed were the best around. Still, she had a sad face; her eyes drooped and her lips stopped short of the twenty-past-four angle. Doris, Milana had always thought, looked as though her face had been taken from the Creator's oven and hung out to dry too soon, causing all the features to run. Even her hairline seemed to have slipped to halfway down her forehead. Maybe gravity had exerted a greater pull on her than others. Doris had said she'd loved a man when she was sixteen and he forty but it hadn't worked out and now he was dead so she'd saved herself the heartache. Instead, she'd put two nephews through university and now, at fifty, she made cakes and sold them to the *panaderia* on the corner.

'Doris wouldn't have to worry about us if you were around more,' Milana retaliated pointedly. She hugged her knees up under her chin, instantly regretting the cruel dig at her mother. 'Father Pancho sent me round there for confirmation lessons,' she suggested trying a new tack. Letty stopped brushing, exasperated.

'Why won't you tell me the truth?'

'You hide stuff from me too, Mum. You don't give me straight answers. Like where you were born.'

'Where I was born?' Letty looked genuinely surprised, 'Who cares? Who asks stuff like that?'

'I do. I read books Mum, and the first thing they tell you is where people come from. Then they tell you what's happened to them and that's what makes them who they are. I know more about people in books than I know about you. Anyways, if Doris was so busy spying on me you know jolly well where I was.'

Letty sighed and tucked her loose curls back under the scarf tied and knotted round her head like a hair band. She passed the back of her hand over her mouth, a sure sign that thoughts were churning under her relatively unruffled exterior. Doris hadn't been totally sure but she had gone up and enquired who's house Milana had spent all that time in. The answer had taken her aback. What business could Milana have at *Señora* Lisa and *Don* Victor Cornejo's residence, when they were known to be in Europe somewhere on some foreign posting?

Everyone in the shantytown knew the kind and charitable *Señora* Lisa. Had Milana gone there for advice or money? Was she in trouble? Did she even know they were away? Letty didn't blame her for going to search *Señora* Lisa out. Once Letty herself had passed the big house but she would never have dared ring the bell however much she might have wished to see *Señora* Lisa's kind face again in order to confide her doubts and concerns about Milana. Letty bit her lip as she remembered *Señora* Lisa's parting words; 'Talk to Milana, trust her.' Three years on, that wise advice remained unheeded. Letty sat down her wide eyes cocooning Milana in the sudden gentleness of regret, her face reflecting all kinds of lights from within. Milana let her hands be taken in the warmth of her mother's. And suddenly it felt as though some invisible defensive shield between them was melting into nothing.

'*Señora* Lisa was like my guardian angel. So many times I've wanted to see her again. If you went to find her, you're braver than I am. I never dared.' Letty stroked Milana's cheek gently and leaning forwards kissed her suddenly.

'She gave so much, I felt I couldn't ask for more. You see she was never like those other women who come to do their five minutes of charity in the shantytown to make themselves feel good. She really cared about each one of us.' Lurching from confidence to confidence, Letty went on in her effort to deepen the rare moment of intimacy.

Milana traced her fingertips over her mother's slender hand.

'Why did she care about us?' she almost whispered, 'I mean, she must have had a reason. I don't believe people do stuff for no reason. She didn't need to come here. And she didn't come with a friend like the other ladies do, like they're trying to prove a point to each other, all self-important and busy. She came alone and kind of loved us.' Milana lifted her eyes and watched her mother who stared down unusually quiet.

'Mum?' she urged. Letty looked up with a self-conscious smile:

'You know,' she confessed, 'she told me once that she'd lost almost everything – even her will to live – and that she'd been rescued from the gutter and found hope again.' Letty stood up and, stepping towards the window, she fiddled with the edge of the plastic there. 'She gave us belief in ourselves, sort of bonded us together, me, Doris, Iris, Ana and Nilda.' Letty paused, as though she had momentarily struggled to overcome some inner conflict, then turned towards Milana: 'She sort of saved me.'

Letty picked up an elastic band off the floor and held it out for Milana to tie her hair back.

'Like I say, I don't blame you going to look for her *Chiquita*, I just don't understand what you found there, seeing as how *Señora* Lisa went away to Europe these three years gone. We would have known if she was back. She'd have come to say Hi.'

Milana recoiled from the faintly mournful note she detected in the last sentence. It annoyed her. She loved her mother's strength and devil-may-care manner; it unsettled her to recognise her pain.

'You're not going to tell me what you were doing there, are you?' Letty sighed and found herself curiously resigned to not knowing.

'We both have secrets Mum, right?'

Letty caught her breath, but she hid the hurt with a little laugh, recognising she had only herself to blame.

'Get on with you girl,' she quipped, pushing her playfully off the bed.

'We've got work to do.'

Milana slipped off the bed, but from the door she looked back at her mother and for a brief moment allowed herself to see the soulful woman that lived under the usual bravado. She ran back and hugged her, pressing her face against her mother's cheek.

'Saved you from what Mum? What did *Señora* Lisa save you from?'

She felt Letty take a deep breath.

'A black hole. But nothing is ever that bad for long.' She paused before admitting, 'I'd be dead if she hadn't turned up.' Letty cupped Milana's face in her hands to prolong the brief moment of tenderness. 'And happiness comes when you least expect it,' she whispered smiling.

Letty's eyes were as large as olives, and the same colour, set wide apart under long, dark lashes. Often when she broke into her trademark smile they remained distant as though they were observing an altogether different reality to the one before them. This time they rested on Milana filling her with love.

'Why did you trust her?' Milana whispered reaching for the enigma behind Letty's smile.

'Who? *Señora* Lisa? I don't know, sometimes you just embrace what God sends you.'

'How did you know He sent her, Mum?'

'I just did. You know goodness, you just feel it in your heart, Milana, 'cause it brings you peace.'

Through the grubby plastic sheet of window, Letty watched Milana disappear down the street to help the other women as she'd promised. Surprised by an inexplicable pressure on her chest, Letty glanced down and found her hand pressed there as if holding down something that had awakened and trembled with new life. It was as though the abortive earthquake had dislodged a rock that for years had restricted the flow of emotion to her heart.

Chapter Two

The sixteenth century church of *Todo Los Angeles* had all but crumbled away in the earthquake of 1984. It was painstakingly reconstructed by the wealthy Hidalgo family as a token of consideration to the people of Barnechea after they sold their land off for new housing developments. The ancient interior was now undergoing a repainting project so the church was temporarily closed. Railings circled the wider church grounds. To these railings Pablo, a shifty, sour-faced youth of eighteen from the shantytown, had tied his colourful kites; a front for his own seedier dope peddling. He would sell these flimsy creations to children from the more affluent nearby developments, while indulgent parents looked on and street urchins skulked around considering their chances of grabbing a wallet or two. Meanwhile, Jose, alias *'Oro Sucio'*, Pablo's mentor and chief pusher in the neighbourhood stood leaning back against a pillar searching the crowds for converts to his drug cult. Jose didn't care who he duped or drugged. He cared only for the rings on his fingers and the shirt on his back and the hairs on his chest that nestled his brand new medallion. It was common knowledge that he had killed a man when he was just a boy. Now, at twenty, he had grown a goatee and bought the bling that separated him from smaller fry like Pablo.

Jose swung from the railings like a sinewy monkey and spat into the gutter as Milana walked by carrying a tray of *sopaipillas*. His spittle crossed her path. She flashed her lively green eyes angrily in his direction. Jose whistled and raised a black eyebrow while Pablo's lustful eyes followed her greedily. Just ahead, a youth moved his plastic bucket, filled with filthy soapy water, out of her way.

'Hello Oscar,' she passed on, innocent of the stares she left in her wake.

'Milana,' Oscar caught up with her. He stood awkwardly, this gentle giant of a boy, his face pink to the ears, a purple bruise bulging over one bloodshot eye. He twisted his dirty car-washing cloth between his fingers.

'I'll carry the tray for you, Milana, it's heavy!'

'I'm fine, thanks.' She made to move on, her heart sinking at the look of thwarted hope on Oscar's face.

'Why don't you go round the other side of the plaza there's more cars need washing there.' Oscar tensed a little at her pointed suggestion. He looked over his shoulder to where Jose and Pablo stood leaning against the railings staring at them. Milana lowered her voice, 'Just don't hang out with them.' She nodded in their direction. 'They're trouble. I've seen the cops watching for them from the bridge. Watch your back Oscar.'

Oscar bit his lip and looked down at his threadbare trainers.

'Come on, take my tray then, if it'll get you to walk away from them.'

'Don't worry about me.' He took a step back feeling their steely gaze boring into him and giving her a sheepish smile, he turned back to his bucket. He knew, better than Milana did, to be wary of Pablo.

All day, under the warm, spring sunshine, Milana went around distributing *sopaipillas* and *empanadas* with icing sugar and selling weak orange squash out of paper cups, while Pablo ogled her lithe figure as she passed back and forth. He felt the pull in his groin like a bothersome itch. No breeze blew to ease the heat. When the fair was over Pablo watched her bending over bags, the contours of her body moulded against the flimsy cotton of her dress as she helped pack up. His eyes remained riveted as she passed with the women, ignoring him. An unfamiliar sensation grew inside him fuelled by irritation and lust as he stared at the little party making their way back across the bridge to the *poblacion*. Then he saw her turn and give Oscar the thumbs up as she passed him washing cars. Inside his pocket Pablo rolled the cold stiffness of his knife across his sweaty palm.

The ground was hard and unyielding on the women's worn-out soles and the sun's glare had tired their eyes. Unsold merchandise weighed heavy on their over-burdened arms. Tempers ran high as they reached Oleander Alley. Iris told Doris the rag dolls she made needed more stuffing and Ana's Christmas calendars needed to be mounted on stiffer card, which caused a few remarks to fly about her pinching clothes from the parish stock for the poor, in order to sell at a profit. Nilda reminded Ana that she had filched baby-wear from the wardrobe sale so she shouldn't cast aspersions, which caused Ana to fly into a rage and everyone to disperse in splendid isolation. Finally Doris, the peacemaker, collected one of her iced cakes and found Nilda dejected and counting *pesos* in her bedroom. She invited her to come and find Letty and Iris so they could all go to Ana's to make up and soothe their frazzled nerves. Meanwhile Milana's brothers, Ricci and Juanito, stayed in the market square to watch the men play roulette. There'd been talk of a dog and rabbit race and Milana had seen the posts with the zip wire for the plastic rabbit and the dog pen with its boxed compartments all ready for the race, so she guessed the older boys would be out late, betting with the men. Oscar would probably be with them. All the same Milana didn't want to risk meeting him again at Ana's. Rather than join the women at tea, she slipped off unnoticed while other shantytown girls hung around the plaza waiting to kiss and cuddle the boys till the cold chased them away.

Milana headed towards the river, past the metal bins where, on other nights, the men folk lit fires and sat around drinking on upturned crates. The place was deserted now. Above her luminous ridges of cloud shaped themselves like flames across the pink sky. Suddenly Pablo stepped out from behind the skeleton of a stripped car.

'Hey,' he called, 'you best watch yourself.'

Milana shrugged and went on.

'You heard me, bitch.'

She wheeled round, eyes mutinous, and stood facing him in silence.

'You watch yourself or your dough-faced sweetheart'll be screwing mud under there.' He nodded in the direction of the riverbed. Milana remained impassive, shoulders back, meeting his predatory eyes. Pablo shifted, fingering the knife in his pocket.

'Screw him,' she said coolly, 'what's it to me?'

He looked her up and down lingeringly, reluctant to let her go, but her dauntless, disdainful gaze debilitated his intention. He passed his tongue slowly over his chapped lips, gripped his crotch and stared after her as she stepped away lightly through the dust. Then he ground the knife against the rusty carcass of the car and took himself off in the opposite direction.

Milana walked on without turning back, unsure whether or not she was being followed. Already she had learnt the power of fearless indifference to shrivel a man's resolve and even at her young age she cultivated an aura of detachment behind which to hide her vulnerability. Unlike so many of her peers she was wary of the opposite sex. El Negro, her so-called 'step-father', had seen to that when he stumbled into their lives and crushed her innocence like eggshells between his clumsy, fumbling fingers. He had come on to her when she was ten while they sat watching telly at Nilda's house. No one had noticed as his hand edged its way along her bare leg and up under her cotton skirt. She had wanted to get up and scream and drive a kitchen knife through his detestable hand with its dirt-ingrained fingernails. But instead, she had remained horrified and speechless while the women sat around her unknowing, un-protecting. Even now, Pablo's weak lasciviousness barely managed to dent the angry carapace that she had built up to shield her from men.

The next time El Negro had sidled up to her when they were alone she had lashed out at him, hitting him across the jaw with the full force of her revulsion. His initial surprise had turned to rage and he had set upon Milana, beating her hard until she got away and ran to the only place she knew his superstitious nature would not allow him access; the far bank of the river under the tall eucalyptus trees by the old dump. All the tales of evil spirits were nothing next to the threat of El Negro's sick cravings that stalked her every waking moment from then on. Even after El Negro left them a year later, the wasteland of the old dump remained her refuge: the place where she would find solace watching the strength of the river carry away boulders and driftwood as the sun climbed high over the snow-capped Andes.

Now, as she sat on the far bank after the day's exertions, Milana found her thoughts drifting from initial concern for Oscar to wishing she had dared ask her mother more questions, cursing the instinct that always held her back from intimacy. Much longed for breezes blew down off the foothills as she gazed at the river dancing over rocks and stones and let her mind wander, sowing a world of promise around her. She had heard of people climbing over the mountains into Argentina, but that was around Mendoza, or down south, not here where the mountains were higher and more treacherous. There was a plane of rugby players on their way to play the Chilean team at the Grange School, that had crashed somewhere up there just beyond the horizon. They had survived eating the flesh of the dead cooked by the sun on the metal casing of the plane. But other than those intrepid rugby players Milana hadn't heard of anyone making it over the mountains to the other side on foot. She sighed and toyed with the earth, digging it out with her hands and letting it crumble between her fingers and tumble away towards the riverbed.

The usual restlessness consumed her again. She dreamed constantly of running away and the more she dreamed the more she endeavoured to keep herself distant and unattached, so that nothing would stop her when the time was right. The books she read only fuelled her wanderlust. Urgency compelled her over and over again to think up means of finding a way out into the world where she would breathe a different air. But to leave required money and there was only one way she knew to make quick money and that was behind the service station. She had watched the prostitutes offer themselves to the well-heeled drivers of BMWs and Mercedes only to turn away in anger and disgust. Theft had suggested itself in unexpected opportunities. But each time, something inside her refused to surrender itself. Meanwhile guilt twisted like a knot inside her, knowing she could leave them all for one shot at freedom from the oppression of the shantytown. Daily she wrestled with conflicting emotions that played havoc with her moods and secretly she wondered how far might she go to achieve her end. She dug her hands deeper into the mud and felt it sucking at her fingers as she pulled them out.

The sun's dying rays caught a flash of colour near the water's edge. Intrigued, Milana reached down to the muddy bank to pick out a piece of painted glass which half lodged in its earthy bed. She passed her fingers gently over it, easing the mud away to hold it up to the light. It was as if all the colours of the sunset had been preserved on its translucent texture. Where had it come from? Who had fashioned it? It was curved so that it could stand on its side and it seemed as magical to her overactive imagination as a piece of stained glass from the cupola of a fairy tale palace. She cradled its smoothness in her hands. This was a treasure indeed. Milana carved her name into the earth with it before laying it ontop and surrounding it with a ring of stones. So absorbed was she, that she never noticed the evening shadows that stealthily gathered about her with the moon now a pale orb high in the sky. Hastily she made her way back across the rushing waters. In her hurry she left her precious glass on the damp earth surrounded by its fortress of stones.

Milana padded across the shanty careful not to get splinters from the rough strips of salvaged fruit crates that made up its improvised floor. Once a small plant had reared its head and been allowed to grow, flower and die there between the thin wooden boards. She glanced to where her brothers sat on the floor engrossed in a kite-making activity unaware of the lateness of the hour. Beside them lay the implements of their work: paint left over from their unsuccessful sale of rocks, an old gluepot, kite paper, sticks and thread.

'Look!' cried Juanito, jumping up and offering Milana his precarious structure.

'All I have to do is put the paper over it and it's ready. Pablo said he made loads of dosh with his kites today and Ricci showed me how to make them. Tomorrow we're going to sell them outside the Chucky Cheese and surprise Mum.'

Milana took the half-finished kite in her hand and, unsettled by the mention of Pablo, she looked distractedly at the sticks glued together to form a star. She knew just as well as the wealthy clientele of the Chucky Cheese Pizza Parlour would, that this pitiful invention would fall in ruins at the first gust of wind. Proudly Juanito retrieved his creation while Milana busied herself putting the kettle on the gas stove. She opened the back door and turned on the outside tap. Water trickled over her hands washing the dust and grit that clung to them. El Negro had employed his sober moments in scrounging lengths of pipe and had tapped into the city water mains. His only useful legacy when he disappeared one day was the operational, albeit basic, shower in the wooden shack that he had stuck onto the shanty's back wall. But, whenever possible, Milana avoided his handiwork, preferring the river. Now she washed her muddy feet under the cold water while the kettle whistled high-pitched and insistent.

Automatically Milana set about the task of preparing tea, as she did every afternoon. She placed a plate of *sopaipillas* on the table and spread a thin layer of jam on them, tomorrow she would serve them with quince that Doris had promised them. She put out three mugs and a jug of hot water into which she dropped one tea bag and stirred in a spoonful of powdered milk. Then she sat down to eat. The boys picked themselves off the floor and joined her in the silent ritual, washing down the *sopaipillas* with the tea to which they added a measured spoonful of sugar each. Ricci got up to switch on the radio. Radio Carolina filled the quiet of their unspoken thoughts with its repertoire of yearning love songs.

19

Later, once the boys had gone back to their kite making and Milana had rinsed out the plates, she stepped behind the plastic curtain that partitioned their living space and, reaching between two apple crates that propped up the mattress, she retrieved a parcel hidden there. Carefully, she unwrapped a notebook, a textbook and a pencil. For a long while after, she sat in the pale light of a low wattage bulb doing English excercises.

Milana's class mates at the 52nd Lyceo had laughed when the new English teacher, a small bespectacled man with a benign smile, had told them that English would open the world up for them. In their opinion, they were doing pretty well just mastering Spanish. The teacher, a temporary voluntary substitute, soon gave up trying and compromised by allowing them to engage in making collages from pictures in magazines instead. But Milana wanted nothing more than the world to open up for her, like Pandora's box, and spill out all its secrets. A month later the new teacher was replaced, but his words, like a small seed, had taken root in Milana's mind and the need to learn English became an all-consuming objective. After much thought, she devised a plan: on the first available half-day at school, she took a bus, paying with two coins she had stolen from her mother's purse, to the house in Vitacura where Iris had said *Señora* Lisa lived, and knocked on the door. A pretty young blonde had opened and to this woman Milana had explained that *Señora* Lisa had promised to help her if she ever needed anything and now she needed to learn English because she wanted the world to open up for her. At first the young woman had laughed; a happy laugh that carried no malice, but it had been disconcerting all the same and Milana had found her eyes smarting. But the woman had stopped Milana gently when she turned to leave and introduced herself as Victoria Williams.

Victoria was the daughter of some English friends of *Señora* Lisa. She explained she was staying at the house while Lisa accompanied her husband Victor on his posting as Ambassador to England. Milana knew nothing about Ambassadors or what any of that meant and was about to turn away again, confused and embarrassed when Victoria, sensing her disappointment and charmed by her intelligent eyes and honest face, offered her ice cream and biscuits. A uniformed maid served them sorbets and wafers under the shade of an old avocado tree in the garden. Victoria told Milana she was studying seismology at the Catholic University and kindly explained what that meant. Milana was fascinated that anyone would come all the way from England to study earthquakes in Chile or that they might be able to put together enough data to predict how and when the earth would convulse. She asked so many questions that Victoria, recognising the girl's natural quickness, ended up suggesting that Milana could come every second Wednesday after school for an hour or so and she would teach her English as best she could.

At first Milana had been a little confused by this turn of events and awkwardly explained she couldn't pay because she had no money and her mother was very poor and sold *sopaipillas* off a cart. This didn't seem to bother the very magnanimous Victoria who laughed again and suggested maybe, if she learnt English well, she'd be able to take care of all her family in the future. Milana remembered she would have to walk the three miles home, so she said she had to leave even though she was enjoying herself more than she thought humanly possible. As luck would have it, Victoria offered to drive her back home. Milana accepted gratefully but not wanting Victoria to come all the way to the dusty dregs of habitation that made up the homes of Oleander Alley, she asked to be dropped off at the Chucky Cheese Pizza Parlour instead. Before driving away, Victoria thrust a thousand *peso* note into Milana's hand and told her to buy herself a cheeseburger. Forsaking the cheeseburger had taken care of her travel expenses for several weeks after, by the end of which Milana had summoned the courage to ask Victoria for a little more bus fare.

Victoria was a good if sometimes erratic teacher. Occasionally she wasn't home on the appointed day, and Milana had to quell her disappointment, but for the most part, in term time, she kept her word and they worked for an hour together using a couple of books Victoria bought for her. There were other things Victoria taught her: Milana learnt about a man called Oscar Wilde and her favourite of his stories became '*The Nightingale and the Rose*' that Victoria had found for her in Spanish. Then there were other books about children being sent away to school and uncanny love stories about vampires. Milana wished she could stay longer with Victoria who was always being called up by friends and spent most weekends away. Sometimes she would show her pictures of young men with surf boards, their arms flung around her, and girls in lovely dresses at parties in stone houses in England.

Milana's school teacher had been right – she felt her world was opening up. While her friends merely ogled magazines, Milana's heart swelled knowing she had a real live person who seemed to have stepped out of those pages to teach her English, in a mansion with biscuits and sorbets served on silver plates; a person who, for one hour at the time, laughed and joked with her and treated her as a friend. There was no way on earth Milana was going to tell anyone about Victoria, least of all her mother who would only be confused and embarrassed and perhaps a little hurt. Besides, telling would break the spell, the magic would be spoilt.

But now it didn't matter anymore because Victoria was leaving. She'd learnt all she had to learn about earthquakes and she was going back to England. They'd had their last English lesson and she'd given her a book, *The advanced Assimil method for learning English*. 'Something to work on till we meet again' Victoria had inscribed inside. Of course they both knew that would never happen. Theirs had been one of those brief encounters that, while they may affect one person forever, become just a quaint memory for another. But for a while longer, at least, as she completed yet another set of excercises, Milana tried to make believe that she would take the bus again to the world of promise, of sorbets and dainty silver spoons, to see Victoria because, right now, Milana didn't think she could bear to think of it being over.

That night Milana lay in bed unable to sleep. She guessed Letty would be back late, having stayed to peel her pumpkins watching telly at Ana's, most likely. Beside her, Juanito and Ricci slept like pups curled up small together, not stretched out luxuriously like kids in films. They breathed evenly, oblivious to the sounds of the night: the shouts, the drunken brawls, the police sirens. Weeks of yielding to wind and rain had caused the plastic sheeting over the window frame to sag and despite all Letty's careful tacking down, at each breeze it blew in and out as though the shanty were exhaling its afflictions into the night air. Lurking in the shadows close by, his back resting against the scant walls of a neighbouring shanty, Pablo struck a match. Meanwhile, from the shanty across the road, Iris's resonant voice reached in through all the crannies.

'That Oscar, he's got a thing for Milana. She might as well get it over with and settle.'

'Saints preserve us, Iris,' exclaimed Nilda. 'She's barely fourteen and besides she's got her own dreams, bless her.'

'Who's she kidding, Nilda? This shit hole'll beat the crap out of her dreams soon enough.'

'She's clever though, our Milana.' But Iris gave a hollow laugh.

'You can't escape this lousy dump, it sticks with you like a bad smell, wherever you go. If Milana's looking for adventure, it'll be with the rest of them tarts by the service station. Oscar's a better bet than that lousy lot of dirt bags. You gotta be rich, Nilda, to rise like cooked gnocci in boiling water and leave the sticky pile behind. Then again, Oscar's well screwed; dumb-ass kid messing with scumbags! I heard them boys outside the church today and it weren't kid's talk. He's just a lousy *pendejo;* wet behind the ears!' Iris paused to draw breath. 'I'll tell you more; them big shot bus drivers Letty hangs with,' she lowered her voice, 'they're using the syndicate for money-laundering, the cheeky sods. Ana's bloke, he's one of them, only I reckon she don't know it or she'd have beat the crap out of the lot of them!'

Meanwhile, Pablo dragged on the stub of a cigarette he'd picked up from the gutter. Lust, like a tick lodged in his skin, was spreading its disease. He eyed the plastic sheeting that stood between him and Milana but the voices of the women warded him off. He tossed the stub into the night and moved away down the alley.

'Ana won't have nothing to do with them pushers,' declared Nilda anxiously.

'Yeah well, like I say, her old man he's too busy with hot shot stuff to see her young Oscar's in shit up to his eyeballs.'

'You must tell her, Iris.'

'Nah, what she don't know...' Iris shrugged, 'she'd just toss the old man out. Then he takes it out on us, says we're lousy braying donkeys the lot of us! Anyway I bet you two cokes that Letty knows what they're up to in the syndicate. She's thick as thieves with them blokes up there.'

'Now don't you start on Letty. I won't listen to it,' Nilda exclaimed truculently. Iris gave an ironic half-smile at her loyalty through pursed lips.

'Letty's covering for them, I'll be bound. Wait till the cops bust the syndicate, they will, you know. Them bus drivers have got too big for their boots, and they don't give a rat's ass for who they screw.' She raised her eyebrows suggestively.

'Saint's preserve us!' Nilda shook her head vehemently

'I didn't mean it literally, but seeing as that's your thought Nilda, I'll back you there. She's a cheap thrill is Letty. Look at her! That orange hair and pink hat, who's she kidding? She likes them coming on to her, makes her feel wanted. So what? I say. Let her have her lousy fun. Truth is them bus driver blokes have got it good,' she ploughed on. 'They've got striking power. You get me? And Letty, she's no numbnut.' Iris paused before setting off on a new tack. 'I told her she shouldn't go letting Milana hang around by herself down by the river. It gives the young lads ideas. You get me? I reckon she'll get done down there by them lousy jerks. Doris heard them at school, while she dished out their dinners, saying they'd like to get a piece of her. I'm telling you, it's just a matter of time before those scumbags make a right dog's dinner out of Milana, and you know what I mean, don't you Nilda?'

Their voices rang clear across the chill night air. Nilda was no match for Iris's sharp tongue and quick wit. Milana pulled the blankets about her and begged sleep to take her but Iris filtered into her prayer.

'I don't blame Letty for pushing her cart all the way up that lousy hill to get away; half way out of here is half way out of hell. I'd like to live without them lousy police sirens, and all the shitty torching and I might just do that, Nilda, I might just go get myself a lousy uptown prison. Yeah, go into service, I mean, in some fancy, *quica* house, better than this shithole! Know what's keeping me, Nilda? Pride. I've got my pride. No need yet to go begging lousy half days or sucking up to the *patrona* being grateful for small mercies. Course, if you don't work hard, they toss you out like an old toaster. Still, sometimes I wonder if I'll just ditch this son-of-a-bitch life and bog off uptown and do whatever sucking up it takes. Truth is there's always them *patronas* that need you as much as you need them, then you cling together, like lousy shipwrecked souls on the shitty waves of life. I tell you Nilda, I know a thing or two.' There was a brief pause, while Iris poured them both a cup of herb tea, before she started up again.

'That Letty, you don't know the half of it, Nilda. But I keep my mouth shut, you know what I mean. I don't want trouble but I can feel it in my bones, trouble's brewing Nilda.'

Under her thin blanket Milana gave an involuntary shudder: Iris was a witch, no question about it, she had to be. She was born in Vichuquen, a hotbed of witchcraft five hours south of Santiago. She was viper-tongued, knife-sharp and knew about spells and voodoo. She understood the properties of all sorts of herbs and grew them in pretty window boxes. Then she gave them out to girls in trouble so their trouble never grew large in their bellies. Besides, she was striking-looking with a single silver streak in her mass of black hair that trailed down all the way to her slim waist. Her coal-black eyebrows gave her a smouldering look when she frowned. She had a feline quality that reminded Milana of cats that sidled up to stroke themselves against you before flashing their yellow eyes maliciously when you had nothing to give them.

But Milana had seen Iris lay the dead out too. Iris was good like that. Everyone wanted Iris to tend their dead. Milana had seen her washing cadavers from head to toe, arranging their hair and applying makeup to dissimulate the pallor of death. She'd watched her dress them like so many helpless babes, pulling on their underclothes, making them look better than they ever had in life. Iris was gentle with the dead, almost loving, but still Milana suspected her of hiding stuff and that she liked the dead because they kept their secrets like she kept hers. And sometimes Milana would stare at Iris just because she knew it made her uncomfortable. Maybe she shouldn't stare, maybe Iris could read her thoughts; Milana passed her hand down her body and over the sheet just to check that Iris's voice hadn't metamorphosed into anything more sinister in her bed.

'You were screaming,' whispered Letty leaning over Milana, gently wiping her temples with the end of the blanket. The grey light of dawn seeped in turning everything monochrome.

'I had a nightmare.' Milana breathed in her mother's fresh scent and felt comforted. She reached up and touched her mother's cheek gratefully. She had dreamt of the many-coloured glass from the riverbank and in her dream power seemed to emanate from it as if it were some magic charm. But her dream had turned into a nightmare as the charm fell from her hands shattering on the river which had turned to glass. Glass that cracked like ice so that the dark waters beneath swirled up around her, the colour of blood, trying to drag her under. Voices reached out to her in the darkness like cats' tongues licking away her skin until she feared there would be no more left of her.

'You smell nice,' she sighed burying her face into her mother's neck in a rare moment of self-surrender. 'You're so soft Mum. Don't go.' How thankful she was for her mother suddenly and it made her heart jump a beat to feel the longing to confide and grow closer. Letty hugged Milana tightly sensing a need yet to be addressed. There would be time later, she told herself. Now the sun was climbing slowly behind the great shield of the *Cordillera* and she must drag her cart up the hill. She glanced at the boys, a bundle of arms and legs interlaced. Releasing Milana she leant over and kissed them fondly.

Outside the window, Oleander Alley lay silent in the half light, but beyond the confines of San Damian, a pinkish glow silhouetted the mountains heralding a new day.

'I've found something beautiful for you, Mum,' Milana called out to keep her from going. She wanted to feel her embrace for longer, she wanted to be small again in her arms.

'I've got my eye on you dreamer-girl,' Letty grinned back shaking her head at Milana from the doorway. The boys stirred and opened their eyes, rubbing the sleep away.

'I took a lace out of your trainer, Ricci. Sorry!' Letty lifted her slim leg with graceful ease to show off the red trainer with the black lace in it.

'It looks weird 'cos the other one's white,' piped up Juanito.

'Who cares?' she blew them a parting kiss, winking at Juanito as the door shut behind her.

Milana didn't want to walk with Juanito and Ricci to school that morning.

'Go on, I'll follow on in a bit,' she told the boys as they grabbed their school bags. But whilst Ricci set off ahead, Juanito dawdled behind reluctant to leave her.

'Where are you going?' he asked when she emerged from the shanty. 'You'll be late for school.'

'I'll walk with you as far as the clock by the bridge,' she said briskly, annoyed at his perceptive persistence. He fell quietly into step beside her. When they reached the bridge he carried on, looking back once, then continuing, head bent, eyes on the pavement. Milana watched him trailing his hand over the railings of the new bridge. Then she headed towards the river, running as fast as she could. At the water's edge she took off her thin-soled shoes and picked her way hurriedly over rocks and stones hidden under the water's surface. The river rushed up with all the force of spring released from its icy winter spell.

By the time she reached the far bank Milana's feet were bleeding from the sharp rocks and occasional shards of glass. The blood seeped into the soft, damp earth. She fell to her knees searching for the curved piece of glass with which she would bridge all the distance and reserve she had placed between herself and her mother. Already she had invested it with healing qualities: it was to be her peace offering, the thing of beauty that she had found to make up for all the ugliness. But it was gone.

An unexpected anguish seemed to want to suffocate her, like smog blocking out the sun, stinging her eyes and lumping in her throat. She lay face down on the ground overwhelmed by a longing to release the love for her mother that she had denied her as a punishment for bringing El Negro into her life. It was as though the earth tremor yesterday had shaken Milana to her senses allowing her to recognise, at last, the self-destructive nature of the rage El Negro had engendered in her, that had caused her to resist all her mother's concern. It wrung her heart now to realise how she had pushed her mother away to present a distant and independent self, behind which she could hide her shock and repulsion, when the truth was all the reverse.

Meanwhile her secret English classes with Victoria had helped to restore the self-esteem that El Negro and his fumblings had robbed her of. In hiding these lessons from her mother she had felt a thrill of autonomy and a way to get back at her. Maybe it was being caught out by Doris, or maybe it was something that her mother had appealed to within her, that now responded with the honesty and spontaneity of the child she thought she had left behind on the sofa that miserable night El Negro had first abused her. The wretchedness was almost unbearable because of the pride in her nature that balked at admitting how much she craved her mother's love to heal her wounds. Milana struggled against the quagmire of self-pity into which she was sinking. Thus the loss of a piece of painted glass became the scapegoat for all her misery. She wanted to dissolve into the earth along with all the other broken fragments lodged there and let it swallow her up, but her sense of dignity impelled her to lift her face from the dirt. That was when she saw him.

Paralysed by the horror and shame of being discovered, Milana remained spellbound as a frightened animal, her eyes focused on the dark bulk of a man not more than twenty yards away from her. Gradually, the form appeared less hostile to her and, watching him, she found herself released from the agony of her previous self-absorption. His black hair caught the sun and hid his face as he bent his head steadfastly over something he seemed to be breaking and stirring.

Chapter Three

The level of his concentration and his apparent obliviousness to all else around him captivated Milana. She edged towards the stranger overcome by curiosity. Intrigued, she paused a moment to wonder if he might be deaf or blind. He sat in the shade of the old bridge working at something on the ground. Challenging any residual fear she might have, Milana crept closer taking care so that her movements did not disturb him, hoping all the while to be able to look over his shoulder at what, for now, was obscured by his knees and the rolled up ends of his trousers. Ever more daring, she came right up behind him and stood but three feet from his shoulder.

He had a stone mortar on the ground filled with what looked like a dusty blue rock. He was pummelling it with a pestle in rhythmic strokes and the mortar was filling with a deep blue powder. There were traces of blue on his fine-boned hands. His hair fell in untidy waves over the side of his face, thick and glossy, obscuring his features and curling over his collar. As she swayed imperceptibly towards him, a sharp stone dug into her injured foot. She gasped audibly. Abruptly, the stranger stopped what he was doing. Milana's hand flew to her mouth in a gesture of apologetic confusion.

She had expected the face of a man, maybe because the coat he wore was big and broad at the shoulders and the muscles of his arms were toned and his whole demeanour expressed strength and purpose, but as his gaze met hers she saw he was just a boy, no more than seventeen or eighteen. His expression was tender in its youthfulness yet strong in the chiselled assuredness of every feature. His eyes were a penetrating deep blue edged in brown under long, black lashes. Her heart pounded as she watched a smile crease the corners of his mouth and felt his impossibly handsome face melt the distrust that had briefly held her emotions in thrall. His expression was one of such unexpected kindness and warmth that she knelt in the earth, head bowed, surrendering to the feeling of deliverance that swelled unchecked inside her as all the unshed tears of years spilled over.

She tried to wipe her eyes with the sleeve of her cardigan to no avail. Through the mist and the blur she saw him get up. At the rivers' edge he leant over the water and washed the powder off his hands. Returning, he crouched down beside her. He seemed about to run his fingers through his hair when, instead, he gently leant forwards and placed his hands momentarily over her flushed, tear-stained face. They were unexpectedly soft and the cool of the water on them soothed her hot skin so her unaccustomed tears no longer stung her eyes. The impression they left warmed her heart. It was as if, in this place that was her refuge, this stranger, by extension, brought her comfort.

'Milana. Is that your name? You wrote it on the earth yesterday,' he explained.

The tears pooled in her eyes turned them the colour of emerald lakes. She pressed her lips together and tasted the salt.

'You've been spying on me?' she asked tentatively.

'Of course not.'

She cocked her head and eyed him guardedly.

'I've never seen you,' she said with a flash of defiance.

'Maybe you just never looked,' he whispered back playfully.

He went back to his mortar and pestle. 'I'm sorry, I don't mean to frighten you, but I've seen you here quite often.' He spoke to her as though it were the most natural thing in the world to sit and cry on riverbanks.

'Why didn't you say anything before?' she asked.

'What should I say? You were happy, back then that is,' he said, glancing at her with just the hint of a smile, 'to be left alone, making pictures out of fragments of clay.'

'You mean you've watched me?'

31

'Not really, but your patterns are clever. You leave quite a few of them about.'

Milana got up.

'Are you leaving?' he asked with what seemed like a passing casual interest.

'Yes.'

'Why?'

She shrugged, 'I don't know.' She realised how much she wanted to stay.

'Don't feel you have to go. There's room enough for both of us on this bank.'

Milana had to smile in response as she glanced at the wasteland around them. She had felt all her natural self possession abandon her; her dignity crushed by the exposure of her misery, and yet it seemed almost funny to try to be anything other than herself with this stranger, so she sat down again.

'I'm sorry about all that.'

'You should never be ashamed of feeling.'

'It doesn't make it any less embarrassing.' She sighed.

He glanced at her, his eyes full of sunlight, 'I guess you don't cry much.'

'Why would you say that?'

'You like being alone, those kind of people rarely cry.'

'Why not?'

'Or rather when they do their tears are real, not for effect.'

Milana realised she'd been paid a compliment. She looked down. She felt his eyes on her .

'You're making me blush like a clam.'

He laughed. 'Clams blush?'

'This one does.' She laughed with relief at her own unexpected candour.

'I'm glad you stayed on, little clam. You've become quite familiar to me over there on the bank creating your mosaics.' He glanced up at her, 'A familiar stranger. There's a paradox.'

She toyed with the earth wondering what a paradox might be.

'Perhaps that's why I've felt safe here.'

'Do I make you feel safe?' He looked at her quizzically.

'I don't know? I just said that? Aren't you safe?'

He laughed again and she saw the even whiteness of his teeth.

'Safe from what?' He looked around him slowly, a mischievous twinkle in his eye, 'From ghosts, from strangers?' He turned his beautiful face on her with a wry smile and raised a questioning eyebrow.

'From loneliness,' she said and moved a little closer to him. The breeze lifted her hair and caressed her face.

'What are you doing?' she asked overcoming her usual wariness.

'I'm grinding lapis lazuli.'

'Cool name!' she cocked her head thoughtfully to one side, 'Hello, my name's Lapis Lazuli, what's yours?' She pondered the idea for a moment, and again recognised the strange sensation of feeling his quizzical gaze on her.

'So who's Lapis? He looks like a piece of sky,' she said facing him enthusiastically with the sudden energy of heightened awareness.

'A piece of sky?'

'Yeah, streaked with grey but deep blue inside. '

He laughed, 'You have a funny way with words Milana. Lapiz here is a semi precious rock used to make jewellery. I'm making blue pigment from it.'

'Pigment? What's that?'

'It's the colour you make paint from.'

'You make paint?' She leaned a little closer to look. 'What for?'

'To paint, naturally.' He glanced at her.

'What do you paint, then?'

'The sunset mostly and the dawn.' Was he playing with her? She couldn't tell.

'Shouldn't it be the other way round; dawn comes before sunset?'

'Or from every sunset comes a dawn,' he shrugged, 'it's more optimistic that way round.'

The blood rose to her cheeks a second time.

'Then it was you who painted that glass I found.' She paused, 'Did you?'

'I try colours out on glass to see how translucent they are. I never meant to leave it in the mud where it could hurt,' he added solemnly.

'Oh, it couldn't hurt,' she breathed, wondering what translucent meant and feeling the fluid transparent nature of the word, then remembering herself she added, 'No one comes here anyway.'

'We do.' He caught her eye. She lowered her gaze to watch the bright blue powder spill away from the rock. Her heart skipped: he had placed her with him on a level with that simple word 'we'.

'I was going to steal it away from you,' she confided with a sudden flash of spirit. 'Would you have minded?'

He stopped grinding to reach behind him.

'Take it, if you want it.' He held out the splendid curved slice of sunset. 'Don't let it cut your fingers,' he warned as she took it, delighted, and held it in the palm of her hand.

'Have you ever painted with blood?' she asked suddenly.

'No, not something I've considered yet.'

'You might if you get desperate. How do you make red paint anyway?'

'From Vermilion.'

'Vermilion? That's another really cool name.'

'What's with the name thing?'

'Oh I just like making up unusual names and giving them personalities, you know, like Lapis I'd say is a quick, clever sort of guy, wise as a mountain, a rock-solid friend. But his girlfriend Vermilion, let's say, is cunning, a sort of snake in the grass person, that can wind herself around you while she sucks the blood from you. It's a perfect name for a vampire!' she smiled a little wistfully thinking of the *Twilight* books Victoria had spoken to her about.

'Where do you paint, then?' she continued, her eyes drawn quickly back to him, but he had stopped what he was doing, a bemused smile playing over his face as he drank in her bright, expressive eyes and the lithe, graceful gestures that accompanied her descriptions.

'Milana Milana!' Urgent shouts pierced the still air, her name pinned to each one. She turned towards the far bank, a sudden panic welling up inside her. She'd forgotten all about school, about everything, the voices pulled at the dream, lifting it away from her, like a treasured balloon she must let go of.

'I've got to go.'

'Go on then,' he urged her gently. 'Before they discover your hideaway.'

'I can't take it with me now.' She stood up, her gaze intent on him as she stretched out her hand. Their fingers met fleetingly on the painted glass as she returned it into his safe keeping.

'Will I see you again?' The words were out before she could stop them. The balloon was being taken by the wind, the string unattached, free.

'Maybe, if you bother to look next time.' She looked back at him once, but he was too far away and the contours of his smile had blurred.

Chapter Four

Shanty dwellers stood outside their shacks on the rutted, dusty streets. Arms folded they followed Milana with their eyes. Rough hands grabbed her by the shoulders.

'Hey? Your name Milana?' inquired a burly man with a weather-beaten face. His open shirt revealed a thick, silver chain on which hung a medal of Our Lady. Milana smelt his odour; a sweet sour smell of stale cooking, onions and cigarettes.

'You Letty's girl?' the question came again, abrupt and urgent.

'Yes.'

The man lifted his heavy-lidded eyes and called out in a deep-throated voice over her head:

'*Hombres,* I've got her.'

An involuntary shudder shot through Milana causing him to let go of her abruptly. He was joined by more men.

'There's trouble. Best you come with us,' said an older man in a vest like the one Ana's husband, Chevo, wore. Milana felt his hand clasp her elbow as he steered her along the alley, his fingers tightening with unnecessary force. Three others, men like himself, rough and badly shaven, fell into step with them.

Neighbours whispered to each other as they passed, a few shook their heads quietly. Milana concentrated on putting one foot in front of the other, aware of the pressure on her arm. It was the only sure thing in this strange charade. One of the men muttered to the other, 'Steady on, mate, she ain't a jailbird.' The one who held her let go in a flash. She sensed his embarrassment. They hung their heads to avoid the stares that stalked them. Doris was standing at the bakery on the corner of Oleander Alley. She held a tray of her sugar-dusted cakes wrapped in cellophane. Milana saw the glint of gold in her front tooth as she bit her lower lip. The sombre group walked past in grim silence.

On the edge of the shantytown the old petrol station had been torn down to make way for the Chucky Cheese Pizza Palace where uptown children could party amidst the maze of plastic tunnels and slot machines. A large yellow bus waited near the entrance to the now deserted parking lot. It was the kind of beaten up vehicle that hurtled through the streets of Santiago scattering pedestrians, stopping at random to gather up passengers, so that at rush hour they hung out of the doors like bees clustered round a honeycomb. The *micro* looked aimless and out of place at this unaccustomed hour. Milana climbed the steps towards the rows of dilapidated empty seats whilst the men watched her in silence. She stopped and looked back at them, these big, burly men, their demeanour awkward, their faces strained, and it dawned on her then; these were bus drivers, the kind that stopped for her mother's *sopaipillas*. The men stared from one to the other and shuffled their feet. They looked back at her sheepishly, guilt-ridden and shamefaced. The smell of air freshener percolated out of a plastic ball suspended from the rear-view mirror.

'They told us, like as not, you'd be down by the river,' chirped a bright voice near her shoulder. Milana turned suddenly. It was the driver. She hadn't noticed him sitting in the driving seat amidst his mascots and rosary beads. A stuffed monkey hung cheekily from the mirror below a psychedelic ball that reflected rainbows in the sunlight. The driver's podgy hands rested on the red synthetic fur that covered the steering wheel. He grinned at her kindly.

'It's better this way,' he nodded her to a seat. The others came and sat around her like silent jailers. They didn't want to answer questions. Instinctively Milana asked none. She felt alien to them, this peculiar brotherhood of sullen bus drivers.

The bus left the shantytown behind. It climbed the hill where the smart new developments were under construction and stopped abruptly in a layby next to a skip. People milled about here like on the fringes of some big gig. The road was new, carved into the dynamited hillside. Lampposts dwarfed the recently planted palm trees and flowering laurels. The hill was alive with bulldozers and cement mixers. For every cluster of brand new homes with cellophane stickers still attached to the glass of the windows, there was another skeleton group with great wire meshes sticking up like eager tentacles from deep foundations, waiting for the cement that would transform them into the walls of up-market dwellings. This was where Letty had chosen to set up her kiosk because she said the construction workers on the housing developments would double her business. They had.

Milana thought of Letty peeling pumpkin after pumpkin chucking the rinds out to feed the alley cats. Night after night she kneaded the flour and lard, adding the pureed pumpkin before rolling out the pastry and cutting out the circular *sopaipillas* in readiness for frying. All the while she sang softly to the love songs of Radio Carolina. Sometimes Iris came from next door and kept her company, sitting on the old cane settee, drinking tea, pouring out the gossip on Ana and Nilda and Nora and the others until it filled the dingy room like fumes from an old gas lamp. Milana would cover her ears then, wishing it to stop, but she had grown used to the women and Letty humming a tune as Iris and the others gossiped.

'Why do you hum, Mum?' Milana had asked her once.

'So as not to hear them,' Letty had laughed.

'But why do you let them come, then, if you don't want to hear them?

'Because they're my friends, they're company, they're all I've got besides you and the boys.'

A few feet away from the bus, Milana looked up at a giant mimosa tree loaded with yellow pom-pom blossoms. They spilled down over the delicate fern like leaves, creating such a mass of colour that it looked as though a thousand yellow chicks had taken residence in its fine old branches. Under its shade

Milana saw Letty's metal cart with its condiments already set out on the counter in readiness. When, later, Milana looked back on this day, her first recollection would always be of the metal cart, parked under the mimosa tree festooned in blossom as though for an Easter parade, and the red jacket her mother wore slung over the pull bar on the front of the cart. And only then, as though inserted in slow motion, the sirens and flashing lights, all strangely out of place here, above the city smog.

Milana shielded her eyes from the sun that reflected off the silver paintwork of a large Mitsubishi Jeep overturned on the new tarmac, its powerful tyres now helpless in the air. Dark rivulets trickled down the hill from where it had spewed oil and petrol. Glass lay shattered like tiny stones everywhere. On the far side of the road a bus lay half on its side in a ditch. Passengers sat by the roadside, some with blankets around their shoulders, others shouting and gesticulating. Noise engulfed her. People crowded about; paramedics, police, firemen, builders with naked torsos and hammers hanging from their leather belts; men in suits, stopped on their way to work, and those that just stared, scattered about, like extras on a film set.

'Are you OK?' asked an elderly woman who was observing Milana closely

'Yes. I'm OK,' the sound of her own voice was oddly comforting. 'Was anyone hurt?' she asked.

'Young chap,' the woman confided, 'still breathing though, the ambulance is just leaving.' As if to corroborate her words its siren started up. They watched the ambulance weave through the confusion and disappear down the hill, lights flashing.

'Were there lots of people on the bus?'

'Not many. They all got out.' Their eyes focused at the same time on the large yellow bus on the far side of the road. It appeared to have been half thrown on its side into the gutter by the impact from the Mitsubishi. Further inspection showed it had been stopped from continuing its otherwise fatal journey into the ravine below by the lamppost which had obligingly bent over backwards to bring the bus to a halt. There was a small crowd around it. They seemed to be checking the damage to the front wheels which were partly obscured by the ditch where the tarmac ended and the pavement had not yet been completed. Milana stared. She took a step forwards but the woman held her back.

'Don't go there,' she urged suddenly.

Milana turned her defiant, terror-filled eyes towards the woman.

'Hey come away there!' someone shouted, but Milana paid no attention. A red trainer lay on its side in the road by her feet. It had a black lace in it. Milana leant over to pick it up. The crowd was getting larger, she could see the paramedics leaning over the ditch.

'They can't reach her! God help her, she's still alive!'

The words thrown up by the crowd encircled Milana's heart like a drawstring. Her teeth were chattering but she wasn't cold, she was hurting, hurting as when strong heat thaws freezing cold. Almost immediately people gathered around her, holding her, she felt pressure of arms, bodies, the breath of others on her face but her own breath was caught as though by great sobs but she could not cry.

'She's still alive,' someone was saying it over and over to her. At first nothing made sense, only gradually could she make out the words, 'She's still alive,' and suddenly they took on meaning; 'She's still alive. She's alive.'

Letty's body was pinned to the ground under the front wheel of the bus that had dragged her like a hapless animal caught in its fender, just short of the ravine. A sun goddess in a picture book, that's how Milana would remember her; her pink cap fallen and her hair spread like frazzled rays reaching out over the earth. Her eyes were half closed. She could barely breathe. One hand lay twisted to the side of her chest. Someone had two fingers to the pulse in her neck. Milana curled up on the earth beside her mother and, putting her head to one side so that her lips touched her mother's hair, she whispered in her ear, 'I love you, Mum.' There was a faint movement on her mother's lips.

Letty's eyelids lifted briefly as her eyes tried to focus. Her whole body responded minutely with infinite gratitude. Milana touched her mother's twisted hand, stroking it very gently.

'I love you,' she whispered. Closing her eyes Milana repeated those three words over and over.

They did not cover Letty with a plastic sheet as was the common practise until the judge arrived. They did not touch the body and no one there dared move the child away from her dead mother.

Chapter Five

Letty's body lay in a wooden chapel that stood in the middle of the shantytown. A ray of sun pierced the gloom like a sword, striking the metal handle of her pine coffin. The lid was open. A smile seemed to play on her lips. Iris had painted them a soft raspberry colour and had expertly dissimulated the surrounding cuts and grazes. The cheekbones appeared more prominent through the taut, wax-like skin, giving Letty a striking, eerily beautiful presence in death that had eluded her in life, or maybe she had wilfully hidden it. Her hands, folded on her chest, looked sculpted, too slender and small to be real.

A steady stream of neighbours came to say goodbye. Some, undaunted by the pall of death, reached in to touch Letty's coldness reverently. Women recited the rosary, the hum of their voices rising and falling like a dismal requiem song. Milana stayed a while repeating the endless litany of prayers but her mind wandered as she watched these women, in their black garb of mourning, hunched over their beads like birds of prey, and she slipped out into the warm daylight.

Milana stooped down to spread her hand over the grass outside the chapel wondering how it could stay so cool beneath the midday sun. The fresh green blades of early spring would soon become parched and burnt by the relentless heat of high summer. On the far side of this little oasis, Milana paused in front of a small stone grotto that sheltered a statue of the Virgin Mary. The peace was disturbed by unfamiliar voices. Behind her, two smartly dressed women were creating a stir by the chapel doors as one called to the other who talked crossly on a mobile phone. A large gold-buckled handbag swung from her shoulder flashing in the sun as she walked this way and that, carelessly unaware of how each word of her irate conversation to her daughter invaded the quiet. Finally, having finished her tirade, they breezed into the chapel together, pushing their huge sunglasses up onto their glossy hair, self-importance quivering about them like an expensive scent.

Milana watched them disappear into the dark interior, these rich ladies, that came to the shantytown with time on their hands and money in their wallets, and a faint sense of guilt at their innate good fortune. They did their bit for charity bringing tea and biscuits and supervising the sale of donated clothes only to find themselves touched for money every which way. Some left indignant and affronted by such shameless scrounging, others stayed longer but eventually they too gave up and moved on. Mostly they came and went like elegant yachts sailing through godforsaken harbours. Milana hoped they wouldn't come in search of her with their well meaning platitudes. Turning her back on the chapel, she sat herself down on the stone seat before the statue of the Blessed Mother.

If only *Señora* Lisa were here now, not these other women for whom each visit to the shantytown was a chore they hoped might pave their way to heaven and widen the proverbial eye of the needle. *Señora* Lisa had surprised the shantytown women from the first by addressing them as equals. She had compared them to soldiers, deployed to this shantytown as they might have been to any other outpost, with a mission to accomplish in God's name and their survival depending on covering for each other. Her unusual vision had excited their imagination and lifted them out of their humdrum existence. She had inspired them to discover where their talents might lie and encouraged them to start soup kitchens and nursing units and even mini businesses with everyone pulling together. That was how Letty had first thought up the idea of her *sopaipilla* business. *Señora* Lisa had never turned a hair at their filthy language. She had taught them the real meaning of love.

A flicker of warmth blew into Milana's heart. She smiled to herself remembering how, for a long time, she had actually believed the gesso statue in the grotto was of this lovely lady that sometimes came to their shanty to leave boxes of goodies and once, a pair of pink glittery slippers. Milana had endowed the pretty slippers with magic powers and still today, long outgrown, they remained on a small wooden shelf above the bed. Even now Milana found she couldn't quite shed the association she had built between her heavenly mother and the ethereal memory of blonde hair and lemon scent left behind by *Señora* Lisa whose features she could no longer recall.

Letty had laughed and laughed when she had discovered Milana's mistake about the statue. Then, registering the pained expression on Milana's young face, Letty had explained that it was *Señora* Lisa who had brought the statue of the Blessed Virgin to the shantytown to replace the one that used to stand there cracked and broken by previous earthquakes. She had distracted Milana from her obvious embarrassment, grabbing her imagination by explaining that Our Lady had her arms outstretched just as she had appeared one night in 1817 to a nun praying in Paris. This Celestial Lady had asked the bewildered nun to have a medal cast of the apparition. Because of its supernatural powers it became known as 'the Miraculous Medal'. Milana had wondered where such a magic medal could be found but Letty had shrugged in her usual dismissive way and said, 'Who's to know but it's a pretty story all the same.'

Now Milana recalled the day *Señora* Lisa had given each of the women a silver plated Miraculous Medal to hang on a silver chain around their necks as her Christmas present to them before she left for Europe. If she had brought down the stars one by one for them, those women, Letty included, could not have been more filled with wonder and gratitude. That medal had become Letty's most prized possession. She was wearing it when she died and somehow it had seemed wrong to remove in death what her mother had clung to in life, so it lay with her now in her coffin.

'Will it do miracles?' Milana remembered asking back then. It hadn't saved her mother. It was foolish to expect miracles she told herself as she sat under the cloudless September sky. And yet, as she took a deep breath she found the place that had previously been stifled by sadness received the spring air gratefully.

A shadow fell across the bench. Milana lifted her eyes to find Oscar's big gentle face looking down at her, his brow creased with concern.

'Them's for you–' he dropped two yellow marigolds into her lap – 'one for your mum, and one for you.'

She picked up the flowers and touched their golden halo of petals.

'Life sucks,' he suggested, thrusting his hands in his pockets and shifting from side to side.

'She was OK, your mum.'

He sat beside Milana.

'Pretty in't she?' he mused.

Milana followed his gaze to the statue. 'Looks like she's moving with all them folds in her dress,' he went on, tilting his head to one side. Beside the statue, stumps of candle rose out of twisted patterns of melted wax.

'Look, one's lit,' he pointed to it with sudden interest.

'I remember my mum lighting a candle here ages back,' Milana responded wistfully.

'Yeah?' Oscar rested his adoring eyes on her.

'Do you ever pray, Oscar?'

Oscar looked back at the statue thoughtfully, struggling to answer.

'Why's she got them ray things coming from her hands?'

'Mum told me they were the graces she brought us to help us live through the dark parts of our life, but mostly no one bothers to ask for them.'

'I'll ask for them, for you, Milana, if you want?' And he waited earnestly for her response. 'There, see, I made you smile,' he declared joyfully.

'I can look after you, if you let me. You know that, right?' he added, overwhelmed by a sudden surge of confidence.

'Thank's Oscar. I'll be fine.'

'You don't believe me,' he looked suddenly deflated.

'Oh I do, but I'll be fine.'

'But I'll show you I can,' he said rising purposefully. 'I'll stand up to them, like you do. I've watched you. I can do it too. You'll see.'

'What do you mean Oscar?' She glanced up a little alarmed. His brown eyes stared back at her loyally.

'It don't matter, you'll see. I can.' And he squared his shoulders a little and looked ahead fixedly.

They remained in silence trapped between the blazing midday sun and the heat that rose from the baked earth beneath. Milana fingered the beads of her rosary. Soon they would close the coffin and there would be no more Letty. No more listening to her singing along to Radio Carolina as she peeled pumpkins into the night, no more sudden bouts of playfulness as she grabbed them and tickled them till they howled. Letty was gone. They would put her into her grave; a hole in the wall where the disadvantaged dead were stacked, coffin upon coffin, with only a thin layer of cement separating each tomb, like the drawers in a hospital morgue.

'I best be going now.'

Oscar's voice jerked Milana back.

'OK,' she whispered.

He lingered for a moment, nodding his head gently as though it were mounted on a spring.

'You know she's in heaven now, don't you?' he said awkwardly. Looking up at him, Milana smiled gratefully.

'I hope so, Oscar, and thanks for these.' She touched the soft orange petals. Oscar felt his heart swell. He moved away, looking back every now and again.

The marigolds, no doubt rescued from Ana's cooking pot by his timely intervention, sat on Milana's lap, their fulsome heads redolent with sunshine. For a moment the face of the stranger on the riverbank came to her unsummoned, his eyes meeting hers, knowing her, but, like a sunbeam between clouds, it escaped again. She stroked the velvet petals feeling their fleshiness cool between her fingers.

Milana reached down and placed the marigolds at the feet

of Our Lady. A gentle breeze stirred the dust around the statue where the tiny flame of a candle fluttered and waned and seemed to extinguish altogether before bravely lifting its little plume of light again.

Chapter Six

Nilda sat down heavily and stared at the empty plates.

They ate everything, bless them, she told herself as she pressed her podgey finger onto some stray crumbs. Her tired eyes rested on the gilt frame that her daughter, Nora, had given her for her fiftieth birthday. She reached out for it. It held a dog-eared photograph of them all: Iris, Ana, Doris, Letty and herself, taken on a beach near Valparaiso. Letty was centre-stage laughing and holding up a bucket and spade, her reddish hair like a rising sun against the horizon. Nilda sat on a rock, looking like a beached whale next to Letty's slim frame. Iris was standing to one side of the photo wearing a purple scarf tied flamboyantly round her silver-streaked black hair. Ana was gesturing in mid-converstion, donning a floppy hat covered in sunflowers that had cost Oscar 10p for his mother at the weekly clothes sale. Doris was on the far side of the picture, sitting on the sand, unwrapping cakes for their picnic. With her simple blue skirt and white shirt, she merged into the surf and the cobalt sea and sky. She was looking at a stray dog that had walked into the foreground to sniff *Señora* Lisa's handbag on the sand, the only indication that *Señora* Lisa had been there too. Nilda replaced the frame and looked around. She pinched the flame of the candle that had remained lit infront of a small plastic statue of Jesus and watched the smoke rise and swirl as it extinguished; our prayers going up to heaven for you, Letty. She smiled. Behind her, in the porcelain bowl that doubled as a kitchen sink, a bunch of lilies protruded from their cellophane wrapper filling the room with their funereal scent. They had been brought by Chevo, Ana's husband, in the name of the bus drivers' syndicate.

The bus drivers couldn't have been nicer, thought Nilda. They had paid for the funeral. It wasn't their fault that the boy in the big Mitsubishi had been driving his father's jeep without permission, or that the bus, had inadvertently crushed Letty as she sat warming herself in the early morning sun. That's how things happened. When you looked carefully, there was always a particular chain of events leading up to an apparently random accident. It was meant to be, Nilda told herself firmly, Letty's time had come. She wiped away a stray tear.

There was a quiet knocking at the door.

'Who's there?' Nilda sighed, heaving herself off the plastic chair. Opening the door, she peered out into the night. The light from inside leaked out illuminating Oscar, hesitantly shifting from one foot to the other.

'What are you skulking about here for, boy?' she said giving him a suspicious look. Her eye rested on the shiny red radio in his hands.

'Here, what you doing with that? In't that Letty's radio, the one she got at the Christmas draw two years ago?'

Oscar looked at the object in his hands as though surprised to find it there.

'Is M... M... Milana here?'

'Never mind Milana, she ain't receiving no visitors, young man,' and she grabbed the radio out of his hands before he could react.

'What's this then, eh?' She turned it over, inspecting it carefully.

'I... I... was b... bringing it b... back.'

'Bringing it back? Her voice rose nearly an octave. Oscar looked awkwardly at his feet.

'I b... best go then.'

'Not so fast.' She looked him over thoughtfully. 'Who put you up to this, boy. You ain't been thieving, 'ave you?'

He stared at the pavement and shook his head.

'I b... best b... be going then,' he repeated helplessly.

'And the telly, did you just happen to find that too?'

His head jerked up at the mention of the telly and a pained look creased his face.

'How'd you know about the telly? I put it b... back,' he blurted out naively.

'You put it back!' Overcoming her initial surprise, she put her hands on her hips and thrust her ample bosom forward as if to impress her indignation upon him.

'Those thieving little oiks, Oscar, will get you into big trouble one of these days.'

Oscar twisted his hands together fretfully.

'D... don't be hard on my b..b..brothers, *Tia*, they don't mean any harm b... by it. They can't help it.' His face contorted into a sudden grimace that he struggled to free himself of. Nilda waited for the violent tick to pass.

'What? They can't help helping themselves to Letty's stuff and her still warm in her grave. What's Ana say to that, eh?'

'Oh M..Mum don't know. Don't tell her.' He glanced up apologetically his eyes startlingly candid. 'I took the stuff b... back soon as I found it in our yard – and they was OK with that.' He seemed suddenly to gain in self-possession.

'OK? I should think they were! You can't cover for your thieving brothers all your life Oscar. They're trouble and it'll only get worse when they get older. I hope Chevo gives them a good thrashing for this.' Oscar seemed to wince and struggle to overcome the onset of another contortion. Nilda noted the dark shadowing round Oscar's eye and the way the bruising seemed to have slid half way down his face, and she bit her lip. ' I'm that sorry for the lot of you,' she added more gently. 'What's with this radio, then? Have you come to tell Milana you rescued all her stuff afore she even figured it went missing? Is that it, young man?' she exclaimed raising her eyebrows. He looked down abashed.

'I didn't mean no t... t... trouble.' And, plucking up all the courage he could muster he looked Nilda in the eye and in short sharp gasps of determination he added, 'I'll look out for her I will. I won't let trouble happen to her. You tell her that and give her the radio back from me.' With that he turned and fled like a cornered animal released.

Nilda watched him retreating, his square frame lit by the occasional streetlamp until it disappeared out of sight. Then she turned back, feeling the smooth cool plastic of the radio as though it were a living thing rescued from a tragic end. She smiled; Oscar was sweet on Milana, no doubt about it. Nilda closed the door and stepped through the front room into the small bedroom where usually she shared the bed with her grown up daughter, Nora, for want of space. Tonight Milana lay there fast asleep with her two brothers beside her. Nilda put the radio down on the table next to Nora's cotton buds. Nora wasn't the sort of daughter Nilda had hoped for, she was a hard-bitten creature not given to affection or sympathy. Still, she was the only daughter she'd got and at least she'd scarpered south to avoid the outpouring of grief, leaving the bed free for Letty's body to be laid out.

Nilda felt a tightening in her chest as she remembered last night; Iris, kneeling where she now stood, gently washing every part of Letty, wringing the blood out of the cloth till the water ran the colour of rust and Ana drained it down the sink. Together with Ana they had dressed Letty in her best clothes and slipped a cross made out of woven palms between her fingers. Iris had applied lipstick and dusted her waxen cheeks with powder and stroked her gently as though she were a sleeping child. Nilda had shied away from touching Letty. She couldn't face the feel of death's cold unyielding film on the familiar softness of Letty's skin. All night they had kept watch over Letty as though they feared the angels might come and snatch her from them if they so much as looked away. Ricci and Juanito had fallen asleep on the bed next to their dead mother but Milana had stayed awake, quiet and distant, sitting under the lemon tree outside, shivering beneath the starry sky.

In the half light, Nilda reached out and touched Milana's hair where it spread over the pillow. If only Letty hadn't dyed hers, she too once had that same beautiful hair before she spoiled it. Why were people never content with what they had, wondered Nilda. She spied with satisfaction her own tightly permed hair in the mirror. Iris had done it for her. Iris was clever that way. Nora, with a daughter's lack of tact, said it left Nilda looking like a prize poodle but Nilda felt that was small price to pay for taking years off her age. Ten years at least, the others had said. Whatever Nora thought of the perm, she had soon shut up when Iris taught her how to roll the brush to give her the big power fringe that all the sales assistants in the fancy shops were sporting.

Nilda settled down into her favourite chair. Moonlight trickled through the open curtains peopling the room with shadows. She remembered little Nora as a baby, fat and round-faced. Nora wasn't born tough as nails, she'd learnt to be tough. Life hadn't been kind to her. Nilda remembered the little grandchild that had been plucked away from them so young. She was filled suddenly by a sort of cosmic sorrow. Tears fell onto her ample bosom and slipped down the polyester flowers of her blouse. She took a tissue from her sleeve and blew her nose noisily. She thought of them all at Letty's funeral and Oscar's thieving brothers hopping in through the window and helping themselves to the contents of Letty's shanty while their own mother, Ana, cried over Letty's grave. What was to become of Letty's children now? An orphanage wouldn't be so bad, she tried to tell herself, but then at fourteen Milana might not qualify. Maybe Ana would take her in, seeing as Oscar was sweet on her. Nilda dabbed her eyes, she knew all too well the kind of ignominious future that awaited street girls. She tucked the tissue away and wriggled in the chair, her generous behind working itself into all the spare places. Soon her chin was nestled into its folds and her large bosom rose and fell with each gentle snore.

Milana woke under the thin bedspread that had been pulled over her and felt the warmth from her brothers sleeping beside her. For a fleeting instant she had imagined her mother, cold and dead between them. A gentle snoring from somewhere close alarmed her. It was several moments before her eyes became accustomed to the dark and she could make out the sleeping form of her mother's most loyal friend, Nilda, in her chair.

Nilda was so plump and round that any wrinkles she might have acquired were smoothed out across her wide expanse of face. Her features were improbably girlish. Her nose, round like a new potato, shone faintly in the moonlight, while her sweetly dimpled chin rose like a tiny island from a sea of flesh. Hair framed her face in a mass of little grey capped waves. If Nilda were a bread roll, Milana had decided long ago, she would be one of those soft doughy ones with sugared icing and cream in the centre. No wonder Letty had loved her so much.

Letty! The memory skipped in and stopped short: Letty gone! Milana tried to push the thought away before it could begin its relentless progress through the brain, like some vile unstoppable cramp. Instead she found herself trying to figure out how she, Ricci and Juanito would manage without their mother. Bleak reality, ever more focussed, seemed to mock her efforts.

Milana closed her eyes and turned on her side covering her face with her hands. Their coldness startled her. Suddenly she remembered the stranger's hands. The memory, unbidden, stirred her. She relived their touch, cold with the water of the river, but warm beneath; their warmth penetrating her skin. The feeling persisted, like the gentlest caress releasing her anxiety with the strength of his imagined presence.

Nilda woke herself up with a loud snore and cast an eye over the children. Peering over them she gasped as she made out Milana's wide-open eyes.

'Heavens, I thought you were asleep, dear child.'

'I've been thinking.'

'You mustn't worry yourself, love…' But before she could carry on, Milana had slipped off the bed and, not wanting to wake her brothers, led Nilda by the hand through the curtain partition into the front room.

Nilda sat while Milana took a jug from the shelf above the

sink that was full of lilies and, filling it with water, arranged the flowers in it and brought them to the table.

'Aren't they pretty,' sighed Nilda stretching out her chubby hand to touch the white blossoms. 'You mustn't worry yourself, Milana,' she continued, gently stroking the fleshy petals as if she were addressing them. '*Señora* Maria will take you in. She'll care for you three. She's subsidised by the parish you know and she gets free milk from the supermarket.'

Milana sat herself opposite Nilda and leaning her elbows on the little table looked earnestly at her.

'I want us to stay at home, Ricci, Juanito and me. We'll manage.'

Nilda looked horrified, 'Bless my soul, anything could happen to you there. You can't stay alone what with all the thieving and torching, all them druggies and thugs about and no one to look out for you. '

'I'll do odd jobs.' Milana went on, ignoring Nilda's concerns. 'And we get free school dinners, we don't need more than one good meal a day, see. We can manage. I don't want us to be split up and packed off somewhere. And I must go to school, Nilda, I must, or I'll be no use to anyone but the guys at the back the service station. I want to be better than that.' She fixed her eyes on Nilda pointedly.

Nilda shook her head pitifully and made a little helpless gesture, 'School?' she grimaced, 'How's that going to help you *Chiquita*?' then smiling brightly she added, 'What you want is to get a good job in service with a nice family. They'll look after you.'

'I can do better than that, if I finish school.'

Nilda pursed her lips, 'You got a streak of your mother's stubborn pride, girl,' and she shook her head again as if to say and look where that got her.

With cool composure Milana persisted.

'If they send me off to *Señora* Maria she'll have me doing all her errands and she'll never give me a chance to get my school certificate. Please, Aunt Nilda, who's going to stand up for my rights if you don't?'

'Rights? What's that then?'

'I'm entitled to be educated just like anyone else. It's the only chance I'll get in life. You only get one shot at it, that's what our English teacher said. He said we had to want it and fight for it and use it well.'

'What's that?'

'Education, learning. You've got to want to learn, else it doesn't work. I really want to know stuff about the world, other countries, you know, people, everything.'

'Your teacher ain't from these parts that's for sure,' Nilda grunted to herself. 'How will all that help you live?' she whined, 'What'll you do for money for the bills, the water...'

'I'll shower at school.'

'What for?'

'To save on water.'

'You still gotta pay for gas to cook.'

'We don't need to cook, we'll eat at school.'

A sort of vacant hopelessness came over Nilda that made Milana want to scream. She grabbed her arm and shook it, 'Aunt Nilda, please, I need you to fight my corner here.'

'Lord knows it's hard,' sighed Nilda, seeming to wake up again to Milana's plight, 'You'll need...' Suddenly she started as though she'd been pinched.

'Oh my,' she gasped, 'Holy heavens! How could I forget?' She pulled herself out of her chair and shuffled to the little cupboard below the sink, flung it open and rummaged noisily through the contents.

'Oh, oh, oh,' she moaned.

'What's the matter? Can I help?' asked Milana, watching Nilda's state of agitation with a kind of objective fascination.

Nilda pushed past the curtain partition back into the bedroom and knelt down on the floor to peer under the bed. She groped the edge of the bed to heave herself up again, her hair dishevelled and her face red.

'It's not there!' She wrung her hands together. 'God help us, those thieving little oiks. I've been robbed!'

Nilda sank into a nearby chair. 'It's the fits,' she cried distractedly. 'They fry my brain.'

'What have you lost, Aunt Nilda? It can't be so terrible, can it?'

'No, of course not, dear. What could be more terrible than the tragedy, Lord knows, the death, the loss... God rest her soul... the telly...' for a few seconds she was silent but then, just as suddenly as before, she struggled up again, her agitation returning, 'Holy Saints,' she cried, 'what did I do with it?'

Nilda resumed her frantic searching. Milana looked on at a loss to understand what all the fuss was about. Meanwhile she stacked the few plates that lay about and, dusting off the crumbs on them, she opened the oven that doubled as a plate cupboard.

'Oh look!' she exclaimed on seeing a large sugar jar sitting proudly in there. She hoped to distract Nilda from her inexplicable frenzy that could easily trigger one of Nilda's frequent epileptic seizures. 'I didn't know you kept the sugar here.'

'Oh, oh, oh,' gasped Nilda nearly fainting at the sight of the jar. 'Thank God and the Blessed Mother and all the angels! Letty would never have forgiven me.'

Milana stared at the sugar jar with some surprise.

'It's only a jar of sugar,' she said picking it up and finding, to her surprise, that it felt quite light.

'It's not sugar, love,' chuckled Nilda and taking the jar from Milana she kissed it before unscrewing the lid.

Milana gawped in amazement as bank notes fluttered out like Kleenex tissues, until a small pile covered the top of the table.

Nilda looked up at Milana.

'She trusted me your mother did, and, Lord knows, after El Negro and his pinching it, she never left her money in the house; said she was out too much and anyone could help themselves to it. She kept it hidden here. Nora doesn't know, mind. Lord knows why I put it in the oven today. Me and my chicken brain! Letty was the one as glued sugar all round the sides so no one would steal it.'

'That's so clever!' exclaimed Milana, reverently picking up a bank note that had dropped to the floor. She had never seen so much money. They were just small notes, collected over time, but it was money, maybe two hundred thousand *pesos*, as much as a maid's salary for a month.

'No wonder you were worried Aunt Nilda, you'd have been sad to lose this lot...'

'Heavens! This isn't mine, love, it's yours. Like I said, Letty gave it me for safe keeping.'

Nilda looked at Milana with infinite tenderness.

'Now maybe it can make the difference for you. Bless you girl, this money will help keep you. See?' Suddenly a shadow crossed her face at the thought of Oscar's thieving little brothers making off with anything they could lay their hands on to feed their drug habit. Hurriedly, Nilda started shoving the notes back in the jar.

'Don't tell no one about it though and hide it outside, somewhere in the ground where no one will find it. There's thieving hands at work, you hear me girl?' But she thought it best not to mention Oscar's visit.

'Wait.' Milana took the jar from her and carefully placed one note neatly upon the other, as she counted them out.

'I'll make Mum proud' she whispered quietly as though she were making a solemn vow to those scruffy notes.

Nilda touched her hand, 'Don't go making promises, *Chiquita*, Lord knows, it won't be easy.'

Two days later, while Ricci and Juanito were over at Ana's shanty playing spin with Oscar, Milana sat on the floor of the room she had been born in, sorting through her mother's old clothes. Neatly taped together pieces of linoleum afforded her some protection from the bare earth beneath. The old shower curtain depicting a seascape of brightly coloured fish was drawn across a wooden pole over the doorway to afford some small degree of privacy. On the other side sat the women, drinking the tea that Iris had brought.

'She can't stay here alone!' Ana was talking as though Milana wasn't there, they all were, regardless of the fact that behind the flimsy plastic divide Milana could hear every word.

'And where the devil will she earn the money to buy food?' Ana's voice was deep and husky; the result of all the cigarettes she smoked.

'They'll have to go to an orphanage, that's all there is to it,' said Iris serving them all one of her strange brews out of a thermos.

'*Señora* Maria's would be better, surely, than the orphanage.' Ana sighed, 'I wish I could take them in with my lads.'

'Poor kids.' Doris shook her head sadly. 'I couldn't fit all three of them in with me. And it wouldn't do to split them up.'

'Course they'll have to be split up. Life's a bugger, you just got to face it.' Iris sat back and slurped her tea.

Their words reached Milana like rodent ulcers twisting their tentacles under her skin. Their combined breathing seemed to float around her like fog obliterating horizons. Milana lay down on her mother's clothes like they were the soft snow of an avalanche calling her to numb her senses in their gentle caress. She thought of the jar hidden in the earth out back, her passport to hope. Beholden though she felt to Rici and Juanito, if all else failed, she would escape the lot of them and the miserable destiny they seemed intent on mapping out for her, and find her own adventure, alone.

The toilet in the shed flushed and Nilda shuffled in through the back door.

'If we keeps quiet, maybe she can stay right here, that's if we don't go round stirring.' Nilda looked pointedly at the others and settled herself back on a chair near the door.

'God help her, how will she manage?' Ana lamented wearily.

'Like her mother I'll warrant,' came Iris's quick retort. 'Only without some ass pedlar scumbag on her case.'

'She's only fourteen,' retorted Ana aghast, 'and already you've got her whoring down the back of the service station. Spare a thought for Letty.'

'I'm just saying she'll laugh at the lot of us and make enough money to keep her brothers in leather shoes and three square meals before she's turned fifteen.'

'You saying none of us have to worry 'cause she'll earn her keep like a good little slut?' Ana glared at her.

'It makes money, if you don't care.' Iris went on airily, 'I never judged Letty. She did well by it.'

There was a shocked silence.

'Well, I can see none of you ever tried to sell your lousy favours,' continued Iris. 'There's them poor sods as don't have any other way, see, they get caught into it, no blame in it.'

'Don't you dare go putting your scummy ideas into that poor girl's head,' exclaimed Ana, indignantly.

'I was just sticking up for Letty,' said Iris ignoring her. 'Anyways if we try and take Milana off to some lousy orphanage she'll do worse than that, she'll cheat, rob and steal to get her own way, like all them lousy horseshit politicians. She'll do what it takes, that girl will. She's got her dad's blood in her.' Iris stopped short aware that all eyes were on her. Then, with a flash of defiance she added, 'I should know. I worked for him I did.'

'Ricardo Romero weren't no politician,' Nilda countered shakily.

'Ricardo Romero is Juanito and Ricci's dad but he weren't Milana's dad,' Iris drew herself up self-importantly. 'That's what Letty let you all think. But I know better see. No, Ricardo Romero was a good decent man, but Milana's dad, well' – she drew it out savouring the moment of revelation – 'he was a real big shot.'

The women stared at Iris agog. In the next room Milana fingered her tears away, wiping her nose on her sleeve rather than risk her snivel being overheard. Usually she tried to let what they said flow away from her, into the river of endless meaningless gossip, but this last was different.

Chapter Seven

'I knew him.' Iris's gaze travelled slowly over Ana, Doris and Nilda. 'He was my boss, see.'

'Bugger me. A big shot dad. That explains why she's always off down by the river, us lot not good enough for her,' Ana declared, folding her arms defensively over her ample bosom.

'Don't you get prickly, Ana, just 'cos Milana won't fall for your Oscar,' muttered Doris beside her.

Milana sat quiet as a mouse behind the curtain, while her heart fluttered like a wild bird caught in a cage.

'Go on, dish the dirt, woman,' said Ana ignoring Doris. Then, glancing at Nilda's pale, strained face she added, 'And if you're going to tell on Letty see you tell your part fair and square, you hear. Letty's watching you, you be sure of that, Iris.' Her warning echoed ominously around the room.

'No need to wake the dead to make me tell it straight. Letty and I, we made a pact we wouldn't breathe a word as long as we both lived and I held my tongue all them lousy years. She didn't want no trouble here. She could have talked, she could have screwed the family. They'd have paid to shut her up. I told her so. She could have struck gold if she'd put her mind to it, but she weren't like that see.'

'She was decent,' muttered Doris.

'That she was,' sighed Nilda.

'Go on,' said Ana impatiently.

Iris lifted her chin self-importantly, 'Remember the old Hidalgo family what lived in the big house over the river, that fell down in the earthquake. Them as sold all the land for the developments and rebuilt the church; the house behind the big gates with them winged creatures on the pillars. That was the house Carlos Hidalgo grew up in; you know, that politician what was on TV lots. Everyone thought he was headed for President. He had a son at that posh English School. I'm talking like fourteen years ago.'

Iris paused to let the significance of this settle on her audience.

'I was a maid in his house, see, when he moved downtown.'

'You were a maid?' Ana let out a low whistle. 'Bugger me! You're a sly one, Iris. All this time I thought you were something better like…'

'I remember,' murmured Doris thoughtfully, nudging Ana back to silence. 'I remember Carlos Hidalgo. Remember his slogan? "Hidalgo for a better Future". It was on banners all the way down Vitacura and Kennedy Avenues. And you, their maid!'

'You said you were a sales girl before you started sewing from home,' muttered Ana remembering. 'You didn't want us thinking you were a maid, that's how come you kept your mouth shut.'

'Lay off, Ana. You want to hear this or not?' snapped Iris.

'Oh, get on with it,' said Doris, 'you know you've got us hooked.'

'I'd only been there a couple of years when it all happened, and Letty, well, she was new. He brought her to work in the house he did, *Don* Carlos Hidalgo himself, and guess where he'd met her,' Iris paused and leaned forwards, 'down by the Golf Metro!' Her eyes sparkled as they danced over her rapt audience. 'Yeah, where the whores hang near the fancy Golf Club for their fancy clientele. The municipality put in cameras now, on all them street corners cos people complained it weren't decent. But that's where *Don* Carlos Hidalgo, the big- shot politician met Letty when she was just a scrap of a girl. Soon as she joined the staff at the house, we got talking see, me and Letty. I could tell she'd never been near a fancy *cuica* house. She talked nice, learnt it off her fancy men I guessed, but she had a knife scar, right across her pretty cheek. That's them lousy scumbag ass peddlars. She didn't tell me that, but they do that, them pimps, put the fear into you, brand you like sheep. *Don* Carlos, he had that scar fixed; took her to a plastic surgeon he knew. Left her face smooth as a baby's bottom. I knew he had the hots for her, a little *mina* like her.'

'You mean *Don* Carlos Hidalgo, the famous politician, was having our Letty on the side, and him all squeaky clean! Bugger me!' Ana shook her head.

'A lousy bird-brain could work it out.' Iris rolled her eyes heavenwards. 'She said he just wanted to help her; said he only paid the going rate to get some privacy with her so them pimps wouldn't get wise to him. Letty claimed he never laid a finger on her, just bought her Cokes and *empanadas* and never got fresh. Now that was some load of horseshit for starters. Who did she think she was kidding?'

'Why would she lie?' asked Doris.

'Come off it, Doris, to protect his lousy reputation. He was kind to her, see, and Letty was decent like that. She didn't want to land him in it, besides she didn't really know me then, so she fed me the old line, *cachai*? She said he told her she was special, different. In't that what they all say just before they screw you?'

'Yeah, and she fell for it. Still, it's no crime,' said Ana staunchly.

'Maybe they was both honourable or don't that enter into your head, Iris?' Doris rebuked with unexpected vehemence and glanced at Nilda who gave her a grateful smile.

'Get on with the story,' barked Ana.

'Like I said, *Don* Carlos filled her head with the usual horseshit; told her she was intelligent an' she fell for it like you say, Ana. But then he got daring see. Oh, he was a crafty one that *Don* Carlos, like all them lawyers. It turned out his wife needed a new maid so he persuaded Letty to get interviewed for the job.' Iris sighed sarcastically. 'Like he couldn't get enough of her on the street corners; he wheedled her into his house so he could have her there, on demand, under his roof.'

Doris rolled her eyes dismissively.

'She had charm see, Letty did, she knew how to make people like her, guess it's part of the job. The *Señora,* she fell for it, thought Letty was the bee's knees, and her a low life whore! Blimey! If the *Señora* had known she'd have had all the carpets that girl ever stepped on, up and out of the house. She'd have had every *cuica,* fancy, sheet she'd ever tucked in thrown out and she'd have had the servants' quarters fumigated. But I didn't tell.'

'Biding your time,' muttered Doris. Iris opened her mouth to counter but shut it again, pretending to ignore Doris as she bulldozed on through terrain that had been left undisturbed for so many years.

'Letty never went out on her days off. "I don't have anywhere to go," she'd say all lame and sweet. I'd tell her to come out with me, but she'd make out like she was too shy to *carretear,* with me. So off I went and left her behind and I guess they reckoned I'd never put two and two together, her and the *Patron.* I mean I liked Letty well enough, but there was the *Señora* to think about. It was disrespectful what they was up to in her own house.'

'What was they up to, Iris?'

'Come off it, Doris. I don't go peeking about *sapeando.* I went out on my days off. But I wasn't born yesterday. Anyways, the *Señora* was always that good to me. Maybe she could be a bit sour; "*Cara raja*" the old cook called her, but I respected her. She walked like she had an iron rod down her back and she had them steely grey eyes and long-fingered hands with perfect dark red nails. Proud, that's what she was. Anyways, one day they got this new gardener, Ricardo, "*El Guapo*" we called him 'cos he was a real looker. At first he was real gentlemanly. He'd carry the shopping for me and stop for a chat, but then Letty started going all coy and flirty with him and I saw how he'd melt for her, and it pissed me off. I mean, it just weren't right, not with her and the *Patron* carrying on. I tried to warn Ricardo. I told him he was getting in above his head, and he just laughed at me. Like I didn't know what was what. That was real *mala onda.* And all the time there was the *Señora* saying wasn't Letty a nice girl and how nice that I had such a nice companion. Like Letty was doing me a favour.'

'That's him right, Ricardo Romero?' Ana broke in. 'The one as we thought was Milana's dad and Rici's and Juanito's. I never knew he was a gardener, blow me! You sure about all this? I thought he was an Argentinian truck driver she picked up at the service station as only dropped by once a year.'

'Yeah well you weren't meant to know shit. But shit gets about and sits half-baked on the road where everyone steps in it and no one knows where it comes from right?' Iris straightened her back and pulled a condescending face at them. 'So, stick with them crappy scraps.' She folded her arms defiantly, 'I can shut my mouth right now and you won't be any the wiser.' Iris's mouth curled into a smile at the wrapt silence that filled the room. 'Hmm, I thought so.'

'Well,' she went on tossing her black mane of gypsy hair back, 'one day the *Señora* gave me this real expensive trouser suit she never wore, just stuffed it in my hand saying, "this should suit you," and in the same breath said, "I see Ricardo's fallen for Letty, they'll make a pretty pair." That was red rag to a bull. I'd had enough of the scheming little tart using poor Ricardo to throw the *Señora* off the scent, and her just a lousy *mocosa,* barely eighteen, but ballsy I'll give you that.'

Ana and Doris caught each other's eye and smirked. They knew jealousy when they saw it.

'My loyalty was to the *Señora* after all she'd done for me,' Iris continued.

'What? A couple of measly outfits and you'd sell out on Letty?' chuckled Ana.

'Oh it weren't so simple see. Letty was pregnant.'

The women quivered with renewed interest. Iris eyed them smugly.

'I saw her getting sick in the mornings. I watched her when she didn't think I was looking, how she'd touch her belly. I slept in the same room with her. She couldn't hide nothing like that from me. Letty was in shit up to her eyeballs. Someone had to stop it all.

'I bided my time. Then one day I overheard Letty and *Don* Carlos talking. It was her turn to serve lunch that day. The *Señora* was out at her book club meeting. Letty took *Don* Carlos his coffee in the dining room. I was cutting peppermint leaves from the herb garden below the open windows and I heard him ask her how everyone was treating her. Then he said' – Iris leant forwards and whispered meaningfully – ' "You're not going to disappoint me, Letty, are you? You will commit to this?" Then I heard him add gently, "Hey, what's up?" I heard his chair draw back, I guessed he'd stood up to get close to her. They was talking too soft to hear but then he changed his tone and said, "Go dry your eyes. Don't talk to anyone about this, just let me sort it out." A long time later I asked her what all that had been about and you know what she said? "Oh *Don* Carlos had a plan to send me back to school so I'd get my diploma but then I told him about the baby and he was cross because he knew the *Señora* would send me away if she knew." You bet she'd have sent her away! School diploma! Who did she think she was kidding?'

'She never actually said it was *Don* Carlos' baby?' declared Doris thoughtfully.

'She didn't want anyone to know it was his baby. I gotta say, I admired her for that later, how she stood by her guns, never told a soul. She could have screwed the family for hundreds of thousands of *pesos*, but she kept quiet instead.'

'Maybe there just weren't nothing to tell. Ever thought of that, Iris?' Nilda spoke quietly from where she sat.

'Nothing to tell,' Iris rolled her eyes. 'Letty took her secrets to the grave she did.'

'She never told any of us nothing,' Doris added thoughtfully.

'She didn't trust no one,' said Iris. 'Not after what happened. She was only a kid; I was that much older I was, I could take it, what came after I mean. But it screwed her up real bad. She never recovered, not really.'

'Here, wait a minute,' Ana sat up suddenly, 'Carlos Hidalgo was murdered, right? Don't you remember? About fourteen years ago or something. Some geezer got into the house and whacked him and then got away, but they caught the murderer…'

Iris, leaned forwards and speaking slowly so she was sure to have all their attention said, 'I know. That's what I mean, see. I was there.'

They stared at her speechless.

'You mean you were there when *Don* Carlos was whacked, in the room, you… Holy Heavens!' Ana's mouth fell open.

'And you kept that to yourself all these years. That can't have been easy,' muttered Doris amazed.

Iris's lip curled into a triumphant smile. 'Oh yeah, all these years I kept it to myself. I'd made a promise, see.'

'Well you'd best unburden yourself now,' said Ana, folding her arms and wriggling impatiently on her seat. Nilda and Doris averted their gaze to avoid disclosing the degree of their curiosity. But Iris was on a roll.

'It was my night off, that particular evening. I met with friends down by *Estacion Central*. I told them I thought Letty was coming on to *Don* Carlos. I didn't want to get *Don* Carlos in trouble, see. I said I was thinking I should tell the *Señora,* and they said it weren't right for Letty to come onto him, and what with the *Señora* being so kind to me, I owed it to her to tell her they was at it together. Besides, they said, the *Señora* might find out and think I'd been in on it from the beginning, covering up for Letty. Then I'd take the rap with Letty and she'd throw the both of us out. So they gave me some drinks and tells me I got to get this off my chest and do the right thing and tell it straight, it weren't my secret to keep they said. Then we was to meet up that next week and I was to tell them how it all went.'

'That's a fine set of friends you had there,' said Doris quietly. Iris shot her a glance.

'Why didn't she just get rid of the baby?' asked Ana.

'She wouldn't. That proud she was of having a baby, an Hidalgo baby!' Iris threw a knowing look about the room. 'She'd hit the jackpot and she knew it; *Don* Carlos would take care of her forever. Only she didn't bargain on what was to happen!

'Anyways, I came home about 10pm after meeting them friends. As I walked up to the front gates, I saw the *Señora* getting out of a car. She took off her glove to look for her house keys. She always wore gloves, she was that elegant.

' "Oh Iris," she said, "do you have your keys? *Don* Carlos has a late meeting and I don't seem to have mine." She has this deep commanding voice that's all silky round the edges, it never fooled me. I knew she was tough as nails that's why I needed them drinks to give me courage. If she'd bothered to look she'd have seen the light coming through the curtains of his study. He was home, sure as I was Iris.

' "If you don't mind coming in the back way," I says, "I've got the back door keys." I was all polite but my heart was pounding cos now I had her alone, to myself. Only she could be that changeable. I could feel she was in her impatient mood. I didn't know if to tell her, but I had the drink in me and it made me bold. So I stopped as we was walking under the avocado tree. She looked at me peculiar-like trying to figure why I'd stopped, see. Then I says, "*Señora,* I know something that maybe I should tell you."

'I saw this puzzled look on her face, then it passed and she gave an impatient little shrug and made to move on.

' "But *Señora,*" I says, "don't you care? It's not right. I ..." but she put her hand up like she didn't want to know, only I wouldn't be stopped, not now I'd started. Then she was walking away from me like I was garbage, not worth listening to.

' "I'm scared, *Señora* Grazia," I called after her. She went on walking like she didn't want to know me, and it made my blood boil. "You've got your boy to think about!" I shouted. She loved that little boy to death. She could be icy, but that boy just melted her. I knew her soft spots, I did. She turned on her heel, so sharp that later I could tell the exact spot for the mark on the stone. She looked that angry I thought she might strike me, but then I reckoned it was just her way and I shouldn't be put off. She stared at me, waiting for me to speak and I, well, I just told her.'

'All your guesses neatly woven together to make a big web,' Nilda shook her head. 'Oh the wrong we do, God help us,' she murmured.

'I told her about Letty and *Don* Carlos.' Iris went on, ignoring Nilda. 'But it was like there was this wall between us, and everything I was saying just fell against it, as if it was a load of rotten tomatoes I was throwing and she was just watching the mess slithering down the wall between us. She had this look of disgust on her face like I was a bad smell. Only it wasn't me, I told myself. It was what I was telling her that she couldn't hack. Then she said, "Iris I think it's time you left us."

'I was gobsmacked! I cursed her silently with all my heart.'

'You did a good job there, didn't you?' Ana quipped looking at Nilda and Doris who only stared at Iris in spellbound silence.

' "*Señora,* I'm loyal to you and this is how you repay me? Your husband is having a baby with the new maid and you throw me out. It's not me he's doing it's her." I know she wanted to hit me then. Her hand rose up and I saw her stop herself. Now I was racing on. I weren't about to spare a single detail. I was going to stick her nose in all the shit she pretended had nothing to do with her.

' "*Don* Carlos, he knew Letty before she came here," I says. "He picked her up by the Golf Metro. You ask him, *Señora.* He had you interview her. She told me herself. Ask her, *Señora,* if you don't believe me."

'It began to rain, one of them sharp, sudden showers. I started towards the house. I meant to open the door to get us in out of the rain, but she grabbed my wrist as I passed. "Go on," she said. She stood there in the downpour, and she made me go on with my story. So I tells her; "I reckons *Don* Carlos has brought Ricardo in to cover for the baby so that Ricardo will say he's the father and it'll all be OK. But it's not right, *Señora,* you thinking Ricardo and Letty are together and all the time it's *Don* Carlos having his way with her. I reckons she's in there with him now. What if your little boy were to go to his Daddy and find Letty with him? Look, *Señora,*" I turned and pointed, "there's light in his study, *Señora,* and you thought he was out. But he's home, see, and so is Letty."

'The rain was pouring down my face, sticking my eyelashes together, coming in at the corners of my mouth. She didn't move but the wall between us wasn't there anymore, it had gone, as if the rain had washed it away.

' "You could just sort it all out, *Señora,* " I said quietly and I could feel her listening. "He's a good bloke that Ricardo, but he's being used. He deserves his job. He's a hard worker, and it's not that Letty doesn't work hard, it's just it's not right her being here what with *Don* Carlos in the public eye and all. I can help, *Señora*. Ricardo can keep his job and I'll make up for Letty not being here." The rain was falling down her face, like she was crying. Only she wasn't crying at all. Her eyes looked kind of frenzied. Her hair, so beautifully done up before, was all tumbling down in the wet.'

'God'll judge you for what you done,' croaked Nilda weakly.

'I told the truth,' retorted Iris proudly.

Doris watched Nilda, who shook her head and stared at the floor.

'Go on, Iris,' urged Ana eagerly.

'"You're hurting me, *Señora*." I had to say it three times; she still had her hand round my wrist. She let go then. I was soaked through by the rain, so was she. "You won't dismiss me will you, *Señora*?" I asked her. "Not now?" But she looked straight through me.

'"Get your keys," she says. I turned the key in the back door. She was right behind me. I stepped aside for her to pass into the house. We walked through the back corridor. The door of the room I shared with Letty was open, the light was on. Ricardo was on the floor with his head on the bed, fast asleep. I tried to shut the door seeing as he wasn't allowed in there, but I was too late, she'd already seen him. He opened his eyes and I could see him trying to figure her out, standing there all wet in the servants' quarters. He stood up instantly.

'"What are you doing here?" she said sharpish.

"I'm... sorry, *Señora* Grazia. I'll go immediately," he lowered his head.

'"Where's Letty?" she demanded. I shook my head so he wouldn't say. Now I was real scared of the *Señora*; she looked glazed over, like a zombie. She saw him glance at me, and turned so quickly that she caught me shaking my head. Then she started talking real soft. I could hardly hear her at first, but it got louder as it went.

'"So you wait down here while Letty is up there with my husband. Is that it?" she says real scornful like, "What kind of people are you? You, Ricardo, you let your girl go into the arms of a married man and you wait for her like some infant waiting for his mother. What kind of man are you? Did she tell you she was having a baby?" She'd taken it all in, everything I said, without questioning it. It felt kind of scary hearing her saying it like it was gospel truth, you know. Ricardo's face was pained. He didn't want to look at her, but he forced himself. I felt that sorry for him, what did he know about it all anyway? It weren't his scheming.

'"I love her," he said. "I'll stand by her and the baby."

'"Fool. Bloody, Fool." Ricardo looked at her and his mouth opened, as if he was going to say something but he never got the chance. She didn't give any more chances.

'"Come with me. Both of you." It came out like a low growl.

"We'd best stay here," I said but I don't think she heard me. She started to walk up the steps towards the kitchen. As we lingered behind, she screamed for us to follow her.

'"Please, I can explain," begged Ricardo. But she silenced him. She was terrifying.

'We followed her into the laundry area and through the kitchen and out into the marble hall. We could see the pale glow of light that came from down the corridor under the farthest door and I could hear the soft rise and fall of *Don* Carlos speaking. She started down the passage, only she went so fast she nearly flew. She stopped outside the study and looked back at us. She pointed to her feet like we was dogs being called to order. I wished then I'd never opened my mouth. I couldn't stop shaking. She waited till we stood beside her then she threw open the door.

'*Don* Carlos was standing infront of his desk beside Letty, his arm around her shoulder. I think she'd been crying. They had their backs to the door.

'"You lying bastard!" she screamed. I'd never heard that language from her. *Don* Carlos wheeled round, his face ashen, like a man caught at last. Letty looked like a startled rabbit and Ricardo was so confused at the sight of Letty with *Don* Carlos' arm around her, he turned to leave. The *Señora* caught hold of him.

'"I know you're all in this together," she declared enraged. "You don't leave this room now, Ricardo. You'll all face the music with me. That's my husband," she pointed to *Don* Carlos for Ricardo's benefit. "And that," she yelled at Ricardo, pointing at Letty's stomach, "is not your baby you foolish idiot, it's his. Yes his!" Then she turned to *Don* Carlos, like a proud queen, "At last, you got what you wanted, Carlos."

'I didn't understand, then, why she said that last bit, but it was like she was all ripped up in inside. She threw back her head and jeering at him she mocked, "*Don* Carlos Hidalgo, *for a better future!*" like the slogan, see. She laughed, a horrible empty laugh. It rang out in the quiet of the house. I heard it in my head for weeks after; that dreadful laugh. Then she looked at Ricardo, her face all twisted, inches from his, and she says, "Don't you want to kill him? Aren't you going to be a man and do something?" I reached out to her instinctively, "*Señora* maybe…"

'"Shut up," she said and shoved me away. Her arm was like iron; I don't think she knew how hard she hit. I fell right across the floor. She didn't even look at me. She was that intent on Ricardo.

'"Go on! Fight the lie. That's all he is. There's no better future. A lie! A big sham!" She pushed Ricardo so he half tripped, half fell towards *Don* Carlos who was so still and silent I still don't know which was more frightening, him or her. And there was Letty beside him, facing us, her hair all scraped back into a pony tail and her little figure, so fragile, so blameless; she looked like a kid herself; her mouth was open, her hands clutched the corner of the desk she was backed up against. The *Señora* took a step back, her eyes fixed on Letty, "She's just a tart, a common little tart." She spat out the words, "And you, Carlos, fell for her, and you've ruined us. Ruined us, you hear. If you wanted a child so bad," she added with venom, "you didn't need to find a whore to carry it for you."

'That's when I knew for sure she couldn't have more children, maybe cos of the diabetes, I don't know, but I guessed that was what was tearing her up. I was staring at Letty, my hand over my mouth, and her so pale and trembling, I thought she would faint. I was sick to my stomach.

'Ricardo leapt towards the *Señora*. I think he would have struck her for calling Letty a whore like that, but *Don* Carlos, quick as a flash, pulled him back.

' "Iris," *Don* Carlos called me sharply. "Get her insulin." I realised then what *Don* Carlos meant, that *Señora* Grazia was having one of her turns.

' "Insulin won't fix me now," she snapped.

'Ricardo tried to free himself from *Don* Carlos who was restraining him but the *Patron* was a strong man, he pushed him to the side so Ricardo fell away. "Stay away from her" he ordered, "She's not herself," then he shouted at me again. "Quick, Iris, get it. Get the insulin. Where is it?" He'd never shouted at me, and I know I was real slow. It was like I was paralysed.

' "Insulin!" screamed the *Señora*, "You think insulin will fix this? It's your poison that's all over me. Your lies and your cheating. And you!" she shrieked pointing at Letty, "You innocent-looking child, with your deceitful, cunning artifice come to rip the heart out of this house. Scheming hypocrites! All of you! Come to disgrace this home. Come to contaminate us, and dishonour us, and drag us down into shame and humiliation. I… I…" she seemed to be having trouble getting her breath but she still turned toward *Don* Carlos, "You made this happen… You… You…" she raged hoarsely. She was so worked up, it was like the words were choked inside her.

'Then it all happened so quick. Out of the corner of my eye I saw *Señora* Grazia grab the marble lamp with the bronze stand and I heard this guttural yowl as she hurled that lamp at her husband. I saw *Don* Carlos's head fly back, and his whole body follow and blood spurt from his forehead; so much blood it was all over Ricardo too. Ricardo half caught him as he fell against the desk and onto the floor. The next second Ricardo had lifted the marble lamp with such a wild look on his face, I thought he'd kill *Señora* Grazia with it, but instead he flung it with all his fury so it smashed through the french window behind.

'The *Señora* fainted clean away across the Persian rug. I

screamed at Letty, "Get her insulin! Get it quickly!" But Letty was deathly pale. She looked sick and her eyes were all red. She just stared at me blankly. Then it was just me and Ricardo facing each other. He was breathing like an animal caught in a trap.

'"Run!" I yelled. "Run man! Before you get busted. You've got his blood on you!" I watched him taking deep breaths like he was fuelling his resolve and then he was gone, quick as a flash. He flung himself through the French windows, only he didn't even wait to open them. He threw himself at them, like he'd thrown the lamp at them, and they shattered and splintered and the crimson silk curtains blew out into the dark, with the rain soaking into them staining them darker.

'I ran over to where *Don* Carlos was lying with his head half under his big fancy desk. There was blood everywhere. I touched his wrist. I thought I should try to find a pulse like they do in films. I bent down close to his mouth. I wasn't sure if he was breathing. He half opened his eyes.

'"Take care of Grazia," he whispered. I hardly saw his lips move and then his breathing suddenly rasped and caught. Sometimes I wonder if I imagined what he said or if it was just the death rattle.

'I got up and went to his phone and picked it up. It was his private line that the President sometimes called him on. I'd never even touched it before. Anyways, I held it in my hand for a bit, trying to think. I could have called the cops. I could have told them what really happened. Maybe they'd have listened, maybe not, but I thought of their son, that poor little boy upstairs in his bed, innocent as a young lamb, with his dad dead, and his murdering mum put in jail for it and I couldn't do it, not even for Ricardo's sake. They'd gotten under my skin, that family. They'd always done good by me. So I shut up, see, and I did my job. I dialled the ambulance. Then I saw, on the desk, what they'd been looking at, him and Letty. They were photographs of *Don* Carlos in his car, stopped near the Metro where the tarts hang, with Letty looking in at the window. I just threw them in the fire and watched the glossy paper curl up in the flame. I found out later it was that ass peddlar, El Paco, that was blackmailing both of them. He wanted Letty back whoring for him and he wanted all he could screw out of *Don* Carlos. Till the day she died, Letty was that scared of that scumbag, El Paco.'

'Where was Letty all the while?' murmured Ana.

'She was there all the time. She's the one that got the insulin from the *Señora's* handbag on the floor. I gave it to the *Señora* as she came round while Letty crouched on the carpet, hugging her knees up to her, swaying to and fro.

'"Where is he?" the *Señora* asked when she came to. I guessed she meant her husband so I told her *Don* Carlos was dead. "He died worrying about you *Señora*," I said.

'Her eyes opened kind of wild-like and her fingers gripped my wrist tight, then she fixed me with her steely stare. "He killed him, Iris. You saw. He killed him. You saw it! You saw it!" She was shaking me. "Ricardo killed him!" She wouldn't stop shaking me hysterically until I said "Yes, *Señora,* I saw Ricardo killed him."

'Then we heard this little voice say "Did Mummy do something bad?" her little boy was stood there in his pyjamas at the entrance to the open door, rubbing his eyes. It made me go cold to see him there, not ten feet from his dead father and all the blood. Letty scrambled to her feet and shot over to him. She took him in her arms and swayed him to and fro like she was soothing him from a nightmare. Then she carried him out of the room, but his big eyes stared back at his mum over her shoulder. Letty lay with him all that night. Everytime she tried to leave, thinking he was asleep, his little hand gripped her tight. Another night we found him curled up where his father had died. Right there on the spot where we'd scrubbed the blood out of the carpet. We never did know how long that kid was stood there that night. He might have seen everything for all we knew and that weren't something to forget, not ever, enough to shred a kid's faith in everything to see his mum kill his dad. But if he did see, he never said a word, and he's a grown lad now, but he keeps his thoughts to himself he does, always has.'

Iris stopped talking. Out in the alley someone shouted,

another voice responded. The sounds of the outside world filtered in slowly.

'So what happened to the *Señora?*' prompted Ana.

'The ambulance arrived and them paramedics took the *Señora* out on a stretcher and left *Don* Carlos, dead, under the desk until the judge came round, about half an hour later. I opened the door and showed him where the body was. We'd covered it with one of them fine linen table cloths.'

'What happened to Letty?' asked Doris.

'Letty came here, to *Señora* Maria's. She was only a scrap of a thing and pregnant. Then the *Señora* found Letty this shanty. She decided didn't want her at *Señora* Maria's cos she said there was too many people prying and stuff and she got me into my place to keep an eye on Letty.'

'So she did fire you after all?' Ana shook her head.

'No, she paid me to keep an eye on Letty. She was good to me. I reckons she just didn't like me around those first years after the tragedy. I reminded her too much of it all. But I was loyal and she knew it. So she kept me on, like, watching over Letty, and after she moved to her new house in the hills, I used to go and keep an eye on things when she was away. Still do sometimes.'

'You'd think she could have got Letty a better shanty,' muttered Ana. 'What with all that money.'

'Letty was lucky to get what she got,' Iris retorted. 'After what she'd done.'

'I ain't so sure what she done,' Doris spoke under her breath.

'Letty kept to herself in those early days. Remember?' said Ana. 'She didn't talk to no one.'

'The newspapers were full of it,' Iris reminded them. 'Letty was scared shitless that that pimp, El Paco, would find her. She kept silent like the grave, with that poor creature that had caused death and destruction growing inside her.'

From beyond the plastic partition Milana laid her face down so her forehead touched the earth floor as though she wanted the ground to open and let her through. A numbness seemed to prevent her from feeling any reaction.

'Don't you go giving that poor babe dark powers, Iris, she's a good girl and I'll have none of your curses in this house,' Doris retaliated with vehemence.

'You could have kept your mouth shut in the first place,' said Ana looking at Iris, 'and no one would have died.'

Iris was thick-skinned. She didn't flinch.

'Didn't Letty try to, you know,' Ana drew her index finger over her wrists and grimaced. 'Didn't *Señora* Lisa find her like that?'

'You're like a dog with a bone, Ana,' Doris reproached, 'Leave the dead to rest. What happened to Ricardo, Iris?'

'It ran like any old thieving and murder story;'the new gardener had thought the maid and the *Señora* were out and hadn't reckoned on finding the husband, and so on. Ricardo was sent to Collina prison with the worst lot of murdering scumbags,' Iris paused, 'but he got out.'

'How?' Ana leant forwards intrigued, 'You don't get out easy like, not from Collina Jail.'

'That was a story and a half!' Iris chuckled to herself.

'Ricardo turned up here more than a year after the murder. That was the night he knocked Letty up with little Ricci and scarpered. It weren't his fault though, he had to lie low . He was on the run from the cops; couldn't stay. He'd been hiding out in a cave on the other side of the river half way up Manquehue hill for weeks before he found us. He came back after that, once in a while. He knocked her up with Juanito a year later. Letty loved him she did, but they was destined to be apart. He went to Argentina. Occasionally he sent money. Then we lost track of him and El Negro came along, and he got his scummy hands on Letty and thieved all her savings.'

'But how did Ricardo get out of prison?' insisted Ana.

'In a coffin! One of the inmates copped it and they put his body in a box ready to be taken out of the prison. The minute word got out that a man had died, Ricardo pretended to have some sort of seizure and got himself into the medical centre. From there he had access to where they'd put the coffin. Every body has to be buried within twenty-four hours of death so there was no waiting around. Ricardo opened the coffin, well, crate more like, and he put himself in with the dead man. I reckon he got help from one of the guards. The coffin was put on the back of a pick-up truck and so, soon as it was on the open road, Ricardo got out; no guards needed for a corpse see, so it was easy. He scared the drivers half to death but they just let him go. It was easier than reporting it and being taken for fools. Anyways,' Iris passed her hand over her face as though she were wiping it clean, 'like I said, I swore to Letty while she lived I'd never breathe a word and I've kept my promise. Now I had to let it all out, see.' She leant back, deflated and exhausted.

'Like confession, eh?' said Ana, nodding her head thoughtfully.

'Yeah, like confession,' Iris breathed out, immensely gratified.

From where she lay, Milana heard the knocking sound first, as it reverberated through the earth floor beneath her, urgent and insistent. It brought her to her senses. She tore out from behind the curtain partition infront of the horrified faces of the women, and ran to where Nilda sat quaking on her chair; the whites of her eyes already showing. A second later Nilda fell to the ground like a sack of potatoes. She lay on her side, shaking uncontrollably, her head knocking against the rough floor.

'Get me a cushion!' screamed Milana. Ana raced to her side. Together they lifted Nilda's head.

'It's so heavy,' Milana gasped, barely able to support it. Ana slipped a cushion under it. Milana tried to embrace Nilda, as if by sheltering her body she might stave the attack. Ana pulled her away.

'You can't stop the shaking, child.'

With frightened eyes the women stared at Nilda, convulsed on the hard floor. It was like watching some terrible force possessing itself of a creature in a fight to the death. Milana looked thin and fragile next to the thrashing body beside her. It was only then, in the juxtaposition of the two, that the girl's vulnerability became painfully apparent. The horror of what they had done struck Doris suddenly, bringing her unexpectedly to her feet.

'Oh God, my poor, poor girl. What have we been saying.' Doris knelt down and taking Milana into her arms she hugged her, whilst the others looked on, appalled now, that they could have forgotten the girl behind the curtain, sorting her dead mother's clothes.

Chapter Eight

'Ricci, don't walk so fast, I can't keep up,' Juanito broke into a run to catch up with his older brother.

'Ricci, slow down, please.' But Ricci showed no intention of slowing down. His face was impassive and his eyes, after a surreptitious glance over the road, were set on the pavement.

'Keep moving, Juanito, we gotta get home,' he hissed.

'What's the hurry, Ricci?' Ricci didn't answer. He kept his head down.

'Hey, dude,' came the gruff shout.

Ricci slowed his step, and glanced quickly at Juanito. 'You go on, Juanito. Go home quickly,' he whispered hoarsely.

'No', said Juanito, 'I want to be with you.'

Ricci glared at him. The two older boys overtook them.

'You in a hurry then?' sneered Pablo always the more aggressive of the two, his brain addled by substance abuse since the age of eight. 'We thought you was running away from us, didn't we Jose?' Ricci looked at them with a blameless expression.

Jose grinned disdainfully, his gold tooth glinting in the afternoon sun.

'Hey, how's your Mum? Pablo told me some,' he interrogated, falling into step with the boys.

'She's dead,' said Ricci staring at the ground.

'That's shit man. She was cool.' He adjusted the cuffs of his black crimpelene shirt, open to his navel. Juanito, quietly keeping up, stared at Jose's dazzling diamante rings. Jose caught his look and winked at him.

'You knew her?' Ricci glanced briefly at Jose.

'I heard an' all.'

'She was cool, yeah,' echoed Pablo as he dexterously flicked a coin over his fingers. Juanito looked on mesmerised. Quick as lightning was Pablo. He could take a watch off any wrist on the subway without detection or slit a lady's handbag and remove the contents and still wolf whistle his unsuspecting victim at the next corner. He was Jose's arse-licking side-kick in the dope peddling racket.

'So you going away then?' inquired Jose, rolling a toothpick over his uneven teeth.

'Nope, why should we? We can look after ourselves. '

'Yeah?' Jose raised his eyebrows as he stepped in front of Ricci blocking his way forwards.

'So Milana gets to play Mum,' he went on suggestively. 'Cool!' Pablo swung in next to Jose, he mouthed her name, savouring the syllables, flicking his tongue out back and forth rapidly like a snake after its prey. They eyed each other. Jose's lip curled into a lecherous grin.

'I don't think it's cool, it's just life, it stinks,' muttered Ricci. He adjusted his school bag. Every fibre in his body was taut. He knew if they smelled his fear he was done for. Jose leant nonchalently against a parked Mercedes, loosening the insignia with practised ease.

'Hey, dude, d'you want to make some *pesos* shifting skunk for us?' Prizing off the insignia he threw it to Pablo, who caught it with two fingers and shoved it deep into the pocket of his baggy trousers. Jose pulled out a penknife with a flourish.

'You know, just errands, no shit.' Jose went on, picking at dirt from under his fingernails with the knife.

'No. But thanks anyway.' Ricci knew he was sticking his neck out saying no, but it was that or be trapped like Oscar. He remembered Letty used to say, 'If you sink too low you drown.'

'Hey,' Juanito piped up, 'I could do it. I'm good at errands.'

'Shut up, Juanito. No one asked you. Go home!' said Ricci tersely. Juanito slung him a scathing look, and raced off seething with embarrassment.

'Hey dude, thanks. We'll look you up,' shouted Pablo after him.

Jose straightened and preened like a ruffled bird. He rearranged his sunglasses on his thick, broken nose and twirled the knife in front of Ricci with a smug grimace.

'Like I said, dude, the offer's there.'

Ricci caught the look that passed between them. He knew they'd try to get to Juanito later. He tried to put them off.

'Juanito's a blab. Can't trust him with anything.' Ricci's heart pounded beneath his white school shirt.

'What you got against us, eh?' Pablo took a step closer. His mouth was open and there was menace in his bloodshot eyes.

'Nothing.' Ricci met his look with a steady gaze. Pablo slung a kick at a passing mongrel dog. It whimpered and stumbled into the gutter. Ricci still didn't dare move.

'You won't grow up to be trouble will you now?' scoffed Jose, a malicious smile spreading unattractively over his uneven features.

'I don't want no trouble,' Ricci's eyes were big and brown and thick-lashed, they hadn't a streak of meanness in them. He turned them on Jose, 'and I'm no trouble to no one,' he added.

Pablo and Jose exchanged knowing looks, laughed and stepped aside suddenly to let him through.

'That's cool, dude. Tough about the old lady. Anyway, if you change your mind, we're here. And tell the squit we'll be waiting for him.'

'He's only ten. He's a blabbermouth. He's no good to you.'

'That's for us to figure,' they smirked. Ricci could hear them still laughing as they watched him disappear into the alleys of the shantytown.

'What did you do to Juanito, Ricci?' demanded Milana as he brushed past her into the shanty.

'Tell him to shut his face. He'll end up in trouble, thick head,' Ricci countered furiously.

'Hey,' said Milana, 'don't you start on him. He only said he'd run errands for someone.'

'Yeah, you know who he's going to run bloody errands for?

81

For Oro Sucio and Pablo.Don't you know nothing? You should listen up sometimes instead of running away to the river all the time.' Ricci's eyes watered and he turned away. His heart was still pounding from the encounter. He'd seen a bird caught by a cat once, and watched how the cat had played with it, its paws shoving it this way and that to encourage it to try to flap its wings. Then, as the little chick had lifted itself up in hope-fuelled drunken flight, the cat, crouched low, had waited for its prey to feel freedom before pouncing like a compressed coil released, its claws splayed, to rip the bird down and destroy it. Now anger burned in Ricci's face.

'I'm not running…' Milana began but Ricci slammed his school bag down with a crash and eyeballed her.

'Just leave me be. You're worse than Juanito and you think you can take care of us.'

He went straight back out, banging the door behind him so the shanty quaked briefly.

'Get back in here,' Milana shouted opening the door. 'You're only eleven you…'

'Twelve next week or maybe you'd forgotten,' he yelled back disappearing down the dusty alley.

That night, Milana woke to hear Ricci sobbing. He was lying on the cane settee with a rough blanket over his head. She pulled it off him and sat down next to him.

'What's up, Ricci?'

He didn't answer. Eventually, exasperated, she got up.

'I'm scared,' he spat out with venom, 'I'm shit scared, OK. Satisfied?'

Milana's face softened. 'Scared of what, Ricci?

He sat up.

'You don't get it, do you? You think you're going to get away with playing house like you're our mum, but they're going to get us, that's what.'

'Who's going to get us?' she retorted angrily. 'Who the hell is going to get us?' The scorn spilled off her words. 'You think I'm scared of the likes of Pablo and Jose. Those jerks?'

'You should be, Mila. They're into all the bad stuff. They're into it big time. The police can't even get them. They've torched the houses of anyone that rats on them, so they get away with whatever, *whatever*... see, and now they're onto us. They want me to do their dirty work, and they've got a *lot* of dirty work. How long before they twist my arm? Huh? Before they get to me, like they got to Oscar and made him work for them and they'll never cut him any slack now. And if I don't do their shit, they'll just torch us in our beds. They don't care. Then they'll go for Juanito. They *kill* people, Mila. I know they do. And toss them in the river.'

Milana's flesh crept as she remembered the feel of Pablo's eyes travelling over her.

'They aren't going to twist anyone's arm,' she countered defiantly. 'And they aren't going to set fire to us and they don't toss anyone in the river, I should know, I hang out down there.'

'You don't know shit. Their dads' are bus drivers. I've been up there with Mum, I've heard their talk. Pablo's dad, he's real tough and he's mates with Jose's dad and there's others up there, they're all big in the syndicate. They laugh at them cops. They don't give a shit. And when the big shots make a law they don't like, they just strike and laugh at the lot of them. You never figured it out? If they run someone over, what with the way them drivers break all the speed limits, do they get done? Never. The syndicate takes care of it. They're like the "untouchables", that's what Mum used to call them and it made them laugh. They're real powerful. And them and our mum were like this.' Ricci held up crossed fingers to show a level of togetherness that in other circumstances might have been touching.

Ricci hung his head. 'They were real sweet on Mum. Always nice and polite with her.' He looked up and Milana saw his eyes well up with tears. 'You think Jose or Pablo would touch us if Mum was alive? No way! They wouldn't dare. We was her kids see. We was untouchable too, but now she's gone and their dads' won't know shit of what goes on, because Mum's not here to protect us, see. Mum's dead.' Big tears rolled down his cheeks.

'Look, it's not like that, trust me, Ricci.' Gently Milana

smoothed his ruffled hair. 'Besides, Mum still looks out for us, only we can't see her.'

'Yeah like she can help us now.' He drew his arm roughly across his eyes to wipe the tears but they kept coming.

'She can help. Remember how she said we've all got an angel,' said Milana brightly.

'Yeah well how come no one gets to see their angel?' Ricci sniffed loudly. 'I don't believe in that stuff.' He felt the loneliness of being an orphan swallowing him up. Milana wrapped the old blanket around them both. He snuggled down comforted by their unexpected closeness while she stroked his head and whispered to him.

'You know what I think, Ricci, I think we're in a long dark tunnel, like the ones they build through the mountains, but we'll come out the other side. You'll see.'

'I don't get you, Mila, but if it makes you feel better,' he sighed again.

'What I mean is I'll go through anything, and I won't let myself be afraid, Ricci if that's what it's going to take to get me through to the other side.'

'Other side of what?'

'This place, Ricci. I'm not going to pull a cart up a mountain every day like Mum did, I'm going to pull myself over the whole blazing *cordillera* into a different life, or through it, whatever it takes.'

Ricci stared up at her, 'Wow, really?'

She shrugged, 'Who knows, but you nearly believed me.'

They laughed together.

She put her arms about her little brother and cradled him, pushing her own fears down deep where they could be hidden amidst all the other buried angers and frustrations biding their time. Peacefully they fell asleep at last on the old settee, fitting into each other's curves like two spoons.

Chapter Nine

Milana stood in the middle of the Chucky Cheese Car Park. It was 7pm and the light was fading slowly. She waved a yellow cloth at another passing car, and, running in front of it, pointed towards an empty parking place. The Subaru Legacy manoeuvred into the indicated space. The car door opened and a slim woman in jeans and a suede jacket stepped out. Four small children piled out of the back. The woman turned to Milana appraising her for a moment, taken aback by the girl with the mass of hair messily collected into a bun and held there in place by an old cracked biro. Her stance was too proud and tall for a shantytown girl, yet her green eyes had the defiance of the oppressed. She was a far cry from old Eliseo who usually worked this spot. The woman dived back into the car for a 500 *peso* coin and handed it to her with a quick, condescending smile. Milana noted the gold bracelet and diamond rings on her fingers. She toyed with the thought of possessing one of these priceless accessories. But what could they do for her? She could sell it and spend the money. Then what? Without an education, a skill… everything else runs out.

'Thank you, *Señora,*' she said receiving the coin gratefully and placing it along with the other coins in her pocket.

Milana hadn't done badly for her first day waving cars into parking spaces. There'd been a bit of trouble with the old man, Marco at the entrance to the car park. At first he'd let her hang around but as soon as Milana started running towards the cars to get their business, he pulled her aside,

'Look here you're Letty's girl in't you? This here's my patch, but seeing as Eliseo in't here today, you take his patch. Just for today, mind. And stick to the back. No running for my business.' Milana guessed she'd got off lightly because he felt sorry for her, still it was a good start.

Cool winds blew off the mountains and played over her bare skin. Milana loosened her hair so that it fell warming her shoulders as she leant against the tall, wire fencing that enclosed the car park. The green mesh boundary pressed into her forehead as she looked wistfully through it to where the land dipped towards the river. A little to the right, but out of sight, was the old bridge. Only a week had passed since that fateful morning on the bank when she had first seen her stranger. Was he there now, just out of sight? Would he be there when at last she could escape back to the riverbank? Milana didn't even know his name and yet, almost every night, she dreamed of the feel of his hands imprinted on her skin. She closed her eyes trying to recall his face. The wind whispered round her ears, lifting her hair, sweeping gently around her neck, carrying the soft minty scent of eucalyptus. She forgot her surroundings, the bright headlights of cars and the purring of expensive engines, the sounds of small children emerging excitedly from the maze of brightly coloured plastic tunnels. She became oblivious even to the sudden wail of sirens and the shouts, she was right there again, reaching out for his hand.

'There's trouble down your way, girl.' Marco was shouting in her ear, breaking into her reverie.

'You's deaf girl.' He cocked his head and she smelt his rancid breath.

'What trouble?' she replied groping her way back to certainty.

'Cop trouble that's what. Go look for yourself. You's deaf as a post girl.'

Even before she turned into dusty Oleander Alley, Milana saw police cars and heard a cacophony of voices. There was a small crowd outside Ana's shanty just two doors away from her own place on the opposite side. Blue flashing lights reflected on the walls and windows of the shanties and turned faces lurid colours. An ambulance backed into the alley and stopped inches from her. Its back doors were flung open revealing oxygen tanks, tubes and metal trays inside. A stretcher was brought out. Milana stood staring at the interior unable to move on from the question: *did they take Mum away in an ambulance?* Her memory of it was trapped somewhere, buried.

Somebody put their arms about her. She felt them sobbing on her shoulder. It was Nilda. But Milana didn't move as she watched the paramedics carry the stretcher back with Oscar on it. Blood trickled from the corner of his mouth. His eyes were closed. The flashing lights reflected on his blank face; red and blue, relentless. The ambulance doors closed. Suddenly Ana raced out of her shanty and threw herself against them, beating on the white metal, screaming, 'Let me in! Let me in! I'm his mother. He's only sixteen.' The doors flew open, knocking her back into the road like a lifeless creature. Hands reached out to her and she was lifted inside by the elbows.

Two armed policemen walked past with Jose handcuffed between them. Head thrown back defiantly, he swaggered, swinging his hips suggestively and, twisting his neck in her direction, he grimaced at Milana.

'Don't worry, princess, I'll be back,' he gloated in a throaty voice, and his lip curled pulling at the scar that crossed the corner of his mouth.

'Scumbag'll be out by tomorrow and Oscar will be dead in a drawer in the morgue,' muttered Iris. 'I'd like to let him have it. Who'd complain?' she spat after him. 'We'd all be shot of him. But nobody will do it.'

'He'll do us all in before anyone gets the better of him, the evil waster,' sobbed Nilda trying to pull herself together.

Milana looked at Iris, her eyes burning. 'Did he do it?'

'No. Pablo's the one as stuck the knife in,' retorted Iris still staring after Oro Sucio.

Milana sank down on the ground as though all the strength had drained out of her and pulled her down with it.

Nilda dabbed her eyes with a discoloured handkerchief. 'You've been away all day, the boys came looking for you... and now...' but Nilda didn't have the heart to tell her.

'Nilda, leave off.' Iris gripped her arm and steered her away.

Nilda, flustered and runny nosed, looked doggedly up at her.

'Iris. She's gotta know sometime.'

Meanwhile somewhere in the dark the murderer roamed free.

Iris stood in the square of light from the shanty door looking down at where Milana sat huddled in the dust outside.

'It weren't your fault, you know, *Chica,*' she said gently as though she were addressing the night air.

'There's some as just ain't cut out to make it, and it ain't nobody's fault so don't you go making it yours.' The pale orb of the moon caused her shadow to fall across Milana.

'I've made tea, Nilda's nerves are all on edge.'

Milana got up from where she'd been sitting silent and dry-eyed and followed Iris into the shanty, afraid that Nilda might succumb to one of her fits. Iris switched on the telly. They sat, all three of them, watching the empty excesses of a Brazilian soap opera until Milana asked:

'Where are Juanito and Ricci?'

'We don't know,' replied Iris truthfully.

'They ran off,' said Nilda.

'Where?'

'Don't know, they must be hiding.' Nilda glanced at Iris searchingly.

'Why?'

'They're scared of them low life scumbags that's why,' Iris muttered. But Nilda put her hand on Milana's.

'They was with Oscar, see, when he got done,' she said shakily. 'Doris saw them at Ana's through the half open door.' Nilda's chin wobbled and she took a gulp of air and hiccupped.

Iris took over the telling:

'Ricci and Juanito, they was sat on either side of Oscar watching telly when Jose called in. Ana was hanging laundry out back, she had the radio on full blast. Jose starts mouthing off at Oscar. Suddenly Pablo appears from nowhere, tearing down Oleander Alley like he has a pack of wolves at his heels. He passes Doris and flings himself into Ana's shanty. Doris sees him flick his knife and yell "peice of shit, squealer" at Oscar and he doesn't lay off yelling "There ain't no out for you! There's only one fucking out and its fucking on the end of my fucking knife!" That's when Pablo lunged forward and stuck his lousy knife right into Oscar. Doris says she couldn't see how it happened cos Jose was blocking the entrance while she's stood outside looking in, but then Pablo pushes right past her as he scarpers out and down the alley. Then she sees what he's gone and done and the blood all pooling out red on Oscar's white T-shirt. Then Jose, cool as a cucumber, pulls the knife out of Oscar's chest, like he was checking a chicken in the oven, and wipes it across Ricci's T-shirt leaving a streak of red. And all the while Ricci's sat there still as a stone.'

'He's a brave kid, that Ricci,' sighed Nilda.

'Neither of them brothers of yours moved a muscle. Then Jose twirls the knife and walks out of Ana's shanty, cocky as a preening parrot,' Iris continued. 'But them cops they'd blocked off the alley and they close in on him right there infront of Doris. He didn't expect that see. "Double crossing bitch, watch your step," he hisses at Doris as they haul him past in handcuffs, as if it's all her fault the cops are there. Anyways, the cops they keeps Jose round back waiting till the police van and them sniffer dogs gets here. And all the time Ana's got her lousy love songs playing out back so she's deaf to all of it. Doris, she's just standing paralysed in the doorway like she's connected to Oscar by invisible thread. That's when Ricci and Juanito make a dash for it. Like the wind, right past Doris, and gone in a flash, just as Ana comes in the room with a basket of ironing. Ana can't see what's wrong with Oscar cos from the back it's like he's still watching telly. Suddenly them cops come swarming in with all them machine guns, like there was a war on. Seems they was onto Pablo for some other shit, but Pablo thought Oscar set him up. Scumbag must have come with murder on his mind.

'Anyways, like Doris said, Ricci and Juanito shot out of there like two bullets right through the middle of them all. Cops tried to catch them, but the boys were too quick. Always in after the kill, them blasted cops squawking about while scumbags like Oro Sucio and his gang torch and murder us and sell their shit to kids.'

'Ana finally figured what had happened to Oscar,' said Nilda very quietly. 'She saw them all looking at him and she put her hand out, real slow, on his shoulder, standing behind him all the while, like she didn't really want to see. Her hand touched his T-shirt and then it travelled over his chest down to where the T-shirt was all sodden, and she lifted her hand off and turned it over real slow and saw the blood...'

Nilda passed a handkerchief over her face to mop up the beads of sweat that had accumulated like a gleaming moustache over her upper lip. Iris squeezed Nilda's hand and took over the narrative:

'Ana just stared at Doris, standing like a sparrow between a lot of crows and Doris saw the horror in her eyes and watched Ana crumple to the floor like a deflated soufflé. Passed out cold she was. She only just came to when the ambulance was leaving.'

Nilda was staring at the floor like she expected to see blood on it. The telly blared out its empty drama, unreal and overacted.

'Least they got Jose,' she sighed wearily.

'Jose's just one turd on the side of a stinking shit hole,' scoffed Iris.

Milana got up and pulled a handful of coins out of her pocket and piled them on top of the telly,

'I made this money today,' she asserted impassively, 'for Ricci. He thought I'd forget his birthday.' She walked out of the back door and sat alone in the dirt, remembering his thin body beside her last night; the frightened hands that had clasped hers. Where was he now? She looked up at the black, starless night, and thought of how afraid of the dark he was.

'We've got to get you out of here, Milana.' Nilda was standing behind her, her eyes wide and frightened.

'Them poor boys, heaven help them out there in the dark with that murdering scumbag on the loose.'

'He won't whack harmless kids like Ricci and Juanito,' Milana whispered without lifting her eyes from the dust, but she wasn't at all sure what Pablo might do. She knew once a line was crossed it could be crossed again.'

'Jose'll be out of that police cell tomorrow you can count on it,' Iris declared. 'Some scummy cop doing his skunk will shift him out.'

'Promise you won't go to the river, like you do,' begged Nilda.'Promise, love.'

Milana looked from Iris to Nilda.

'I'll be OK,' she said calmly, 'don't fret, Aunt Nilda.' Looking past her she gave a little gasp of surprise. Nilda and Iris wheeled round. Chevo, Oscar's father, was standing in the doorway in a vest and with his trousers rolled up to the knee.

'We've been and combed the dump and riverbank,' he said gruffly. 'No sign of them boys, Nilda. But rest yourself woman, if we can't find them, there's none as will, so they'll be safe, I reckon, for now. There ain't no sign of that scumbag Pablo. But he won't get away with this, his dad's going to answer for this, I'll bust the whole bloody lot of them, even if I goes down with 'em.' And he turned and left before they could give him sympathy for his dying son.

Iris switched off the telly.

'They're sensible boys, Ricci and Juanito. They'll take cover. You'd best go home, Nilda. I'll stay with Milana tonight.'

Milana looked at the scant plastic sheeting over the windows and thought of Pablo prowling the darkness like a hunted animal, and silently consented to her company.

Milana lay on the cane settee remembering how, curled around the thin body of her brother last night, she had felt his shoulder blades jutting out under his skin like the bones on a hungry dog. Her arms longed to console him, and Juanito too. She thought of the sumptuous orange marigolds Oscar had dropped in her lap, their soft furry stems alive with sap and his earnest face and eyes brimful with benevolence and how his promises of care were now reduced to a trickle of blood from the corner of his lifeless mouth.

That night, Milana's dreams metamorphosed the shanty women into harbingers of disaster, as with soft furry faces and eight legs they crawled around her, talking incessantly, busily weaving a web to wrap her in. Milana thrashed about to wrestle free of these silken threads so strong she could not break them. All the while the gentle spiders pushed and prodded, tossing her this way and that with their giant claws, pleased with their work, like they were wrapping a baby in swaddling clothes. She woke and dozed again while thoughts twisted and re-formed, growing gigantic and irrepressible in her head. She wrestled with these demons, unable to reconcile herself to sleep, whilst Iris snored next door on the bed that Letty had shared with her children.

Finally, Milana threw off the single blanket that covered her and opened the back door. Usually the moon's silver-blue light filled the tiny cement back yard, but tonight clouds scudded low obliterating their light. She knelt by an old flower pot that was covered by a battered aluminium plate. Removing the plate she reached in to find her bag of treasures collected over time from the wasteland. In the shaft of light from the open back door, she laid them about her on the dusty earth; a collage of pretty fragments, broken pieces from other people's lives.

Iris found her in the morning, sunlight pooled around her reflecting off the bits of coloured glass and china. Milana was icy cold and curled in a foetal position in what looked like a magic circle of broken stones. For one terrible moment, Iris thought she was dead.

Chapter Ten

'I've made you a sugary tea and now I'm off,' called Iris from the door.

In the next room Milana pulled a grey tunic over her white shirt.

'You get yourself to school now, girl, or they'll just fill your place with another lousy kid.'

Milana appeared in the doorway knotting her school tie under her collar.

'Thank you for staying, Iris.' Then, recognising the peculiar bond that had existed between Iris and her mother and wanting to trust her, she added, 'My mum said you'd been good to her.'

Iris paused, her dark eyes flashed towards Milana, she looked momentarily afflicted.

'Like Ana said, I could have shut up and no one would have died.' She gave a tiny intake of breath as though something cold had touched her skin. 'Jealousy! It beats the crap out of you.' Then, mustering a bitter sweet smile, 'Go on with you, you'll be late, *Chica*,' she said coolly, 'and keep away from the river while that scumbag's on the loose.'

The 52nd Lyceo School was buzzing with gossip and speculation. Pablo was said to have been spotted in all manner of unlikely hideouts, including the ghost train at the local amusement park. There were those that imagined he would wreak vengeance in the school refectory, appearing at lunch time and spraying bullets about the place, and conjectured all kinds of variations on this theme. The teachers were understandably on edge. A violent, drug-crazed ex-alumni with a grudge was an unsettling prospect for everyone. So when the final bell rang at 3pm, far more parents than the usual meagre scattering of devoted mothers were at the school gates to escort their offspring home.

Ricci and Juanito were used to walking home together, leaving Milana to make her own way, but today they might have found themselves looking about for her anxiously if it were not for the fact that Juanito and Ricci had not appeared in school at all. In all the commotion no one had noticed their absence. Milana passed a few of their friends loitering near the kiosk and asked casually if they'd seen them. They looked back at her with blank faces and shrugged and shouted to another group of stragglers, but no one had seen Ricci or Juanito.

Milana hurried away. As she crossed the bridge that linked the school to the shantytown she scanned the banks. The river snaked far beneath, possessing itself of that lonely place, hissing over the rocks, swelling in places like a boa constrictor digesting its prey.

Defying all warnings, Milana turned sharply at the end of the bridge and slid her way down the steep bank, then ran along the rocks until she reached a shallow expanse. Leaving her shoes behind on the bank, she waded across, keeping her eyes down to avoid slipping into deeper water. She came to the underbelly of the old bridge, with its ancient graffiti and mossy stone walls, and gazed at where she had last seen him, her boy-stranger, pummelling his lapis stone to powder. But he wasn't there. The place now seemed bereft of its magic, lonely and abandoned.

Eyes down, she walked upstream hopelessly scouring the rocks for some splash of colour, some shard of painted glass, any proof that he was real, until she was almost dizzy from staring down at so many rocks and stones and bits of fossilised wood. She reached the point where the river ran its course through the abandoned banks of the old wasteland under the shade of great eucalyptus trees. This was the place beyond which no one ventured. The place where *El Cuco* of folklore was said to roam. The air seemed to grow chill, prickling her skin, but all the cautions only served to goad her on. She wrapped her arms around herself and quickened her pace.

From where he sat in the graveyard, under the shade of the jacaranda tree, Santiago made out the figure of a girl. He flicked his hair back from his eyes in a quick gesture of sudden interest. Leaving his work to one side, he got up and, after a moment's hesitation, began to walk briskly along the high bank from where the land fell away towards the river. The girl moved fast along the lower bank, feet barely seeming to touch the ground as she twisted lithe and agile, this way and that, avoiding rocks and boulders in her path. Struck by the fluidity of her movements his artist's eye captured the fusion between her figure and the force of the wind against it, in all its abstract beauty. He stood still staring after her.

A hundred yards on Milana stopped and sat on the bank. The scent of eucalyptus, warmed by the afternoon sun, filled the air. She stayed there catching her breath. Her thoughts drained out of her, her feelings numb. The absence of him, of Letty, of her brothers, seemed to consume her. There was just the wind through her hair and the sun on her skin; she concentrated on them, wishing they could fill the emptiness inside her.

'Hey? Hey,' he said again, 'are you OK?' The sun played on her eyes so she couldn't see his face at first. He crouched down beside her.

'What are you doing this far down stream?' She perceived a flicker of concern in his question and the intensity of his eyes resting on her made her stomach flutter. For a moment she couldn't speak. But then words surged up longing for release. She hesitated, holding them back, to filter them appropriately.

'I can't find my brothers.'

'Ahh.' He glanced back upstream pulling his hair of his face, a smile playing on his lips. So that's who the boys were. He'd guessed as much from what Atilio, the church caretaker, had told him. He could see it now, a similarity in the eyes, the dark lashes and the wide clear forehead.

'Some of the men from the shantytown are out looking for them now but they've gone the other way, downstream. No one came this way. They never do,' Milana explained quickly, unsettled that he had so suddenly materialised before her.

'Look, I think I know where your brothers are.' His gaze darted quickly about them as though he were afraid they might be overheard, then rested on her face where it became immersed suddenly in the urgent, vividness of her eyes as she tried to figure him out. For a moment neither spoke.

'Come, I'll show you.' He reached out and, taking Milana's hand as though they had done this before a thousand times, he pulled her up. As his skin touched hers he felt an inexplicable connection; the recognition of something trapped somewhere within, suddenly unbound. He let go, but glancing at her, instinct told him she felt it too.

He led her along the riverbank. After a few hundred yards, he turned up the bank and through a small, gated fence. Soon they were passing the headstones of carefully tended graves. They came to a wall of plaques, behind which were sealed the coffins of the poor who could not afford a plot of land.

Milana stopped suddenly. 'My mother's grave,' she said solemnly. She glanced back at him. 'She was lying on a road dying that first time I saw you.'

'I heard about that from Atilio, the caretaker here. I'm sorry.' And his eyes held hers undaunted by the pain he perceived there.

She felt his sympathy.

'Please show me where my brothers are.'

He led her to a tiny chapel and opened the door. The stone altar was covered with a white cloth. A simple crucifix stood centrally on it. Bending down, he lifted a corner of the lace trimmed linen. Under the altar, Ricci and Juanito lay fast asleep beside the remains of a sandwich wrapper.

Milana gave a little gasp of surprise.

'Did you bring them here?' she whispered.

He shook his head, letting the cloth cover their hiding place again. 'I just bought the sandwich.'

Outside in the warm sunlight Milana looked bewildered. 'Who brought them here then?'

'They came by themselves. It's a safe place to rest.'

'They came here to feel safe?' She broke off looking at the graves around her. 'Here of all places?'

'Your mum's here. They can still feel her presence here, don't you see.'

You've lost someone too. She recognised it instinctively and there it was, in her eyes when she looked at him, something absolute that drew him in.

Amongst hundreds of slabs that covered the niches in the wall, Milana reached up and touched the one that read *Letty Romero*. From a respectful distance he watched her fingers trace the letters as he leant against a statue of an angel. The stone was unexpectedly cold. He was reminded of the great marble mausoleum in the National Cemetery in which they'd laid his own father to rest. The memory brought back the pungent smell of lilies that had filled the cold space; the marble slab taken down and the black hole into which he had watched them manoeuvre the heavy ebony coffin. Someone had given him a white rose and lifted him up. 'Throw it in, Santiago,' they'd whispered. He'd tried gripping it tight to throw it all the way into the cavernous space, so huge to his young eyes, but a thorn had hurt his finger and the rose had fallen on the crisscrossed marble of the floor. He'd cried then, so loud, so terribly, they'd rushed him away. How many times had he stood there since, in front of the dark marble slab into which his father's name had been carved in gold, feeling he had not loved his father enough, and now he was destined to love him too much; an unfulfilled love that yearned for what might have been.

'What are you thinking?' Milana's question brought him back to the promise of her eyes, reaching out to him, searching him for clues. He drew his fingers through his hair and smiled at her. Again her stomach lurched as the smile creasing his handsome face showed more poignantly the sadness in his eyes. Neither seemed to want to move, even the air was still here. It was like time had stopped to give them a chance together.

Milana rested her head against the wall of tombs with a wan smile. 'Do you think death is just another prison?' she ventured. The expression on her face was so intent it made him want to know all the thoughts behind her clear, intelligent eyes.

'Have you ever wanted to die?' she asked him suddenly.

'I think everyone has at some point in their life, don't you?'

'I've thought of it. Cutting my veins with a fragment of glass. Like last night, in the dark. I thought of it.'

'What stopped you?' He took a step closer. She wasn't sure what she was doing speaking as she was; whether she was responding to something deep in him or in herself.

'Oh I could never kill myself. Not really.' She flashed startled eyes at him and then, with a touch of merriment, 'I collect what's been chucked out. I guess I value that sort of stuff, you know, broken bits of glass and china. So I'd hardly be able to toss myself out cos of a bit of heart break. More likely I'd keep myself in a box and reinvent myself as a collage.' His eyes rested on her intrigued, their warmth drawing her in.

'Heart break?' he echoed.

'Whatever.' She shrugged again. She was aware her heart felt as though it were beating to an independent rhythm that the rest of her hadn't yet caught up with. What was she on about? He was making her say the strangest things.

'But what stops you, really, when you have those thoughts?' he repeated with genuine interest.

She stared up at him curiously. 'You mean what keeps me going?'

'Same thing,' he replied.

'Hope,' she asserted.

'Hope,' she repeated quietly looking back at the cold slab that carried her mother's name.

She sensed his eyes on her and after a while she felt herself released as he turned away and moved to where the ground fell away towards the river. A chill tingled down her spine as though the sun had left her in the shade, and a flurry of anxiety put all her thoughts in disarray. She looked back eventually to check he was still there. He was facing away across the river, solid and real against the ethereal light of early evening. A few moments later, her self-control exhausted, Milana came and stood beside him. She stole a glance at him; his shoulders set squarely against the wind, his hands thrust in his pockets, as he seemed to survey the mountains and the river. They stood silently looking in the same direction.

Finally he raked his fingers through his hair and rested his hand on the nape of his neck. 'Sometimes, I feel if your heart doesn't break, just a little, all the dreams contained in it can never see the light of day.' He glanced at her with a wry smile. 'Maybe all the best in us gets a chance to spill out of a broken heart.'

On a sudden impulse Milana turned towards him and buried her face in the crisp fabric of his shirt. He stayed quite still, his arms by his side, her warmth spreading through him. She heard the pounding of his heart, strong and rhythmic and lost herself in its certainty. Gently he placed his hand on her shoulder and, for an instant that she caught and made timeless, she felt the strength of his protection as, for an all too fleeting moment, he stroked her hair.

Chapter Eleven

Doris, the one with the sad face who baked cakes, was also a dinner lady at the 52nd Lyceo and usually picked up a fair bit of gossip from dishing up the meals in the school refectory. So she was more than grateful when the lunch hour passed uneventfully on Friday and Pablo didn't turn up wielding a gun. She lost no time finding Nilda and informing her that Ricci and Juanito hadn't shown up at school. While she baked fresh cakes for the weekend orders, Doris filled Nilda in on the gossip going around, and, after a few weak teas, they had fabricated a theory that Pablo must have Ricci and Juanito in some hideaway, scrounging for food for him, and getting them to pick-pocket and thieve for his benefit. They were mildly disquieted when Iris turned up reporting that Milana had arrived back from school all of two hours late, grubby and breathless and quite unbothered to hear the boys hadn't appeared. Meanwhile Nora, Nilda's sour-faced daughter, recently returned from her visit down south, breezed in after work telling them that it was all around work that Oscar was in a coma in El Salvador hospital and Ana was keeping vigil. Nora asked a few apparently innocuous questions of her own about Milana, before slipping away saying she had to pay the parish priest a visit.

The others remained gossiping till late evening and Iris, having indulged in a few tipples of straight pisco that she kept for special occasions, quite forgot to look in on Milana. Their unease about the boys' whereabouts grew overnight and by the time Doris picked up Nilda on Saturday morning on their way to the clothes sale in the Parish Centre they had resolved to call in on Milana and question her to see if she really was that unconcerned and, more intriguingly, why. But Milana had padlocked the wooden door of the shanty from the inside and there was no reply. They looked through the blur of plastic at the window, but Milana had nailed a cloth up so they couldn't see in. Giving each other a resigned look they left her to her slumbers. As they walked on, however, they began to wonder if she hadn't perhaps set Ricci and Juanito up to something, some sort of ploy to avoid *Señora* Maria's orphanage that she was so set against or, more darkly, Iris, when she joined them, suggested the possibility that Pablo had some sort of hold over her too.

'Well, he looks at her like a dog looks at a steak,' Iris declared suggestively. Which reduced the others to ruminative silence.

It was unusually quiet when Milana finally woke. In one night she had made up all the hours of sleeplessness that had preceded. She got out of bed with a new sense of vigour and pulled down the cloth that served as a curtain. The spring warmth filled the little room. Glancing about her for her clothes, she delighted in insignificant details: the sun pooling on the bed and spilling onto the patch of linoleum floor, the dust sparkling in its path. Even the feel of her clothes delighted her and she hugged herself for a brief instant, as though she had suddenly found herself reunited with an old friend. She thought of Ricci and Juanito curled up safe under the big stone altar of the little chapel and taking a deep breath as one might before any leap of faith, she accepted that Letty was watching over them, even if she had taken the guise of a rather more attractive than usual angel of deliverance.

Absorbed in her thoughts she did not at first hear the knocking at the door, until it came again; a gentle tapping.

'Who is it?' called Milana from inside.

'A friend of Letty's,' came the soft disembodied reply.

From her silk blonde hair to the tips of her black suede boots that peeked under her jeans, the woman at the door looked exquisitely, effortlessly expensive. She clasped Milana's hand between both hers, with undisguised feeling. They were fine hands, slim fingered with unpainted, almond shaped nails.

'Do you remember me, Milana? May I come in?' Milana stood aside to let her pass, following her graceful movements with rare admiration.

'Letty made it so pretty here. May I sit down? You were just a child, Milana, when I saw you last.' The woman kept her eyes on Milana just long enough for her to read their sincerity. Milana watched her sit, crossing her slender legs, where usually the shanty women slumped like lumps of lard. The woman placed her suede bag on the floor beside and leant over to search for something inside. There was a quality about her; a freshness, both sensual and fluid, like the river, that filled Milana with a feeling of well being. This was *Señora* Lisa. It had to be even though she seemed different. There was no other woman of this class who would have called herself a friend of Letty's.

'Here we are,' she smiled, taking out a packet of chocolate chip cookies, a small box of tea, a bag of sugar and a carton of milk in quick succession.

'Have you had breakfast yet?' she enquired brightly.

Milana shook her head. From the safety of the stove, she studied *Señora* Lisa in this new light of recognition as she bent to look for something else. She was fine featured and delicate. She wore hardly any makeup which enhanced the gentle kindliness of her expression. Her golden hair, that Milana remembered she had always worn up, giving her a regal air, now fell across her face as she leaned forwards so that she pushed it behind her ear in a girlish gesture. No one had blonde hair in the shantytown, unless it was so dyed that it looked like yellow paint had fallen on it, missing all the roots.

'I'm sorry to turn up like this, so unexpectedly,' she said adding a fresh loaf of bread and a packet of cheese to the little collection on the table. 'Maybe you're busy?'

Milana smiled at the improbability. *Señora* Lisa continued, 'You see, quite by chance, as I was walking through El Salvador Hospital I came upon Oscar on one of the wards. Poor Ana was with him, she won't leave his side incase he wakes from the coma. She told me everything that's happened. About Letty,' she paused to let the significance of her feelings be weighed out in the silence, before adding, 'and about Ricci and Juanito.' Her look conveyed such frank sympathy that it reached though Milana's defences and drew a gasp of feeling from her heart.

'You were in El Salvador...?' Milana responded, swiftly deflecting the attention from herself and equally baffled that this elegant woman should have visited the public hospital, downtown, where only the poor people went. It was a far cry from the uptown clinics of the rich.

'I used to visit El Salvador regularly,' she went on, perceptively, allowing Milana time to compose her emotions. 'You see we only returned from England a few days ago. I heard Esperanza our old cook had been taken ill, and I went to see her. And then I looked around the hospital again. Four years is quite a long time though, I hardly recognised anyone who worked there.'

'But who did you used to visit there?'

'Just people with no one to talk to.'

'What exactly does it mean to be "in a coma"? Will Oscar die?'

'He's unconscious. They don't know if he'll ever wake up again. Ana is going to stay with her sister downtown to be close to the hospital. I'm glad she's agreed to it. I believe Oscar hears her. I told her she must speak to him and tell him she loves him, tell him everything she feels, and if he dies he will take all her words with him.'

'That's a lovely thing to say to her.' The kettle whistled and Milana busied herself with it.

'I wish you could have been with my mum before she died,' she said quietly.

'But you were there, Milana. That's what mattered. You comforted her.' Clutching the kettle with a hot rag, Milana looked solemnly at *Señora* Lisa.

'Your mother died in your arms. She died in your love, Milana. What more could a mother want?'

In the look Lisa gave her, Milana recognised the strength that would have bound her mother to this woman. Tears lumped in her throat. She turned to rummage in the cupboard and finding two fine china cups with pretty gold rims that her mother had never used, she poured the tea into them.

'I am OK. I mean about Mum,' she said huskily, 'I haven't gone to pieces or anything.'

'I'm sure you are strong and capable, like your mother. Victoria told me you came to the house and that she gave you English lessons. Was she a good teacher?' her eyes twinkled at Milana, 'That was very resourceful of you, Milana, to get her to teach you.'

'I didn't do anything. She was just kind. I miss her. But that's all over now,' she added with cool composure, and balancing the tea cup and saucer carefully so as not to spill any of the slightly overfull contents she handed it to *Señora* Lisa.

Lisa felt a wave of unease at such dispassion and chose to ignore it. Maybe the child had inherited her mother's rare capacity to dissemble.

'You must keep up what she taught you. I can help you sometimes, if you like, when I get myself organised. I'd like to. Your mother must be so proud of you.' Milana smiled at her, she liked the fact that she had used the present tense for Letty, it forged an understanding between them and she imagined *Señora* Lisa would share her belief that Letty was looking after the boys too.

'Mum did go to pieces though, once, didn't she?' she said, turning away again to bring the sugar. It was a crude but urgent attempt to seek out the information she always felt her mother had kept from her.'

Lisa surveyed her over the gold rim of her tea cup. Milana sensed that she was biding her time, as though there was something altogether different she wanted to say and she shifted uneasily under the shrewd gaze.

'Extraordinary suffering shaped your mother's determination and her strength. Never let anyone tell you otherwise, Milana.' She put the cup down. 'I would have liked to have come to her funeral.' She sighed.

'Why did you come here to San Damian, *Señora* Lisa?' Milana asked, on an impulse, 'Why did you help us like you did? And why did you go away again?'

Lisa stopped herself giving a stock answer. She could feel Milana's keen eyes on her, challenging the truth. It seemed to her Milana's question was directed to an altogether different part of her conscious being than the one she dressed and put forward for social occasions. It was precisely the person she kept back, that Milana seemed to address with breathtaking candour.

Lisa wrestled with the answer remembering what her husband, Victor, had told her those years back. *Your duty lies in caring for the children you have, the family God gave you, not the one He took away from you. You can't let the shantytown consume you like it was a debt you must pay. Let it go and you'll find peace in the end.'* She had left the shantytown and walked away from the tangled emotions it stirred in her, even before her husband had received his posting to England, and had not visited again. But the peace Victor promised would come, had eluded her. Guilt still ate away at the corners of her life. And now here she was again, drawn back by fate or by her anguished heart that still sought out what had been lost to her.

'I just wasn't very well, Milana. Then we went abroad for a while.'

'Are you better now?'

She gave a little laugh, like a gentle exhalation of breath, 'I don't know,' and her eyes rested on Milana, wistful and infinitely tender.

'How are you going to manage, Milana dear, have you thought?'

'I am managing. I'm fine.'

'But what about your brothers, Milana? I hear they haven't come home.'

Milana responded with unexpected vehemence.

'Of course they ran off after what happened at Ana's, wouldn't anyone? They'll come back when the heat dies down.'

'Milana, I know you're very capable, but don't you see you're too young to live here alone.'

'I've been looking after my brothers ever since Mum worked on the hill. There's no point protecting me now, it's too late for that,' she retorted coolly.

'You're barely fourteen Milana, we can at least try.'

Milana's heartbeat accelerated like that of an animal that senses a trap.

'They sent you didn't they? Who was it, Father Pancho? School? Nora? I know she's itching to get her hands on our place, Iris told me.' Milana lifted her chin defiantly and narrowed her eyes. 'They got you to come and tell me nicely that they've vacuum packed my life like they do the meat in the supermarket, so it can fit into some neat little plan that makes everyone feel better about themselves.' Milana sank onto a stool as if she knew the effort to resist was futile. 'If Juanito and Ricardo hadn't been at Ana's that night, if that hadn't happened to Oscar, they'd have left us alone. Now they want to fold us up and put us away before we become a nuisance.'

Lisa was struck by the intuitive cleverness of the girl.

'I offered to come, Milana. No one told me to. I would have come to see you anyway. But you must see this is no place for you to grow up alone, there's too much trouble here…'

'It's the only home I've got,' insisted Milana. 'It's all I've got left of Mum. And Pablo doesn't scare me.'

'But I believe there's a better alternative, Milana, one that will be good for you all. The boys will like it. They can't live in hiding, Milana.'

'The boys will come back. You'll see, *Señora* Lisa. I know where they are.'

'Where are they?' she retorted with surprise.

Milana hesitated. 'They went to Mum's grave. They've been sleeping under the altar of the little chapel.'

'How did you find them?'

Milana's eyes lit up, 'Someone showed me. He'll look out for them.'

Señora Lisa frowned, 'Who?' The simplicity of the question hung heavy. Milana realised how ingenuous she must seem. She had cried in front of him, told him her innermost thoughts, even embraced him, and yet she didn't know his name.

'I don't know. He didn't say.'

'Why wouldn't he tell you his name?'

Milana grew more anguished, 'I never asked him.'

'Well, where does he come from?'

'Under the bridge...' even as she uttered the words she wished she hadn't.

'Does this person live under the bridge?' Her question was gentle but urgent.

'I don't know.'

'Oh, Milana. There are all sorts under the bridges and they're mostly petty criminals. You can't trust any of them.'

'Who can I trust then?' cried Milana throwing the angry challenge at the gentle guest.

Lisa put her hand on Milana's.

'Let's have more tea,' she suggested. 'These cups are lovely, they were your mother's favourites. She bought them with me in Valparaiso. Did she tell you?'

Discomfited, Milana shook her head.

'Do you know Valparaiso?'

Again Milana shook her head.

'Huge cruise ships anchor there and people crowd down the gang planks into the shops and markets buying up all our little trinkets like they were raiding the lost ark.' She laughed a soft mellow laugh that seemed to soothe Milana's anguish. 'They take these treasures home and show them proudly to their families and they say, "We brought this all the way from Valparaiso," as though it was the greatest adventure to have been here.'

Milana knew *Señora* Lisa was coaxing her into submission but she still marvelled at how effortlessly she changed tack. Lisa was smiling. She had the familiar creases around the mouth that Milana had so loved in her mother. She wanted her to keep smiling like that.

'I took your mother to Valparaiso once. We went to the markets like the tourists do and guess what she bought? These teacups. She said they were so delicate and fine that they carried with them the experience of elegance.'

'What could she want with fine teacups?'

'Something different perhaps. Do you like travelling, Milana?'

'The furthest I've ever been is to your house on the bus,' Milana retorted.

'Wouldn't you like to?' she persisted ignoring Milana's ironic tone.

The same chill as before came over Milana. That which she would have longed for just days ago now became a threat.

'I know so much has happened. It's all been so sudden and so shocking,' Lisa went on exhaling kindness in every word. 'You know, your mother had friends down south. She always hoped to take you down there, but she never got round to it. *Señora* Lucy runs a home for children on a farm near Panguipulli. Her two sons are grown-up and coming to Santiago and she could do with more help round the farm and with the little ones. Nilda's daughter, Nora, was just down there. Nora told them all about you.'

Milana couldn't help rolling her eyes at the mention of Nora's name, anything Nora suggested would always have no one but Nora's best interests at the heart of it, and generally a fair amount of scheming.

'This is a wonderful opportunity for you and your brothers.' Lisa paused, leaning towards Milana, 'Your brothers would love it there, and they'd be out of harm's way…' She got up and poured Milana another cup of hot tea, placing it in her hand.

'Panguipulli is very beautiful, Milana. It's a little town on the shores of a lake. There are hills and rivers bursting with fish and if you look across the lake you see the Villarica volcano. It's active you know. I actually saw it erupt years ago; the most impressive thing I've ever seen. Now it has a tiny cloud above it, like a little puff of smoke as if to tell people, "I'm breathing, I'm alive, I can do great things".' For an instant Milana was reminded of her mother and that lyrical far away quality her voice sometimes had, and she forgot what she was saying and just listened to the inflection of the words.

'On clear nights, Milana, you can see a pin-prick of light like the glow of a cigarette, it's the glow of heat from the crater. You can go right up to the crater and look inside and smell the sulphur.'

'But not now, *Señora* Lisa, not just yet,' interjected Milana, coming to her senses. 'Please, not yet. Let me finish the year at school...let me stay until, at least December, please.'

'It's magical, Milana. They've got horses and there's so much space. You'll love it. Nora can take you, on one of those buses with beds... with your brothers, and no one will get to you there.'

'I wouldn't want Nora to take me round the block let alone on some bus south, she's about as different to Nilda as a toad is to a rabbit. It's hard to accept they're even related,' said Milana looking at Lisa with a sinking heart. Lisa looked a little taken aback and a touch amused, but she went on seamlessly from where she'd left off.

'And in going, Milana, you have nothing to lose, and everything to gain.'

But how could *Señora* Lisa know all that she had to lose.

'I can't even think about it then, can I?' pleaded Milana.

Lisa squeezed her hand by way of answer, but seconds later she relented: 'Of course you can. I suppose you can finish the year and be down there for Christmas. Why not?'

'I'd like that,' said Milana brightening about as much as a low energy light bulb. 'What will happen to this place?'she enquired dismally.

'Oh,' Lisa looked over the miserably makeshift walls plastered with old wrapping paper to conceal gaps and patches of damp and the plastic sheets over the window spaces. Her eye travelled over the nails from which a few clothes hung and the plastic curtain with seascapes that divided the one space from the other. 'Nora will look after it,' she concluded brightly. 'I have an idea *Señora* Lacy's boys from Panguipulli could use this place and do it up, put in proper windows, that sort of thing... so it would be here for you.'

'Nora will never let us have it back. She'll say it's payment for all the cokes Nilda's bought us over the years. You don't know Nora, *Señora* Lisa. She hates us.'

'She doesn't hate you, Milana, she's jealous of Nilda's affection for you and your brothers.'

'What's there to be jealous of?' Milana looked incredulous.

'You'd be surprised. She's had more than her fair share of hardship. She's been scarred by suffering, a mother's suffering.'

'Well Nora's as insensitive as a rock and she's about as maternal as a hyena, she'll never have children. You know hyenas eat their prey, bones and all, and they'll eat their young too.'

Lisa couldn't help smiling but she saw fit to persist despite Milana's resistance.

'Come and sit here beside me, Milana. I want to confide in you.'

'*Señora* Lisa, you don't have to explain stuff to me. I know you mean well, I do,' she said, seating herself next to her on the little settee.

'Nora had a baby girl called Sarita when she was sixteen.' Milana looked disbelievingly and Lisa paused and nodded as if to verify the statement.

'When the baby was about a year and a half old, Nora left her in Nilda's care. Nilda had one of her fits. She fell on the hot coals of the brazier she used to cook on, whilst still holding the baby, so the baby was trapped under her weight. Doris heard her screams and raced over and saw it all. Nora arrived moments later and used her considerable strength to turn Nilda over and get her off the brazier. It all happened so fast that, at first, Nora didn't realise that her mother was holding little Sarita. Nilda's grip on that baby was iron hard. There was nothing that could have been done to save the child by then. The baby's shoulders and the back of its head were burnt away. Nilda survived pretty much unscathed save for her arm. You could say it was Nora's baby that saved Nilda's life or at least saved her from far more life threatening burns.'

Lisa pressed Milana's hand. 'I'm sorry to be so graphic but I want you to understand what she's been through. She was only a couple of years older than you are now. For some people like Nora, it's as though their heart freezes in order not to face the pain. Besides, that's not the only horror Nora witnessed in her life, Milana. As a little girl she was found watching television with the dead body of her father hanging from the light fixture in the centre of the room. He'd killed himself and she'd just come home from school and pretended nothing had happened. She was hugging herself in a little ball and swaying back and forth, when they got to her. She wouldn't let anyone take her away from the television. She screamed if they tried to move her. She wouldn't look at anyone. Her eyes were riveted on the TV as though that screen would save her from everything that was happening.'

'How come no one's ever mentioned this stuff?'Milana asked, her scepticism helping to keep her empathetic nature in check.

'Because we hope what isn't mentioned will wipe itself away.'

'That doesn't really work though, does it?'

'It does for other people. They forget your pain if you don't keep reminding them. Eventually they never refer to it again. I know Nora makes herself difficult to love but think of what she's lived through and it might make it easier to forgive her for being cold and uncharitable now.'

Milana looked dubious. 'I can try, but it's hard. There's others who have loved and lost and are kinder, *Señora* Lisa.'

'Nora's closed up her heart so as not to feel, but deep down there must be a terrible unspoken resentment of what her mother did. It filters out against you and your brothers, who have survived where her own child has died.'

' She's against us that's for sure. Nilda should talk to her and help her.'

'Nilda's the last person who could talk to her. Nilda never knew exactly what happened; you see after a fit she doesn't remember much. Doris took that burnt baby away wrapped in a blanket and gave it to the parish priest who buried it himself. Doris will keep the secret of that death from Nilda, to the grave.

'Why? Is that right? Shouldn't Nilda know exactly what happened so as to be able to make it up to Nora?'

'Maybe, but some things are covered up instinctively. I don't think Nilda could have borne the truth of her part in it all and, for all her faults, Nora has never breathed a word of blame to Nilda. I know Nora can't have any more children, which must make it even worse for her. We criticise people's shortcomings so quickly, but their strengths, Milana, their rare moments of fortitude are often their most silent moments, only God sees those.' She paused and looked down at her fingers, twisting her wedding band, 'People's lives and sufferings are far more complicated than we imagine.'

'Why does God let stuff like that happen?'

'Accidents happen. God doesn't make them happen, but God can help us through them if we let Him in, but people don't Milana, they blame Him for disasters and close up their hearts so His love can't reach in and heal them. They need our compassion not our criticism to overcome their bitterness.'

Suddenly Milana's face softened. 'All the best in us gets to spill out of a broken heart,' she murmured.

'Where did you learn that?' asked Lisa with genuine curiosity.

Milana shrugged but her heart raced as she repeated his words and a sudden warmth flushed through her as though she'd just brought him into the room with them.

'Can't you help Nora, *Señora* Lisa?'

'She doesn't want to be helped, her only comfort is her pain, can you understand that?'

'Maybe because it's the only feeling she's got left. She doesn't have any other kind of feeling that's for sure.'

'You're a clever girl and you do have a sympathetic spirit, though you try to hide it.' She smiled and tilting her head to one side she observed Milana. 'It helps that you're a dreamer and your heart loves so much.'

Milana looked alarmed, but Lisa laughed and placed her hand reassuringly on hers, 'It loves the sunset and the river and your collection of old stones.'

'Oh. So you know all that too?'

'Letty always spoke about you and how you loved nature. Loving nature is God's way of bringing us close to Him.'

'I don't know much about God,' sighed Milana.

'Oh but you do, much more than you think.' She stood up and gave Milana a soft scented kiss.

'Your mother suffered but she had a noble heart too. She'll watch over you. You know that don't you? Pray to her, won't you? And for her. Souls see us when we pray for them.'

'Yeah. Mum used to tell me that too.'

'We'll see each other again soon, Milana. Father Pancho knows where to reach me anytime.'

Lisa left a twenty thousand *peso* note on top of the old, broken television as she left.

Milana sat, staring at the gold rimmed cups and the gifts of food that *Señora* Lisa had brought. Gradually the exquisite smell of perfume she left behind became more like the warning scent of change. Rather than peace Milana felt herself consumed by sudden apprehension. What if *Señora* Lisa went back and told the parish priest that Ricci and Juanito had been taken by some man on the riverbank and the police came looking for him and locked him up? She cursed her confiding nature. She should have kept him secret. The restlessness she had suppressed during the visit bubbled up inside her, urgent and irrepressible.

Moments later she was running through the narrow alleys past mangy mongrels and dodging piles of garbage, twisting her way over rocks and boulders, sliding down earthy banks until she came at last to the open plain of the river. She stopped then, to catch her breath and lifted her face to the morning sun high above the mountains. She felt safe here, alone in the open. The Andes like timeless Gods of wisdom seemed to embrace her in their breathtaking proximity, calming her. She welcomed the chill in the air and the familiar feeling of the wind flowing through her hair, caressing her skin as though it were weaving its magic around her. Plunging her bare feet into the icy waters, she recognised the recklessness that drove her. Standing in the river, her heart hoping against hope, she could no longer deny that already nothing mattered more to her than seeing her stranger again, whoever he was, and that this was the cause of the uneasiness she wrestled with.

Chapter Twelve

They were standing way up-river, up to their ankles in water, all three of them, without, it seemed, a care in the world. The midday sun illuminated them in a haze of light and the water pooled like molten gold around them. The feeling that washed over Milana when she caught sight of them made her giddy. Or maybe it was the heat or the fact that she had run so fast. She stood at the water's edge forgetting everything but the unrestrained vehemence of her racing heart.

'Hey Mila, Mila, we caught a fish,' cried Juanito catching sight of her.

'We didn't, Santiago did,' corrected Ricci grinning widely.

So that was his name: 'Santiago'. It was strong. It was the name of the capital city. Milana liked it. Santiago looked at her from beneath the hair that flopped over his eyes as he bent over the rocks, his bare hands dripping with water.

'Breakfast?' he suggested, his indescribably handsome face creasing into a broad grin. She came a little closer. There on a rock was the fish, flapping its life away.

'It's big,' she observed, standing over it and touching its silver scales, feeling foolishly self-conscious and a little cross with herself because the reaction he produced in her was unfamiliar and disquieting.

'River trout,' Santiago came up behind her. She felt his proximity shiver through her.

'Get some twigs, boys, and some dry grass.'

They ran to do his bidding. Santiago gutted the fish expertly with a swiss army knife and cleaned it in the river, then he placed the twigs and grass on the rock, and took a tiny gold rimmed glass lense from his pocket and held it up to the sun's rays until a thin thread of smoke rose from the dry grass. He blew softly on it, whilst the children watched him intently. The grass caught fire and then the twigs.

'Wow,' they gawped, fascinated, 'how come it never works for us?'

'You've got to be patient, Juanito, and keep it very still, that's all there is to it. The midday sun helps of course, and the right kind of lense,' he winked at him.

'Cor,' said Juanito in admiration. Santiago sharpened the end of a stick and skewering the fish, held it over the fire, turning it occasionally.

'See those big *llanten* leaves over there,' he said, 'they can be our plates.'

The boys scampered off again to pick the huge green leaves. Milana remained watching Santiago's movements warily, as though she were trying to grasp the nature of his know-how. She noticed the knife was engraved with the initials SH in beautiful sloping letters.

'Don't worry about them,' Santiago nodded in the direction of the boys, noting the troubled look that had crept into her eyes.

'We've spoken about what happened, they're cool.'

Milana asked herself truculently how witnessing a murder and having the bloodied knife wiped over their T-shirt could suddenly be talked away, or how two terrified kids, who'd sought refuge in a graveyard for three days could be 'cool', except literally. In some darker recess of her mind, she resented that Santiago should have such a powerful though apparently benign influence on the boys, it somehow detracted from the exceptional nature of their own meetings, which served to annoy her more.

'Why do you come here, to the river?' challenged Milana, thinking of the suspicion on *Señora* Lisa's face when she had mentioned him.

'Same reason as you, I guess.'

Why did she come to the river? She thought about it. To get away, to dream, to look for hidden treasure and now; *I came*

116

looking for you. He was smiling, a candid playful smile. *Can you read my thoughts too?* she asked herself slightly rattled. Despite her frustration she tried to smile back, a small, rather sheepish smile of uncertainty.

The fish was delicious. It tasted of milk and smoke.

'Hey, this is brill, in't it Ricci?' Juanito sucked on his fingers. Milana, resigned to the ease of Santiago's company with her brothers, walked a little further upstream and bent over the water trailing her fingers through it, letting it wash over her wrists, then lifting her hands so that it trickled down her bare arms. She walked aimlessly in the river delighting in its icy freshness, slipping over mossy stones and laughing, despite herself, as she regained her balance.

'We've fished this river lots but we've never caught nothing have we Ricci?'

'Nope,' Ricci grinned at Santiago, 'will you teach me, I mean, to do it just like that, just with my hands?'

'I can try.'

Santiago sat against a rock, his hands resting behind his head. Milana felt his eyes following her and, moving a little closer, she let them rest on her, thawing out the distance between them. He watched her slim, graceful limbs as she shifted positions, her blouse lifting so that he could see the lovely curve between her waist and her hip. Finally, she turned towards him slowly. Her lips soft and full, her eyes wide and questioning; the innocence in her beauty took his breath away.

'What do you paint then? Will you show me?' she asked.

He watched her perfect eyebrows draw a little closer into a frown. *You have no idea of the effect you have,* was the fleeting thought that crossed his mind as he observed her distractedly.

'Don't you keep them in some scrapbook?' she persisted.

'No, I don't keep them in a scrapbook,' he laughed. 'But yes, I will show you if you're patient; if you don't ask too many questions.'

'Don't you like questions?'

'Who needs questions when we have all this?' And his arm swept over the river and the Andes and the remains of the fish and the four of them sitting there in the middle of it all.' She realised what he meant.

'Just take it or leave it as is,' she said slowly, thinking how *Señora* Lisa wouldn't approve and how there were no clear answers to the questions she wanted to ask.

'Exactly,' he eyed her with renewed interest. 'No boxing up for convenience, just let be!' He sighed contentedly.

'Only real life isn't like that is it?' she said with a hint of annoyance.

'It is today,' he retorted with an easy smile.

Santiago pulled out his watch which was on a chain round his neck.

'That's a funny place for a watch,' exclaimed Juanito.

'I lost the strap, no time to get a new one.'

But you have time to sit here with us, thought Milana.

'Do you live round here?' asked Ricci scampering close while chucking pebbles downstream.

'I don't exactly live here but I feel alive here. Will that do?' He tossed a pebble so it collided perfectly with Ricci's.

'So where's your home, then?' asked Milana.

'Not far,' he said rising, 'there you go with the questions,' he flashed her a wry smile and glancing towards the boys he added, 'and now I must go.'

'But it's a holiday today,' they reproached in unison, keen to prolong their moment of happiness. 'You said it was September 18th, Independence Day, that's how come you were so early and there was no school. Remember?' cried Juanito urgently.

Santiago flipped the fish tail at Juanito playfully, 'Sure I remember, but I still have to go.' Suddenly he crouched down near the boys; 'I tell you what, I'll come back later this evening but you've got to do something for me.'

'Yeah, anything.'

'You know the old shack just a little further down the river?'

'What, Old Whitebeard's?' asked Ricci incredulous. Juanito opened his eyes wide, *'El Cuco's,'* he breathed and gave an involuntary shudder.

'Did you know him, Whitebeard, I mean?' Ricci asked Santiago in a respectful whisper.

Santiago raised a dark eyebrow at him by way of response. '"Whitebeard!" good name! I just called him "Old Man River". Do you know his shack?'

Milana shook her head dubiously. 'We don't know anything about him or his address, except that if we were bad they said he would draw us down the river to his lair and do unspeakable things to us and turn us into mist. Frankly none of us thought of looking him up.'

Santiago laughed, her defiance stirred him. 'But he was real all the same,' he whispered back knowingly.

'Do you think he was a werewolf or a wizard?' piped up Juanito breathlessly.

Santiago ruffled Juanito's hair, 'Just a sad, old guy, Juanito.'

'I saw him once,' Ricci paused, remembering, 'I think, in winter, walking along the bank, a long way off, but I was scared of what people said about him, so I ran away.'

'Well nobody's going to see him now because he's dead,' Santiago assured them. 'He died a couple of years back.'

'Makes no difference,' said Juanito, 'his spirit'll come, they said so, didn't they? Even the bad guys like Pablo won't go down past that bend in the river. They were told, same as us, that Whitebeard would get them if he saw them and make them sorry. They said he feeds off old cats so he can see in the dark. All us kids are scared of him.' Juanito was so excited, he barely drew breath as he talked.

'You know Pablo?' said Ricci cutting in, 'The guy that stuck the knife in Oscar. I heard him say that Whitebeard was a rich man, really rich; he kept his treasure buried in the riverbed. We kids always thought they worked for Whitebeard, all those drug pushers, but they don't; they're scared of him just like us, ever since that guy was washed up dead.'

'That guy drowned himself,' corrected Milana.

'No.' Ricci shook his head vehemently. 'Whitebeard got him. He was one of Oro Sucio's gang. They were that scared of Whitebeard, even those tough guys.'

'Ha!' Juanito let out a yelp of delight at the thought of them being scared.

'Ok guys, look, Whitebeard can't hurt you, I promise. Forget all that stuff.' Santiago glanced at Milana for support but she was looking downstream lost in thought.

'If you go down past the sharpest bend in the river by the ancient eucalyptus tree, on the far bank, you'll see his shack. Get firewood; lots of twigs and driftwood and I'll meet you there later. We'll make a bonfire, they won't see us that far down river. I'll bring stuff: *empanadas* for us to eat. We'll celebrate Independence Day together. It's kind of fitting.'

'What d'you mean?' Juanito had perked up considerably.

'He means it's our independence too we're celebrating.' Santiago shot Milana a look, struck again by her quickness of mind, but Milana only sensed his hurry to be gone.

'All of us?' Milana asked.

'Sure, you too, Milana.' But to her mind he seemed caught up in some other thought.

'And I'll tell you the story of Old Man River and why he lived here, if you like.'

'Wow,' Juanito gave a low whistle.

Milana watched Santiago stride off over the rocks, sure-footed and purposeful. He cut a striking figure, his hair black and uncompromising against the faint blue of the sky. She ran after him suddenly, stopping him in his tracks.

'You don't have to do this, you know,' she gasped breathlessly. 'I mean look after us or anything. We're OK.' She shrank back from the look that he flashed back at her. He glanced back at the boys. 'Really?' He looked at her with dark intensity. 'You think a couple of fish for breakfast can heal the shit they've been through?' he added with unexpected vehemence. Milana felt her cheeks burn with embarassment and frustration.

'No. Of course not,' she retaliated. 'I meant you don't have to feel sorry for us, that's all.' She turned away but he held her back, gripping her arm, his fingers firm against her skin.

'If I felt sorry for you, that would mean I thought my life

was better than yours. That's not something either you or I should try to judge.'

Milana thought of Letty, it was the kind of thing she'd say. She tried to look apologetic but it only seemed to antagonise him further and she felt his hold still fixed on her.

'Look around you, it's a bloody wasteland, there's no one watching us, no one cares about us. There are no rules here. We can do what we want and be who we want to be. If I meet you guys tonight it's because I choose to, and I'm sorry you think you're such a waste of my time.'

'I didn't say that.' She met his eyes with sudden fire.

He drew his hand away and pulled his fingers through his hair, as though he wanted to pull some deep seated anguish out of his mind.

'Don't come tonight on account of me, or whatever kindness you think I'm doing you,' he said impatiently. 'Come because you want to.'

Milana watched him go, before turning back to the boys with a wan smile to cover her confusion.

Chapter Thirteen

'This place is so spooky.' Juanito stopped walking and looked about him. A light mist rose from the water. Along the banks, tall eucalyptus trees shuddered and grew still as a desultory wind passed over their desiccated leaves.

'You sure he meant this far? It feels like we've walked miles.' Juanito's arms were weighed down with twigs that stuck out at uncomfortable angles.

'You don't have to drag the twigs everywhere,' muttered Ricci.

'But Santiago said he wanted twigs to make the fire, right?' They were standing upstream from the graveyard. They had left the familiar old bridge with its iron railings far behind and beyond that, the huge concrete Americo Vespucio overpass that straddled the riverbed, its endless traffic speeding out of town down the steep incline of La Pyramide to join the Pan American Highway that led north all the way up through the Atacama desert to Peru and on.

'Look! There!' Milana pointed to the far bank where a solitary eucalyptus stood majestically bestowing its shade over the carpet of crisp fallen leaves beneath. There beside, rising out of the rocky bank like a strangely symmetrical organic growth, was a small shack made of weathered wooden planks nailed together with a corrugated roof, only a tiny bit bigger than Nilda's outside toilet.

'That must be it,' said Milana staring at it curiously.

Juanito yelped in horror and, dropping all his twigs, ran to where Milana was standing.

'What is it?' Ricci looked about nervously.

Milana saw what had scared Juanito. It sent a shiver up her spine. Five crosses had been staked into the ground to the side of the shack. They were carved out of huge bits of driftwood. Around each cross, six feet long and about two feet across, there were stones marking out a perimeter.

'They're graves,' said Milana quietly.

'I don't want to stay here, it's... it's horrible,' stammered Juanito taking a step back but not wanting to separate himself from the others.

'No wonder no one came here. He did kill people, right? Like they say?' Ricci's expression reflected the horror of standing so close to unexpected graves whose occupants you couldn't be sure about.

'What's different to the graveyard, Ricci?' suggested Milana genuinely interested. 'You were OK to hide out there?'

'Are you nuts, Mila? The graveyard's for people who die and are buried like they're meant to be. Not like this! These guys have all been *murdered* or why would they be left here? Maybe Whitebeard even buried them alive. Please let's just get out of here.'

'No,' said Milana firmly. 'We've come this far and found it and now we'll stay; or at least we'll stay nearby. If Santiago said he'd come he will.'

'How come you know him so well suddenly?' Ricci challenged her. 'He's OUR friend, right Juanito?'

'I don't know him at all,' replied Milana calmly.

'Mum told us not to trust strangers,' murmured Juanito uncertainly.

'Everyone's a stranger till you know them,' retorted Ricci. He came up close to Milana, trying to be out of earshot of Juanito. 'I like Santiago too, but how can we be sure about him? I mean, where's he come from? Why won't he tell us? What's he doing round here, anyway?'

'We can't be sure, Ricci. It's instinct we have to rely on; gut reaction, like a good or bad smell.'

'And you think this guy's like a good smell.'

'Yeah. Don't you?'

'I guess, but still… why bring us here?'

'So we won't be bothered by anyone.'

'What, like these guys weren't bothered?' And he shot a look towards the five crosses.

They circled the shack but never dared look through its single dirty little window. They tried to ignore the graves by keeping away from them. Milana searched the shallow riverbed for pretty rocks and pebbles while the boys amused themselves finding misshapen bits of driftwood and searching for fish. The afternoon turned chilly and the mist rising from the river swirled about them, damp and eerie.

'I hope he comes,' muttered Ricci. 'It'll be dark soon.'

'Aren't you having fun?' Milana lifted her head from the pile of smooth rounded pebbles she had gathered.

'Kind of, I mean, I'm a bit spooked.'

'Me too,' said Juanito. 'But it's an adventure, right?' He grinned back at his sister.

Milana noted the gathering shadows, an idea, a way to freedom, half forming in her mind. Suddenly she was standing over her brothers.

'Hey, don't spook us more,' cried Juanito looking up,

'What's up?' Ricci registered the earnest expression on Milana's face.

'Don't you guys go telling anyone about this place, you hear. I mean not ANYONE, not even your best mates or they'll want to say they saw it too… and it'll be over.'

'Geez, Mila! Don't get so cross. You're freaking me out.' Ricci dried his wet hands on his T-shirt.

'What'll be over, Mila?' asked Juanito in awe of her vehemence.

'I'm serious. NO ONE must hear about this.'

'OK sis, don't bust a gut,' said Ricci.

'Swear that you won't tell a soul. Swear it now.'

'OK, OK, I swear.'

'And you, Juanito, both of you…swear on our mother's grave, swear it.'

The two boys straightened and swore solemnly on their

mother's grave that they would not tell a soul about this place. Satisfied, Milana went back to her pile of rocks while they exchanged puzzled looks.

'You don't think this place is bewitched?' whispered Juanito after a while.

'Why?' Ricci glanced nervously at his brother.

'Well you know' – he nodded in Milana's direction – 'she's come over all funny.'

'No, silly! She's not bewitched, just a bit of a witch at times.' Juanito laughed inspite of himself. Still, Ricci wondered what had come over his sister and it made him uneasy.

If thoughts of ghosts weren't bad enough, Ricci hadn't forgotten that Pablo was still at large. He feared him more than any ghosts, but reason reminded him that Pablo, for all his murdering instincts, was scared witless of Whitebeard and the old legends, and that meant that this godforsaken place was still the safest of havens. Suddenly he understood what Milana meant.

Thin ridges of cloud criss-crossed the sky streaking it pink. It promised to be one of those fabulous sunsets that turned the skies vermilion and set the Andes on fire, just like the one the night before Letty died. Juanito raced over to Milana and huddled by her. 'There's someone coming,' he whispered.

'Oh heck!' said Ricci seeing a bulky figure approach out of the misty shadows. 'It's coming from the shack, from the graves.'

'It's a ghost. I know it is. I know it is,' cried Juanito burying his head in his hands and curling up beside Milana.

'No, it's him,' said Milana.

'Who? You can't even see a face,' said Ricci.

'Santiago. Who else silly?'

'How can you know it's him?'

'I know how he walks.'

'He's got something over him. You can't see how he walks,' Ricci hissed back.

'It's him I tell you.' Milana backed away whilst Ricci and Juanito stayed put, their eyes riveted on the approaching figure. Moments later Santiago was beside them.

'No fire?' he said, looking at the boys in mock disappointment.

'We didn't bring matches,' muttered Juanito.

'We didn't think it could get so cold down here. It's colder than those nights in the graveyard.' Ricci shivered.

'It's the mist, it gets into your bones.' Santiago tossed the boys a lighter, one of the cheap plastic sort bought in kiosks. 'Keep it, you never know when you may need to start a fire.'

From the shadows, Milana watched Ricci and Juanito fanning the tiny flames from ignited twigs. They fed it with dried eucalyptus leaves that released a final exhalation of minty perfume as they burnt. Milana picked up another stone, smoothed by years of erosion, it felt soft as skin. She rolled it in the palm of her hand as she watched the fire take and the sparks lift like fireflies into the night and Santiago sihouetted against the flames. She didn't want to move, or speak. She wanted this moment to last forever.

Santiago had taken off the long poncho he was wearing and left it on the ground.

'Wrap that round you and help yourselves,' he said indicating the large paper bag next to it that he'd been carrying. The boys fell on the contents eagerly, lining up two, litre bottles of Coke, a bag of *empanadas* and a huge bag of things that looked to them like cotton wool balls. Ricci grabbed the bag. 'What's this, Santiago?'

'Marshmallows.'

Santiago took a long twig out of the fire. 'Open the bag and stick one on the end here.' He held the marshmallow over the heat. A blue flame enveloped it. The smell of burnt sugar filled the air. He handed the stick with the marshmallow to Juanito.

'Take care, it'll be hot.' Juanito licked the caramelised crust, then he bit into the soft interior.

'Wow!' he crooned, his mouth full of sweet, creamy substance. 'It's incredible!'

Santiago handed another skewered marshmallow to Ricci and put the bag between them, 'Go for it boys. Happy Independence Day!'

Santiago turned towards Milana. She realised he'd been conscious all along of where she was and felt a tautening inside her. She was still smarting from their earlier exchange but whether from embarrassment or another kind of heightened self-awareness she couldn't say. His eyes swept over her and a half smile of amusement curled his lips, as though he was aware they were playing some sort of game. She felt the blood rise to her face and looked away, suddenly annoyed by his insouciance. He crouched beside her. With the back of his hand he brushed her cheek in a fleeting gesture of concern, 'You're cold,' he said, 'I'm sorry I couldn't come earlier.' He made no reference to their last parting.

'It's kind of a weird place for a picnic,' said Milana flustered by the effect he had on her.

'It's private.'

The quickening of his senses on seeing her had discomfited him, so he had, at first, chosen to ignore her. Now, having distracted himself with the fire, he felt at ease and wanted to reassure her. She looked cold as she sat gracefully leaning to one side, her hair falling about her shoulders in a mass of tangled curls. He cast his gaze over her face and it rested on her mouth… her eyes met his suddenly. The realisation of being caught in an unexpected feeling sent a jolt through him. He stood up abruptly.

'Why does it need to be so private?' There was an accusatory edge to her tone.

'The boys don't want to be found. Isn't that why they were hiding amongst the graves?'

'This isn't much better, is it?' She felt herself being deliberately provocative.

'It's a whole lot better. No one else dares venture here. Do you want the whole shantytown coming to our picnic, or maybe just Pablo?' Santiago thrust his hands in his pockets and looked intently upstream. Milana tried concentrating on *Señora* Lisa's distrust of him to counter the unnerving attraction he produced in her. She felt her blood pumping faster as she drew up the courage to confront him.

'You're not on the run or something?' she ventured, her cheeks flushed with daring.

'On the run? Why? Do I look it?" he countered, shooting her a cursory glance. His surprise turned to a frown. 'You met me under the bridge. I wasn't exactly running.' He turned away more rattled than he dared admit. There was a fieriness to her that seemed to ignite some unexpected wick within him and send a wave of heat straight through him. He pulled his fingers through his hair disconcerted as much by her sudden mistrust as by the galvanising impact she had on him. As he turned back towards the shack a thought struck him.

'You know those aren't graves, don't you? They're just memorials in a man's tragic life.' Then, noting her confusion, he added, 'God, girl, I'd never ask you to meet me by a lot of godforsaken graves! Is that what you thought?' Not waiting for an answer, he walked away to feed the fire over which Ricci and Juanito were still gleefully melting marshmallows.

Santiago sat with his long legs stretched out infront of him, and his elbow resting on the mossy bank. His shirtsleeves were rolled up and there were traces of paint on his arms and across his hands. His jeans were tucked into a pair of scuffed leather riding boots the soles of which were thick with mud. He too skewered a marshmallow and watched the flames lick the white substance until the whole blackened crust slid off exposing a soft melted cream that was consumed by the flames.

'Hey! Don't waste them,' exclaimed Juanito. Ricci immediately threw a marshmallow at Juanito and soon they were chasing after each other. Milana came up and stood by the fire with a dignified air of self-possession. Santiago glanced up at her briefly and smiled to himself.

'Can I try one?' she asked gravely. Santiago skewered one, toasted it and handed it to her, before turning his attention back to the fire. She watched his face lit by the flames, his handsome features now distant and impassive, as though the moment he turned away from her, she was forgotten.

For the boys, the shack with its lurking ghosts and gruesome graves had lost its menace, now that Santiago had come.

Together, they warmed the *empanadas* he had brought by wrapping them in foil and laying them on the glowing embers of the fire. While Santiago played with the boys, Milana turned them once or twice.

'They're done,' she called finally and the boys, all three of them, breathless and hungry returned and sat by the fire. Santiago handed them out, removing the hot foil in one quick flick and wrapping them each in a llanten leaf. He offered one to Milana. She looked at him seeking to make up for her blatant distrust as she took it from him, but his eyes passed over her, his look inscrutable. Suddenly Ricci shouted, 'Juanito, watch out! Behind you! There's a ghost!' He screamed. Then he fell about laughing, but Juanito was freaked out. He had forgotten the significance of the graves and it was a shock to remember them. Santiago put his arm around him, 'Hey, Juanito, there are no ghosts here.'

'But the... the graves are just there.'

'Those aren't graves, Juanito.'

Ricci sat up attentively.

'So what are they?'

'You really don't know about this old man and why he lived here?'

'No.' They shook their heads.

'Tell us. Tell us who Whitebeard really was,' said Juanito.

'Yeah, tell us who he was, please,' urged Ricci.

'You promised, remember?' whispered Juanito. Santiago glanced at Milana who had wrapped herself in the discarded poncho.

'Come nearer the fire, it's getting colder,' he urged her suddenly, but in the darkness she couldn't see the twinkle in his eye. Gratefully she got up and sat between her brothers wrapping the poncho round them too.

'It's a pretty sad story,' he began, coming closer to the fire himself and placing his hands over its warmth.

'He wasn't always an old man with a white beard; once you wouldn't have told him apart from any other dad at the Chucky Cheese, eating pizza with his kids.' Juanito sat in wrapt attention.

'He was clever too. If you'd gone to see a doctor for an operation, you might have found yourself sitting in his waiting-room and a nurse would have come and ushered you into an office. He would have been the surgeon, sitting in the white coat with a stethoscope around his neck and asking you about how you felt, and you would have sat there telling him your problems, trusting he would solve them.'

'He was a doctor?' gawped Ricci.

Santiago nodded, 'Doctor Alfonso Carrerra, a brilliant young surgeon. All sorts of honours decorated his walls. And if you looked on his shelves you would have seen pictures of a pretty young woman with dark hair and brown eyes, laughing out of the frame at you. And on the wall behind him you'd have seen a big black and white photo of three boys running at the camera through the flowering desert and at the very front running wildly with all her little locks blowing in the wind, their little sister; barefoot…timeless beautiful children. And some people would wonder; is it just a lovely poster or are they really his kids? And so they'd ask and he'd tell them they were his four kids and that the smiling lady was his wife.

'His house was up in the hills, built in the middle of a walnut grove. If you went to pick up your kids from one of his children's parties you'd see him racing about the garden, chasing them or playing football with them, or climbing the walnut trees and making them all squeal with delight, and you'd stand around thinking, what a great dad. I wish my dad was like that. I wish he'd bother to come and play at my parties.'

'Did you think that, Santiago?' Juanito was gazing up at him with his wide inquiring eyes.

'I didn't go to his kid's parties,' he answered casually.

'Then one summer he bought a plot of land and had a beach house built in Zapallar.'

'Where is that?' asked Ricci.

'Just north of the port of Valparaiso, there's a tiny, beautiful bay with little fishing boats painted all colours and occasional dolphins and seals and even penguins nearby. Perched on the hills above the beach, between splashes of brightly coloured bourganvillea are some of the loveliest houses. It became Alfonso Carrera's getaway, his little paradise. After work on a Friday, he would drive his family to their fabulous new beach home. He never liked to miss a weekend. Their life was as perfect as any life could be. They had money and happiness and love, and then one day the whole thing fell apart.'

'Oh,' gasped Juanito, who sat with his knees up to his chin, totally transported. Santiago stared pensively into the darkness, the fire sparkling in his eyes.

'It was a Friday night. Alfonso had been operating. The operation went on much later than scheduled. He wasn't able to phone home, so his wife had packed the car and got everything ready to go to Zapallar. When he still didn't come home, she put the children to bed and stayed up waiting for him. Finally, very late, she saw the lights of his car turn into their steep drive. He came in apologetic and eager, "Have you got everything ready? Let's leave for the beach right away!"

' "It's too late to go now, Alfonso," she reasoned, "let's go tomorrow."

'But he insisted. "It's going to be a beautiful weekend. If we go now we can wake up to the sound of the waves and the smell of salt and pine trees." She tried to dissuade him, but he was so enthusiastic and so determined that they put the sleeping children in the car and set off.

'The roads were empty as he drove towards the river from up there.' Santiago pointed towards the hills of La Dehesa, where the lights of smart homes twinkled in the distance. 'At some traffic lights, they met friends on their way home from a dinner party. Alfonso wound down the car window and they chatted. The lights turned green and Alfonso shot off way in front of them, tooting his horn in farewell, as his tail lights disappeared round the slip road to join the Americo Vespucio fly-over that straddles the river just downstream from here. Meanwhile the other couple took the underpass along the riverbank. Seconds later they heard a horrific smash, like an explosion behind them, as a car flipped over the protective barriers of the flyover and shot through the air above them landing upside down in the middle of the river beside them.

'Alfonso's colleague screeched to a halt and for several seconds stared in disbelief at the scene. Then he opened the door and ran wildly towards the upturned car, screaming something. His wife watched, paralysed with shock. Then she realised what he was screaming above the persistent whine of the car's horn – "It's Alfonso's car! Get help." He waded into this river to save them, just a few hundred yards from where we are now.'

Milana stared downstream at the dark ribbon of river.

'What happened next?' urged Ricci.

'Ambulances, fire engines and police came, but it was no use. Two of the children had gone through a side window and were lying across rocks killed on impact. The eldest and the youngest were thrown, jumbled together, to the front of the car. When the car door was opened they fell out, their limbs relaxed. They had died instantly while they slept. The beautiful wife that smiled out of the photographs in the doctor's office, was thrown through the windscreen, her body half splayed across the bonnet, her neck broken. They were all dead. They thought Alfonso was too. His face was pressed down on the steering wheel. He was the only one they couldn't get to. They had to cut him out of the car. He was alive, but only just. For months he was in hospital, in intensive care. People came to see him daily but he was too ill to know them, too ill to be told the fate of his family. He never saw them lying dead in their coffins, he never said goodbye…he never even knew they'd died, till weeks later.'

Santiago paused to throw another piece of driftwood on the fire. The flames licked round it hungrily and reflected in the wide expectant eyes of his little audience.

'Please don't stop,' whispered Ricci.

'Eventually he was well enough to come out of hospital. Friends came and drove him home to his house in the walnut grove. He walked into the house and saw his children's drawings and his wife's notes on the fridge and the photographs everywhere and the toys on the kitchen floor…everything just as it was left on the fateful night, and he broke down and wept. Then he walked out and never went back to his beautiful home; he never went back to his office or to the beach house in Zapallar. He came here. He sat on the riverbank with his head in his hands and told people that he'd killed his beautiful family. He said that his wife had begged him not to go that night but he had gone ahead and killed them anyway. No one could coax him back home. For years they tried but he refused to leave here.

'"This is my home, here on the river where they died, where they left their souls forever," he would say. Friends came and they put up a tent for him. Then they put up this little shack for him. He never shaved again; he let his hair grow wild and he fashioned these six graves out of boulders from the river. Over the years he carved these crosses with a penknife. And when someone asked him why there were six he pointed to the last one; it's further away than the others, on its own, down there,' Santiago pointed into the darkness. 'And he said, "That one's mine. I don't deserve to be with them."'

'For years, almost every day without fail, his old colleagues and friends hung a bag with food, on that tree over there by the old road. That's how he survived. When no one was about, he would come and get it. Then one day he didn't come for his food, neither that day nor the next nor the one after and that's how they knew something was wrong. They came to look for him then and they found him dead on his bed in that shack. His heart had just stopped. They took him away and buried him in the family mausoleum in the *Cementerio General*. His tomb is like a palace compared to the shack where he spent more than twenty years of his life.'

'How do you know all this?' Milana asked in a whisper.

'He was my grandmother's doctor. My mother knew him too. She went to his funeral. I saw him in his coffin, through the glass lid. With his white beard he looked like Abraham might have looked.' Santiago looked away from them. 'There's peace on the faces of the dead, like they can rest at last.'

'Yes that's true,' said Milana.

'So there's no people really in them graves. I mean it was

just like pretend?' asked Juanito trying to make sense of the thing. 'Why would he do that?'

'To remember them, silly,' said Ricci.

'So he'd have his guilt to look at every day,' whispered Milana, 'so he'd never forget he killed them.'

'He could have tried to forget, no one would have minded,' suggested Juanito.

'Yeah, but he didn't want to, did he?' countered Ricci, 'Come on let's go see them.'

The two boys left the fire and stood solemnly side by side a little distance away staring down at the crosses on the grave, the sadness of the story countering all their fears.

'I'm sorry I doubted you,' Milana said tentatively breaking the stillness as they stared into the fire. 'I mean, I'm sorry that I thought...I thought...' she trailed off.

'It's strange,' mused Santiago, lost somewhere far away in his own thoughts, 'when you think that behind every face, there's a story of love and loss and hope and longing... and what do we know when we see faces? We can't read their lives there; we can't hope to judge their inner struggles.'

'Wow!' exclaimed the boys returning. 'And we thought that old man was the bogey man, when really he was so rich...' chortled Juanito immensely relieved by the story. 'What happened to his money?' Juanito brought Santiago back from his distant place.

'Well Juanito, he didn't care did he?'

'No,' and Juanito shook his head in wonder that anyone could choose to live in a shack when they had a house in a walnut grove and one by the sea.

'Do you think we should pray for him,' said Ricci suddenly. 'I mean seeing as we're here.'

'What, so his ghost will be nice to you?' teased his sister trying to forget her own confused feelings.

'But what should we pray?' asked Juanito enthused by the idea of making contact with this extraordinary and wealthy gentleman.

'We could pray that he's forgiven himself at last,' said Milana entering into the spirit.

'And that he's with them all in heaven,' said Ricci.

'And with Mum,' put in Juanito.

'Ask him to watch over the three of you now,' suggested Santiago.

'You sure about that?' Juanito looked dubious, 'I mean he won't turn up or anything then will he?'

Santiago suppressed a smile.

'It's a bit spooky,' said Ricci.

'Souls watch over us and protect us when they die. Didn't you know that Juanito?' said Santiago.

'I didn't know they could look after us like that. I mean even old Whitebeard,' Juanito turned his eyes heavenwards with a happy grin.

Milana watched Santiago rise and gather his things together.

'You're always going off. Where are you going now?' Juanito pressed him.

'Home. Like you young man.' He looked back at Milana and then, almost as an after-thought, he threw her a sudden smile.

'Are your paintings in there then?' She nodded towards the shack unable to contain her curiosity.

'No.'

'Can we see inside?'

'Are you kidding,' Juanito look horrified.

'Don't worry,' laughed Santiago, 'it's locked. Someone came and put a padlock on it when he died and no one's been in there since.'

'Oh.' Milana sighed and folding the poncho she handed it up to him.

'Come on,' he said gallantly, 'I'll walk you back. Ricci! Juanito!' He shouted over to them. 'It's time you guys went home. You can't stay in graveyards forever.'

Santiago went to put out the fire, but his eyes strayed back to Milana. He watched her stand up and brush down her old jeans, cropped just above her slim ankles. She tossed back her hair and wrapped her bare arms momentarily about herself as the cold penetrated. Wordlessly he stepped behind her and placed the poncho back around her. She drew it to her again.

Suddenly he laid his warm hand over hers. 'You're still freezing,' he whispered before letting go.

They started walking back along the riverbank, the four of them picking their way over the stones.

'Do you live in a big house, Santiago, like Whitebeard did?' asked Juanito bounding beside him. Santiago didn't answer.

'Are you rich?' Juanito shot out the next question.

'Oh don't be silly, Juanito,' said Ricci crossly. 'Look at his clothes and his long hair. He's not like all them guys as come and meet on the bridge in them fancy cars and smoke and get... you know.'

Santiago looked away to cover his amusement.

'What guys are you on about Ricci?' Milana looked concerned.

'You know. Them rich kids that come and buy stuff off Pablo and Jose.'

'You hang out there with those guys, Ricci?' Milana's voice rose involuntarily.

'On Friday nights they come and get the skunk so we go and check out their cars,' piped up Juanito. 'Cool cars!'

'Skunk?'

'Yeah, skunk and other stuff,' said Juanito, like his sister was dim. 'You know.'

'Shut up, Juanito,' said Ricci sharply. Milana shot Santiago a quick look. The moon had risen now and it reflected off the water. Santiago's expression gave nothing away.

'Anyway, Santiago might be rich too, so there,' countered Juanito. 'Whitebeard was rich, and *he* lived in a shack,' he added triumphantly.

Santiago stopped abruptly. 'Juanito why does it matter to you what's in my wallet, if, infact, I have one at all? What difference does it make to you?'

Juanito looked defiant suddenly. 'Well if you're rich, you're not one of us.'

'I'm walking with you. We've had a picnic together. What makes me not one of you, Juanito?' he persisted with a half teasing smile.

'You won't tell us things, that's what,' Milana said suddenly, her tone quiet but bold. 'You won't tell us where you live or why you come here…and you won't let me see your paintings.'

'Is that what this is all about?' the gentleness in his voice seemed to dissolve all kinds of unseen barriers within her. 'I'll show you my paintings if you want, but not now; I don't carry them around and they're certainly not in Whitebeard's shack, but you can see them, if you really want.'

'Yes,' said Milana. A new kind of assurance possessing her. 'I do want.'

Juanito looked from one to the other. 'What paintings?'

'Come on, Juanito,' Ricci called him. 'It's girl's stuff.' He shrugged, 'It don't matter to us, Santiago, what you are. We had a really good time. Thank you,' he added graciously.

'Yeah those marsh thingies…' agreed Juanito.

'Marshmallows,' corrected Ricci.

'Yeah them. Weren't they brill?'

Santiago and Milana walked on in silence side by side until they came to the edge of the shantytown. Moonlight played through the iron railings of the old bridge. Milana's forthright manner had made unexpected inroads. She felt a new rapport growing between them. They had stopped walking and she slipped off the poncho to return it to him.

'Keep it. Wear it. It's a present. Look,' he added avoiding the awkwardness of being thanked, 'if you really want to see these wretched paintings, wait for me under the bridge, tomorrow, after 5pm. Right there,' he pointed to the place where Milana had first seen him. 'I'll come for you.' She felt his eyes on her, but in the shadows Milana could not make out his expression. A meagre light shone out from the shanties on the far bank and, in the distance the yellow and orange neon lights of the Chucky Cheese obliterated the stars. Ricci and Juanito were already half way across the river. Milana reached up and kissed him on the cheek. She turned then and ran, pulling off her shoes before wading through the river, not caring about the cold water that rushed knee high over her torn jeans.

Chapter Fourteen

Santiago was already there the following day, leaning against the bridge on the far side of the bank, when Milana arrived flushed and out of breath.

'I couldn't get away from my aunts… I thought you'd give up waiting.' She looked up at him gratefully.

Santiago placed himself squarely in front of her, his broad smile absorbing all her misgivings.

'So you have many aunts? And you gave them the slip?' he enquired, tilting his head very slightly to one side as he adjusted the woollen hat pulled over her tousled hair, so that he could see more of her face. The unexpected closeness accelerated her already racing heart.

'They're just neighbours, not real relatives, you know.' He was aware of the rise and fall of her chest under her flimsy cotton top as she struggled to regain her breath.

'Everyone calls people aunts and uncles in the shantytown. We're just one big happy family.' She gave a little sarcastic grimace. 'I told them I was off to buy bread.'

'So when you don't come back, what then?' His eyes danced over her.

Milana shrugged. 'They'll gossip for hours. Then they'll start wondering when they last saw me and forget again.' She flashed him a smile. 'Who cares anyway?' Her green eyes sparkled with excitement. 'Let's go.'

Milana wrapped her cardigan more tightly around her as they walked briskly along the riverbank. The clouds hung low and threatening.

'What about Ricci and Juanito?'

'What about them?' asked Milana.

'Are they OK? Didn't they want to come?'

'Yes. No. I dunno. I didn't tell them. You never asked them,' she added, a touch defensively.

'No, I didn't did I? Ricci didn't seem very taken with the thought of seeing paintings,' he grinned catching her eye.

'Yeah, well they don't care about paintings,' she laughed.

'And you do?' he ventured.

'Yes. They speak to me, like writing. You know, feelings, thoughts, emotions, all there in lines and colours.' Santiago gave her a searching, slightly droll look. She caught it.

'I mean it,' she insisted. 'It's like they're alive, all those lines; soft, hard, sad, beautiful, twisted, making their magic.' She moved her hands expressively as she half skipped to keep up with his long strides. 'A kind of witchcraft really, casting its spell on the unsuspecting.'

'Whoa!' Santiago, looked taken aback. 'Spoken like a real artist.'

She half turned then and went on walking backwards for a moment her face flushed with enthusiasm. 'I've seen all kinds of pictures in books,' she went on earnestly. 'There was this book of paintings of the stations of the cross by a man called Pedro Suberca-something. I wanted to look at them all the time. I couldn't figure, was it the painting that was beautiful, or that he'd given life to Jesus in those lines and made it kind of holy.' Milana bit her lip noticing how Santiago was looking at her; an intent look that seemed to be directly linked to her heart.

'Subercaseaux, Pedro Subercaseaux. I know those paintings. You're very eloquent today,' Santiago quipped to cover the momentary awkwardness.

'I don't know what that means,' she replied, moving on ahead of him.

'Expressive, you're very expressive.'

'Don't you like that?'

'I love it.'

She moved so easily over the rocky ground as though the fluency of her speech was perfectly reflected in her movements;

she played and walked and talked around him as lightly as the spring breeze.

'You ever read that bloke Oscar Wilde. He's my favourite. That story about Dorian Gray. You know it?' she enquired eagerly.

'You bet I do. I loved that novel.' Santiago shook his head in disbelief at her. 'You're full of surprises,' he half whispered to the wind.

'Yeah, the painting gets the soul and the guy gets the looks. I wish I could see what that painting looked like.'

'Why don't you draw what you think it looked like. Have you tried painting?'

'Yeah, with old bits of charcoal. I went round drawing people's smiles, you know, little prim ones, fake ones, cruel ones, all sorts. The hardest of all to draw were the kind ones.'

'Why?' Santiago found himself quite gripped by the images she conjured.

'Cos they take in the eyes and I was just doing the mouths.'

She continued to walk in silence, the rush of excited chatter was replaced suddenly by a cool, almost haughty air, as though she were self-regulating and decided she'd overdone the enthusiasm. Even her stance as she picked her way over rocks became undeniably dignified. He found himself suppressing a smile, this girl was the most unusual mix of insatiable eagerness one minute and worldly insouciance the next.

'I wish I could paint,' she said moments later with a sigh, 'but they don't sell those sorts of paints in the Lider Supermarket. They sell kid's paints and...'

'Make your own paints, Milana. Like I do.'

'What?' She swept round.

'It's easy, I'll teach you.'

'You'll teach me? Really? Just like that?'

'Yes, like they did in the old days; egg tempera. If it was good enough for the Great Masters, it's good enough for Milana.'

'Do you mean it? Really mean it?'

'Yes,' he laughed and took her by the hand as if grabbed by sudden inspiration. 'You're going to start painting right now, girl!' He broke into a run along the riverbank, her hand firm in his, so that she had to relinquish her sudden decorum and run even faster to keep up with him. Her heart seemed to be levitating and she couldn't quite tell if it was the running or the idea of painting or simply his hand holding hers that made it lift so.

Santiago led her swiftly up through the old graveyard, past where her mother was buried, and the tiny chapel where they'd found Ricci and Juanito, through an old wrought-iron gate and across a wide open courtyard of orange trees until they stood before a pair of impressive oak doors.

'But this is the church!' she gasped.

'You want to see my paintings don't you?' Stooping to search behind a huge terracotta urn that stood nearby, he pulled out an old key.

'And you want to paint don't you?'

'Yes but,' she laughed nervously. 'I can't really paint in there.'

'We'll see about that,' he retorted as he placed the key in the ancient lock. Milana took a few steps back to get a better look at the building. It seemed very imposing and very old, but recently restored and painted white. Beneath the single bell tower she could see doves roosting. There was a round window above the door and she could just make out that it was painted many colours. It dawned on her then, just as the heavy door swung open onto the cavernous interior, what he might mean.

Santiago let the door shut heavily behind them. She found herself engulfed in what seemed like total darkness while her eyes adjusted to the gloom.

'Is it OK?' she whispered.

'Is what OK?' he replied in a teasing voice.

'Why are you shutting us in?'

'So no one will find us here.'

'Why? Why mustn't they find us?' breathed Milana, anticipation coursing through her. It was so cold that she clasped her hands together and blew into them to warm them. Santiago came right up to her so she could feel his coat against her. His hands came over hers.

'The sun barely penetrates through the thick walls, but you get used to it,' he whispered and she felt his fingers rest on hers so softly that there was no pressure, only the awareness of his warm touch on her skin.

'You can't paint with such cold hands.'

'Why mustn't they find us?' she whispered back. 'Aren't we allowed?' He leant forwards so that his forehead nearly touched hers.

'Because it's none of their business.' A shiver went through her body like electricity and concentrated somewhere in the pit of her stomach. Her eyes locked on his. In the shadows it was hard to see what thoughts might be hidden there.

A muted light percolated through the stain glass windows, shrouding the interior in a mist of faded colour; spectral and sublime. Their closeness seemed to stretch into timelessness as each split second fused into the next and still he didn't move. His hand slipped away from hers and searched for something in his coat. Suddenly a brilliant light filled the space between them; so bright that for a moment it dazzled. But still he didn't move away. His smile reflected the warmth of his eyes and seemed to absorb her completely. He was holding something that looked like a black pen, but in place of a nib it had a powerful halogen bulb that threw a pool of light up at the ceiling. Milana followed the light until it came to rest on a magnificent painting behind the altar. The mural depicted the Virgin Mary, her arms outstretched, like the Madonna of the little grotto outside the chapel they had laid her mother in. She wore a veil of cobalt blue so that just her hands emerged from beneath. Golden rays from her hands streamed across the blue of her gown and merged with the background from which she seemed to radiate like a vision. Milana stared at it in awe. 'You didn't paint her, did you?' Santiago laughed warmly.

'Me, paint that? Why of course not.'

Milana's eyes remained riveted on the painting. 'She's almost real, like she's going to walk out and touch me.' Santiago kept the torch shining on the beautiful lady, and followed Milana as she walked, mesmerised, towards the painting, until they were standing just feet away from it.

'Her face is so gentle, so full of love.' Milana reached out, touching it reverently. 'It's painted on the wall!' she gasped, 'But that's such a pity. You can never pick it up and take it away.'

'She belongs here. She's not meant to be taken away,' he whispered amused.

'I know, but what if the wall falls down in an earthquake or something?'

'Then I'll paint her again.'

'You *did* paint her?' she swung round in disbelief. Now it was him she studied in the glow of the torchlight, the smoothness of his face, the creases around his smile, the way one eyebrow arched whimsically as his eyes held hers, their ardour galvanising her heart.

'How did you learn?'

'I just painted. I've always painted. I started by painting on old logs in summer camp and the head of the summer camp entered them in a competition without me knowing and I won first prize. It all sort of went from there; I was asked to paint more stuff and here I am,' he shrugged. 'Look, do you like these?' As the torchlight fell on the walls on either side of the nave, Milana saw, one by one, the fourteen stations of the cross, each one depicting a different moment in the twenty-four hours of the Passion of Christ. Some were finished, some were only part drawn and part painted, but from each one Milana experienced a sense of being drawn right into the extraordinary depth of the experience.

'You did them too? Wow! I mean, Wow!'

'Now you sound like Juanito,' teased Santiago, his voice very close.

'I've never seen stations of the cross painted like this, I mean for real. We only have carvings out of wood in the shantytown chapel. They're just still forms…but this, they're more beautiful than the ones in that book I saw.'

Santiago was behind her. She glanced over her shoulder at him but his eyes were on the paintings. She turned back towards them, transfixed as much by their beauty as by his proximity.

'Someone must have taught you to paint like this,' she murmured.

'I don't know, I just rough it.'

'But someone must have, or does it all just spill out from inside you.'

He laughed again. 'I guess one needs a little inspiration.'

He could feel her waiting for him to speak, to tell her more, to fill the silence and suddenly it seemed churlish not to answer.

'Once, years ago, I was sitting alone in a church. I was very sad just wishing the ground would swallow me up when this woman came up to me.'

'Go on,' she urged, sensing his hesitation and drawing herself imperceptibly closer so she could feel his intake of breath.

'She had a lovely face and she looked at me with such sympathy I felt she understood everything I was feeling. She was wearing a white habit and her veil hid all her hair except for a curl that had escaped above her ear.' Milana felt Santiago's hand gently touch her hair. It sent a shiver of delight through her. He noticed but she could not see the smile that crept over his face, only that he too drew closer, 'I so wanted to pull the veil off to see her hair,' he whispered playfully.

'How old were you?'

'Seven, maybe eight.'

Milana felt her woollen hat gently slipped off her head so that her hair cascaded down over her shoulders. She knew his lips were close because she could feel the warmth of his breath as he continued, 'She knelt beside me and held her hand out to me.' Santiago's hand found Milana's where it rested at her side and lacing his fingers gently through hers, he held her hand tracing his thumb over her skin causing such commotion to her blood flow that she felt light-headed.

'She took me round the stations of the cross, I'd never really looked at them before, and in front of each one she told me what was happening. When she'd explained them all to me, she sat me down beside her and said; " He's so alone. Walk His Passion with Him." I asked her what that meant.'

Santiago stilled his hand.

"To walk Christ's Passion is to dare to love with all your heart. That's how He loves you. You know He loves you, don't you?" she asked me, but I shook my head. I wanted to say yes, to please her but I really wasn't at all sure that He did love me. She was totally unfazed by my reply, she just said, "When you think no one in the world loves you and they've all let you down, that's when He's loving you most. But you have to be very still to feel it." So I tried to be very very quiet.' Milana felt the warmth of her hand in Santiago's, the exquisite sensation of his skin against hers and the excruciating sweetness of desire flooding through her.

'I remember the silence in that church. It felt like a presence you had to stop and listen to. She made me feel my sadness was part of something bigger and more significant that I couldn't quite see.'

Santiago took a deep breath and it seemed a sort of shudder went through him. Milana found herself swaying gently back against him. Her whole being aching to be enveloped by him so her loneliness would be gone forever. In the same moment he drew his hand away, albeit slowly, reluctant to let go altogether. She felt him separating from her. His tone became lighter, more matter of fact; 'Since then I've always wanted to paint the stations of the cross, and Our Lady there,' Santiago pointed with the torch to the painting behind the altar, 'has the face of the nun who spoke to me in that church.

'Milana,' he cried urgently, his arms around her instantly, holding her up. 'I thought you were going to faint, are you OK? You're so cold.'

'I'm just hungry,' she murmured. His face was full of concern but she closed her eyes unsure of how to face the feelings that overwhelmed her.

Chapter Fifteen

Atilio was short, dark and past sixty. He had only three fingers on his left hand and was missing several teeth, but this in no way diminished his zest for life. He spat on his palms and rubbed them together with gusto before taking up paintbrush or spade or any other tool of trade. He tended the graves, cleaned the pews and had helped the decorator, Andres, paint the outside of the church. Together he and Andres had helped the young Santiago to prepare the interior church walls for painting. He had helped the carpenter put up the great crucifix over the altar and he watered the orange trees in the front of the church. He hosed down the courtyard every evening before taking his lunch box under his arm and walking home to the small bungalow he shared with his wife and her elderly mother.

At first Atilio was suspicious of the girl that came from the shantytown to meet the *caballero* who was painting the church. Atilio had been at the church the first day Santiago had come there. He had seen the boy step out of the large Mercedes with the Monsignor and the Mayor. He had observed how the Monsignor, dressed in his full length black cassock with the fine purple sash around his waist, put his arm about the young boy's shoulders as they walked around the church and how the Mayor constantly smiled and nodded his approval. Atilio had been there when journalists came to take pictures of the boy in front of the church, along with several suited men and one tall smartly dressed lady who, he guessed, was his mother. Atilio's wife, Guillermina, got the newspaper from the lady she cleaned for, and Atilio had seen the pictures in it; there was even a picture of his lunch box, just visible in the corner behind all the people.

So Atilio never called Santiago *joven* like he called some of the other lads that age; he called him *caballero* as a mark of his esteem. He was not taken in by the shoulder-length hair the boy sported or the scruffy clothes. He could tell at once that this boy had breeding. Years of working as a butler, before he lost his fingers in an accident with a faulty liquidizer, had trained his eye to these things. Yes, this was a real *caballero* with a recognised talent.

Atilio had observed, admiringly, as the boy traced out the lines of his huge painting behind the altar. He had watched him mix colours and he had helped him collect plants and resins for his paints. His respect grew as he perceived how much the boy knew and how lightly he carried his knowledge. When the girl turned up she was, as far as Atilio was concerned, a usurper of his place and an unwanted distraction to their work; besides, she was too lowly to be a worthy companion to this *caballero*. On that first afternoon that he had found her standing in the courtyard, reverently touching the oranges on Atilio's carefully nurtured trees, he had sent her packing. She had not dared come the second day and only on the third day did she come and hide behind the church. Santiago had gone to meet her as soon as he'd seen her, as though he had been expecting her. At one point as she spoke to him, he had swept the hair out of her eyes and shaken his head. Atilio had seen it all from where he was scrubbing the large clay urn that had been splashed with paint. Santiago had caught him looking and smiled at him, raising his eyebrows and, in a confiding sort of way, giving him a secret thumbs up that the girl couldn't see. Thus, cleverly, Santiago had made Atilio a fellow conspirator in his new interest.

The girl, Atilio soon realised, had not come to distract, far from it. She was kind and funny and forgave Atilio his initial brusqueness. She welcomed his help as she learnt to mix paints under the watchful tutelage of Santiago, who sometimes even let her paint parts of the cobalt sky or fill in bits of the stations of the cross. She watched and worked meticulously and Atilio could not help but notice how carefully and lovingly she traced her paintbrush over Santiago's drawings. Once in a while, when they did not know that Atilio was there, he had seen how

Santiago taught her, his hand over hers, guiding each stroke of the paintbrush, as he stood leaning behind her, his lips almost touching her auburn hair.

She came every day even when, on occasions, Santiago wasn't there. Atilio would find her in the shed behind the church sitting on the workbench, studying the glorious gold crystallised rocks from which Santiago would obtain orpiment, or king's yellow. Or she would be grinding lapis or turquoise or even cinnabar to make vermilion; that rich crimson colour that Santiago used in his skies and to depict the blood of Christ. Atilio would remind her that the dust from cinnabar was poisonous and suggest she wore her mask so as not to inhale it, but Milana would shake her head and say, 'I hate masks, Atilio.'

Atilio had never seen anyone make paint. He had not known or thought about paint except as something bought in a metal tin. He was mesmerised by the rocks and crystals that Santiago brought to the shed in tupperware tubs. Enthralled, he watched Santiago grind them and mix the powders with alcohol, or knead them with wax and water and press them through fine cloth. Finally a rainbow of colours, vibrant and splendid, were collected in rows of little tubs, and from these, Santiago would mix his paints, creating egg tempera. This egg business had made Atilio laugh and he joked with Milana that the 'Maestro' made 'paint tortillas'. Milana followed attentively as Santiago separated the yolk from the white of the egg, expertly transferring the yolk from the palm of one hand to the other, never dropping or breaking it and then piercing the yolk sac and allowing it to drain into a container. Milana practised and practised and soon she could mix and knead and dilute and separate egg yolks and create paint almost as well as Santiago.

'I told them I would paint this church in the style of the Old Masters,' Santiago explained, 'and that I would create paints from natural sources and do the whole thing as Giotto might have painted his frescos.' And Milana and Atilio would smile enthusiastically despite their ignorance of Giotto.

Atilio and Milana shared a mutual admiration for Santiago. But while Atilio knew the boy's place in the hierarchy of wealth and position, Milana knew nothing of Santiago's background and Atilio never thought to enlighten her. She remained spellbound by his enormous talent and his generosity in sharing it with her. Both stood in awe of how Santiago treated them as friends, imparting his knowledge enthusiastically and on a level. He managed to make even the most complicated ideas sound simple and they delighted in listening to him. The long afternoons they shared felt as vibrant as the colours they made together. They were beautiful, creative days, full of warmth and laughter and Milana thanked God for them. Neither Milana nor Atilio knew who these 'Great Masters' were or what 'frescos' were, but little by little they learnt much more than that. Simply making the paint and sourcing the minerals, earth or clay from the river, was more thrilling than anything Milana had ever done before. The concept that paint could be made from rocks, earth or bones, leaves or flowers was something so magical to Milana, that daily she would stop on entering the church and gaze on the great wooden crucifix thinking *the world is a treasure trove in which I can find all I need to make me rich.* Hope coursed through her veins and filled her with courage and a thirst for learning greater than any she had experienced before.

Santiago rarely spoke while he painted. Even when he watched Milana paint, it would be in a deep contemplative silence that you could almost hear. She asked him once, 'What are you thinking in the silence?'

He had laughed good-naturedly, 'Wondering at it all.'

'Wondering? Is that like praying?'

'Maybe. When you open your soul and let it be filled.'

'Filled by what?'

But he didn't answer.

Later, Santiago would make up for his silences as they mixed or ground the pigments. He would tell them about art; how Giotto was a funny ugly man who revolutionized painting with his creative personality, 'He must have been notably ugly for it to have been recorded, and yet he created so much beauty.'

Santiago always seemed to have a half smile on his face, as if he never really took himself seriously. Yet he spoke with such vigour and strength that Milana was captivated. To her these were lessons like none she had ever known and she drank in all he said. She came to understand how closely art and religion were intertwined then, and how one was conceived from the other. He told them about the Gothic cathedrals soaring higher and higher to try and reach up to the heavens and she heard about the genius of the Renaissance revolution; Leonardo da Vinci, who while thinking up flying machines and submarines and how the blood circulates, painted the Mona Lisa and her famous, and in Santiago's opinion smug, smile. 'Because really it was Da Vinci's smile on her face,' he quipped.

One day, in late spring, Santiago stopped painting for the day earlier than usual and pulled Milana outside.

'Look, it's beginning to bloom,' he exclaimed pointing to the jacaranda tree. 'Have you ever seen anything more spellbinding than a jacaranda tree in full blossom? Come and lie under it.'

He lay on the cool earth with his hands behind his head, staring at the sky through the shimmering buds and first opening flowers. Milana moved a few paces further to where the sun pooled on her face between the branches. As the heat of early summer burned her skin she felt his eyes on her.

'Come and lie beside me,' he said quietly.

She came and placed herself a little awkwardly next to him staring up at the sky, feeling the tension that fizzed like an electrical charge every time they touched. He turned towards her then, propping himself up on his elbow, his candid deep blue eyes riveted on her.

'We've lost touch with our soul, Milana, that's why there are no Michelangelo's anymore. We've lost our inner strength, our core, to a world of cynicism that's eaten away at all man's finest disciplines.' He sighed, and reaching out he touched her hair as it spread its silky softness around her. He curled the soft ends around his fingers and his hand and watched them slip themselves off back to the ground.

'I don't want my life packaged and tied up with ribbons of

convention and presented to me. I want to carve it out of the rock of who I am,' he mused as though he were answering some private conversation with himself.

Milana smiled to herself, 'You're more like a river, or a rainbow or an ocean than a rock,' she murmured. Santiago flashed her a piercing look and picked up another elusive lock of her hair.

'I don't think anyone could ever package you,' Milana added turning towards him, and despite her mischievous smile, her eyes held his steadily. He felt a corresponding warmth well up and a sweet ache inside him that made him shiver. She reached up and touched the dark wave of hair that fell over his forehead.

'How can you paint with all that hair in your eyes.' She flicked the hair back and laughed to watch it flop back against his brow. The desire to kiss her laughing mouth was so compelling that he closed his eyes. But she didn't stop, her hand brushed his hair back again and the tips of her fingers lingered on his skin, he felt them trace his eyebrow and rest on the furrow of his brow. He leant into her, feeling the length of her body warm against him. *I want to know everything about you,* he mused.

'You look a little cross,' she said still tracing her finger over his brow.

His lips creased into an inevitable smile, how could he tell her it took all his concentration to resist her. He opened his eyes, she was looking directly at him, her gaze unwavering in its new and deliberate intent. His physical reaction was immediate and inevitable and to recover himself he got up and walked away, calling her moments later, to where Atilio was cleaning and drying paintbrushes in the sun.

'Why did you stop?' she said.

'Stop what?'

'Talking.'

'Oh.' He paused and suddenly laughed, 'I haven't stopped I could go on all day.' But he didn't. He stayed quiet.

'What are you thinking?' she asked softly after a long while.

'The Scream,' he grinned in order to distract her from the

subtext of his feelings, 'I'll show it to you one day: Edvard Munch's brilliant comment on us all, on the whole of the twentieth century.'

'Go on,' she ventured. 'What about the twenty-first century?'

'That can't be summed up yet. It's only just begun. But it'll be an answer to that "scream", that's my bet,' he added with a twinkle of humour. 'It'll be our great awakening.'

'You think we're asleep?' Atilio glanced up and thought he'd never seen two young people more awake to each other.

'Yes, I do. I think we're asleep in our souls. We need to scream. We should scream. *By God I feel like screaming.* Don't you ever want to scream?' And his voice, its energy and its strength, resonated inside her.

'I suppose I do, yes,' and she laughed. They all laughed, even Atilio, laughed and then, watching them together, his smile faded and he remembered what his wife had said, 'No good will come of it, you mark my words.'

Atilio had often watched how Santiago looked at Milana while she painted. Once, Santiago caught Atilio's eye at just such a moment and he gave him one of his broad smiles. 'Atilio, she has such talent,' he had confided later, 'God must have brought her here to paint for Him.' Atilio had nodded but it was not her talent that Santiago had been watching so closely, Atilio could not be fooled... and why not, he thought, Milana was beautiful.

'The loveliest lassie you ever saw,' said Atilio to his wife. 'Like she was an angel sent from heaven to help the *caballero*... and she don't talk, not much. She just watches and learns and paints, quiet as a mouse, and turns over them crystals for them pigments in her hand like they was magic. And she listens to him like he was a young god. She comes every day, rain or shine, always there after school, and sometimes they work late. I know cos Claudio at the kiosk tells me.'

One day in mid November Santiago presented Milana with a new canvas and a box of paints all of her own. Milana asked Atilio to sit for her so she could draw him. Day after day, Atilio would prop himself against a gravestone, with his lunch box at his feet, while she laid her paints on the coloured gravel of some stranger's tomb, and set to work. As she painted she would confide in him how happy she was. That was why it was such a surprise to Atilio when, one day in the heat of December, she did not come. And when the day after that, she did not come. And when a week went by and still she did not come.

At first it seemed to Atilio that Santiago didn't think it mattered, so absorbed did he seem to be in finishing off the chapel. But then, one evening, Atilio spotted him sitting by the water's edge, his head in his hands, his fingers pulling through his thick black hair again and again as if he were wrestling thoughts out of his head. When at last he looked up, he had remained, staring downstream lost in thought. Atilio approached him then and sat near him; the boy looked younger and more vulnerable than he had ever noticed before.

'In't she coming back, *Don* Santiago?' he ventured, intrigued to discover what might have happened to drive the girl away so suddenly. For a long while Santiago didn't answer, he couldn't trust himself to speak. The tremendous sense of loss that overwhelmed him could only be contained in silence. Atilio stayed beside him, a kind of unspoken loyalty to the boy in his hour of need keeping him there.

'Our angel has flown,' he murmured at last.

'Some things aren't meant to be, *Don* Santiago,' Atilio soothed sagely.

Santiago closed his eyes, how could Atilio, or anyone understand how this girl, who found beauty in the simplest things and gazed with the disarming wonder of a child upon the world, had stirred his soul. She had reached inside him and awoken some intense longing that for years had searched for an answer, and he, in turn, had reached out to her hoping that she would restore the inspiration to love that he had lost so long ago. He lowered his head, his conscience racked with guilt, wishing he could have said something to reassure her. She was a mere child after all, no wonder she had run from him when he had reached out for her before she fully trusted.

'Atilio, I'm nearly done here. It will be Christmas next week,' he added stirring himself out of his introspection. Atilio went home then, broken hearted by the sadness he perceived in the boy wondering what could have occured.

Chapter Sixteen

It was December the fifteenth when it happened and their world unravelled; a shimmering hot afternoon with hardly a breeze to disturb the heat haze. Above the riverbank the jacaranda tree spread its blue canopy beneath the lapis sky. In the past few days Santiago and Milana had barely stepped outside the cool interior of the church to lie in its shade, so absorbed were they with finishing the final mural.

Milana stood up a ladder in the side chapel, poised precariously so as to avoid the shadow of a powerful spotlight that, directed as it was onto the wall, illuminated her every stroke. It also added its own occasional gigantic and nightmarish projections if she got in its way. Her hair was pulled up and off her face in a tangle of waves held in place by a single paintbrush inserted through the middle. Her palette was vibrant with colour; vermilion, king's yellow, ochre and lapis blue. The colours streaked her hands and fingers and even her neck, where she had applied the pressure of her fingers to alleviate the strain. At first her brush had dared only tentatively to add the beginnings of a sunrise to Santiago's splendid mural of the fishermen with their nets overflowing. But over days, under his guidance and encouragement her strokes had grown bolder. Santiago stepped back from the figure he was putting the finishing touches to.

'Give it more colour there,' he called up to her, 'just go for it! Feel the rays wanting to burst through, like when fire eats the edges of paper.'

When finally Milana climbed down from the ladder, Atilio had gone home and they were quite alone. She could tell from the way the colour had drained from the stain glass window that it was later than usual. Ricci and Juanito would be growing restless at Nilda's, but in the rarefied atmosphere of the church all those petty squabbles lost their urgency.

'It's perfect,' said Santiago coming up to her and turning her to face the mural. 'It's magnificent! See what you can achieve, Milana, when you finally break through your inhibitions and believe in yourself. You can't restrain natural talent, see.'

'You really think I can paint?'

'I don't have to answer that, look at it, it speaks for itself.'

Santiago let his hands rest on her shoulders and leaned into her, 'When I paint,' he whispered, 'it frees me, really frees me. Don't you feel that too?' She turned to look at him and he saw it again reflected in her eyes, something vital, essential in her that seemed to exist just for him. A smile creased his features chasing away the urgency that she perceived fleetingly in his eyes.

'Hey,' he brushed her face with his hand but the depth of her intuition drew him closer.

'It's almost finished, isn't it?' she sighed. 'I don't mean the mural, I mean the whole thing. Atilio said they were opening the church up in time for Christmas.'

'I know.' He felt something trapped in his chest pounding to be released.

'We'll just live on here in the dark in our paintings on the wall.' She gave a little laugh and shrugged, 'You know, like flat faces and figures from the old times, remember? Nothing revolutionary like taking up real space, right?'

'Wow! You really were listening to all my bullshit.'

'Now you sound like Juanito.' She gave him a weak smile. 'Well, it's not like we'd make 3D, right?' she said turning away to hide her face but he pulled her back wordlessly.

Had she really implied what he thought?

They stood facing each other sensing the significance of the moment. He felt her gaze pulling him into her and he lost the will to fight it. He put his arms around her and suddenly he was reaching out to her through the pain and sadness of years. *Rescue me* was the cry from within that made him tremble suddenly so he could barely breathe. The silence grew more intense as the recognition of their mutual desire absorbed them. He touched her face, moving his fingers over the softness of her skin as though he were learning it by heart. He traced the lines of her eyes, her nose, her mouth, coaxing her every nerve ending to tingle and commit his touch to memory. His eyes held hers all the while, taking courage from the depth of what he saw there. Every fibre in each of them seemed somehow connected. As anticipation pulled each nerve taut, the closer they inevitably drew. Suddenly she felt the strength of his arms gathering her to him as his lips met hers. Feeling hers gently yield he kissed her deeply as he had wanted to for so many weeks, while an exquisite agony seemed to tear through him, liberating him.

Above them the spotlight fused, like a shot exploding. Milana pulled away with a sharp intake of breath, Santiago let go, stunned by the sudden noise.

Bats swooped blindly in the dusk, dipping and diving through the graveyard in her wake. Milana raced along the riverbank, tripping and stumbling over rocks and driftwood, disturbing lizards that slumbered in the dying light. She waded barefoot across the swirling mountain waters of the river and crawled up the slippery bank, ignoring the rats that scurried away under the faint glow of shanty lights. She didn't stop running all the way to Nilda's shanty, but when she got there it was empty. She ran still faster to Oleander Alley. Adrenalin coursed through her blood and mixed with the euphoria; she wanted to live forever in that moment before and never let herself be pulled back to the present. She ran, past the kiosk, past Iris who was talking to Doris and stopped to stare; past the boys slouching and smoking against the wall of the alley shouting lewd remarks at her; she ran until she reached the wooden door of her shanty.

Through the half open door Milana saw the women inside: Ana was nearest the window, her hair now streaked with grey since Oscar's death. Nilda sat beside her, her shoulders slumped, her face crumpled into submission. The boys, Ricci and Juanito were cross-legged on the floor at her feet. Standing in the middle of the room with her arms akimbo stood Nilda's fifty-year-old daughter, tough old Nora the supermarket sales person and sometimes taxi driver who wasn't afraid to work nights too. Now she folded her arms over her ample bosom like a self-important budda. She was holding forth while the others listened. For all the sufferings *Señora* Lisa had spoken of that had befallen her, Nora looked hard as steel, unbendable in her decisions and unable to grieve. Maybe her tears had been frozen way back and maybe that's why she avoided death which wasn't easy when death hung all around; births and deaths, common as the commas and fullstops in every sentence. Truth was, some people just couldn't help being nasty and Nora was relentless in her nastiness. Her bellicose rantings reached Milana where she waited bent over the dusty ground, recovering her breath.

'You don't do them kids any favours Mum,' she barked as Nilda sank further into her chair as though she were hoping to merge into its unfeeling frame. 'They got to face what's due them and toughen up.' Nora turned and spotted Milana through the plastic sheet of window.

'Get in here, girl,' she bellowed. Milana's heart pounded as she surveyed their strained faces. Milana crept in among them, her eyes ablaze with an intensity that Nilda had never seen before. The others merely looked at how her hair hung tangled about her shoulders, how her legs were streaked with mud and how her bare feet left dark footprints on the rough floorboards. Her canvas shoes dangled from her paint-covered fingers. Milana followed their gaze to the empty place where the TV had stood that morning.

'It's gone, who took it?' she said blankly, breaking the sudden inscrutable silence.

Nora laughed sarcastically. 'Yes, it's gone! You think we took it? One of us?' she mocked. 'It weren't one of us, it was them as know you're never here so what's your need for a telly or a radio eh? And they'll come for the rest soon, and then maybe the shanty and… maybe they'll just make merry with you too and who'd help you then when you get knocked up with some bastard kid? My mum, that's right; soft hearted, soft brained Nilda! Yeah, she'll look after you won't she?' Nora went on like an unstoppable bulldozer carving its way through soft earth. 'This is fair warning; cops or no cops your nice lady friend, *Señora* Lisa, can't keep shit from happening and now that Iris told the police your diddlysquit brothers were outback with Ana and saw fuck all, there ain't no suspect to pin Oscar's murder on and Doris hasn't got the balls to own up to what she saw, so we're all just as fucked as we always were and them two cokehead killers are strolling about Christmas shopping.'

'Nora, you know very well Pablo's left the shantytown and he won't dare come back. Not while *Señora* Lisa has promised to clean up this shantytown. Like she said at Oscar's funeral, and she's got backing too for it, they're going to make an example of San Damian,' countered Nilda, quietly from her corner.

'I've seen it happening already,' Ana assured them. 'There's cops all over the bridge at night so Oro Sucio's moved off down Barnechea way, he won't risk his neck in these parts. No shit's going to go down while she's on our case.' Ana looked boldly back at Nora.

'Promises, promises, you just keep hoping your boy didn't die for nothing, but let me tell you Ana, Oscar's death ain't going to swing it for San Damian, *Señora* Lisa or no *Señora* Lisa.'

Turning her beady eyes from Ana's quivering chin to Milana, Nora went on with renewed vigour;

'AND... what's this famous Christmas project, eh? Doris hasn't heard of any "Christmas Project" and she doles out them school dinners. We went looking for you this afternoon, after this happened, see,' she pointed a fat stubby finger at the empty spot the TV had occupied, 'Before anyone else figured Letty's shanty was a free-for-all Christmas market, and guess what, miss smartypants? There weren't no one doing any famous "Christmas project" at the school. And my mum here says you got some important project to finish but I think there never was no project. I think you just dumped them brothers of yours on her and she's too big hearted to stop you and you knows I'm too busy to notice, while you been mucking about…you been mucking us all about for weeks now! Been with some man, I'll bet.' Nora turned to the others. 'Remember what Iris said. She fair warned us.' Nora looked back at Milana with a triumphant sneer all over her face, 'Or more than one. Yeah, servicing a whole heap of good-for-nothing trash, catching their filthy diseases, while my mum sits there serving up your brothers' tea at my expense. You're a sly little slut, you are. I'm not taken in by your tricks. You must have made a pretty penny at it all these weeks. Was you thinking to run away eh? Yeah! You're a crafty little whoring bitch ain't you.' Nora turned back to the others, 'What's the point of being all sanctimonious now. '

Ana stood up seething with contempt. 'Knock it off, Nora! You got no right spouting off in here of all places.'

Nilda was crying into her apron.

Nora turned on Ana, 'I'm the only one round here as will sort them brats out.' She pointed to Ricci and Juanito, 'I've booked them out on the bus south and I'm going to take them to the bus terminal in my taxi this very night, see. That's more than you freeloaders will ever do. I won't sit back and watch them being robbed and ruined like the rest of you and I'll get lads up here from Panguipulli to look after this place and nobody will dare pinch stuff again. So don't you tell me where to get off. You hear me, woman?'

'Don't make out like you're so squeaky clean, I know you, Nora! You're just a greedy meddling witch,' Ana retaliated angrily.

'Oscar don't give you the right to speak to me like that. Thanks to me them kids won't be following behind Oscar. I've good as saved their lives, getting them away from here. I should have left the little whore to make her own way but I paid for them bus tickets for tonight out of my own savings, I have. What have you ever done for them, eh, Ana?'

Milana was grateful that all eyes were on Nora and Ana, so that her own feelings could pass undetected as she stood with her heart on fire and the fingers of both hands covering the lips Santiago had just kissed.

'She's packing her bags this minute!' shouted Nora defiantly.

'No!' cried Milana, emboldened by the strength she felt inside her. She turned to her brother, 'Who took the telly, Ricci, didn't you see?'

'I saw,' piped up Juanito. He had curled himself up in the corner by the back door.

'Shut up! He's always courting trouble that one. He probably had…'

'Shut it, Nora!' snapped Ana

'It was Raul, him and a friend,' squeaked Juanito.

'Doris's sister's boy?' Nilda gasped in surprise. Everyone knew Nora paid Raul to run her errands. Milana stared at Nora. It seemed incredible that Nora could have staged this little burglary to justify her intention to get her hands on their shanty. But Nora was a clever schemer and Milana knew to be wary of her. It was best to pretend to go along with her plan, then split. Milana had plans of her own. She wasn't afraid to hide out in old Whitebeard's shack. If it had been good enough for him for twenty years it would be good enough for her. Atilio would help her. He wouldn't talk and she would get him to buy her food from the kiosk, but she would need the money Nilda had given her. She couldn't manage alone without it. The south might be good for Ricci and Juanito but not for her.

'OK. I'll pack,' she said quietly, feigning submission, then she turned towards the back door.

'What's to pack out there, Milana?' yelled Nora.

'I want to get the washing off the line,' she answered quickly. Nora stomped over to the back door and flung it open.

'No washing on no line, see. Little liar…' and she narrowed her eyes. She wasn't taking any chances with Milana. Milana knelt down and pretended to comfort Juanito, who sat there with eyes wide and frightened by so much yelling from the big women. She whispered in his ear, 'Juanito, in the yard just by the wooden post next to the flower pot, you'll find the earth's loose, dig it up. There's a jar hidden there. Bring it to me but don't let Nora see.' She ruffled his hair affectionately before rising and looking at the others. 'Leave him alone, he's only small. You're scaring him.'

Juanito was forgotten. He slipped out and started digging. There it was, the old jar, so cleverly disguised by Letty. Juanito pulled it out of the gravelly earth and looked at it. Why would his sister want a jar of sugar? He began unscrewing the lid to check the contents, 'Juanito? Where are you?' called Ana.

'He's probably run away from fright,' Juanito heard Nilda say. Ana stood at the back door. 'Juanito,' she laughed when she saw the jar, 'Eating sugar! The little monkey.'

'See, he's not upset,' sneered Nora

'Come here love,' called Nilda

Juanito shuffled over to her, trying to keep the jar out of Nora's eyeshot.

'You'll have it good down south,' Nilda put her arm around him. 'There's fishing and swimming on the lake and making fires. It'll suit you, you'll see.' Juanito nodded obediently aware of the jar in his left hand and thinking only of how quickly he could get out of the room.

'Just a minute. You been stealing our sugar?' Nora glanced at Nilda, 'You been giving him our sugar, Mum?'

'Nora, leave it be. He's not stolen it,' murmured Nilda.

'That's one of my jars, them as I bring back from the supermarket.'

'You think you're the only one with them jars,' chimed in Ana.

'Well Juanito in't got any that's for sure.'

Nora held her hand out for the jar. Juanito hung his head and reluctantly released it into her clutches. Bemused by its lack of weight, Nora looked at the jar more carefully. That was when Nilda realised what it was. Her hand went to her mouth and she gave a little involuntary gasp.

'Get packing,' Nora waved Juanito quickly on. But Nilda's gasp wasn't lost on Nora.

'So quick to protect them aren't you, Mum?' she said turning on her. Nora's fat fingers curled around the sides of the jar. 'Go on, get off with you,' she roared at Juanito, but Juanito just stood there staring at her with big reproachful eyes.

'You little thieving oik,' she muttered as she opened the jar slowly with supercilious disdain. She didn't even look inside for a moment or two, but when she did, she covered the jar without saying a word.

Nora clutched the jar full of Letty's hard-earned *pesos* and told the boy to get lost. The flicker of a smile turned her look gloatful. Nilda stood up quietly and went behind the old shower curtain into the bedroom where Milana was stuffing a few belongings into an old plastic bag.

'It's all gone,' Nilda mouthed, the words barely audible as she sank onto the bed. 'Nora's got it and opened it and there's nothing we can do, or she'll just make up stuff about how you got it whoring and thieving and it'll be worse for you.' Nilda's eyes brimmed with tears.

Milana stepped out eventually from behind the plastic curtain, a small, grubby bag in her hand. 'I'm ready,' she said standing up to Nora with her accustomed self-possession. Ricci and Juanito came and stood beside her. Behind her Nilda sobbed uncontrollably into her apron.

'Good,' said Nora, looking Milana up and down suspiciously, 'I'll be that glad to see the back of you, you scheming strumpet.'

Standing between the Monseigneur and the Ministers for Arts and Culture and Education at the official reopening of the church, Santiago smiled dutifully, if somewhat stiffly, for the cameras. Later, while the assembled dignitaries marvelled at the fine interior and commented on the faces of pain so exquisitely portrayed in the stations of the cross, Santiago joined Atilio where he sat under the jacaranda tree eating his sandwich. Around them falling petals formed an oasis of deep blue, while they sat sheltered from the heat of a late December sun. Voices reached them on the breeze like ghosts of times past. Santiago spread his hands on the warm wood of the trestle table and looked into the middle distance. Atilio got up and left, returning a few moments later with a canvas in his hand.

'You can have this,' he offered in a croaky voice thick with emotion. He was fond of the picture, but the boy needed it more. 'She left it behind, I guess she's not coming back for it.' 'Seeing the face of Atilio on canvas, smiling his crooked smile at him in bold strokes that nevertheless caught the kindness in his eyes, made Santiago laugh, but maybe it was to stop tears that he laughed so heartily and slapped Atilio on the back and told him only Milana could have turned him into a handsome old rogue.

The University press chose the mural of the fishermen with their nets to illustrate the front cover of their monthly magazine, delighting in how the sunrise seemed to set the picture on fire.

Everyone, even Doris and Nilda and Ana and Iris, when they eventually went along to see what all the fuss was about at their local church, found themselves oddly moved by the bold and brilliant beauty of the paintings.

'Some young bloke painted all this,' Ana whispered knowingly to Nilda. '*Señora* Lisa told me.' Lisa herself came with them and walked through the church perusing each painting thoughtfully. At the back of the church she picked up an issue of the Catholic University magazine and read the article about the young artist inside. She was studying the photograph of Santiago when Nilda shuffled up to her.

'Milana, now she'd love all them paintings,' she commented wistfully. 'Pity she in't here to see 'em.'

'Don't worry Nilda, I'm sure she's relishing the beauty of the Chilean south. It's the best thing for her,' Lisa replied absently.

'He's a dish and a half,' sighed Nilda looking at the photograph that had Lisa so absorbed. 'And to think we had him hanging about here all these months painting them walls, and all Milana ever picked up on the riverbank was them broken bits of china.' Nilda sighed dreamily but Lisa glanced up from the photograph, a glimmer of understanding flickering suddenly in her eyes.

PART 2

THREE YEARS LATER

Chapter One

The morning sun poured its hot soothing balm over Santiago, penetrating through his closed eyelids, turning his world the colour of gold. He could hear the gentle lapping of the water on the shore as he floated between sleep and waking: cocooned in semi-consciousness. His blanket was the heat of the Chilean summer and his bed was the sand of the Chilean south and he was lying naked between the two, save for his red swimming trunks still damp from his earlier swim in the lake.

Santiago let carefree insouciance sweep him up like a wave and dared himself to be carried unreservedly upon it. Though his eyes were closed, a smile played on his lips as he surrendered to the easy, unruffled oblivion that washed over him. He was thousands of miles away from the constraints of his English university, away from books, papers and articles and the dark-panelled rooms of his college. He was a whole hemisphere away from the rain that ricocheted off the window-sills and ran in rivulets along the gutters outside his digs; the constant drizzle on his face and the damp that permeated his bones and his moods. It had been a soggy autumn. He had watched the trees once more turning their glorious hues as decay crept over them. He had braved his bicycle through the relentless winds that blew over the Cambridgeshire flatlands tearing leaves off branches and sending them swirling from lofty heights to an ignominious death. But England had dissolved into its now all too familiar mists as Lan Chile Airways delivered him back home for Christmas and nineteen glorious days of summer.

'Hey, wake up!' The soft female voice wafted over him like a breeze. Santiago opened one eye reluctantly. Beside him a pretty blonde girl in a turquoise bikini lay on her stomach with her head turned towards his face, smiling. He shut his eyes again.

'For one awful moment I thought I'd see the face of my alarm clock calling me back to the dismal damp.' He spoke coolly with a hint of amusement, which was his usual way.

She was seeing him in profile his face lit by the sun's rays, his tousled hair flopped back in thick black waves. She had to control herself not to reach out and touch it, instead she leant over him and blew an insect off it.

'Come on, it can't be that bad. You just say that so we won't feel jealous that you get to study where we go as tourists.'

She watched the corner of his mouth curl into his familiar lopsided smile.

'You know what you're really jealous of? That I get my degree after three years and you here don't get anything for five.' He clasped his hands behind his head and breathed in the warm summer air. She watched the way his lungs expanded and the suntanned skin lay smooth and tight across his chest and the flatness of his stomach.

'By June I'll be free as a bird.'

'What'll you do then?'

'I'm giving myself a year off. I'll get a studio in Bellavista and dedicate myself to painting. Then I'll sell the paintings to a gallery in New York, make my name there and leave these tranquil shores for the East Coast.' He let a minute or two go by then risked a sideways glance. Her eyes met his, awkward and self-conscious she lowered them. It hurt that he could speak so flippantly of leaving Chile. She couldn't be sure if he was just toying with the idea or speaking in earnest. She had seen him, once in a while, on the brink of betraying some real emotion, then take cover under his customary conspiratorial charm and she guessed he was keeping her at bay by being purposefully vague.

'Surely you won't paint forever. You'll get bored.'

Santiago laughed off the thought. But it was a hollow laugh. She regretted the remark and tried to justify it.

'It's such a lonely occupation,' she persisted,

'And compelling and totally absorbing.' His voice was deep and languid. 'You can't feel lonely when you're engaged in the creative process, it's impossible.'

'Didn't you ever feel lonely in England? During those long winter evenings?'

She felt him grow more distant and the atmosphere between them become suddenly strained. He stared up at the cobalt sky.

'I've never felt lonelier than in the company of people I don't want to be with,' he murmured.

'Hey, Santiago, Isabel! We're off to the *pueblo* with Diego and Cristobal to get some fresh bread and meat for the barbeque,' a tall young man with shaggy dark hair and navy blue shorts shouted across to them. As his dusty sailing shoes drew level with the towel on which she lay, Isabel looked up. His car keys jangled between his fingers.

'Want to come?' he offered.

'I'll stay here.' Isabel lay back and closed her eyes. 'Can you get me some chewing gum and the latest issue of *Cosas*, I'll pay you back later, JP.'

JP was an English abbreviation for Jean Paul, typical of the Grange School they'd all been to together, and it had stuck.

'I'll come.' Santiago stood up. 'I'll pull on some jeans.'

'Hey man no fuss, you're not in England now!' he laughed.

Santiago stretched and breathed in as though 'no fuss' was something you could savour. He glanced at Isabel but she had turned the other way to cover her disappointment.

The four boys climbed into JP's jeep glad to be in each other's company. Though they had each gone their separate ways at university, their friendships had been forged on fourteen years of shared experiences.

'OK, I'm on a mission, I must find something I can paint on.' Santiago opened the window so that the warm wind rushed into his face and through his damp hair.

'You could paint the *cabana* walls,' laughed JP referring to the wood cabins they had rented by the lake for their week-long holiday. 'Just think it would put up their value no end.'

'I know what you can paint on,' said Diego suddenly.

'Well?'

'A hide?'

'What?'

'An animal hide, the skin; they're always skinning animals here, get a cowhide.'

'That's brilliant, Diego, wait till I tell them in England, if you can't find canvas round my way you just paint on cowhide.'

Diego was Santiago's closest friend. He had been a star rugby player at school, he was tall and blonde with a ruddy complexion and wide, laughing mouth. He was often teased for his big hands and size twelve feet 'like the oversized paws on a pup' and his boundless enthusiasm. But his powerful frame and buoyant charm belied a deep insightful character that surfaced in the gentleness of his soft brown eyes.

'No, I'm serious, I'll talk to the butcher, I bet he's got something.'

'What'll you do for paint?' interjected JP, shifting a pile of tennis rackets wedged between him and Cristobal, a short sandy-haired boy, known to be the fastest downhill skier among them.

'Use cow blood!'

'Hey, not bad, Cristobal, never painted in blood before but it's natural, it's a great dye.'

'Oh come off it, that's disgusting.' JP swerved just for the hell of it.

'Someone suggested it to me once,' murmured Santiago. The memory of Milana produced a strange sensation inside him, like flying over a bump too fast.

They drove into the village down the dusty track that wound through tall ferns and wild hazelnut bushes and parked the Jeep opposite some artisan stalls by the old church. Diego strolled past the little open market thinking of his girlfriend who was holidaying in Europe with her parents. Cristobal called to him from across the road. Diego held up some complicated dangly earrings with feathers hanging off them. 'Dream catchers,' he called back, 'for Anita.' Cristobal rolled his eyes and waited kicking a stone along the pavement while Diego bargained with the stall holder. Meanwhile Santiago followed JP into the bread shop.

'Aren't you going to check out the butcher for cowhide?' JP suggested as he watched Santiago selecting freshly made *quesillo* and the local *queso mantecoso*. Santiago shook his head, 'No way man, leave it to the experts, besides I'm longing from some fresh-baked *pan amasado.*'

'Give me five or ten minutes, and I'll have the bread steaming fresh out of the oven,' said the young woman in the white apron as JP deposited the cheeses on the counter. 'I can get you a coffee and a pastry or you could take a walk round the square while you wait,' she went on brightly to JP, 'or you could look in the church, it's been done real special.' Santiago turned from where he was perusing some salami. 'What's special about the church?' he inquired.

'It's been painted real nice. It's got quite a name round here. It's open, you can just look in.'

'Hey, he paints churches too, or did. Better go check out the competition,' JP laughed at Santiago's undisguised interest.

'I'm not exactly dressed for church,' Santiago looked down at his swimming trunks. 'On second thoughts I'll be back in a minute, you coming JP?'

'You go, I'll take the coffee and the pastry. Meet you back at the car.'

Santiago ran to the butchers. Slabs of meat were displayed on trays and sawdust covered the floor. The back door of the small establishment was open and just outside he saw Diego inspecting the carcass of a huge pig.

'Diego, quick, lend me your T-shirt will you? I want to take a look in the church.'

'Hey, come and check this out,' retorted Diego.

Santiago grinned and shook his head, 'I'll pass. Thanks.' Besides the smell made him want to gag.

Diego pulled off his white T-shirt and threw it to his friend. 'I hope you're serious about that cowhide, they're rounding up the cow now for the slaughter.' Santiago rolled his eyes. 'Where's Cristobal?'

'He's just here checking out pig's blood with the butcher. 'Want a sip?' Cristobal stuck his head round the door and grimaced. Santiago laughed and gave him the thumbs down, glad to have an excuse to get out of there.

From the window of the little shop where he drank his coffee at a tiny metal table waiting for the bread to come out of the oven, JP watched Santiago stroll across the square towards the old church. He smiled to himself remembering the first time they'd all come to Lake Panguipuilli together. They'd been twelve years old and Santiago's mother had been invited round Yugoslavia on the yacht of some Greek shipping magnate. Santiago had been thrilled not to have to go with her. It had been the best holiday ever. Santiago had dared them all to swim to the next cove at the dead of night. The boys had set out but underestimating the distance, by the time they got to the next beach Cristobal got an attack of croup and Santiago had insisted on climbing up to a nearby house and waking the sleeping residents to come and rescue him. The rescue had developed into a strange affair with the mother of the household spending the rest of the night in the hot shower with Cristobal so the steam could ease his cough and his desperate battle to breathe. Meanwhile the boys had played ping pong with the two older boys of the house who, woken by the commotion and not willing to miss the excitement, had stayed with them till dawn. Finally the gardener had driven them all back to their *cabañas* along with the two boys who Santiago had magnanimously invited to stay for lunch and to corroborate their story. They'd all become firm friends after that and their capers had become increasingly more thrilling with Santiago's irrepressible spirit of adventure.

Santiago had joined them for many more summer holidays and fortunately parents never wised up to half of their escapades which, at fourteen had involved illegally driving one of the Jeeps along the dirt tracks to rescue Diego the time he'd twisted his ankle. The summer they all finished school they had rented horses and ridden across the Andes to Bariloche and done some of the most dangerous white water rafting they were ever likely to experience again.

Now, as he stared after his friend, JP considered how it was always Santiago who had pushed further, taken more risks, as though he were forever searching for the boundaries that would make him safe. One occasion came vividly to mind. They had been skiing off piste in Portillo and had come over the brow of the mountain when suddenly the whole massive slab of snow on which they stood had moved. Santiago, ahead of them, had felt it first and turning warned them, with his finger to his lips, to ski to the side and had watched them do it. Then, to their amazement he had continued to ski down at a phenomenal speed, clearing the avalanche that followed, seconds before it might have killed him. That day they had seen that death itself held no fear for him or, as Cristobal had commented watching him go, 'That's called a death wish.' It had shaken them all. It was not showmanship they had witnessed in that moment but a kind of desperate recklessness. He'd shrugged it off later saying: 'You only really appreciate living when you face dying.'

Although always singular in his ways and strongly individual in his approach to life, Santiago had changed now. The clean-cut youth had matured during his years in England. His raven mane seemed thicker and more unkempt and his handsome face now seemed to sport a permanent shadow of stubble. The darkness of his look only served to accentuate the piercing blueness of his eyes that searched you and then relinquished you unsatisfied.

He had arrived off the plane just days before, with his usual carefree insouciance in the unlikely garb of an English country gent, which he had laughed off saying he'd gone straight to Heathrow from some Hampshire shooting party. He proceeded to tease his friends that his English ancestors were influencing him from beyond the grave and that he'd finally discovered his English roots and caused much hilarity all round by mocking the plum-in-the-mouth English accent, which he pulled off with remarkable ease. The following day the suede moccasins and tweed jacket had been discarded and replaced with his trusted leather boots and jeans but it had been a revealing insight. Their hearts went out to him. They knew too well this

173

was a man who would not be moulded to his surroundings. Santiago couldn't fail to stand apart; his whole demeanour, the dark smouldering strength of his look couldn't be subdued by any uniform of convention that he, or maybe someone else, some girl there, might be trying to tailor him into.

Now they noted a deeper transformation in him; the idealism of before had changed into a bold resolution, a toughness born of spirit and stamina that was at first difficult for his friends to adapt to because it was powerful and concentrated and an unknown quantity. It was as though, unbeknownst to him, some inner force had broken through the attempted conformity of his younger self. His gentleness had shaped itself into a more commanding presence, especially in the way he threw back his head and laughed at situations, a warm laugh unresolved as yet whether to mock or placate. The strength in his unwavering gaze remained unchanged but still there was a restlessness in his eyes at times that disconcerted his companions even though it often appeared cloaked in his characteristic easy charm that belied emotion.

It was not easy at the best of times to know Santiago. He rarely spoke about himself. Only to Diego, once or twice, had he revealed thoughts and feelings, lightly and briefly giving the topic little importance. All the same Diego was the one who knew him best. Santiago had spent more holidays with Diego than with his own mother. When girls wanted to know about Santiago, it was Diego they asked, for, as one of his friends had once remarked; 'Of all the horses in the stable Santiago is definitely the darkest.'

Poor Isabel, she adored Santiago, but he didn't even seem to notice.

'He won't commit to anyone,' some would say, 'he's wrapped up in his art; all artists are, they're hopeless companions.' But Santiago wasn't a hopeless companion, he was as good a friend as anyone could hope for. JP remembered how when they were fifteen, the Grange School offered an exchange programme for a semester with an American school. Santiago had always longed to get away and he grabbed the chance to go to school in America.

Diego too was desperate to go, his sister had just died in a tragic skiing accident and his parents were on a rollercoaster of grief that threatened to split them completely. They both signed up for the exchange but Diego just missed the selection programme, Santiago got picked. Then suddenly Santiago signed off the programme and Diego got to go instead. Santiago told everyone it was because something else had come up. But when the boys came back from the exchange, at the party to welcome them home, the headmaster told Diego, 'You've got a loyal friend in Santiago, it's good to know who you can count on. Keep it to yourself, Diego, I just thought you ought to know.' That's how Diego discovered that Santiago had gone to the headmaster and quietly resigned his place on condition Diego took it. Diego knew better than most the measure of Santiago and he had shared the information with JP. With women it was different, Santiago didn't want to be cornered by them, or forced to do their bidding. 'They start manipulating your life, they can't help it,' he'd once said to Diego and JP. The others didn't really mind that. They liked their social life being organised by their girlfriends. It was quite a relief. But Santiago never let the girls get close enough for that.

The young woman at the bread counter had been observing JP with interest for several minutes. Watching his changing expressions was like seeing light and shade chase across the water. It was a mystery what boys thought about, she sighed to herself, when you asked them they always said 'Nothing'.

'Bread's ready *Caballero*,' she called across, 'are you going to pay for your friend's stuff too?'

Chapter Two

The church in the middle of the little *pueblo* of Panguipulli was old and like so many similar churches in Chile it had suffered the effects of numerous earthquakes. The stone facade had been patched up in places and huge cracks along the wall had been filled in and painted over leaving great white scars. It was built centrally on a grassy plot where someone had lovingly planted and tended white and red rose bushes that were now in full flower.

Strolling around it in his red bermudas, Santiago circled the church until he came to a small side door that was half ajar. He slipped into the quiet interior. The roof had been recently restored and a skylight incorporated allowing the bright sun to stream in. Above the altar a small red light burned day and night showing the sacred presence of the consecrated host in the tabernacle.

Santiago knelt and, head bowed, made the sign of the cross. Then, rising, he clasped his hands behind his back and walked slowly down the aisle. On either side, the stations of the cross were painted on wooden panels in deep vibrant colours. Behind the stone altar a large crucifix had been painted on the wall to look like it was occupying real space; the trompe d'oeil effect had been stunningly achieved. Painted rays of light emanated in such a way that it seemed that the cross was superimposed on a magnificent sunrise, and on the furthest edges of the sunrise there were angels rendered in whites and yellows, as fine and ethereal as the spirits of light they represented. Santiago stepped back and stared spellbound at it for a long time before turning towards the stations of the cross, beginning at number one:

'Jesus before Pilate' and on through to 'Jesus laid in the tomb'. He walked very slowly; any observer would have thought he prayed, such was the reverence with which he gazed at each individual picture, his unsuspecting heart galvanised by the shock of the violent and unexpected emotion that racked his whole being.

The stations of the cross took him all the way around the church until he found himself back in front of the altar. He knelt there for a long time, not moving. His friends who, intrigued, now watched him from the back, dared not speak or interrupt, caught by the solemnity of the moment and the surprise of seeing Santiago, the rebel, kneeling before God.

'You don't think he's going to become a priest?' Cristobal whispered to JP.

JP gave him a withering look and pushed him quietly out of the church. Diego followed but looked back. There was something deeply compelling about the intimate moment of such a private man. Meanwhile, oblivious, Santiago sat back on the front pew and, placing his head in his hands, he breathed in deeply.

Nothing had prepared him for this. If he had had some inkling of what had been waiting for him inside the church, his well programmed defence mechanisms would have kicked in. Instead, the memory that he had kept locked in the innermost part of his being, these three years past, had been released. It was as though some unseen hand had twisted its way through all the layers of flesh and blood and, tearing into his heart, had wrenched out its best kept secret and splashed it onto the walls for all to see. He felt wrung out. Why couldn't he control this as he had controlled so much in his life? The force of his emotions seemed to tremble through him breaking into the darkest recesses of his being; cold tombs where he had tried to lay to rest the harrowing ghosts of his past. A host of unstoppable memories overwhelmed him like a mighty wave that, building up unseen, towers suddenly in all its awesome power. Before he could figure it out his strength dissolved. He was left a vulnerable and miserable wreck on a distant shore of unanswered questions from which he struggled desperately to return to the here and now.

When, finally, Santiago emerged into the sunlight Diego was sitting on a bench by the rose bushes.

'Where are the others?' inquired Santiago in his usual jovial manner.

'I sent them home,' said Diego. 'Told them I'd wait and we could walk.'

Santiago nodded and managed a smile, a real smile, 'I could do with a five mile walk,' he teased. But then he put his arm briefly around Diego's square rugby player's shoulders, 'I could do without their banter right now, Diego. Thank you.'

'You had quite a revelation in there,' said Diego as they walked.

Santiago shot him a look, 'What? Were you there too?'

'Only for a minute. You took so long, man. We all came to check out the church.'

Santiago shoved his fingers through his hair, then he pulled off Diego's T-shirt and handed it back to him. 'All thanks to your T-shirt.'

'Santiago, you don't have to joke all the time.' Santiago raised a playful eyebrow at him. Diego sighed exasperated.

'Look. I don't know what happened to you when you were painting that church by the shantytown three years back; you know the one by the river, that you got that big national prize for. I know something happened there, it changed you. Just now you looked like you'd seen a ghost. Maybe it's none of my business but...' Santiago stopped in his tracks and put his hand up for him to stop. For a moment Diego didn't know if he was angry or just thinking or what. They had walked out of the *pueblo* and had set out across the hill following a small beaten track through ferns and huge fleshy green leaves. Santiago looked up at the uninterrupted blueness of the sky. He passed his hand over his face. The redness of his eyes was not lost on Diego.

'Sometimes, Diego, in our very ordinary and mundane lives, something happens. It's like somehow in the fabric of life there's a tiny tear and you see something awesome, uplifting, like a banquet that would feed your soul; food you never knew existed for a part of you that has searched for it forever. You want to reach out and take it, but you can't.' He looked at Diego. 'That's it, that's what happened when I was painting the church back then.' Then he laughed. 'Look at you, Diego. You must think I've lost it completely.'

Diego looked puzzled and remembered Cristobal's comment.

'You didn't have a religious experience did you?' he threw the question out awkwardly as though trying to distance himself from it at the same time.

Santiago threw his head back and laughed, releasing Diego from his discomfort.

'Not the kind you're thinking,' he twinkled at him, 'But you're still looking at me like I've lost it.'

'No, I don't think you've lost it at all, I think maybe you're trying to find "it".'

Santiago straddled a huge fallen log, then he lay down on it and stared up at the sky.

'It,' Santiago sighed, 'the elusive 'it"

'A woman?' suggested Diego, 'In England perhaps?' he ventured playfully.

'I don't seem to be very good at relationships, Diego.' He sighed

'You don't trust women. They want to love you but you give so little away, it's kind of one-sided. It doesn't make for lasting relationships, Santiago.'

'Whoa, you sound like Anita now.'

'Yeah well, maybe that's just what you need, a girlfriend. There are several interested candidates, by the way.'

'What are you, some kind of broker?' Santiago shot him an amused look. Diego shrugged, 'Anita tells me stuff, she says you go out with girls, you sound interested in them, but you never make a move. Why don't you go for it?'

'I'm trapped, Diego, between a rock and a hard place, as they say in England.'

'Look,' Diego faltered unsteadily, wading into unknown territory, 'I'm not good at this but, shit, why man, why d'you

179

hold back?' Santiago laughed, a real good-natured laugh, 'Diego. You're doing a good job,' he reassured him jokily. 'Damn, I wish a had a drink now.'

'Drink?'

'Yeah, that's all you do during those long winter nights in England, drink to get warm, drink to forget, drink for fun and drink for courage.

'Courage? What have you ever needed courage for? You'd dare anyone to anything. That hasn't changed. So...'

Santiago arched one eyebrow. 'Some might call that kind of courage recklessness or desperation.' Diego didn't answer.

'Thanks anyway.'

'For what?'

'Understanding.' Santiago threw the word out dismissively. 'Man, I don't understand! That's just it.' He laughed a slightly hollow laugh and shook his head. 'I know it's none of my business.' He lifted a hand up to indicate he was backing off.

Santiago immediately recognised his friend's embarrassment at having broached such unexpected intimacy.

'Well you did in there! You sent them all packing, that's what I mean.' Diego looked gravely at Santiago, like he was trying hard to make him out.

'Look I know you guys must think I'm selfish, irresponsible and reckless.' He took a deep breath. Neither spoke for a long time. Neither felt the need to fill the silence. A caterpillar crawled lazily past and butterflies danced merrily overhead.

'The thing is Diego,' he said at last, 'that all my life I've felt like I don't belong. Not in the house I was born or to the mother that bore me. Then the feeling stops, like a ghost chased away by the sunlight, and I forget it. But then suddenly it returns stronger than ever, like a question I must answer. An uneasiness pursues me like some horrible poltergeist in my mind throwing around all kinds of weird thoughts. I found peace from it only once in my life, briefly, when I painted the church in San Damian. For those few last weeks I could live without the restlessness and the nightmares. Nightmares that you wouldn't wish on your worst enemy, Diego. I can't run or hide from them, but maybe they are what make me reckless. They seemed to get worse under the dank oppressive clouds of England. So I painted those nightmares. I had to get them out of my system. There's nothing like endless hours of dark English winter to make my demons surface; they were monstrous, cathartic paintings. They actually frightened people but of course they loved them in England. Thank God I was in England. Ironically, those weird pictures made my name there. Here they'd have had me locked up.' Santiago passed his hand over his face again. Diego could see the tension in his muscles. Santiago fell silent again but Diego could feel the churning up of those still waters that had hitherto run deep and impenetrable.

'There are things in my past, Diego that I don't understand,' he said at last. Santiago shot him a look; deep, penetrating and earnest without a hint of his customary joviality. 'I was too young. I relive them sometimes, but only in dreams, where they take on these grotesque forms. To get rid of them I have to find out the truth but there's no one I can talk to.'

'Is it about your father's murder?' asked Diego tentatively. 'Is it about the guy who killed him?'

'In my dreams, it's not some guy,' and then, almost inaudibly, he whispered, 'it's my mother.'

Diego wondered if he'd heard right but he knew he couldn't ask, he couldn't even speak, he remained shocked and still beside his friend trying to push away the awful implication and pretend he'd never heard it, so that life could go on as normal.

'But, it's only a dream.' Diego countered at last, relieved. 'Dreams play shit games with you. Can't you see someone about it?'

Santiago stood up briskly, 'Doctors know shit. They mess up our brains with their questions and toss in new cans of worms that were never there. I just need someone who was there. I need the truth. But I know I can't ask. It's killing me, Diego.' Santiago walked on a few steps and looked back the way they had come.

'Then, in there, Diego, I find it again; that tear in the fabric of my shitty life through which I can glimpse heaven. Food for my starving soul, the promised land. I want to reach out and take it but I can't, because it's just paint on a wall. God, Diego have you ever loved? I didn't think I had it in me to even say the word, but have you, man, really?'

Diego stood shaking his head, 'Not like that, no. Not so hungrily.'

Santiago tugged his fingers through his hair and laughed, because he was so used to laughing through the pain.

'You're right, Diego, I'm too damned hungry, I've been starved for too long.'

'Hey man,' Diego shrugged and gave him a sudden impish smile to cover all the imponderables, 'no need to starve. Take Isabel, she's pining for you as we speak.'

'Poor Isabel,' Santiago's faced creased into that familiar good-natured smile, 'You know the story of Adam and Eve and the tree of life, Diego? The only tree they wanted to eat from was the one that was forbidden. Funny that.'

'They only wanted it because it was forbidden,' said Diego simply.

'No,' said Santiago, 'I reckon it was forbidden because they wanted it so much. That was their test.'

'Diego looked momentarily perplexed but then he shrugged, 'Yeah, well they failed the test, right?' said Diego, 'And we all failed it with them, so don't beat yourself up about it.'

They went on walking, the moment of truth had passed.

That night at the barbeque on the sand, beneath the perfect luminous curve of the moon drawn onto the velvet star studded sky, Santiago was ceremoniously presented with a calf hide by Cristobal, sporting feathers on his head and a grass skirt in a mock ritual. With much hysterical sashaying and chanting by Cristobal, Santiago was requested to take this gift from the natives back to civilisation and lie on it while he revised for his finals and he would be magically empowered by the spirit of the Great Southern Cow. After all the fun and the games and after they had sung to guitars in front of the campfire into the small hours, as they staggered back to their respective *cabañas*, Santiago walked up to JP.

'Any chance of borrowing your Jeep early tomorrow, JP? I'll be back before you miss it.'

'Sure, it's all yours.' He tossed him the keys. 'Where are you going?' he added yawning.

'Only into the village.' Santiago tucked the keys into his jeans and disappeared into the shadows so no one would find him and offer him their company. He wanted to be alone.

From a distance Santiago watched the others scatter off to bed. He pulled his jacket close. The night was cold without a bonfire but Santiago knew he could not survive the confines of the *cabaña* tonight. He gazed along the little row of wood cabins with their outside verandas and wooden tables, and the lanterns flickering in the darkness. He had missed this holiday for the past three years. Term times in England had eaten into the Chilean summer and his mother had used his time in England as an excuse to spend Christmas in Europe, then skiing in Gstaad where his godparents owned a chalet. Naturally he felt obliged to join her, wishing all the time he could be back in these *cabañas* on the shores of Lake Panguipulli. Even at a distance there was, he found, a peculiar comfort to knowing where his friends were. This was what they did, just like they skied in La Parva in the winter and spent the summer on the beach in Zapallar and here on the shores of Lake Panguipulli.

Their families had been friends for years and Santiago always came here with them, rescued from the tedium of being otherwise forced to holiday with his mother on the manicured yachts of the super rich off the coast of Yugoslavia and Sardinia. Politely he had continued to decline the invitations to join her, as much as he could, preferring the company of the friends he had known from childhood. Amongst them he was included as just another member of their families as they wind-surfed and water skied, went on riding expeditions or cruised the lake in motorboats meeting friends and having picnics on the secluded beaches along the shores.

Santiago listened to the faint lapping of the water. The sky of the southern hemisphere spread out above him in all its glory. He lay down on the cool sand and watched the myriad of constellations such as he had never seen anywhere else but here. Occasional stars shot across the sky and died. He let himself imagine that somewhere close she could see them too. The stars became her eyes holding his and he let himself revisit all the emotional power they held for him. Her gaze had seemed to hold the wisdom of the ages, as though she had drunk in every sunset and sunrise, the mountains and the rivers, and delivered it all into his aching heart to resurrect him. Discovering her, her courage and her faith in him, had banished, albeit briefly, the darkness within him. With her he had experienced the single most liberating feeling of his life; the intensity of first love in all its facets and, as she had never held him to ransom, his love had surrounded her like the air she breathed until she could hardly distinguish one from the other, both equally essential. 'Milana,' he whispered into the darkness as though she might be listening.

Atilio alone had witnessed their relationship and understood it without ever needing to judge it. But Atilio had not seen the kiss that had tipped the delicate balance that lies at the heart of all human relations. Why else would she not have come back? All Santiago could imagine was that he had frightened her with his intensity or that whatever admiration he might have felt from her, had been simply for the art he taught her. And yet, when he asked himself could she, young as she was then, have been capable of responding to his love, every instinct told him yes.

He was shaking now as he shook so often when he thought of her. But today the spectre of her had risen to take hold of him in a grip from which only her real presence would release him. He remembered her as he had seen her that first day, face down on the riverbank. To her he could have bared his soul now. She alone, instinct told him, possessed the courage to face the darkness inside him.

Chapter Three

Santiago drove JP's Jeep into the *pueblo* just after sunrise. Already the women were about their work, lighting their mud ovens to make bread for the menfolk before they left on bicycles and pick-up trucks to tend the crops on the *fundos* near by. He parked the Jeep by the church. An old woman carrying a bucket of fresh milk smiled a toothless welcome. He watched her climb the hill and disappear over the brow. Finally he stepped out of the Jeep and walked across the square towards the main post office. As he passed a yellow painted cottage, the front door opened. He saw into the interior where a small group of people were gathered. A priest came out and the door closed behind him. Santiago stopped to let him pass.

'Good morning, Father.'

'It's been a long night in there,' the priest looked back up the little garden path.

'Has someone died?'

'Yes, *Señora* Hilda, at last. She was so ill but so very young to die, God rest her soul. You don't live round here though?'

'No, I'm on holiday.'

'Good, God bless you, son.' The priest made to move on.

'Father, I saw the church yesterday.'

'Ah yes,' the priest turned back showing sudden interest, 'the paintings, you like them?'

'They're beautiful,'

'You know about art?'

'A little.'

'It's very good isn't it; the art, in there?' the priest sought his more learned confirmation.

'I think so. Does the artist live close by?'

'Milana? Why yes. Just down the track there. There's a courtyard with a drinking well, that's *Señora* Lucy's house for children. That's where she lives. So, you think she's good?' The priest smiled immensely gratified and walked away across the square.

Santiago watched him go, his heart racing. Anticipation seized him like some kind of euphoria inducing drug. For a moment he barely knew which way to turn. He wanted to prolong the feeling inside him, the thrill and the excitement that made him feel suddenly intensely alive. He had known of course from the first moment he had seen the painting of the sunrise in the church that she had done it, he had guessed she must live close by. He knew she'd gone down south because he had returned, a whole year later to ask Atilio what he knew of her. But now to have it confirmed so casually, to know her suddenly within reach, for sure, was overwhelming.

Though part of him thought maybe he should wait, come back at a more sociable hour, prepare himself, he found himself turning at the corner of the lane and walking slowly down the dirt track the priest had indicated. A dog on a long chain barked savagely as he passed. Blossoming white and lilac veronicas lined a white picket fence which ended abruptly in a large courtyard. Hens of various sizes pecked the dust by an old well in the centre of the yard. Around the well there was a circular brick step to allow people to reach the iron handle more easily and on this step a small girl sat crying with her knees tucked up to her chin. The early morning rays threw Santiago's shadow across the ground in front of her and she looked up. After scrutinizing him for a moment she looked down again in continued misery, her small frame shaking with the force of her sobbing. Santiago walked over to her and sat on the step next to her.

'What's wrong, little one? Can I help?' She looked up again and stared at his face, taking him in bit by bit as though somewhere in his features she might discover the answer to her troubles. As she looked, her eyes, though brimming with tears seemed to widen in hope, but then she broke into another sob.

'She's gone, Milana's gone.' She repeated it three times until she was satisfied that he realised how shattering this news was.

'Where's she gone?' he whispered. How could the little girl know the enormous impact of what she was saying, or the significance it held for the handsome stranger.

'Don't know.'

'Did she say why?'

'No, she just went. She never even said goodbye.' At this the girl dissolved into a new bout of tears.

A woman came running into the yard from the building beyond, scattering hens in her path.

'Oh, Ines, there you are! Thank heavens! They'd told me you'd gone after her.' The woman scooped Ines into her large dimpled arms. Then she looked Santiago up and down.

'Can I help you, sir?'

'I just wanted to meet the girl who painted the church.'

'Oh heavens!' The woman brushed Ines' hair off her face and planted a motherly kiss on her forehead, 'I need the chickens fed, Ines, and I've got a heap of leftovers in a bucket by the stove. Will you go do it for *Tia* Lucy, please?'

Ines nodded and walked off, looking back several times.

'Heavens, Sir. It's been all topsy turvey this morning and I've not told the *Padre* nothing. He doesn't know. I barely know myself what possessed the girl.' She raised her thick sunburnt arms heavenwards in a gesture of helplessness. 'You had some business with her?' she asked, looking at Santiago with interest.

'The *Padre* directed me here. I don't suppose you know where she's gone or when she left?'

'This morning I thought I heard her footsteps early. I was sure she'd be on the farm with the pigs or looking after one of our little ones, but... she's gone. She must have walked to the crossroads where the bus comes. I reckon she's gone off to one of the big towns. She had so many people coming round here after she painted the church. She wanted to travel she said, to the capital or to see the desert in the north. She was always that restless. She was here but she wasn't, you know what I mean? Like them birds that are about to wing it. I knew she'd go.

Thought she'd leave the very day she came, she was that distraught poor girl. Inconsolable! Wouldn't talk to no one.' She wiped away a tear, and went on. 'I got Father Juan over, and gradually, he talked to her, dunno what he said, but he's the one who brought her the paints and the sketch book, and that's how come she stayed. He'll be that upset. He brought that kid out of her misery and it was his idea she paint the church. Oh there was that amount of umming and ahhing about the wisdom of it but it was done and well done too, and good for him is what I say.'

'But how can you be sure she's really upped and gone? Aren't you going to look for her?' Santiago asked after a long pause.

'Wouldn't know where to look. Father Juan might.' The woman shook her head. 'But what's the point, see?' Out of her pocket she brought a piece of paper. 'She left this.' At the sight of the letter *Señora* Lucy's chin wobbled. 'You read it to me. Such a talented child.' She waved two sheets of paper that had been torn out of a school exercise book at him. Santiago took them. They were covered in neat straight writing. His smile disguised his emotion. He read slowly taking the words right into his heart before he could speak them out to the woman beside him.

'*Tia Lucy,*

You've been so kind and patient with me from the first day I came. You and Father Juan gave me back the will to live again and the courage to try. I will never forget your kindness. Now, thanks to you, I am strong enough to leave and take responsibility for myself. Tell Father Juan that I will make something of myself, I promise him. I will never stop painting. It is God's gift to me. I know that now. Tell him he helped me believe it and I do believe him and I am grateful to God and to him and to you, dear Tia Lucy. And now I must go. Don't worry about me please. I am strong, and I must be free now to find my way. I have questions I must answer and a life that I left unfinished back home.

Panguipulli was my beautiful refuge when the world turned

188

sour on me. But now I am healed and the world looks a brighter place and I want to go out into it. I am doing what Father Juan asked, I am making something of myself, please be happy for me.

I will come back Tia Lucy one day and see you. I have left a note for little Ines under the loose brick by the well. Remind her when she is sad that I took the wooden bead bracelet she made me and I will wear it always. I've left her my mood ring that changes colour.

I love you Tia Lucy and Father Juan. Please show him this letter.

Thank you for so much,
Milana.'

'You knew her!' *Señora* Lucy's voice broke the spell. Santiago looked up and saw that she had her head to one side and was watching him curiously. Santiago nodded and looked back at the letter. They stood in silence for a moment.

'You'd like to keep that wouldn't you?' she gestured at the paper. 'Well it's no good to me, I don't read that good. Why don't you take it to Father Juan, and then if he don't need it you can keep it.'

'You wouldn't mind?'

'No,' she smiled, 'I got her here in my heart. I seen her every day for all these years.'

'I knew her a long time ago,' Santiago hesitated, 'when the world "turned sour" on her.'

'Don't go taking that personally. There was a lot happened in her life. Father Juan, he told me and it's no business of ours.' Then she folded her strong arms and stood back a moment. 'You an artist too then?'

'Yes, I am actually.'

'You're not the bloke that taught her to paint?' *Señora* Lucy was nodding her head with that look of countrywomen who often could not read or write but when it came to human beings seemed gifted with some sixth sense.

Santiago breathed in deeply and pulled his hand through his hair.

'Yes, you was! And here am I standing talking to you. I get to see you as taught her all this beautiful stuff.' And suddenly she opened her arms to Santiago who, though somewhat embarrassed, allowed himself to be wrapped in her strong embrace.

'Come in. Have some fresh bread with us.'

'Maybe I should go and find Father Juan.' As he spoke Santiago surveyed the circular step on which Ines had been sitting until his eye caught a loose brick. He leant down and lifted it. 'Look here's where she put the letter for Ines.'

'Oh, pick it up and I'll give it to her, there's a good lad.'

'Why don't you tell her where it is and let her find it. It'll be like finding a little treasure from Milana.' *Señora* Lucy looked at the impossibly handsome man, and grinned, 'You got the heart of a kid, my lad,' then she stepped a little closer, 'you don't think it would be wrong if you just read it to me once?' Santiago smiled, more thrilled than she could know to oblige, and picked out the folded sheet of paper.

> *'My beautiful little Ines,*
>
> *I am going on an adventure like I always told you I would, remember? We all have to have our special adventure and one day it will be your turn. So you must be very happy for me and help Tia Lucy with the hens and look after Molly our donkey.*
>
> *Ricci and Juanito promised they would take you on Molly one day to look into the crater of the volcano. Ricci and Juanito will miss me they said, but I told them that they had another little sister now, and they must look after her. That's you, Ines. That made them happy. They are good brothers and they will always look after you.*
>
> *I took the bead bracelet you made me. It will be my good luck charm and I will wear it all through my adventure and bring it back safe to you one day. I left you my mood ring that you like in your red shoe. Wear it and think of my love always round your finger.*
>
> *Milana. xxx'*

Señora Lucy wiped her eyes while Santiago folded the note and replaced it under the brick. 'You go tell her,' urged *Señora* Lucy, 'it'll be more special.' She watched as Santiago walked over to where the little girl stood on the far side of the courtyard feeding the hens. She watched him crouch down in the dust so that he was level with the child's face and she watched Ines listening to every word he said. It was longer than the brief message she'd given him to pass on, but the girl's eyes grew wider as he spoke and a measure of happiness entered her face, and eventually, when he stood up, she ran across to the brick and lifting it, squealed with delight and took her letter away somewhere private.

'She don't really know how to read yet.'

'Oh I shouldn't worry about that,' said Santiago. 'Thank you, *Señora* Lucy, it's been a pleasure meeting you.'

'And you, son. Hey, you never told me your name.'

'Santiago, Santiago Hidalgo.'

'Ooh,' she said, 'like that murdered politician, Carlos Hidalgo. My dad, he worked on the Hidalgo estate he did, when he was a lad that's how I come to know them folk in San Damian shantytown where Milana's from.'

'Carlos Hidalgo was my father.'

'Ooh.' Her hand shot to her mouth. 'You poor, poor boy.'

Santiago broke the awkward silence, 'It was a long time ago, *Señora* Lucy,' he smiled at her to dispel her instinctive misgivings.

Santiago stepped into the silent, empty church, and sat down to recover. The words from Milana's letter filled his head with their stark message; *Now I am healed and the world seems a brighter place.* He knew that he was not healed.

The night Carlos Hidalgo was killed, everything he had ever loved was taken from him and a crushing burden of guilt had fallen upon the young Santiago's shoulders. Santiago carried the events of that night deep within, trying to block out their meaning so that he might be able to live and smile and laugh and call his home a home. But he was torn between being a part of what his heart rejected; his mother and what he had seen her do, or being utterly desolate, and as good as orphaned, so he chose the lie. Over the years he had sought refuge in the love of God because that was not within man's power to take from him. Gradually the 'lie' had eased and he accepted and received the love of his mother but his nightmares tormented him and shocked him all the more because he could not control them.

Now, something about her letter seemed to reproach him; *face truth, whatever the consequences* it whispered. Maybe it would purge his soul to speak at last. Diego had tried to reach him and Santiago had done his best to meet him. But he had sensed how Diego, while embracing his friendship, had buckled under the burden of trust and pushed away the implications as instinctively as he himself had for so long. It had seemed so much easier to live with the lie than to face the truth. But now he understood that while he ignored his demons he would never be free. Never had he understood this more keenly than at this moment, bereft and disheartened. He felt left behind, not by Milana's departure but by her intrepid spirit, that had liberated itself and now had moved on undaunted, ready to take Life on. It was that spirit that he had felt feeding his soul with its strength and courage while he painted the church, the same spirit that, had she seen into his soul now would, he believed, have called him a coward.

'My son,' he felt a hand on his shoulder. It was Father Juan. 'I thought it might be you. Did you find her? Did you see Milana?'

Santiago stood up abruptly as though by doing so he could shift the anguish weighing down on him.

'She wasn't there, Father.' He took Milana's letter out of his pocket. '*Señora* Lucy wanted you to see this. Milana has gone but she left this letter.' The priest took the letter and walked to where the sun shone more directly through the skylight.

'This is good news.' He beamed and folding the letter gave it back to Santiago. 'I will leave you, son, with your thoughts.'

Santiago reached out to him as he turned away, 'Father Juan.'
'Yes?'

After a pause the priest took Santiago's hand from where it still touched the edge of his sleeve and held it for a moment.

'I'm here to listen, son, to anything you need to say.' Santiago met his eyes and the priest saw the look he had seen so many times in his long vocation.

'Son,' he reassured him, 'whatever you tell me in the confessional, even the most heinous crime committed, I cannot speak of it to a living soul. Your secrets will die with me.'

Chapter Four

The yellow bus hurtled up President Kennedy Avenue. The driver, a youngish man with a swarthy complexion and a pair of psychedelic sunglasses, eyed the pretty girl in the cotton dress that sat next to the old lady. The girl held a yellow rose on her lap that she had bought from a street vendor. The *micrero* shifted his glasses to check the colour of her hair that cascaded over her shoulders catching the sun in soft auburn waves, then he swerved the bus abruptly and glanced again in his enormous panoramic rear-view mirror. Her eyes, green under dark lashes, flashed him a look of annoyance; he grinned and promptly swerved the bus again, just to see her stunning eyes flash at him again. But Milana looked away to where, beyond a row of shops advertising car parts and bicycle repairs, the shantytown she grew up in extended down to the river. She fingered the wooden beads of the bracelet little Ines had given her and wished she could have said goodbye properly, but she knew it would have just made it more difficult to leave. And leave she must. The restlessness in her heart had left her no choice.

Many times she had walked the two miles from *Tia* Lucy's to where the bus passed on its long route back to the capital, and so many times she had watched after its tail lights in the cloud of dust it left behind, having failed to sum up the courage to leave. Not a day had passed in all three years in Panguipulli that she had not thought, even fleetingly, of returning to the river where all her dreams lay washed up on the bank. The only thing that had held her back was that she had no money. So, when eventually money had arrived, she knew it was a sign that the time was right to leave.

The bus rattled past the huge Lider shopping-mall. A little further on where the road forked to the right up the mountain towards the elegant ski resorts of La Parva and Valle Nevado, the bus veered left at such speed that Milana was thrown against the little old lady next to her. The yellow rose she held in her lap rolled against the old lady's bag. Milana apologised taking it back again. The wizened woman with skin like creased leather was wrapped in a black crocheted shawl that gave her the appearance of a small fly trapped in a large spider's web. This effect was further enhanced by a huge pair of dark glasses. Milana noticed the bus driver looking again and it made her uncomfortable. 'Do you know the church of *Todos Los Angeles?*' Milana asked the old lady by way of conversation, but the woman did not hear her.

The bus veered right and left again, throwing passengers onto each other and causing bags of shopping to fall and oranges and apples to roll along the bus floor. Milana looked up crossly at the driver. He was looking at her again. She had the distinct impression that these manoeuvres were undertaken for her benefit, to thrill her, regardless of the confusion and discomfiture of his passengers. She was relieved then, when the bus screeched to a halt before the tree-lined avenue behind which she recognised the stone courtyard of the church. She avoided the driver's eyes as she stepped off the bus and turned to reach for her heavy black hold-all, but he had come from behind the wheel and with unexpected gallantry handed it down to her. He returned to his seat and waited while the little old lady negotiated the steps clutching her handbag and was helped off the bus by Milana. Then with a toot of his horn he was off again.

'Flirt,' said the old woman crossly.

'I'm sorry?' said Milana,

'Flirt, that driver. A flirt,' she humphed.

'Yes, I know, he could have got us all killed.'

'Huh?'

'He was going so fast,' said Milana loudly.

'Don't know about that. They all drive like that. You not been around much then?' She lifted her dark lenses.

'What's your name, girl?

'Milana,' and then a little louder, 'Milana.'

'You better get used to them buses if you're from out of town.' She looked at the bag in Milana's hand, 'Come to stay a while?'

'Yes, I've come home.'

'Never mind. I can't hear a thing anyway,' and she started to walk away muttering, 'Pretty girl, face like an angel.' Milana watched her go, dragging her slippered feet across the street in her huge shawl and wondered how often thieving hands had wrenched that handbag or one similar out of those determined fingers, and she smiled at the plucky old woman.

Señora Silvia shuffled home where she informed her daughter and son-in-law, Atilio, that the girl with a face like an angel had come home again. Atilio and his wife looked at each other and rolling their eyes heavenwards nodded and let it pass. Señora Silvia was prone to make bizarre claims and they put it down to advancing dementia.

Wistfully Milana looked over to the old wooden doors of the church. She did not have the courage yet to step inside; instead, passing the orange trees that Atilio tended, she walked towards the graveyard stopping in front of the small plaque that denoted her mother's slot in the wall. She hesitated a moment, gazing at the yellow rose in her hand as if she felt she should leave it there. But there was nowhere to lay the rose, so, touching the plaque she mouthed the words 'I love you, Mum.'

Beyond the shade of the jacaranda tree, a new grave reflected the sunshine. An old and weathered statue of an angel stood on the earth that covered the coffin beneath. Decorative chips of green stone had been scattered on this bare earth for want of grass. The grave was edged in little bricks that had been painted with white gloss to form a gravelly garden six feet long by two feet wide. At regular intervals yellow pansies had been planted between the stones. A woman knelt here, carefully dead-heading the flowers.

'Is that you Doris?'

Doris heard but, as she bent her ear towards the freshly

turned earth of the grave, considered briefly the possibility that she might be encountering the voices of the dead. She turned slowly and gasped with surprise.

'Milana! You've come back.'

Milana stepped up to her and hugged her. 'Is that the angel from your yard?'

Doris nodded proudly. 'It's the right place for it.'

'It's beautiful, so solemn and gracious.'

'Nilda loved my angel. I should have given it to her before, but I gave it to her now and she can see that can't she?' Doris's chin wobbled as she clasped her old and dusty hands over Milana's. 'She asked for you. All the time she asked for you, I... I so hoped...but it was too late.'

'No. Don't think that,' said Milana. She knelt down on the hard earth and placed her rose by the angel, 'Thank you dear Aunt Nilda. I know you're still looking out for us. I know you somehow made Nora send me back that money. Thank you. I'll always pray for you, Aunt Nilda.'

'What money, Milana?' Doris looked bewildered

'Why, my money. Didn't Nilda ever tell you? My mother saved money for us and gave it to Nilda and she kept it in a sugar jar and gave it to me when mother died. On that night we left the shanty, Nora took it from me. Well, she sent it back to me last week, the exact amount. It's not much, but I can make a start, and I left some for Ricci and Juanito. They're doing just fine down south.'

'That was your money? Well, well! Nilda didn't tell no one about that, but the morning she died she called Nora over while we was all there and she said, "You send it back, you hear Nora, every last penny. You send it back to that girl or I'll never rest in peace. You hear me."' Doris laughed, suddenly comprehending, 'Nora looked that frightened. But she paid for this here grave she did.'

'Well, like I said, Nora did send it to me, every last *peso* so I guess she is well and truly more afraid of Nilda dead than she ever was of her alive.' They both laughed and then, together, fell silent and stared at the angel and thought about Nilda lying there six feet under.

'I look after the church now, ever since it re-opened just after you left,' explained Doris standing and stretching her back. 'I do cleaning and Atilio, he helps. He does the graves and keeps the shed and the courtyard tidy and waters the orange trees, but I do the pews and the woodwork and the sweeping and just keep an eye on things. But you don't know Atilio, do you?' She squeezed Milana's hand. Milana just smiled.

'Shall we go and talk in there?' Doris motioned towards the church. 'We can sit down private like. Just you and me.' She patted Milana's hand and looked at her in quiet admiration.

'Can't we go to that lovely tiny chapel instead. The one we saw when Mum was buried. Let's go there. It's more intimate.'

'But you have to see the church, dear. People come miles to see it.'

'Dear Doris, I didn't come to sight-see.'

'But you haven't seen anything till you've seen this,' Doris continued, unable to curb her enthusiasm. 'It's a work of art. I mean real art Milana. Not the rubbish they call art these days. I know what I read in the papers. You've got to see it.'

Milana longed to be alone in that cool interior and feel Santiago there beside her again, but not with Doris.

'Doris, it's you I want to spend a little time with. The church can wait.' Doris relented and with enormous relief, Milana followed her as she led them towards the little chapel. Only then did Milana glance back at the church doors. For her, the essence of Santiago was trapped forever in that church. As a perfume recreates for an instant the presence of the one who has worn it, Milana wanted the walls of the church of *Todos Los Angeles* to bring back the love she craved.

'There was a big clean up in the shantytown, but you knew that.' Doris was saying

'No I didn't.'

'The bus drivers that were caught up in money laundering got rooted out and thanks to *Señora* Lisa's husband, Pablo got put away. He's in Collina jail. Jose's doing time too but he's in the city jail.

'And Iris?' Milana particularly wanted to know about Iris.

Doris shook her head. 'After all that woman said about being in service, she upped and went back to being a live-in maid; said she was lonely and wanted to be part of a family.'

'Where, Doris? Where did she go?'

'We don't know. She's not come back to visit. I expect she will sometime. I did see her at Nilda's funeral. Don't know how she knew, but she was there at the back of the church; standing by the doors with a big handbag and a nice coat. That's what she likes; all them presents of clothes she gets from the *Patrona*. She said she had to get out of this "shit hole". That's what she called it. I reckon *Padre* Pancho here knows where she went.' Doris stopped suddenly and looked serious. 'You know you've got no home don't you. They did tell you about what happened to Letty's place?'

'Yes, they told me.'

'Well I don't know what really happened, Nilda never knew either. The place was torched one night. Just like that. We went there after, to see if we could find anything, but there was nothing, just a load of ash and muck and a few broken bits of stone and glass and stuff and them gold-rimmed teacups that were your mum's, all smashed up. You know you can come and stay with me,' she said with feeling.

'Doris, that's very kind, but I was given the name of some people. They're expecting me,' Milana lied sweetly so as not to hurt Doris's feelings.

'Oh,' said Doris meekly, not daring to insist. 'If you've gotta go, and it's fixed and all. I'd have liked…' she fell silent.

'I'll come and see you when I get myself sorted. I promise.'

'Good. There's only me left now.'

'What about Ana?'

Doris shook her head sadly. 'No. No Ana.'

'But, Ana would never move away.'

'Ana was never the same after Oscar died. Never really came round to it. Not really.'

'But I saw her after Oscar died. She was fine. She was a tower of strength,' Milana insisted.

'Oh Milana. You're too young to understand. Why should

you? The real hurts; we don't wear them on our sleeve see. Them as have real hurts they're down so deep no one can see them. Not even them that know how much they hurt. It's all buried so deep. It's only when you touch them where it hurts they flinch and sometimes they smile to cover it up so as you won't get to know where the hurt is. You just don't go touching them there again; know what I'm getting at?'

Milana was very quiet.

'Ana's been hurt bad before and Oscar going like he did, well it hurt deep. She smiled but nothing could take away the pain see. So she took it away only way she knew how.'

'What did she do, Doris?' Milana spoke the words so quietly that they were barely audible.

'Iris found her. She'd pulled the flex of the light bulb in the ceiling and she'd wound it round her neck. Just like Nora's dad did. She was still warm too.'

'So that's why Iris went back into service. Now I understand.' Milana bent her head so that her tears spilled onto the waxed wooden floor that Doris had polished so beautifully only that morning.

'Atilio doesn't come on Wednesdays,' Doris whispered. 'I'm going to have to lock up the chapel now. There's been a lot of thieving so we're taking no chances.'

They stepped out into the early evening sun.

'There's a wardrobe meeting tonight with the ladies from up town and I'm in charge of the keys.'

Milana smiled, 'Ever busy, Doris. Bless you.' She kissed her on her well-lined cheek. 'Don't mind me. I'll stay; I want to sit and pray a while in the graveyard.'

'You sure?' Doris looked worried.

'Doris, I'm OK.'

'Whenever you want, you come and stay with me, you hear?'

Milana nodded and gazed after Doris as she walked down the road and past the kiosk where Atilio bought his lottery ticket every Friday.

Milana turned back across the courtyard and walked to the

rear of the church. There by the shed, where Santiago had stored his pigments and taught her how to mix paints, Milana sat under the jacaranda tree. All around her there was a carpet of rich blue fallen blossoms. Leaning down she gathered up a handful of flowers and felt their soft wax-like petals.

'This is my favourite tree, first it is ablaze with blue and then the blue drips gently off it until it forms a pool all around it.' It was something Santiago had said, and she had laughed and replied, 'Not everything is about paint Santiago.' Now she sat remembering how he had grabbed her hand and pulled her down and said, 'Yes it is,' and they had stayed like that, she lying across his lap, he looking down at her. Then with the tips of his fingers, so soft and gentle he had touched her hair, her face, her lips and the tips of her eyelashes and he had ruffled her eyebrows and she had laughed again. He had placed one hand over her hand as it lay on the ground beside her, so gently that only his fingertips touched hers and she had watched him all the while, his look concentrated and slightly puzzled, the powerful muscles of his tanned arms visible where the white shirt was rolled up to his elbows. In the silence of this strange embrace she had felt the quickening of her pulse. He had laced his fingers through hers and pressed so hard that his strong hand seemed to want to crush her tiny one in his. His eyes had held hers, dark and intense, their stunning blue shaded by a softer brown. The stillness had scintillated with the tension between them. She had grown serious under his quizzical gaze. He had lifted her then, his arm beneath her shoulders, raising her up towards him, his face bent over hers so that his thick, beautiful hair touched her skin and she breathed the fresh smell of limes.

She'd closed her eyes, unable to suppress in any other way the longing to close the gap between them. Her whole body was so powerfully magnetised by him that it was as if he were drawing desire, like threads of electricity irresistibly through her. She had opened her eyes, gasping at the new, overwhelming sensation. His mouth was so close to hers that she shook in anticipation of what she longed for, sensing through her skin the electricity that rippled through him too. She had felt the intake of his breath and then the desperation of feeling herself suddenly released. He had stood up and walked away then, as he often did, silent and elusive, never imagining that he was leaving her breathless and confused, locked in a spell of yearning from which she thought she would never recover. Even now the memory of him hit her in the solar plexus and left her winded.

For a long time Milana stayed under the jacaranda tree. Gradually the shadows lengthened and it grew colder. The breeze against her suntanned skin made her shiver. She looked around her as if to ensure that there were no prying eyes. Then, taking her bag, she stepped across the graves and came to the high bank where the land sloped down to the river. Below her was the gate through which Santiago had first brought her to find Ricci and Juanito sleeping beneath the altar of the little chapel. Throwing a final look back over her shoulder to where the graveyard stretched towards the church, she edged carefully down the bank and through the gate to the river's edge. The wind blew against the flimsy material of her dress. It circled her face, her bare arms and legs, and she shivered again, not because of the cold but because of what she was about to do.

Chapter Five

Old Whitebeard's shack could have been removed, torched like her own home, ransacked and left open to the elements, yet here it was, apparently undisturbed over the years. The chain and padlock were in place exactly as they had been on the night they had all picnicked here over three years ago with Santiago. She had come expecting to find it.

Milana wrapped her fingers around the smooth cold metal of the chain cutter she had taken from *Señora* Lucy's tool shed, leaving in its place an envelope with money and an apology. She pulled the heavy instrument from where it lay at the bottom of her bag and, lifting the cutter to the now dulled chain, applied all her strength. As she did so the chain slipped over itself and fell like a loose arm hanging down from the padlock which was attached to the metal hook of the door. As Milana moved the cutter the rest of the chain fell, like some uncoiling snake, at her feet. It was then that she noticed that the padlock hung unlocked.

Tentatively, she pulled open the makeshift wooden door until she stood facing the space that had been Alfonso Carrera's home for twenty years. It was hot and stuffy and smelt of liquor. A shaft of evening sun poured into the small space through a single sheet of acrylic that had been fitted into a wood frame. It created a hazy mist of light in which dancing particles glittered like magic dust. Santiago had said the place was padlocked after the old man's death and yet as she stood in the doorway, looking in, she knew immediately that Santiago had been here. On one wall hung her canvas of Atilio, on another a sketch of the graves and the jacaranda tree. The far wall had been used to attach a rough wooden work surface and in one corner there were pencils and paintbrushes sticking out of an old jar. Possibly Santiago had stayed here, but the boy on which her eyes came to rest, stretched out on the narrow metal bed that took up exactly half of the living space, was not Santiago.

Milana remained in the doorway, letting the cool air circulate through the muggy interior. She waited for the boy to stir or open his eyes. She took a step inside and peered at him. Although she guessed he must be at least eighteen, the way his short blond hair curled about his face gave him a much younger look. His features, what she could see of them, were soft but well formed and the blond bristles on his chin showed that he had not shaved for some days. His head lay over the side of the bed and one arm hung down so that his hand trailed the ground. A shotgun lay on the floor just out of reach of the boy's sleeping fingers. An empty bottle nestled in the crook of his other arm. She lifted the bottle out from its warm embrace and smelt it. The label read 'Malt Whisky' and 'Special Reserve'. It was not the sort of whisky bottle she had ever seen in the bar in Panguipulli.

Milana looked the boy over. His old rugby shirt, his designer jeans, the leather belt, the Reebok trainers, all proclaimed his moneyed background. His blondness was typical of upper-class kids, the *gente linda* as they were called, 'the beautiful people'. Milana guessed he would not wake from his drunken sleep for hours. She crept past him. There was a small cupboard attached to the wall above the work surface. She found a mug, sugar and coffee, an unopened box of long-life milk, matches and a small battery-operated boil in the cup boiler. She had not seen one of these before and noticing it said 'made in Germany' she took it down, eventually guessing from her limited knowledge of TV, what it was for. Milana put it back. She picked up the carton of long-life milk and looked at the sell by date. Sometime last winter he must have been here. Who else would have put up her half-finished canvas of Atilio or the sketch of the jacaranda tree?

Milana noticed a blanket which had been pushed to the floor. She picked it up. It was made of finest alpaca wool, a far cry from the rough, grey blankets that had kept her warm for years. She took the blanket outside and, sitting down on it, she leant back against the warm wood of the shack wall and let the rays of the sinking sun play on her face. As the breeze lifted again, she took a thin bar of chocolate and some bread out of her bag and made a chocolate sandwich. She ate it wading barefoot in the river watching the water eddy around her feet. Finally, as evening drew itself across the sky in shades of mauve and lilac, she lodged a boulder against the open shack door so no wind might blow it shut in the night, and unrolled a sleeping bag. She climbed inside it and felt the soft nylon cling to her thin figure like a cocoon. Folding her only cardigan into a makeshift pillow, she fell asleep across the open entrance of the shack.

Milana woke abruptly feeling, at once, the stiffness of her joints. The ground was hard beneath her and the cold of the night still lingered in her bones. Someone was touching her hair. The sun dazzled her eyes. She put her arm up to shade her face. Sleep had wiped away all sense of place. She grappled to comprehend where she was and what she was doing lying in the warming sun. Like a telescope bringing the distance into focus her mind unfolded the events of yesterday and by the time her eyes rested fully on the boy that crouched beside her she knew exactly where she was.

'I'm sorry,' said the boy, his pale eyes studiously taking her in. 'I couldn't see your face so I tried to move your hair off it and I suppose I woke you up.'

Milana sat up. 'Are you OK?' she asked by way of answer.

'Me, yes, I'm fine,' he said defensively. 'I thought no one used this old shack...' he trailed off awkwardly. Milana arranged her dress around her and unzipped the sleeping bag.

'I've been away,' she said standing up and shaking the sleeping bag briskly before rolling it up.

'Oh. I knew the old guy died, I thought... I'm sorry... are there more of you?' he asked nervously, looking around suddenly.

'Don't be silly, there's just me,' she said and laughed. 'I didn't live here, but I might from now on, if you don't mind. I think you probably have a perfectly nice home to go back to.'

The boy sat back thoughtfully taking in the vision of loveliness before him. Milana shot him a glance as she pushed the sleeping bag back into its nylon holder. Her poise and self-confidence intimidated him but at the same time it sent a flutter of excitement like adrenalin coursing through him.

'Don't *you*?' he asked, catching her look and the brilliance of her eyes.

'Don't I what?

'Have a home too?'

She straightened and felt the freshness of the air fill her lungs with a giddy sense of deliverance.

'No, not really.' Suddenly overcome by the exhilaration of total liberty she stretched out her arms as though they were the wings that had brought her this new found freedom and turned round in a circle, taking in the river and the mountains and the hills under the blue summer sky.

'This is my home, if you don't mind vacating.' She stopped right in front of him a little breathless. He found his heart beating a little faster.

'My life is a clean sheet from today,' she declared, 'and I'm going to start drawing my future on it right now. And you,' she added with sudden warmth, 'are the first line of it.'

'How's that work?' He looked bemused as though it had never occurred to him that he could figure in anything.

'Because you are the first person I saw on the first day of my future. That's why.'

He gazed entranced at her green sparkling eyes and her hair that in the sunlight cascaded in golden waves over her shoulders, lifting with the breeze as she turned; the same breeze that pressed her dress against the slender, graceful contours of her figure.

'Have you been here all night?' he enquired sheepishly, drinking in her presence, her energy, and how the rays played over her skin.

'Yes. Looks like you've been here a while too.' He didn't answer but looked away awkwardly.

'Hey, I don't give a stuff who you are or what you've done. I've been around, and you don't look like danger to me so relax, I'm just settling in here and when you're ready you can move on and leave me to it, if you don't mind.'

'You mean you don't mind if I stick around for a bit?' he ventured shyly.

She shrugged, 'You're free to come and go as you please, seeing as you ask so politely.' And a playful smile spread over her face emboldening him.

'Look,' he exclaimed, suddenly grabbed by an idea, 'if I go to the kiosk up that road and buy us something for breakfast, will you still be here when I get back?'

'Me? Yes. I'm not going anywhere. I told you I've come home.' She noticed how he instinctively checked the back pocket of his jeans.

'It's OK, I haven't stolen it.'

'What?'

'Your wallet, what else?'

'But I didn't mean–'

'It's OK. We're strangers,' she said dismissively, 'but I'll be here, if you hurry.'

'Yes, yes, right.' Her face was so gentle and beguiling that his eyes remained riveted, his spirit lifted by her loveliness. 'I'll be back,' he called, looking back at her as he half ran, half stumbled over the stones and boulders in his path. At the top of the bank he stopped to look back again as though he feared the apparition might have dissolved into the sunlight. He waved back rather too eagerly.

Milana smiled to herself as she brushed her hair and changed her crumpled dress for a fresh one from her bag. It was sky blue, her favourite of the two. Like her yellow dress and her red cardigan, it had been given to her by a girl in one of the big summer houses that *Señora* Lucy took care of on Lake Panguipulli. The simple cotton dresses were the loveliest things she had ever owned and these two and her jeans were all that she had brought with her, apart from the canvas shoes on her feet. She rinsed the yellow dress in the river and draped it over a large boulder to dry out its creases in the sun before turning back to the shack to take another look inside.

The bed had been smoothed down and there was no sign of the shotgun she had seen last night. Intrigued she searched for it, finally locating it lodged down the far side of the bed. The empty whisky bottle had been placed neatly in a corner. Stepping back outside into the bright morning sunshine, she lay down on the blanket and closed her eyes until she heard the boy scrambling back over the rocks. Soon he was breathlessly depositing his purchases like so many offerings on the blanket; a few oranges and pears and grapes, some bread, a carton of milk and *quesillo*, freshly made that morning.

'There wasn't much to choose from I'm afraid.'

'This is a feast,' sighed Milana, sitting up, remembering another feast in this same place and how suspicious she had been. 'Thank you.'

He sat down opposite her on the blanket.

'I don't know your name,' he smiled.

'Mi... Malala,' a pang of conscience striking her as she changed the 'm' into the first name that came into her head, as if by reinventing herself for him she was reaffirming her autonomy over her new life.

'Malala, that's nice. I'm Juan Carlos Miranda. My friends call me JC.' He held out his hand. She laughed, because it was a world away from her experience where people did not shake hands or present themselves with surnames, and threw him an orange.

Milana opened her bag and unwrapped a knife, a fork and a spoon.

'I came prepared,' she said, passing him the knife as he wrestled with the orange peel. JC dissected the skin of the orange in four parts before deftly peeling it back and offering her the fruit.

'I've never seen anyone peel an orange like that,' she said. 'Thanks.'

While he carved up his own orange his face grew more serious.

'Did you see me last night, then?'

'Yes.'

'Weren't you afraid?'

'Of you?'

He glanced up, sensing she was teasing him.

'I mean of this guy, just lying there.'

'Drunk, with a shotgun,' affirmed Milana.

JC sighed and stopped peeling the orange.

'I thought you might not have seen that. How did you know I was drunk?'

'Because you were cradling an empty bottle of your father's whisky for starters.'

'My father's whisky?' he looked surprised.

'Well,' said Milana sitting very still, 'if I was going to get myself drunk in order to shoot myself, I don't think I'd go out and buy the best whisky. I'd be more likely to steal it but you don't look like you could steal to save your life. I reckon you took it from your father.' Her eyes met his gently, allowing him the time he needed to build a bridge of trust.

'Then you know everything?'

'I know nothing, Juan Carlos. Nothing at all about what really matters.'

'What's that?'

'Why you would want to die?'

'Die?'

'Or did you bring the gun to shoot some fish, or maybe strangers?'

Milana watched emotion constrict his breathing and conflicting feelings tear through him. For a moment he stared down at the orange, confused and finally he pulled himself up and stood staring towards the river, his hands in his pockets, his face tense, biting the inside of his lip. Then drawn by the eyes that watched him he looked back at her. She gave him a little shrug and made a sweetly helpless gesture with her hands as if to say 'Oh well, there it is.' He exhaled a sort of hopeless sigh and she noticed his fists were balled up in his pockets.

'It was so stupid,' he conceded awkwardly. After a moment's hesitation he added, 'I wish there had been no witnesses to it.'

'I'm not much of a witness,' retorted Milana. 'You'll never see me again and you can forget this ever happened.'

'No,' he said after giving it some thought. She offered him a segment of orange. He took it slowly, looked at it and shook his head as though it were communicating with him.

'I can never forget. Like the leprechauns who are indebted forever and a day to whoever saves their life,' he shot her a shy look. 'If I hadn't fallen asleep blind drunk like the fucking loser I am, I'd have pulled the trigger.' He threw the orange segment as far as he could and watched it land in the river.

'That was a perfectly good piece of orange,' whispered Milana. He glanced back at her, 'Pity,' she said.

'Why did you leave the door open?' he asked staring at her intently.

'I don't know,' she said simply.

He crouched down beside her.

'I woke up, in the night,' he said quietly, holding her gaze now with a kind of manic vehemence. 'I grabbed that gun and thought, *Do it now.*' His anxious look seemed to want to communicate something far more intense than mere words could encompass.

'It was like the gun was my only certainty in this bitch of a life. I put my finger on the trigger and I thought, *Oh God, I really am going to do it now,* and then I saw the open door and there was this bundle there. My reprieve, that's what you were. If the door hadn't been open,' he shook his head at the thought, 'I might not be here now.'

'I don't know why I did that, why I left the door lodged open,' she breathed thinking of how careless she had been of the destiny weighing on that otherwise insignificant decision.

'You see,' he went on compelled by the need to communicate, 'I got up and walked over and saw your arm and your hand in the moonlight, so thin and delicate and your hair... I thought I was dreaming.' His ears suddenly burned. He lowered his eyes and stopped. Milana reached out and touched

210

his hand with the tips of her cool fingers and gently whispered, 'Hey it's OK.'

'It's just that suddenly, weirdly, I was terrified of wanting to die... I saw you and I saw the gun in my hand and I was so scared it might go off. I lay on my bed wishing I hadn't got the gun, and then I fell asleep till the morning. So, technically, on the first day of your new life, you saved mine.' He echoed her earlier helpless gesture.

'Wow! That's the greatest thing I've ever done and I was asleep,' laughed Milana but her eyes were full of concern.

JC grinned.

'Last night I thought I'd never smile again.'

'Moments pass,' she said gazing at the water. 'We should never react on the spur of the moment. Life's like this river, it's always moving on, the worst moments move on with it and so do the best.' She turned back to him. 'Why are you a "fucking loser"?' He looked taken aback by the question.

'Your words not mine,' she shrugged, 'they're kind of harsh.'

He scrutinized her, testing that tenuous bridge of newly laid trust.

'Don't you think some things are best kept to oneself?'

Milana shrugged again.

'Where do you come from?' he asked her.

She nodded in the direction of the shantytown. 'I used to live there. I know this river like the back of my hand. It's home see.' She paused, thinking, 'I guess guys like you come here because it's a wasteland.'

'What guys come here?'

'You. Old Whitebeard. Just blokes.'

'Whitebeard? Oh, you mean the old guy. Yeah, he was a sad case.' JC brought his knees up resting his chin on them and stared at the swirling waters.

'So why are you a loser?' she pressed him. His gentle eyes met hers and her heart went out to him, he seemed so young and guileless. He stood up and shoved his balled fists in his pocket again and looking at the ground he toyed at a loose stone with his foot. 'So tell me. I saved your life. Remember!'

'Why do you care? Am I the first loser you've met?'

'What have you lost?'

'What have I lost?!' he exclaimed. 'OK.' He laughed, 'That's clever but it's…'

'Just think, and then tell me.' She lay on her stomach eating a pear.

'You're something else,' he kicked the stone into the river.

She felt his eyes on her but she resisted the temptation to speak as he paced around her and then wandered off down the riverbank. She laid her face sideways on the soft wool of the blanket and watched the tiny blades of grass that grew between the stones, dance in the breeze.

'OK,' he said arriving back suddenly and sitting down beside her, 'but tell me something. How come you're so smart?'

'Smart?' She looked surprised.

'So clever, observant. How come you understand people like you do.'

'Do I?'

'Yes, yes you do,' he affirmed tensely.

'I guess, I just read a lot. I get to know people and their feelings in books, you know, like why they do the weird stuff they do. We think people are weird until we know what motivates them, then we understand. Soon as you understand you can't think stuff weird because that would make you odd for understanding it, see?' She grinned to herself without looking up, wondering how long before his restlessness would calm down and he would open up to her as she knew he longed to.

'So, I'm just like another person in a book to you?'

'I don't know what you are to me. You haven't told me anything much yet.'

'What do you want to know?'

'Your story. Like it was your story in a book.'

'Don't some stories suck, so you don't want to read them?'

'Stories never suck if they're true.' She gave him an easy uncomplicated smile.

JC got up again and walked to the water's edge. He cupped

his hands together and splashed water on his face and hair, combing it back with his fingers so that it trickled cold down his neck. A memory flashed through Milana's mind and caught in a missed heartbeat. He came and sat cross-legged beside her. His face still had the slight roundness and softness of childhood, rather than the angular strength of a man. It was a face as yet unlined with experience or distress, it gave nothing away, not a whisper of the anguish that could have made him bring a shotgun to this place to kill himself. *Old people have their lives and their sins etched into the lines of their skin, but the young can hide what tortures them*, thought Milana.

'Where shall I start?'

Milana cocked her head and looked at him.

'OK, think of your life like a pair of really cool trainers, designer label, expensive, the best. You're just happy to be wearing them and suddenly they start to hurt, maybe it's just an ache, or maybe a pinch, but something is sore. Start there, the point where they first rubbed but you carried on wearing them, 'cos let's face it they were the only ones you got.'

JC laughed, then he grew serious and thoughtful and stared dumbly into the middle distance. All the while Milana waited patiently for him to figure it out in his mind.

'OK, here's the riddle,' he said at last. 'I did OK at school. I came top of my class then I came top of my school, then I went to university and got brilliant grades in my first term. You'd think my dad would have been happy but my dad...' he shook his head, 'I was invisible to him. All he cared about was whether I made it to the football team or the rugby team. Whatever else I did, however good, it wasn't good enough for him. To him I was just this loser kid.' He met Milana's quiet scrutiny; 'Where did I fuck up?'

'That's it?'

'Yeah, pretty much.'

JC ventured nothing further.

'That's it? That's why you were going to shoot yourself?'

'Putting it into words makes it sound pathetic.'

He looked down a little awkwardly.

'Gay,' he muttered.

'Gay?'

'My dad thinks I'm gay and to him being gay is like having leprosy.'

'So? Are you gay?'

'Of course I'm not gay,' he exclaimed crossly.

'Well what's the problem then?'

'My dad thinks I'm this fucking loser gay guy.' The blood rushed suddenly to his face and he stopped. 'You don't get it either.' He turned away.

'Then explain it to me?'

'Explain? Isn't it obvious?'

'Nothing's obvious except in your own mind. Explain it to me,' Milana insisted.

'What's the point? What difference will it make?'

'What have you got to lose?'

'My dignity.' He lowered his eyes then raised them to meet her gaze. 'OK, that went last night,' he conceded.

'Tell me about your dad,' she coaxed. 'I've got all day.' Her sympathy sent a tremor through his heart.

'You must think I'm so weak and contemptible.'

'I'm not your dad.'

JC laughed bitterly.

'Does it matter so much what he thinks?'

Looking into her bright green eyes none of it seemed to matter, except that he might have never got to live today but for an accident of circumstance. The anger against his father rose suddenly like bile.

'When I was a kid and I cried he'd shout, "Are you gay or what?" Then when I didn't get on the rugby team but got selected for the school musical instead he said, "Don't you turn gay on me." When I said I wanted to learn the piano he shouted at my mother, "What the hell is wrong with this kid, why's he so different from the rest? Why's he want to fiddle about with the piano. You deal with him!" Then one awful day he got me in the car and said, "Right, I'm going to wise you up, my boy," and,' JC hesitated, embarrassed, 'he drove me to a whore house.'

Milana let her unwavering gaze shepherd him on, 'He walked in there like he owned the place and said to the Madame, "Make a man out of this kid",' JC gave a hollow laugh, 'It makes me cringe just to remember it. He put all this money on the counter. I still remember thinking, wow! He'd spend that on making me a man. I got taken up to a room by this big woman only she turned me off so much, with her painted face and musky smell, that there was nothing in the world that could get me to function. So they got another one in and then another, these half naked women – all I could think of was the sleazy men they'd just been with. I wanted to disappear! I dreaded them and their advances. I wanted to cry but even my tears had dried up. Maybe that meant I was gay, what did I know anymore. I just remember him coming to pick me up and the Madame saying, "*Señor* there's nothing we can do for him." My father wouldn't speak to me.'

'Weren't you revolted?'

'With myself or with the women?'

'By your dad! Who else! Wow, you cut him a lot of slack don't you? Who wants a fat tart for his first date. Major turn off!'

JC paused, 'He's just my dad. I guess he thought he was doing me a favour?'

'I'd say he was just another messed-up git, an abuser, like I've known a few.'

'Really?' His keen eyes rested on her with sudden interest.

'Go on. What did he do after that?'

Caught between his fears and his longing to keep Milana just where she was, JC went on, surrendering to the thrill of confiding.

'Well, there was this one time he threw my best friend out of the house because he saw him hug me at the door. I'd just got the top grades in the school and this friend came over to congratulate me. He knew how hard I'd worked. When I opened the door he gave me this bear-like hug that lifted me right off the floor, and dad was passing and shouted, "What the blazes do you two think you're doing? Get out, the two of you!" It was like Whoa! Overreaction or what? He never heard about my grades and I was so angry I couldn't tell him. Never did. He was so obsessed with his fear of me being gay, no one could believe how he behaved but they thought there must be something in it. Even my sisters came up to me all confidential saying "It's OK you can tell us, we'll stand up for you". My mum, she had these screaming matches with him defending me. I thought they'd bust up because of me.' JC turned to Milana, 'Have you heard enough?'

'No, I want to hear more,' she declared firmly.

'It feels good to tell you.' He smiled at her a little perplexed.

'This year I started university here. I don't know who told them but some guys there found out about my father and how homophobic he was and they all thought it was very funny. For my initiation they got me drunk and sent my father pictures of me with a feather boa round my neck and some guy draped over me. He went apoplectic with the university, my mother, everyone. In the end he directed his anger against me. He threw me out. Said he didn't want to set eyes on me. Mum was pretty cut up seeing as every kid they know at uni lives at home. I tried to tell him it was all a set up, but he just threw the photos at me, yelling at me to take my fucking ruined reputation with me.'

Milana was very quiet.

'Hey?'

'What?' she met his look.

'I don't know,' he murmered. 'Say something. I feel so fucking pathetic.' His face creased apologetically into an ingenuous smile.

'Don't. You're not.'

He shrugged. 'Anyway, who cares? Right?'

'I do,' affirmed Milana without hesitation. 'I think your dad's gay.'

'What?'

'Makes sense. He's paranoid about you because really it's him.'

'Gees, Malala. He's about as straight as they come.'

'You seen the uptown tarts? They hang around smart residential streets. Ever looked closely? They're tall, great legs and stunning. They're all men. I asked Iris, she was a friend of my mum's. She knows stuff like that. "They're there for all them married blokes." That's what she said. Then I figured it out.'

'Gees!' You can't just say stuff like that.'

'Why not? Life's complicated. Maybe he's one of those guys with no conscience I read about. Sociopaths, that's it! Born without a shred of conscience. They cover it up with charm and bluff but you can tell cos they don't give a toss about anyone but themselves. Anyway, what happened next.?' JC looked even more taken aback.

'It just gets more pathetic.' He sighed.

It was something in her look that connected to him and seemed to be steering him through his own life story. He realised her presence was filling his heart, expelling grief, and he experienced an inexplicable feeling of security as he sat there in the midday sun pouring out his heart to this random girl.

'I moved into a flat subsidised by my mum. Dad didn't object he just didn't want me around. Then one day I got off with a girl at a party. I guess I just felt sorry for her, like I felt sorry for myself, and...' he broke off. He covered his face with his hands in part to give himself a moment to adjust to the strange emotions that were overwhelming him. He felt Milana's touch on his arm. 'Go on,' she encouraged, her warm discerning gaze melting into him. Milana let go of his arm, leaving the imprint of her kindness.

'We ended up sleeping together. She was just a druggie hanging with pushers. I should have known better. No wonder she looked lost, and dumb as I am I was faintly attracted to her. We went back to my flat. I guess I was past caring. Think what my father would have said about that too,' he gave an empty laugh. 'I suppose she told her friends about me. They were quick to ferret out that my dad had money.' He paused, struck suddenly by his own naivety, and lowered his eyes.

'Don't worry,' said Milana, quick as a flash to take in the sudden thought that had occurred to him, and he could hear the all-forgiving merriment in her tone, 'I don't have to finance a drug habit. I don't need his money! I won't be blackmailing you.'

He bit his lip, still unable to meet her eye.

'Next thing I know two punks turn up at the flat asking for money. I tried to shut the door but they stuck their foot in and shoved a photo in my face of me handing money over to some random beggar boy. I recognised the kid. He'd been following me about, pestering me for money. I'd wanted to tell the kid to get lost, but I tried to be nice and give him some coins to get rid of him. More fool me! The guys told me that if I didn't get the money off my dad, they'd send the photos to him and tell him I'd done it with the kid for money. I told them no one would believe them. "Really? Think about it," they sneered. "We'll be back," they said and walked off laughing. The more I thought about it, the more I realised what they meant. That's when I flipped and right now that's where I am.'

He looked up at Milana. 'The minute I leave here, those guys will find me and they'll tell my father their lies and…well, if it's not them, it'll be something or someone else, it just won't go away. I'm so fucked, I might as well be dead. I think my dad would be thrilled if I copped it. I really do.' The sadness returned, all the more powerful for the momentary reprieve he had felt.

Milana averted her eyes feeling he needed space to realign his feelings. After a while JC got up and walked to the water's edge. From a safe distance he turned and looked back to where she sat.

'You know, for a moment there I was free of it all; there was just you, and you talked of the first day of a new life. My God, I envy you.' He looked away again and bent his head.

'It's not so bad,' said Milana.

'Oh don't worry, I won't cry, my dad dried up my tears years ago.'

'You've just talked yourself into being a victim.'

'But I am a victim. That's just it.'

She got up then and moved over to him and turned him abruptly towards her. She put her hands on his shoulders so he could feel the firm grip of her slender fingers and looked into his eyes.

'Your dad's done this to you. You were just a kid with good grades who liked piano. He's a bully. A coward who can't love even himself. I've given this a lot of thought in my life, believe me. Tell him to cut it out. Tell him you're proud of who you are. Believe in yourself and, in the end he will too. We can't always rely on our folks to give us self-belief 'cos, sometimes they're too messed up and don't have any self-belief themselves and we have to do it for ourselves. And that story those scumbags are threatening you with about you doing it with some beggar kid, it's just a load of horseshit, that's what they'd say in the shantytown. Laugh at them, and if you can't do that, just tell them you'll get the cops onto them and ask them who they think the police will suck up to, them or a member of the Miranda family? That's your surname isn't it?'

She looked him squarely in the eye. Even though he dropped his gaze to the ground, her fiery strength galvanised his heart. Her touch, on the other hand was startling and unsettling.

'It's not that simple.'

'Make it simple. Lose the fear, that's what gives them their clout.'

'But I *am* afraid.'

She let go and with a momentary pang of distress he watched her arms fall by her sides.

'What of?'

'I don't know. Everything.'

'Can I tell you something only please don't be cross with me?'

JC looked back at her, 'I'll try, but you kind of get under my skin. You say some pretty tough stuff.'

She sat down a few steps away, not realising how much he craved her closeness again.

'Look, I'm hearing your story, like I was reading a book, right? And it makes me hate your dad. I think to myself, why do I hate his stupid dad? I've never even met him and then I get what I hate about him. He's cheated you. He never loved you. All the while you're imagining you've lost his love because you did something wrong and that's what's killing you to the point

219

you'd just as well shoot yourself, when really he's never loved you. You didn't destroy anything, he did. That's why he's so mad at everyone. If he had loved you, really, you wouldn't want to die, you'd want to win him back. But there's nothing to win back, cos you never had it in the first place. See? That's why you're so confused.'

'So that's meant to make me feel a whole lot better,' he said sarcastically.

She beamed at him in return.

'Yeah. Soon as you figure out he never loved you in the first place you'll be free of all his baggage. He's just another messed up git who's never lived up to his own expectations and you're his scapegoat. See, Juan Carlos. You can be the strong one and he turns out to be the weak one. Maybe if you cut the crap he's shifting onto you, he'll have a chance to face himself and grow into the man he's wanting you to be. Maybe you can help him, but you gotta be independent, trust yourself, believe in yourself, don't wait for him to do it first, he can't. We're only human you know, and we're all of us pretty fucked up. You've got to forgive and move on.'

'How the heck do you work these things out?'

'Because you have to figure things out to be free.' She sighed, 'People are always out to shovel their shit on you. You've got to learn not to fall for their bait. If fish could figure that out you'd never be able to catch them.' Milana lay back down on the blanket, 'We get caught by our weaknesses,' she murmured thoughtfully.

JC came and lay beside her, not too close but close enough that the cotton of her dress touched his jeans. He propped himself up on his elbow.

'You must have known a lot of tossers in your life, to have figured all this out.'

'Most people are just thinking about themselves, even when they're looking like they're interested in you, they're just trying to figure their own shit out.'

'Is that really what you think.'

'I don't know. But I read stuff and I can tell you that's what loads of people feel. They think life's unfair, they feel empty and then they have sex. Like you did. Then they try to make out that because they still feel empty, there's no love, no God, and nothing's beautiful anymore and they don't search cos they don't think there's anything worth finding and they just vegitate; or do drink or drugs or more sex. I think life's what you believe it is. It's really that simple. You gotta make it what you want.'

They lay side by side in silence for a while looking up at the uninterrupted blue.

'Is this as unusual for you as it is for me?' he asked suddenly.

'The two people getting to know each other bit, or lying on the ground looking at the sky?' she asked facetiously. He wanted to point out that he didn't actually know anything about her but he stopped himself. She had been more generous to him than anyone. She had listened and spoken her mind freely and with disconcertingly brutal honesty. He glanced at her lying there with her eyes closed, her hair spread like sunshine about her.

'I know what you mean,' she added more thoughtfully, sensing his quiet scrutiny. 'When you go off track, things get more interesting.'

'Malala, are you really going to stay here, in this shack?'

'Yes.'

'Come home with me. I wouldn't ask anything of you,' he said quickly.

The rushing river filled their silence. Then he tried again, 'You can't stay here alone, anything might happen to you. I've got a good apartment. It's got two bedrooms. You'd be safe there, and independent. I won't disturb you.'

She turned on her side to face him. Her green eyes held his and he felt them boring right into him so that even the hard tiny pupils seemed to pin him down for scrutiny.

'Did you really just say that?' she said at last, her tone almost accusatory, 'You realise you know nothing about me.'

'I know you're wise and kind and very clever.'

'You shouldn't trust so quickly. You'll get yourself into shitloads of trouble.' He felt the blood rush to his face, but he knew from experience it was less obvious to others than he imagined, so he remained coolly quiet and waited for the heat to subside.

'But you wanted me to trust you, didn't you?'

She caught his eye and smiled. Then after appearing to give it some thought she said, 'I can't go home with you. There's stuff I've got to do. There's stuff that you have to do as well,' she reminded him. He looked at her, downcast as a child who on finding a stray kitten is told he can't take it home as a pet.

Chapter Six

Milana made her way up the narrow flight of stairs that smelt of wood polish and disinfectant. She had pulled her hair back off her face and twirled it up into a bun, she had then carefully applied some eyeliner and lipstick; priests, she had observed, never looked too closely at women if they wore lots of make-up. Milana felt satisfied that, after three years, Father Pancho would not recognise her. The last thing she wanted was to be sent back south by the well-meaning parish priest.

The door opened and Father Pancho looked round. Warm brown eyes shone out of the deep lined creases of his face. He peered at the woman in front of him.

'Ah yes, you have come for confession?'

His kind eyes reminded Milana of Father Juan back in Panguipulli.

'No, Father. I'm not here for confession. I'm a cousin of Iris Cardenas,' it was only a small white lie, 'I'm up from the south and I was hoping you might tell me where I could find her.'

'Ah, yes,' he sighed, showing no trace of recognition. 'Come in, come in.'

He waved Milana into his small office, littered with papers. Blankets for the poor lay heaped in one corner. Boxes of goods waiting for distribution were piled precariously against another wall. A bread basket full of rosaries balanced on an assortment of papers on his desk, next to a pile of baby clothes. Milana sat on the edge of a chair and tried to jog his memory:

'Iris was the one that discovered the suicide of her friend Ana Rosas in the San Damian shantytown. It shook her up and she needed to get away after that.'

'Ah yes, yes, what a terrible business. Yes, of course, of course, Iris Cardenas, tall... yes.'

'Father, could you give me her new address?'

His slim, boney fingers travelled over his papers lifting one here and there. Finding an address book he peered inside, humming gently to himself. Finally he pursed his lips and said thoughtfully, 'She went to work with...let me see.... Menendes, I think it was, or...Velasco one or t'other.' He appeared to examine Milana again in this new light.

'Are you family?' he smiled kindly, revealing a set of neat false teeth.

'Yes, I have some news for her.'

'Ahh,' he nodded briefly and picked up the telephone. Milana noticed, as his fingers curled around the receiver, how clean and manicured his nails were. He spoke to his secretary. It took a while to spell out the surname several times. Finally, after what seemed an interminable wait, the door opened and a small, well dressed woman came in with an address. 'Ah here we are. Now let me see.' He perched his glasses on the end of his nose and examined the writing on the card in front of him. 'Jorge Velasco, Los Nogales 1253, La Rayan, Phone number 230460.'

'Thank you, Father,' said Milana, noting down the address on a scruffy bit of paper. 'I'm very grateful,' she added rising quickly so as to prolong the interview no further.

From where he sat, Father Pancho proffered an ancient hand. Milana let his cold, long fingers gently encircle her own, then, hesitating only for a moment, she turned and left the room.

Once outside his office she stopped at the top of the stairs and looked back, not wanting to leave, yet knowing the moment had passed. Her heart raced with indecision. Father Pancho would know the whereabouts of the boy who had won the National Arts Prize for painting the interior of his beloved church, but Milana hadn't dared mention Santiago for fear that it might draw her into a conversation from which it would be difficult to extricate herself.

'Excuse me dear,' came a voice just beside her. Milana started. From the threshold of her little office the elderly secretary eyed her with concern. 'Are you alright, dear?' Unable to explain herself Milana ran down the stairs and out of the building.

She found a telephone booth and dialled the number she had written down and got a continuous tone. It was either incorrect or Father Pancho had confused one of the digits. She tried dialling 5 instead of 6 but they didn't know any Iris there. She tried replacing the 3 with an 8, but that didn't work either. Dejectedly, she replaced the handset and walked back to the river.

The excitement that had fired her when she left Panguipulli was draining away. Her sense of purpose seemed to have ebbed out of her. The last ten days she had been painfully aware of her own solitude, and staring at the river and the wasteland she realised there was no pre-determined path for her to follow anymore. The life she had left behind here was all but erased. She had been dreaming something might be waiting for her in this place that had held so much magic for her, but the dreams were insubstantial. She must forge her own way. Finding Iris would have been a start. She wanted to find her mother's birthplace, to retrace her life in order to place herself in the context she had always felt was missing. But life suddenly weighed heavy on her and she felt more and more unequal to the task. Alone under the great open skies with the Andes mountains towering on the horizon and the river running its immutable course to the sea, she realised how inconsequential she was and how vulnerable. If it were not for JC she could die here and no one would be the wiser.

Milana sat on the bank watching the sunlight dancing over the water that twisted over rocks and boulders like a moving mass of shimmering snakes.

'Hi!' called JC as he approached and sat down beside her. She wasn't surprised to see him, he had come nearly every day since they met.

The morning after their first encounter Milana had seen him standing ankle deep in the river smoking as she approached the shack from the road.

'Where've you been?' he had asked rather too proprietarily for her liking.

'What's it to you?' she had retorted without giving him a backward glance as she entered the shack and delivered a few provisions onto the bed. When she turned he was standing at the door blocking the view.

'You're like those pesky muts that won't leave alone,' she had added, rearranging the blanket on the bed.

'What pesky muts are those?'

'The ones that are hungry and hopeful and end up washed up with the driftwood.'

'Whoa! Where did that come from?'

She straightened and looked at him squarely.

'What do you want with me?'

'Are you always this confrontational?'

She shrugged. 'Just don't get any funny ideas. You rich kids think you own everything. I'm not for sale.'

'But I just bared my soul to you yesterday, or have you forgotten?'

'That was yesterday, today is another day. I don't want you hanging about, that's all.'

'Why not?' he had said smiling suddenly. 'Have you got anything to hide?'

'I've got my life to live and you've got yours and we don't have much else but the ground we're standing on in common. What's the point?'

The old JC would have backed off at this point but he kept faith in the generous hearted girl of yesterday and determined to find her again.

'What's the point of anything, then? Don't you ever go with the flow, just see what happens?'

'Sure, but you're not exactly in my flow, if you see what I mean.' She couldn't help an apologetic grin.

'I wanted to see you again. Is that a crime?'

226

She sat down on the bed and softened.

'No,' she sighed.

'Where did you go, just now?'

She raised a warning eyebrow.

'You don't have to answer, I was just asking,' he added with a quick gesture of apology.

She pulled her hands through her thick beautiful mane of still damp hair.

'I went to the municipal pool.'

'Oh, for a swim?' He looked a little bemused, 'I'd have thought you were more of a river nymph myself.'

She smiled to herself and looked down a little awkwardly, 'They have showers there, and soap.'

'Oh, yeah.' He tore his eyes away from her to glance out at the river and thought about how resourceful she must be to live like she did.

'Look, I brought you a book, I hope you don't mind,' and he tossed a copy of Isabel Allende's *House of the Spirits* unceremoniously onto the bed. 'I thought you'd like it.'

He watched her pick it up gingerly. He could see how she touched it almost reverently, letting the tips of her fingers experience its glossy cover. She had opened it and continued the same ritual then she lifted it to her face and smelt the paper and smiled. 'It's new.'

'Yeah?' he felt a curious happiness lifting his heart as she raised her face to look at him.

Why? Why this book?' and losing himself briefly in the sea green eyes that questioned him, he murmured:

'Because it's eccentric and memorable like you.'

She had laughed. Then she let the book fall from her fingers and pushing past him she stood bathed in sunlight tossing her hair to dry it.

'Let me start reading it to you, come on. Don't say no, I haven't anyone else to be with right now, please.'

She had raised her head and looked at his pleading grey eyes and the softness of his features, not strong enough to be handsome yet. It was a pleasant, kindly face with a hint of seriousness that made his enthusiasm all the more charming.

'Chapter One,' he began, lying outside on the blanket, '*Rosa the Beautiful.*' He glanced up to see if she was listening. Milana was leaning against the warm wood of the little shack.

'Go on then. No one's ever read to me before.'

Today Milana could sense his excitement, a slight breeze toyed with his dishevelled hair. His eyes shone and he stood in front of her, his legs apart and his head thrown back with an unaccustomed air of self-possession that she noticed was rather attractive.

'I did it, Malala! I did it!'

He settled himself beside her. 'I tossed those tossers out. They came back you know, trying to eek money out of me and make me afraid but I told them I was on to them. I laughed at them, and told them I had the place covered, that there were security cameras everywhere. "You sad fuckers," I said, "you think I haven't had to deal with this shit all the time. You think you're the first couple of hopefuls who've had this little brainwave? Well wise up, because there's others behind bars for this kind of scam, and if you don't want to go that way, get the fuck out of here or you'll be fried so quick you won't feel the burn." You should have seen their reaction. I was so into playing my part I forgot to think of what they'd say back.

' "OK man, OK, chill, chill man, we're out of here," ' he said imitating their voices, ' "No more trouble. Chill. We didn't mean no harm, just a laugh. Chill man!" but they were out so damned fast they literally ran out of the building. And now I just can't stop sporting this inane grin, so I've come to hide here with you.'

Milana gave him the broadest of smiles. He felt his whole being unburdened and melting into unknown joy. Nothing mattered as much as this extraordinary liberating feeling that seemed to wash away the sadness of years and lift him to a place without fear where anything was possible. He leaned over and kissed her on the cheek.

'I've got a favour to ask you, Juan Carlos,' she said gravely in response.

'Anything, Malala, anything.'

Milana explained how she needed to find Iris who'd been a friend of her mother's. She told him about her visit to Father Pancho, and how she'd had to wait all week for him to come back from holiday and then how she'd noted down the address but had the wrong telephone number.

'Hey, stop! No need to go on. I'll take you. Do you want to go now?'

Milana produced the piece of paper she'd written on and handed it to him and watched his serious profile lit by the warm summer sun.

'Jorge Velasco! I know him. He's married to Grazia. They're friends of my parents,' he added brightly. But she had turned away. With a sigh of annoyance she got up and moved to the water's edge.

'What is it? What did I say wrong?' She glanced back at his earnest and uncomprehending face, and walked further away. It was foolish to think of this boy as a friend. A strange exasperation seemed to well up inside her. Then she felt the touch of his hand on her shoulder.

'Don't just shun me like that, Malala. I'm so grateful to you. I don't understand why it matters that I know these people. I don't care about them, I care about you and helping you.'

Her first impulse was to want to cry but she checked that impulse, knowing it would bring his arms around her, and feeling too frustrated to figure out if that was why she wanted to cry in the first place she said crossly, 'I'm just tired and hungry.'

'What?' What's got into you?'

'It's not good for us to meet. Don't rely on me. Why do you come here, anyway?'

'Hey,' he said taking her arm in an attempt to turn her towards him. She snatched it away.

'Don't do this, Malala. I'm not relying on you, in fact you were about to rely on me and that's what this is all about isn't it? You did me a favour but now you won't let me return the favour. I'm your friend, remember.'

She gave a little laugh. JC took a step towards her again and held her arms so she couldn't move away.

'You're like a forest animal, mistrustful and so quick to dart away, but I want to make you trust me and I want to help you if I can. Please let me.'

She stared at how the sun made a golden halo around his hair and wordlessly she lowered her eyes.

'I'll take that as a yes.' She felt his grip loosen and immediately wished she could feel the force of his fingers digging into her skin again. But he stepped away afraid of the impulse that made him want to throw his arms about her and kiss her, really kiss her, not on the cheek but deeply, possessively. If he did, he feared she would run, disappear from his sight forever.

'Come here, sit beside me,' he ordered her. 'We're going to plan the next move for finding Iris.' He smiled encouragingly at her. 'You're not going to frighten me off you know.' He felt empowered, and happy in the knowledge he had won a little victory, for she quietly took her place beside him.

'The best time to find this Iris would be when Grazia is out. That way you'll have some time with her. Most of my mother's friends have pilates or bridge classes or tennis in the morning. How about we try tomorrow morning?'

Milana looked at him darkly.

'But what if she doesn't go to her class?'

'It won't matter.'

'What if she sees you?'

'I don't care if Grazia sees me with you. It'll give her something to gossip about.'

'Juan Carlos I'm only another *rotita,* a girl from the shantytowns.' JC stopped suddenly, his clear eyes looked slightly troubled.

'Is that really true? I find it hard to believe, honestly. It's just that...' he wanted to say 'you're too clever,' but that sounded wrong so changing tack abruptly, he shrugged, 'Who cares anyway. In that dress you could be a princess for all they know.' Milana looked away and felt loneliness mingled with a tremendous longing for happiness.

'You know what I think, don't you Malala? I don't have to spell it out do I?' He paused. 'I'd give anything for you,' he said quietly as though to no one in particular.

'Don't say that.'

'Why?' Her gentleness gave him the courage to take her hand from where it rested by her side, 'Can't we try being more than just friends? You might like me.'

'I do like you, JC, it's just that I can't. I'm, well… my heart is somewhere else.'

'Maybe I can bring it back.'

She smiled shaking her head.

'No one can, except the person who put it there.' The moment she'd said it she wished it unsaid. Put into words her foolish hope was risible. A hope based on a dream, a memory. JC let her hand go.

'My God. Lucky, lucky man. Where is he? How can he give up such precious time with you. Thank you, whoever you are, for giving me a look in.' He spoke to the air around him. But his words seemed to mock her folly and make her more vulnerable. 'Still, don't mind me loving you. It's my choice and if it makes me feel good, you don't have to do a thing about it. Everything's cool.' His eyes darted over her with sudden earnestness.

'God girl, you look so uneasy. Do you know how alive you make me feel? I was ready to die before you came along.'

'Love's a big word. It's not fair if I can't love you back,' she sighed.

'Who said love was perfect or fair. You've made me happier than I've ever been. You set me free and made me feel stronger than I've ever felt. Don't you see?' he said trying to counter her misgivings. 'Surely that's the very best kind of love. I can make do with that for now. Besides loads of guys love girls who make them feel like shit.' Suddenly JC put his arms around her. 'Now you've got to let me hug you because you look like you need it and you don't have to hug me back.' But she did, laughing because there was nothing threatening in the happiness he exuded. His arms felt strong and safe and she surrendered to the feeling of relief they brought her.

Chapter Seven

JC glanced at Milana as he steered along the winding lanes of La Rayan and shook his head.

'Can I tell you something without you biting my head off?'

'I don't think I'd like to bite your head off. Not while you're tearing round these horrible bends at any rate,' she retorted savouring the thrill of speed. She had never been a front seat passenger in a car but she felt foolish admitting to it.

'I'm a bit uneasy about you living the way you do. You're pretty exposed, I mean any day or night, if some gang found you there's no telling what they might do to you.'

'Those kind of jerks don't go that far upstream, they're all cowards. Believe me, they won't go near the shack. They're too superstitious, or plain scared.'

'I still don't like it. I don't think you should tempt fate.'

'I like it, JC, I'm free, I'm happy, and maybe it's easier because you're around.'

JC shot her a look. 'You mean it?'

'Don't get any ideas,' she grinned, 'but I do mean it. We all need a friend, and you've been that to me. You don't give me a chance to feel lonely, and look, what would I have done about seeing Iris if you hadn't been around. Sitting here, driving up to La Rayan in this fancy car… it makes me feel like a star.'

'This is not a fancy car, Malala, it's a second-hand Suzuki Jeep.'

'Well it is to me. Remember I've not been around much.'

'Malala, I've been thinking. If Grazia is in, I'll chat to her, ask her about her son. He's sort of a friend of mine. Well, that is we were at the Grange together but I'm a bit younger and he's far cooler than me.' He laughed a little awkwardly. 'Meanwhile you go round the back and see if you can find Iris. If Grazia isn't in, I'll just get Iris for you and wait near the car, OK?'

'Whatever you say. You're the one sticking your neck out here, not me. I don't want to get you into trouble.'

'By the way,' he added casually trying to disguise the fondness in his tone, 'I like you calling me JC, stick with it from now on, please.'

The road they were on had bordered the river for a while before it began to wind up into the hills where, a little way up it forked. JC pointed to the left. 'That's the road up to the mountains. Have you ever been skiing, Malala?'

'I've never even touched snow.'

'That's so cool.'

She glanced at him puzzled.

'It's cool to have new experiences when you're older. If you've seen and done it all when you're a kid, you have nothing to look forward to later.' He threw her a happy grin. Milana liked hearing JC call her Malala. With her new name, albeit a small variation on the old, had come a new life, a new beginning. Her mood had lifted, the momentary fearfulness had evaporated like the river mists. She felt strong again.

The road climbed more steeply now while the hills around were dotted with imposing walled villas in Tuscan or Spanish style with high security gates.

'Wow!' she exclaimed, 'These guys have money, just look at the houses. They look like fortresses.' After a while she stole a look at JC, 'Come here often then?' she enquired.

'There are some good parties up here. I'll bring you next time.'

'No way.'

'Scared?' JC glanced at her.

'You bet.'

He smiled. 'Ironic that.'

They turned at a pair of tall iron gates. JC pressed the security panel. A voice asked his name.

'Juan Carlos Miranda.'

The gates opened instantly.

'That was easy,' sighed Milana impressed.

'It's my father's name too. I'm just Juan Carlos Junior, but they know my dad, so hey presto.' The wind had blown his hair off his face so it stood thick and dishevelled rising proudly from its roots. She watched the way his hands controlled the steering wheel, smooth and decisive in their movements, as they drove up past the front of the house and round to the far side, parking between two huge palm trees.

'She's not in,' JC assured Milana as he stepped out of the car.

'How do you know?'

'The garage is shut. When the cars are in during the day they tend to leave it open.'

'So you know them quite well.' She gave him a slightly admonishing look. The front door opened. A man in a butler's uniform looked out. JC waved. The man smiled in recognition, 'They're down south, *Don* Juan Carlos, they're not back until tomorrow.'

'Oh, well, how's everybody?'

'Fine, *Don* Juan Carlos. Yourself?'

'Never better, Enrique. I've brought a friend. She wants to see Iris.'

'Iris the maid?' he looked a little surprised.

'Yes,' JC smiled, 'she used to know her.'

'I see,' Enrique smiled politely at Milana. 'I will get her for you.'

Moments later, Iris appeared in the doorway. Her hair was scraped back in a bun and she was wearing a navy blue uniform edged in a white collar and white cuffs. Milana did not recognise her immediately, she looked somehow diminished. Iris looked from JC to Milana.

'Oh my!' Recognition swept over her and she took a step forwards.

'It's OK, Enrique,' she said quickly to the butler who hovered close by, evidently interested. Enrique turned on his heels and his footsteps echoed into the interior again.

'I can't believe it. You're so grown, such a woman.' Her eyes examined Milana, boldly travelling over every part of her. 'Nilda never got to see you. She… she would have been so…' but she trailed off as Milana stepped forwards and hugged her.

'Seeing you like this, so suddenly… You bring it all back,' she whispered pulling away from her, notably flustered. 'It's been so,' Iris paused, 'terrible.' Iris shook her head as though to change the pictures in her mind, 'You're all grown up, girl.'

'You look so different in uniform, Iris. I hardly recognise you.'

'I couldn't stay, not after…' she trailed off again but she raised her chin and held her head high defying the emotions that threatened her composure.

'What's happened to Nora, Iris?'

'Working as usual. Taken over Nilda's house. Got some man living in, I don't know, I don't care. What's with you, my girl?' she looked at JC where he stood a little way away looking over the panoramic view and whispered, 'Looks like Enrique knows your fancy friend. How did you hook up with him?'

'It's a long story.'

'Not bad. Not bad. But be careful girl.'

'Of course, Iris.'

'You got a kid yet?'

'No Iris. I'm barely seventeen and I'm not like that.'

'Just checking. Just want the best for you. It's good to see you.' There was a slight pause as a shaft of suspicion pierced Iris's thoughts.

'How did you find me?'

'*Padre* Pancho.'

Iris threw her a more searching look and her pupils seemed to want to bore right through Milana. 'If you found me, it weren't just to pass the time of day.'

JC strolled a little further away to survey the garden. He stood with his hands in his pockets leaning against an archway that was drenched in flowering bourganvillea.

'I need to find Ricardo Romero, Iris.'

'Ricci?'

'No, Ricardo Romero, their father and maybe mine too for all I know.'

Iris raised her eyebrows and for a brief telling moment curled her lip with a touch of knowing arrogance.

'I just want to talk to him, Iris.'

'He doesn't want memories of them cruel years,' she said dismissively. 'Besides, I don't know where he is. Somewhere in Argentina. He can't never come back into Chile.'

'But you could find out, couldn't you, Iris? For me? Please?'

'Look here, you just gotta forget them things you heard. They weren't meant for your ears. I should never have told them stories.'

'But they are true.'

Iris breathed out a reluctant sigh, 'If I weren't so full of it and you weren't sat their listening that night, there'd be no trouble now.'

'There is no trouble now, Iris. I just want to find him.'

'I told you, I don't know where he is. Some place over the border like San Martin but that was a long time ago.' Suddenly her looked softened, 'Why don't you leave it be Milana, what good can come of it?'

Milana came a step closer, 'How can you say that? My mum hid all her past from me and now she's dead, and that Carlos Hidalgo that you say is my father is dead, and Ricardo Romero is nearly as good as dead.' She paused and her hand touched her chest in an involuntary emphasis, 'But the connections I feel to these people, they're very much alive and they keep me awake at night and I feel them pulling for answers, pulling inside me, moving me to do something. I can't just do nothing. Don't you see?' She looked keenly at Iris. 'What if there's a reason I'm feeling this, what if it's my mum, Iris, doing this. Maybe she had stuff she wanted to say, and she died before she had the chance, or maybe she sees stuff now she's dead, that we can't see, and she's trying to tell me something.' She reached out to touch Iris as though to help her meaning flow into her and animate her to some response, but Iris remained unmoved as a statue.

'At least, if you can do nothing else, tell me where I can find

Carlos Hidalgo's widow, she might be able to help or even his son, surely that boy has questions about what he witnessed that night that he has tried to answer.' Iris looked at her strangely. Milana watched her expression change as one might watch a total eclipse of the sun, fascinated and horrified at the same time. She saw the colour drain from Iris's face and fear enter her eyes.

'What I said I should never have said. I got it wrong, all wrong that night. Don't listen to me, girl. Leave it alone. Some things are best never said. It's the devil's got into you girl. Stirred you up. Don't listen to them pullings, them voices. It's the voice of darkness. I know these things. Leave it alone. Shut your ears to it.' She spoke in short staccato sentences, as she backed away from her like a frightened animal.

'Iris, please. You're the only door to my past. Please don't shut it in my face.' And the more Iris retreated the more Milana believed the secret Iris had so eloquently divulged three years earlier. Meanwhile Iris stared at the expression on Milana's face with something close to genuine pain.

'Forget the past. It don't matter.' Iris nodded to where JC stood looking out over the hills. 'Be grateful for what you got. Don't stir up the past.'

Milana leant forwards and looked her in the eye. 'I can't Iris, I've got to know.'

And suddenly Iris grabbed Milana's hand, 'Look, if I tell you this, you gonna leave me be, because I got no more than this to tell and you know I care, Milana, I really care for you. Your mum told me she was born in Alhue by the big house that came down in the '65 earthquake. She told me they called her the devil's daughter and that's why she'd turned out so bad. She was really down, that was just before *Señora* Lisa found her half dead, the day she near took her life, but I wasn't to know that then. I told her not to be so silly and she turned to me and says, "I was cursed at birth, Iris I've never known my mum or my dad, I was a foundling that's what they told me."'

'That's so horrible, Iris. What did she mean?'

'Don't go taking this stuff to heart. It's, you know, them stories you hear, in them places, but if you're going to mess with the past, you start there, Alhue, it's a Godforsaken spot I know that much, but it's all I got for you. I've gotta go, kid. They just sent me up on the bus ahead to get the house ready for them. Good luck. You turned out good.'

Pale and shaken, Iris turned and walked away.

'How long have you been standing there?' asked Milana, sensing JC just feet from where Iris had been talking to her. He was leaning against a gum tree, his arms crossed, looking serious.

'Get in the car. Let's go. She's a bit of a witch, your Iris.'

Milana looked puzzled, 'Witch?'

'She gives me the creeps.'

'Iris has been a good friend to my mum,' she said thoughtfully

'Didn't look like it.'

'Why? What do you know, JC?' She looked at him.

'She's well…you know..'

'What?'

'I care more for you than she ever will, OK.' And he took the turn out of the drive so fast, that the tyres skidded and the dust rose in a cloud behind them.

Chapter Eight

That night was clear and balmy but Milana couldn't sleep. Fragments of her brief encounter with Iris kept coming back to her, distorted and sinister. She lay huddled on the metal camp bed in the shack wishing she was not alone. She longed more than ever for JC's easy company. Thoughts kaleidoscoped in her mind and her imagination seemed to bring to life a thousand sleeping shadows that took the shape of devils and witches.

Milana had let in the spirits of her past and now she could not still their voices. She was afraid of the empty graves outside the shack. The imagined ghosts of Nilda and her mother and all the other spirits in the graveyard and those that left their souls in the river seemed to haunt her now. Tormented by what Iris had told her about her mother and what JC had implied about Iris she found herself trapped in an agony of morbid agitation. The spirit of Whitebeard seemed to curl up beside her on the bed. She tried to close her eyes but the sounds of the river, of the wind, of the creaking wood, crept in like evil imps at play. She tried opening her eyes. Moonlight filtered in through the acrylic window and fell over the bed onto the floor in a silvery pool turning the familiar, unusual and frightening.

Face down on the bed Milana began to pray the Our Father in her head, but she could not silence the voices in her mind. She tried the rosary instead, reciting it slowly out loud, listening to the sound of her own voice, her eyes tight shut, her hands gripping the edges of her pillow, her face buried in its darkness, her breath trapped against the softness.

As she lay there, it seemed to her that the door of the shack opened and a chill wind blew in. She felt a presence close and sheer terror freeze her over. She went on reciting hoping she would not feel the thing that might kill her now. For a while there was stillness, as though the room held its breath. She went on, afraid to stop, afraid to listen and it seemed time passed but she couldn't know how long, just that she repeated the prayer again and again and after what seemed like an age, very softly she heard a whisper like an echo. As she said the words of the prayer someone else was saying them with her. Her heart seemed to stop beating, but her mind was racing. Evil would not whisper the rosary to her, would it? Her whole body lay clenched in the grip of uncertainty and suddenly she stopped reciting. The voice went on very softly getting closer, until she felt the warmth on her hair, but now it wasn't the words of the rosary that were being whispered.

She loosened her desperate hold on the ends of the pillow and very slowly turned her face to the side, her eyes still tightly shut. Lips brushed her mouth. She felt their warmth, like colour and light flooding into her tormented mind. Fingers touched her skin like the softest breeze. They traced her features awakening her memory to their touch, bringing her senses back to life.

She turned her whole body now so that she lay on her side and for an agonising moment the lips moved away. Then she felt the whole weight of him lie down beside her, his hands stroking her hair. She smelt the familiar, well remembered freshness of his clothes and felt the cool cotton of his shirt on her skin. She pulled away the blanket and touched the contours of his body beside her, the smoothness of his jeans and the roughness of his belt. Slowly her hands reached up over his arms and circled his shoulders and the broadness of his back and she felt the strength of him pressing her small frame as his arms embraced her. She felt herself being gradually charged by his presence, warmth began to consume her from within, waking up desire that, after years of suppression to the quiet centre of her being, ached for release. This agony was sweeter and more painful than anything she had ever known. He kissed her eyes and whispered, 'Open them.'

'I can't,' she said, 'you might not be there.'

'I'm here, look at me.' He gazed at the sweep of her dark eyelashes and the perfect oval of her moonlit face. He watched as slowly her eyes opened and focused. Like pale green pools reflecting the silver light, they spilled over with tears.

He touched her tears, kissed them and buried his face in her warmth. She put her hands up to his hair, it fell through her fingers thick and soft.

'I can't believe I've found you,' he murmered.

'Maybe we're dreaming?' she whispered. With her fingers raking through his hair, she pulled him to her lips, crushing him to her, returning the kiss that he had left imprinted there three years back. 'I want to kiss you forever. Never stop, never never never.'

'Oh God, I never thought love could be such agony.' But he was smiling lifting himself up, taking her with him as he pulled her to him rocking her in a tight embrace, 'I've waited so long to find you again. I want my whole being to be inside you, Milana, nothing else is enough.'

'Lie on me, let me feel your weight on me, I might just melt into you.'

He laughed, his beguiling carefree laugh. 'Can this be for real? he hugged her to him. 'Impossible dream. Can you be so in harmony with me after such inconclusive, inauspicious beginnings?'

'You kissed me, have you forgotten? There was nothing inconclusive in that kiss.' She touched his face. 'I'd loved you with a silent passion all those months, hoping your kindness was more than that. I thought you must have so many girls, how could you possibly care for me. All those times you held my hand I told myself you thought of me as a child, you couldn't know what I felt. But you didn't make me feel like a child. Still I was never sure until that kiss. At first it nearly destroyed me then it kept me going.'

His eyes lit by the moon held her gaze and she touched how his smile creased his face.

'There is so much I want to learn about you,' he murmured.

Milana seemed to shrug this off. 'You know me so well, already. I grew up in those three months under your care.'

'Just because I taught you to paint, surely not?' She saw the whiteness of his faintly mocking smile.

'Because you loved me,' she said covering the smile with her hand. He grabbed her hand and crushed it to his mouth. Her trust disarmed him as nothing else could.

'Milana, I can't stay.' His words were so urgent that they seemed to be said more for him than her.

'You're here, just be, for a moment longer, please.' Her hands touched his lips again, 'You love me.' She sighed.

'You have no idea how much,' he laughed.

'I loved you from the first day, when you put your hands on my blotchy miserable face. I knew I would never dare tell you. It made me angry to feel it sometimes. I thought you'd laugh at me, so I tried to learn everything you said and to paint with everything I had in me, to show you how I felt.'

'And I barely dared face it myself, Milana. It frightened me to feel so much. I couldn't understand what it was about you. Whenever I came too close to you I walked away from you remember. I sometimes imagined you like some forest nymph come to taunt me and lure me to distraction. Maybe I was cruel, Milana. I tried to suppress those feelings like I have so many others but I couldn't. It made me angry too, sometimes, perhaps you noticed?'

'Do you understand it now? I mean what it was about me.'

He smiled. 'Yes, I've had alot of time to figure it out.'

'Won't you tell me?'

He shook his head playfully and kissed her. 'You've got to work it out for yourself.'

'I always believed that if I painted with my heart, my paintings would be like love letters to you and you would feel them and understand. That last evening,' she breathed, 'I knew you felt it too, without a doubt. I was so in love I could barely think when they sent me south. Then I got there and I was lost without you. I thought I'd burst, I had all this love inside and I'd never told you. I wanted to run away, but then I started to paint. I painted like you taught me, a whole church. It has my love for you in every stroke. I made love to those walls with my paintbrush, it was the only way I could release it and survive.'

'I know, I saw it, I couldn't breathe when I saw it.' His hands cupped her face, his thumbs tracing her lips as he reached down to kiss her again.

'You saw the church?'

'Yes.' He kissed her again, 'And I saw little Ines crying her eyes out for you, and I saw Father Juan. I hope you didn't leave all your love on those walls, I hope there's still some left here.' She heard the laughter in his voice but she felt the strength and warmth of his hand on her chest connecting with her beating heart and she pressed it down into her and felt him catch his breath.

'I've made love to you almost every day' – he confessed – 'in my thoughts and often in my dreams. You were trapped inside me and I couldn't release you. I'd shake sometimes just thinking of you – weird – I even cried, but that could be the weather in England it's very depressing.' He laughed again, playfully so close to her, 'You worked your way into my heart and breathed it back to life and it's made a mess of my emotions. I can't get you out of my mind it's like you're linked to every feeling part of me.'

'Let me stay there then, please don't try to get me out,' she touched his hair now shorter but still falling in a dark wave over his eyes, she touched his sensuous mouth that made her want to kiss him all the time, even more so when he was serious.

'I want you to make love to me like you never have and never will to anyone ever, only me, for always,' she whispered. He laughed with relief and because she had grown up and all his fears of stealing her innocence were wiped out in one fell swoop by passion shared more completely than he could ever have hoped.

'And I will Milana. Every day. But...' his breath caught again as she kissed him deeply. Her fingers unbuttoned the crisp cotton of his shirt. She could feel his stomach tensing, his heart pounding; every nerve ending alive to her touch and she felt her whole body responding to his.

He held her hand, stopping her. 'Milana, I can't stay.'

'You don't even need to touch me and I'm on fire,' she whispered in his ear.

'Oh God, God help me,' he groaned. 'Think of a volcano when it's going to erupt, think of how the solid earth sends out tremors that shake everything. Feel how I'm shaking, and think of molten lava deep within the earth that will explode the solid rock of the mountain when it comes and understand why I can't sleep with you and leave. You're too linked to my emotions. There's a lot of heart ache in there and a lot of darkness that I'll tell you about one day. Milana, if I sleep with you it would destroy me to leave you. I couldn't be so reckless.' Their lips met again, insatiable, desperate for each other. Milana stopped, breathless.

'How did you know I was here?'

He was breathing so hard he could barely answer, 'I guessed.'

'But how? All these years have passed.'

'Enrique, the butler, mentioned that JC had come to the house and that he'd had a girl with him, called Milana, who talked to Iris. Don't you see. You came to my house, Milana, just hours before I arrived from the south.'

'I was at your house? Oh God! You mean I stepped into where you live. And Iris?' she opened her eyes wide with incredulity, 'She works for you then? She makes your bed and tidies your clothes? Oh God, I'm so jealous of her, so jealous.' And she hugged him to her.

'Don't be, I'm never there. I came back just to get my things and go to the airport, and then, as I loaded the Jeep, Enrique mentioned JC's visit. I think he was fishing for info. He didn't know what he was saying.'

'What did you feel?' whispered Milana.

Santiago sat up pulling his fingers through his hair down to the nape of his neck in a gesture she remembered so well.

'My heart stopped,' he looked at Milana bathed in moonlight and his eyes held hers intently. 'Then it raced so fast he must have seen it pounding under my shirt. I was so restless, I could barely eat. I didn't know how I'd get here, but I had to try. It was the only place I might have a shred of hope of finding you. There was a dinner, people wishing me well, endless niceties. I got away. I said my goodbyes. They knew I had to go to the airport. I just left a little earlier and made the guys stop at the club, just around the corner from here. That's where they are now. Thank God they know better than to ask me a load of questions. I told them there was something I must do,' he paused, touching her face very gently, 'They're waiting for me there now. I have to catch my plane back to England.'

'Why?'

'I'm studying there. But I'm nearly done. Just a few more months, Milana. I have to finish my university degree. I'm in my last year. I'm probably late as it is.'

'What club?'

'The Polo Club. It's just up the river, minutes away from here. The boys are having a drink there. I can't miss my plane. I have exams coming up. But now I'll live with hope not sadness.' He cupped her face in his hand. 'I've lived for this moment. I drove here, but I never really dared think I'd find you.'

'Why did you drive here? How could you know?'

'Because it's what I would have done. What I did in fact do for a while. I came and painted here just to feel closer to you. Now these snatched minutes must see me through the rest of the year in England. There's so much I want to say, explain and...' he smiled, 'do to you.' He stared into her eyes as her gaze sent a familiar tremor straight to his heart. 'If I slept with you I'd leave you pregnant right now, against any odds, no doubt about it.' He sighed.

'I wish,' she whispered. 'I wouldn't care,' she added, 'then if you never came back, I would still have something of you.'

'I will come back, Milana.'

'England is so far away. It's so tiny on the map.' She pulled off the beaded bracelet on her wrist. 'Take this back there with you.'

He took it and felt the beads between his fingers.

'The bracelet Ines made for you?'

'Oh! You know about that too?' she smiled. 'Keep it. I told her it would never leave me, I can't break my promise to Ines.'

He rolled the little bracelet, impregnated with her scent, her warmth, onto his wrist; 'So you'll never leave me while I have it. That's your promise?'

'You've understood perfectly,' she said.

'Milana, what are you going to do? You can't stay here.'

'Oh don't worry, this is my home, remember?'

'I don't want to go.' Suddenly he seemed so young and beautiful, like the first time she'd seen him, and his eyes looked at her despairingly.

'Miss your plane.' She smiled hopefully at him.

She felt her heart being torn apart as an answering smile creased his handsome face and she sensed the strength in him that had made her feel so safe. Santiago took off the heavy silver chain that he had always worn around his neck. He pulled off the medal of Our Lady that hung on it and pressed it into her hand. 'Keep it. She'll protect you. I consecrate our love to Her.'

He left as quickly as he had come. Moments later she heard a car engine start up. Clutching Santiago's medal, Milana curled in the warmth that he had left and slept.

Chapter Nine

'They really are lovely, JC. I've never...' she trailed off '...and they fit!' Milana lifted up her foot to take a closer look at the elegant heel in the afternoon sun.

'Why shouldn't they fit?' said JC, looking pleased with himself, 'I know you by heart.'

She felt herself redden as though he'd somehow struck her.

'I've never worn high heels. I'll fall over,' she replied awkwardly lowering her eyes and fiddling with the shoes.

'You're not wearing them to walk over these stones and boulders, I'm going to take you out tonight, if you'll let me that is.'

'Can't we just stay here and rest and watch the sun set.'

'Rest? I can't imagine you get many interruptions round here that will spoil your rest. Besides I think you'll be interested in where I'm taking you. That's why I bought you the shoes.'

'So I'd look the part?' she raised an eyebrow at him.

'Yes. So you'll look wonderful and everyone will say, "Who is that girl JC is with?" and I'll be dead proud and you'll get to see something I think you'll like.'

Carefully, Milana untied the yellow silk ribbons that wrapped around her ankles and slipped off the pretty sandals. She looked at them thoughtfully.

'What's the matter?' JC stared at her curiously from where he stood ankle deep in the river water, with his trousers rolled up, smoking a cigarette.

'Nothing.'

'You're distant.'

Milana was silent.

'You're a million miles away.'

She curled the end of the ribbon round her finger. He threw the cigarette into the river and thrust his hands in his pocket.

'You want me to go?'

Milana shook her head.

'Then what?' He came up and sat beside her. 'You can trust me. Remember. My life is in your hands.'

'Not anymore,' she smiled.

'No, I'm my own man now. Don't worry I don't have to lean on you, but it's nice.'

'I'm confused, JC, that's all. With things that Iris said. Things about my past.'

'I'm not sure I believe you, Malala. That's not all.'

'Why wouldn't that be all?' she looked surprised.

'I don't know.' He looked at her as though he were weighing up whether to say something.

'This morning when I came you were still sleeping. I sat here for a while and I saw this,' he glanced at her. 'Well, it's pretty obvious you haven't even noticed it.' He picked up a rock covering what looked like a one thousand *pesos* note, 'I found it like this, just one edge sticking out.' I left it and went shopping without you.'

'What is it?' Milana held out her hand.

Across a green one thousand *peso* note, a bold hand had written "WRITE TO ME". Underneath, Milana read "Trinity College, Cambridge University, Cambridge, England." There was nothing else, no hearts or crosses not even a name, nothing telltale.

'She glanced at JC and caught him watching her.

JC laughed, 'Come on Malala. It wasn't there yesterday. Besides your colour's up.'

'Maybe it's been there for ages, only we've just noticed it.' Milana shrugged, feigning innocence.

'What I want to know is why you won't trust me?'

'JC, what are you talking about?'

'You asked me to take you to the Velasco house, right? To speak to their maid, Iris, and that just happens to be Santiago's home, you know, the guy I told you I knew from school, and Iris happens to be the family's maid, and then his address just happens to crop up here under a stone. I mean it could just be a coincidence, right?'

'I guess so,' Milana shrugged but her insides had tautened at the mention of Santiago and the memory of the previous night.

'You were there, JC. You heard my conversation with Iris. Nothing to do with this guy you know,' she said faintly.

'OK. I'll believe what you want me to believe, Malala. You don't have to tell me.' He stood up and threw a stone as far as he could.

'I think you came here to the river to meet him and he didn't show until now.'

'No, JC, honestly.' Milana reddened slightly.

She saw a flash of anger in his eyes.

'Please don't be annoyed.'

He laughed, emptily.

'Don't laugh, you don't want to. You're cross with me. Maybe you hate me.'

'I don't want you to lie,' he burst out.

'I won't lie then. Why won't you look at me?'

'I don't want to see what you're thinking.' He bit his lip furiously, embarrassed by the awkward turn the conversation had taken. Milana sensed his discomfort. She followed him with her gaze weighing up what to say, torn by the need she felt to be honest.

'I knew him three years ago when my mother died, that's all. He helped me then. He showed me this place and I haven't seen him since.'

'Until last night?' he suggested almost shyly.

'OK, until last night, but only for a minute. I guess he came to get something. That's some of his stuff in there. He was on the way to the airport. He never expected to find me here. He's just kind to me, that's all. Please don't make a thing about it. It embarrasses me. He left me money see?' she looked at the note he had left and turned it over as though for inspiration. 'and he was worried about me living here. He told me if I got into trouble I should write to him. He'd help me, like he did before. I didn't think he meant it but, see, he left his address, so he did mean it. Then he left very quickly. Iris working there is a coincidence, I swear I had no idea.' Without raising her head Milana risked a glance at JC. He thrust his hands in his pockets and looked back at her choosing not to persue a tack he didn't want to face anyway.

'Hmm, maybe Iris put him up to it, to get you off her back. She looks like a Machiavellian schemer. Anyways was that so difficult? Now we're even. You know so much about me, now I know something about you. We can forget it now.' He strode over to her with a slightly contrived air of assurance. 'And don't worry, I won't tell a soul. His mother would have a fit.'

'What do you mean?'

'Well, darling Malala,' he put on an affected air, 'she's a frightful snob. Pedigree comes first and last for her. She weeds out all but the finest hot-house flowers for her son. Poor Santiago. She guards him ferociously. What a judgement this would be on her. Serve her right,' he laughed carelessly.

His last words cut Milana to the quick, although she knew he meant her no harm. She turned away abruptly. 'I told you there was nothing to tell.'

He took a deep breath and tried to swallow the feelings that threatened his happiness. 'Now please let me take you out tonight,' then, looking at her more intently and a touch wistfully he added, 'you'll really want to come, trust me, when you know where I'm taking you.' His tone was unfamiliar, a touch ironic. She felt sadness engulf her, all the more overwhelming for the happiness that had preceded it.

'Where?' She tried meekly to appease the misery within.

'I'll tell you later. Put on that very pretty dress and bring the red cardigan and don't forget the shoes.'

'I wish you'd tell me where we're going.' JC put his finger to his lips. 'Humour me, please, just this once. And I don't mind if you're a million miles away, thinking your own thoughts. I'll let you be. I won't even talk to you in the car if you don't want me to.' He took her hand and pulled her to face him. 'Malala, you don't have to pretend with me. It's me remember? I'm all done pretending, thanks to you.'

'We all have to pretend sometimes,' she said looking him in the eye, 'it's part of our survival.' He watched her walk up to the shack and close the door behind her. He was with her and that was all that mattered.

When she stepped out again, he whistled his admiration. Milana smiled weakly, and started to take off the sandals.

'What are you doing?'

'I can't walk over stones in these heels, can I?'

JC stepped forwards, 'At your service ma'am,' and with that he swept her off her feet and carried her over the bank to where the grass grew nearer the road. As he set her down he picked up the medal that hung on a cheap chain around her neck.

'You haven't worn this before,' he said, feeling its weight.

'I thought I'd wear it tonight.'

'It's the Miraculous Medal of Our Lady. Who did it belong to?' he asked. The question was innocent enough, but it took her by surprise.

'It's mine.'

'I know, it's just that I thought maybe it was your father's or some heirloom. It's rather beautiful heavy silver, the chain's rubbish though.'

'I know, I bought it from a street vendor.'

'It deserves to hang on something better, but I guess being round your neck makes up for it.' And JC opened the car door for her to get in.

They sped along the left bank of the river towards the downtown area of Bellavista where residential homes of past decades had become fashionable studios and cafes. Artists and craftsmen mingled with the young and trendy. Art Galleries and restaurants nestled in converted houses, spilling out onto pretty courtyards overhung with bougainvillea. Unlikely Spanish villas had transformed themselves into smart nightclubs or seedier Jazz venues. Stalls on the narrow pavements sold leather and jewellery; lapis lazuli, malachite, quartz and alabaster.

Sitting next to JC in the car, Milana found the memory of

her extraordinary encounter with Santiago receding into the realms of the imagination, like some implausible invention of her own making. It had left no tangible impression on the real world apart from a green bank note with a written message left under a rock, and a silver medal. He had come like a reprieve from all the terrifying images of the night, bathed in a silver light like an apparition, and he had faded back into the night. The sleep that had followed had taken the reality all too quickly into that other worldliness that he had come to inhabit in her dreams. He had materialised too quickly, too briefly. When the morning sun had crowded in blazing its warmth through the small acrylic window of the shack, there seemed to be nothing left to tell her it had not all been a dream. Only the effect of that extraordinary chemistry that still left her shaken and breathless testified to what had happened. JC's very real and often demanding presence, on the other hand, acted like a bright spot light that seemed to blot out the tenuous shapes of an implausible craving.

'You look annoyed, Milana,' he said glancing over to her. 'Relax, enjoy this, please. And let me show you off.' He released the steering wheel and squeezed her hand fondly. 'Humour me. Go on.'

She felt the muscles of her face relax and realised she must have been frowning. 'I feel like I'm acting a part and I don't even know what part I'm playing. How can I relax?'

'Well you might at least enjoy the ride.' He pulled her hand towards him and kissed it quickly. He would have let it go but a sixth sense told him it was OK to keep holding it.

Milana looked at his hand on hers and reluctantly accepted that she was grateful for its protection, its real warmth penetrating her skin telling her she was not alone.

A man holding a yellow duster waved frantically at the car, '*Señor, Señor,*' he called, 'I make a space for you.' JC manoeuvred into the parking space whilst the man with the duster manually pushed the cars together to make way for JC's. 'Leave the handbrake off, *Señor,* OK? I take care of the car, *Señor,* OK?' Milana watched the man race to another car to try and squeeze it into the row of parked cars, shifting them this way and that to make room for more.

'I did that once,' she confided to JC.

'Did what?'

'Waved cars into parking spaces, but I didn't have to push them around like he does,' Milana laughed suddenly and it broke the ever increasing tension between them.

JC, took her elbow to steer her through the crowded pavements.

'Where are we going?'

'Just across the road there.' He pointed to where hibiscus plants placed either side of an old arch, marked the entrance to what looked like a private club. Men in dark suits flanked the doors. Three Mercedes Benz limousines with blacked out windows waited parked outside. Behind one of them two more men in suits with dark glasses chatted.

'They look threatening,' whispered Milana nervously.

'Don't worry about them, they're just bodyguards.'

'Bodyguards?'

'The President is probably in there. He and Grazia are quite close.'

Milana stopped dead. 'I'm not going in there. I can't meet people like that.'

'Oh come on, never mind the politics.'

'JC, I'm not thinking of politics, I don't know shit about politics. I'd never dream of judging anyone who had to run a whole country. I'm just not used to this. I can't do this.'

JC, pulled her back into a small alcove covered in climbing ampelopsis.

'You're with me, Malala. I won't leave your side. Besides, where's that tough girl who taught me to stand up for myself? You're worth more than the lot of them in there. Please, will you just trust me?'

Milana nodded gravely. He made to move on, but she stayed put.

'I may not look like a kid from a shantytown to you, JC,' she whispered, 'but I am, and if I open my mouth they'll figure it out and I'll come flying out of there like a rotten egg.'

'Are you nuts? Nobody would dream of throwing you out of there, Malala. God girl! Besides you're better read than most of my friends ever will be.'

'I'm not up to this right now.' Her eyes flashed darkly at him. 'I've got to be strong and confident to survive now and I don't want to go places that undermine my confidence.'

JC looked at Milana with a curious mixture of irritation and pleasure; pleasure because she produced a sense of happiness in him just by being with him and irritation because he perceived her inflexible stubbornness and he had been very much looking forward to leading her into that club.

'OK. I understand.' JC perched on a low stone wall and patted it. 'Come, sit here.'

'No, I want to stand.' He sighed and crossing his arms leant back.

'Have it your own way, but just hear me out on this. I wanted to surprise you tonight but seeing as you won't budge I'll explain it to you. Last night you obviously saw Santiago. I don't know how you know him, that's your business, but our families are friends since way back. I didn't have the faintest idea you knew him until I saw that address written on that one thousand *peso* note outside the shack. And yet,' he paused as the significance of what he was about to say was only just sinking in, 'I had planned to bring you to this "Opening" here, days ago.' Milana shrugged. She didn't know what an 'Opening' was, which increased her general feeling of unease.

'You love art and I wanted to show you some of our best Chilean art. So I planned this for you. Now here's the coincidence Malala: do you have any idea who's paintings are hanging on the walls of this fancy nightclub that is hosting tonight's private view for all society top cats?'

Milana looked completely perplexed. Her nerves and her high shoes were making him difficult to follow.

'Why should I know anything about it?' she said defensively.

'Santiago's,' breathed JC. 'This is his show. It's his paintings in there.'

'But he's in England,' gasped Milana, the colour slowly draining out of her face.

'Of course he's in England, but his art is here. In fact, knowing him, he probably timed his departure to miss this Opening Night. He hates all the fuss. Don't you see, Malala, I was going to bring you here anyway. There's a coincidence!'

Milana sat down beside him and folded her hands on her lap. He noticed she was trembling slightly and taking off his jacket placed it gently over her shoulders.

'I had no idea that you knew him. I just thought it would be fun to come down to Bellavista and hang out and see some art, seeing as you said art is your thing. So, having come all the way here, surely you must be a little bit curious to see in there.'

JC got up and thrusting his hands in his pockets leaned against the arch, watching her. Her curls moved in the light breeze, a slight tremor seemed to run through her occasionally, but she seemed completely oblivious to his presence. Finally he came and stood directly in front of her.

'If you don't hurry up I'm going to start feeling I'm kind of crazy to bring you to see the paintings of a guy you're clearly besotted with, when really I wish you felt that way about me.' He paused feeling the blood rise to his face. 'In fact maybe you shouldn't see them at all, it'll just make everything worse for you and me.' He turned towards the car, but Milana didn't follow. Instead she remained on the low brick wall sitting between clusters of flowering japonica and held her head in her hands. The sun was still warm and it caught her hair, flecking it with gold as it cascaded down over her face in soft waves. JC relented and patiently rested one foot up on the brick wall and leant towards her:

'There are no coincidences, Malala. I'm sure of it now. There's a bigger picture and if you don't go in there now, you'll have failed yourself.' He paused for a deep intake of breath, 'You'll have failed yourself because you were afraid.'

Milana looked up suddenly, JC appeared immensely wise and superior leaning towards her in this attitude of assured benevolence. She reached for his arm, her eyes glittering with sudden determination, and held it tight, 'OK,' she said.

JC bent down and kissed her cheek.

'You'd better have your jacket back. I'm OK now,' she added with new found defiance. Afraid is something she abhorred being.

As he slipped the jacket on, feeling immensely pleased despite all the other conflicting emotions, he announced casually, 'I'm going to introduce you as my girlfriend, OK? That's my perk for the night and I think I've earned it.' He held her close by the arm and whispered, 'I'm so lucky to have you beside me.' She barely heard him. Her eyes darted worriedly towards the entrance to the club.

'Come on. Let's have some fun. That's the cream of society in there.'

Milana's heart beat like a mad thing under her thin cotton dress and her ankles felt weak and unsteady in the unaccustomedly high heels. She gripped his sleeve more tightly. JC felt a wave of manly pride move through him lifting his spirits heavenwards.

As they stepped past the two suited men, there was a flurry of activity and before they could enter through the black double doors, two men opened them and stood holding them back. The President of Chile, dressed in a dark suit came out flanked by two men. He walked slowly and caught sight of JC who nodded a salute. The President smiled warmly at Milana, as she stared at him in awe.

'Excellent show in there,' he remarked and moved on.

'Wow!' Milana breathed, 'That was, I mean...'

JC nodded, grinning at her excitement.

'I can't believe he noticed me.'

'I told you, I'm a lucky man, even the President can see that.' And he covered her hand briefly with his.

The room was filled with elegant people in the latest summer fashions. Jewellery sparkled under the tiny halogen lights that glittered like stars in the velvet-black of the ceiling. The pictures were spot-lit so that they made their own individual statement in isolated pools of light. Milana longed to get close to them but at every step they were stopped by glamorous guests in silks and chiffons of scintillating colour.

JC propelled her into the throng; fashionable people with perfect faces and whitened teeth that smiled and kissed and murmured, 'Hello.' Maybe their smiles, like their make up, hid a more mundane truth, but to Milana they were spellbinding with their bronzed skins and glistening hair, like so many genii called up from the pages of those glossy magazines in all the kiosks. If she heard their names at all she instantly forgot them. Their talk spilled too fast for her. She could not relate to them, yet here she was, rubbing shoulders with the jet set in her little yellow dress that somehow, demurely, fitted in. In her new sandals with their silk ribbons wrapped around her shapely ankles, Milana could imagine for a moment that she had fallen through a looking-glass into a sparkling world of make believe. Trays of canapés passed under her nose, too exquisite to eat. Tiny morsels nestled in miniature bamboo boats, with little bamboo forks for sails, riding on a white porcelain sea. She stared at them in wonder. JC placed a glass in her hand. She sipped champagne for the first time ever and felt a warm glow spread through her. 'Can we go and look at the pictures?' she asked tugging at his arm.

They were remarkable drawings, flawless in their attention to detail, yet achieved with a minimum of strokes. '*People on the London underground*', humourously captured the quintessentially English indifference to another's proximity. In one drawing, a man read a newspaper, whilst a couple writhed beside him in a passionate embrace. In another, a man stood impassively in the crowded carriage, looking away, whilst near by a woman sobbed. In yet another, a man lay on the floor of a carriage filled with foreigners each staring at him, faces contorted with horror or concern whilst in the middle, an English man sat displaying dignified disinterest. The characters were carefully observed, their attitudes accurately reflecting frailties and defences. 'They're brilliant and so funny,' declared Milana with undisguised admiration. 'He's so clever. Look how he reads people. He unmasks them all.'

'JC are you going to introduce us?' said a low drawling voice tinged with mockery.

Milana turned towards the distinctive voice behind her.

'*Señora* Grazia, this is my girlfriend, Malala,' JC announced without hesitation.

Grazia Menendez, Santiago's mother, was stunning. Her pale cat-like eyes surveyed Milana with interest, her black hair fell in a perfect wave over her pale face, curling around her angular jaw. She stood back slightly and tilted her elegant head.

'You look familiar, my dear.' Her earrings, clusters of black pearls set in tiny diamonds peeked out from under the silken veil of hair. Her dress, a rich salmon pink trimmed in black plunged a tiny bit lower than propriety demanded revealing a glimpse of lace beneath. Milana breathed in her heady Chanel perfume.

'JC, you are full of surprises,' she twinkled at him. Her eyes turned to Milana, their perfect symmetry showing a glimmer of uncertainty,

'I didn't catch your name, my dear.'

'Malala Romero.'

'Romero,' she repeated a touch wearily.

'Have you met my nieces, JC? Gloria come,' she uttered the words as one who is used to command and her hand stretched out to clasp Gloria's arm. Gloria, tanned and in a strapless calypso dress, turned and smiled, her highlighted hair shone under the lamps. 'And this is Marie Louise Risopatron and this is Carmen Irrarrazaval, she said introducing the other two girls with similarly highlighted hair and equally diaphanous dresses, before turning away to speak to others who waited for her attention.

'Aren't they fab?' gushed Gloria enthusiastically about the drawings, 'I was at school with him. But he was older. We all had crushes on him.' Gloria giggled, 'Where are you at school?' she added politely.

'Malala's left school,' JC put in quickly, 'she's been studying art.'

'Really? What, abroad?' But Milana wasn't listening, she longed to be left alone to gaze on each picture at her leisure but she could see Grazia's feline eyes were turned in her direction and even at that distance seemed to penetrate. Milana's hackles rose and she tugged at JC's arm.

'Please let's go, JC,' she whispered urgently.

'Really?' he smiled. 'But you're such a hit here.'

Eventually they said their goodbyes and, reluctantly, JC led the way towards the exit.

'JC, before you go, come, do look at this.' At the sound of that drawl Milana's heart sank. She had sensed it immediately: Grazia had identified easy prey and the cat would have her mouse. Intrigued JC followed Grazia.

'Now tell me JC, what do you see?' Grazia's elegant hand draped his sleeve momentarily as the perfect nails tapped out their impatience on the fabric. They were standing before a charcoal portrait which had several smaller studies radiating off it, all of the same girl, and as JC turned his eyes on it, Grazia smiled triumphantly. His look of amazement said it all.

'I knew she looked familiar,' Grazia declared smugly. JC looked at Milana, who, hanging back a little, stared at the sketched picture of herself as she was three years ago.

'Now, I'll tell you a secret,' breathed Grazia, 'I pulled this one out of his luggage last year. I was quite intrigued by it and I included it in this show. Santiago has never painted a girl quite like that before.' She turned pointedly towards Milana, 'Who do you think this is, my dear?' Grazia's eyes searched her with frightening intensity. In that instant someone took a photograph and Milana saw the gracious smile that Grazia donned and lost, as the flash subsided.

'It's you, my dear. Most definitely. Do you know my son?' Although her manner was laced with charm, her tone was icy.

Milana gazed back at the painting that, lit up as it was, seemed to announce itself as irrefutable proof of their love; its bold strokes legitimizing her presence amongst this breed of people with whom she shared so little. She felt strength galvanise her spirit as though he himself were standing beside her. Silently she turned her glittering eyes towards Grazia and returned her gaze without wavering as she recognised the unexpected status the painting had bestowed on her.

'It's quite possible, I've known Malala off and on for a while,' JC promptly answered for her.

'Quite intriguing, isn't it? Where did you both meet?'

'Down south,' Milana shot him a complicit look.

'When I gave her a lift in my car,' JC smiled imperviously.

Grazia gave a perfunctory smile and reached out her hand, unfurling her slender fingers and waving her perfectly painted red nails towards a pretty girl who was just passing.

'Isabel, do come and say hello to JC,' Grazia drew out her vowels pulling her into the conversation. 'I'm sure you two have a lot to catch up on.' Then she turned to face Milana squaring her shoulders and positioning her bust like a rampart between them. 'Isabel here is Santiago's girlfriend,' she stated coldly. Milana sensed her intention to wound and kept her eyes lowered to avoid her scrutiny. More people interrupted and Grazia glided away with them but she had made her point. The woman was a pro at nailing her adversary and, despite her momentary sense of rebellion, Milana felt like an ant speared by a stiletto heel. The warm glow she had felt, blew out like a candle.

If Grazia Menendez had poured a glass of icy water down her back she could not have done better in bringing Milana to her miserable senses. Grazia had needed no further words to express her contempt. The warning had been unequivocal. In cruel contrast, Isabel was sweet and smiley and greeted Milana warmly.

'Hey JC, she's lovely,' she whispered and turning back to Milana, 'We thought JC, well, you know, that he played for the other side,' she confided, 'that's what Daddy calls it, isn't it a funny expression. Anyway, you'll squash all those silly rumours now,' she smiled welcomingly at Milana and turned to JC. 'Santiago always said you were straight.' She giggled coyly. 'You must know him quite well,' she said looking up at the portrait and then back to Milana. 'Did you go out with him?'

'No,' Milana assured her.

She smiled, clearly relieved. 'Were you a model?'

'A model?' Milana looked bemused.

'A painter's model you know, like in Paris, like at art classes.'

'Maybe he just saw her once and drew a quick sketch, like all these,' said JC hurriedly.

'Oh yes, no reason to know you at all, right?'

Milana nodded, no longer able to speak.

'We've got to dash, Isabel,' JC excused them, 'lovely to see you again.'

'And you JC, and your lovely girlfriend.'

As they turned to go Milana's foot slipped on a piece of paper. It was an invitation to the show that somebody had dropped. She picked it up and stared at it; 'Santiago Hidalgo and Hernan Garcia, Studies and Sketches.'

'JC, why does it say this here?' she said pulling him back and pointing to the name.

'That's the other guy who did all those abstract drawings in the other room. Quite clever to contrast Santiago's work with Hernan's. He's good too.'

'I mean the name, "Hidalgo".'

'That's his name, silly.' He seemed almost impatient now as he tried to make his way out of the building. But Milana stood still for a moment looking down at the engraved card in her hand. Surnames didn't figure in her life. She realised Grazia Menedes was Santiago's mother, but the boy of course would take the name of his father.

'Why isn't it Velasco. Isn't his father Jorge Velasco?' she persisted, catching up with JC.

'Jorge Velasco is Grazia's second husband. Santiago is from her first marriage to Carlos Hidalgo. Poor Carlos Hidalgo came to a bit of a grizzly end.' JC was walking a step or so in front of Milana, leading the way out so he never saw the impression his words made on her as he so casually spoke the name of the man Iris had claimed was also Milana's real father.

From that intangible place where hope and despair are born in equal measure and love finds its home, Milana heard a gut wrenching cry that silently swelled and rose and reverberated through her ears screaming 'No'. In one long endless echo it pulsated through her and seemed to stop her very blood as it tore through her veins and arteries with its hateful message and for an instant seemed to stop her heart. A passing waiter steadied her. Then a silence followed, more terrible for the emptiness it filled as her brain made all the fateful connections and hope drained. She bumped into someone and their glass fell shattering and spraying perfectly tanned ankles with champagne. But she saw only the blood Iris had described spurting from fateful wound and the little boy Letty had rescued from the murder scene, the one Iris had found curled up asleep on the spot where his father bled to death – Santiago, her Santiago? She turned then like one stricken and looked back at Grazia, seeing her for the first time as the woman Iris had saved from jail.

As JC reached out to open the car door for Milana, two things happened simultaneously; he saw a wretchedness in her eyes that turned him cold, and a young man stepped between them and flicked a knife in her face. In an instant the pick-pocket's hand had clasped the medal around her neck. A second later her knuckles smashed into his jaw so fast and furiously that they cracked audibly. He reeled back in pain. Before he could retaliate, JC had moved in and twisted his arm causing the knife to fall. He pushed the man to the floor and placed his knee in the small of his back and yelled at the bouncers across the road to help. He looked for Milana but could not see her. JC attributed the look of anguish on Milana's face to the fact that she must have seen the attack coming instants before he had.

In no time a crowd gathered and the security police pushed through. The cheap chain was still caught in the man's fingers. The police prised it off him.

'We'll be holding this chain as evidence of theft.' But Milana was desperately searching the pavement. She spied the fallen medal lying in the gutter, inches from a drain. *Leave it there, you have to give him up,* whispered the bitter voice of reason inside her. But moments later, someone's foot stepped into the gutter, dislodging the medal, shifting it even closer to the open grate.

'Oh,' she cried and stooped down to rescue it. JC watched

her as she straightened up. Before he could say anything a policeman addressed him.

'You'll have to come to the station to press charges, or we can't hold him, Sir.' JC looked back at Milana. She stood in the gutter her fist closed over the medal, her other hand resting on her neck. Her shoulders were slumped as if she had been struck in the stomach and he couldn't see her face for the waves of hair that hid her features.

'You'll be doing us a service, Sir. We'll take him to 34th precinct, do you know it?'

'Yes. We'll drive ourselves there shortly thanks,' said JC, stepping towards Milana and placing a protective arm around her. He felt her rigid and unmoving.

'You were awesome,' he whispered, 'let's get out of here.' And he led her to the car while the pick-pocket was led away in handcuffs.

'Wow! You tossed that right hook faster than any guy I know,' marvelled JC in the car. 'I guess you really know how to deal with these low lives. You're so impressive.' He glanced at her quickly as he turned onto the huge six lane highway, Avenida Kennedy. Milana looked fixedly ahead.

'I hope your knuckles aren't broken,' he went on, a touch awkwardly, for on reflection he judged his last remark might have been insensitive. On the whole JC was, at this point, impervious to the nature of Milana's feelings because they were too far off his own. He felt masterful. He had successfully grounded the culprit. It had been so quick and effortless with him and her acting together in perfect unison. He felt a wave of happiness and huge satisfaction at his own unaccustomed strength.

'Tell me about Carlos Hidalgo, how he died?' Milana asked. Her voice was thick and strange to her ears but JC didn't notice anything amiss. Conversationally, he continued.

'Oh it was terrible, my mother told me about it, but everyone knows the story, though it's never talked about now. Carlos Hidalgo died in a dreadful accident years ago, Grazia married again.' He opened a bottle of water and offered her a drink.

'They had a son?' she whispered hoarsely.

'Yeah.' He took a quick swig. 'Poor Santiago was about four or five I think. The gardener was accused of the murder…'

What she feared, knew already, was confirmed. In her mind the overwhelming and inevitable attraction not of lovers but of brother and sister suddenly explained everything. Why else would they have found each other so compelling, why else would a boy like Santiago have noticed the likes of her.

'JC! I'm going to be sick!' JC swerved off the road. Milana wrenched open the door and stumbled out of the car. She leaned over, her hand on her stomach, her whole body convulsed as she threw up every last canapé. JC got out of the car. He watched her bent nearly double, her body shaking, her hair cascading down. At first, he barely dared go over to her. The attack was so sudden and so violent that he wasn't sure what to do. But when he saw her lift her head slightly and clutch the nearby lamppost, he came up and gathering her hair into a pony-tail he held it off her face as she was sick again. As she continued to retch, her head thrown forwards with the effort, he placed his hand gently on her forehead for support. Finally, she breathed in deeply and taking a step away, sank down on the grass verge. JC brought water from the car and wiped her mouth with a handkerchief. Beads of sweat stood out on her temples and her hair clung to the sides of her face. Pale as death and worn out she met his look before turning her head away in pain. He sat beside her in silence and after a while he picked up her hand and cradled it in his own.

'What's the matter? Maybe it's the shock of the attack, after the nerves,' he whispered. She was unresponsive.

'Shall we go?' he suggested tentatively as an alternative.

She didn't move and didn't answer.

'Let's go,' he said standing slowly and reaching down to help her up. She looked at him so pitifully that he sat down again.

'Are you ill? What's the matter?' he repeated gently. She breathed in deeply. 'Did that idiot hurt you? Shall I take you to hospital?'

She shook her head turning her face away.

'Come. Let's go,' he repeated soothingly. 'I'll talk to the police while you wait for me in the car and rest. Let's get it over and done with.' She let him pull her up and help her to the car.

They drove in silence. JC glanced at her every couple of seconds and stroked the back of her head, barely able to see her face for the hair that fell obscuring her profile. Lovingly he swept it aside every now and again. When they drove into the police station car park he stopped the car and looked at her. She seemed to be sleeping. He leant over her, his hand touching the softness of her hair that curled over the edge of the leather seat as he reclined it for her. Then he took off his jacket and covered her with it.

'I'll be back in a minute,' he whispered but she made no answer.

When eventually JC returned to the car, his jacket was on the seat but Milana was gone.

Chapter Ten

Occasional lampposts lit the residential streets. Barely a car passed. The pavements were empty and silent but for JC's solitary footsteps. He turned around several times, trying to imagine what Milana would do, where she would go. As he searched the dimly lit streets, he thought of her walking alone, ill and dazed. Finally, he came to a corner where, a few yards away, he could see flickering candlelight through the windows of a small restaurant bar. He headed towards it, flung open the door and breathlessly examined the rustic interior. Copper pots and pans hung from the ceiling and empty wine bottles of varying shapes stood massed on shelves and reflected in the many little mirrors that lined the walls. The young people who sat huddled together deep in conversation barely noticed him. As he turned to leave he caught sight of a lonely figure sitting on the verandah outside, hunched over a solitary table.

'Malala,' he called coming over to her, 'you gave me such a fright. Why did you go away?'

She raised her eyes to him. Dark circles accentuated their vacant expression. It frightened him. For a fleeting instant he wondered if she might be mentally ill, somehow on medication she had forgotten to take and he remembered how she had warned him of his all too trusting nature. But his eyes fell on her slender hands folded demurely one over the other, her tiny wrists and the delicateness of her that he had never quite appreciated and his heart went out to her. Her vulnerability was breathtaking, almost intoxicating. He wanted to sweep her up in his arms that very instant.

'Come on. You can't stay here. Let me take you home.'

'Why?' she held her head in her hands. 'I want to stay here,' and then she added, 'What home?' JC drew up a chair.

'You're sick. You're cold and you're shivering. It's my turn to look after you.'

'What for?' Milana stared at him absently.

JC touched her skin with his fingers and felt its cold clamminess.

'Did you drink too much?' He searched her ashen face for clues. She closed her eyes.

He leant over her then and whispered, 'I'm going to take you to my place, Malala, so you can sleep.' His voice seemed to soothe her. She murmured something indistinct. He rose from his chair then and with sudden resolution he placed his arms around her and scooped her up like a child. He felt her surrendering. Her limbs were soft and pliant and her face rested against his shoulder. He felt both intimidated and exhilarated by the sudden intimacy of the moment. As he walked towards the car his arms tensed drawing her a little closer and he felt her breathing warming his skin beneath the fibres of his shirt.

He drove to his flat in a pretty residential street of Vitacura lined with mimosa and flowering laurels, and helped her out of the car in silence. Her slim frame subsided into his arms as he steered her into the elevator, her head rested on his shoulder, her hair massed around in soft waves over his arm. Helpless as she was, she still had the power to waken his senses whilst his thoughts despaired at her condition. He unlocked his front door on the sixth floor and switched on the light. Only then did he realise she was barefoot. Her feet sank into the soft thick pile carpet and she crumpled to the floor as though it were a haven on which to rest. He picked her up and took her through double doors to a room with a wrought-iron bed and a duvet untidily draped over it. He laid her down on his bed and placed a pillow under her head. Like a docile ragdoll she let him. Then he sat down on the bed beside her and stroked her hair. She closed her eyes and turned away from him.

For hours JC sat on a chair by the bed and watched her. He couldn't tear himself away from the sleeping form of the girl who filled his every thought and every waking moment. How could she know what she meant to him? Today he had learnt to whom her heart was pledged and he had seen enough pictorial evidence to suggest that Santiago loved her too.

To watch her was a privilege. To see her yielded to sleep was to witness the surrender from her for which he longed but never dared hope. She was devastatingly beautiful in the most overwhelming sense of the word. Every line of every feature was as perfect and soft as the curls that splayed themselves upon the pillow like golden waves. He stared so long at her lips that he could have drawn them perfectly; two high ridges with a gentle dip in the middle, the flesh full and soft and tinged with colour. He stayed beside her until the first rays of light turned the room a dim, colourless grey. She turned then towards him, her eyes wide open. He slipped from the chair and knelt by the bed. Her face was wet with tears, her hair tangled, her eyelashes glistening. He touched her face and closed his eyes, shielding her from their intensity.

'Why don't you sleep?' she whispered.

'I can't sleep. I can't stop watching you.'

She closed her eyes and he watched tears catch in her lashes and finally, wrestling themselves free, roll down her cheek. 'That's silly,' she said.

'My stomach is tied in knots and I can hardly breathe.' He smiled self-consciously.

She put her hand out to his. 'Not for me. Please not for me.'

'I can't help it.'

She opened her eyes then and he felt himself swimming in their gentleness.

'I wish with all my heart I loved you, JC,' she said this last so desperately that it gave him hope.

'Just to be here with you is enough,' he whispered.

'How? How can it be enough?'

'Nobody else will ever share this moment with you. To see you like this is almost like being made love to by you. Don't you see? It's your soul I want to reach out and touch and it's your soul that's crying now, dissolving all over my sheets and that's just one step away from dissolving over me.'

Milana held out her arms, tears now falling unchecked.

'How can you say such sweet things? How can I hold back from you what you so want? You can do what you like with me, JC.' The pain in her heart had left her past caring. JC lay on top of the bed in her arms feeling her body beneath him shaking with the sadness that seemed to rip her up inside. He kissed her soaking face tasting the salt of her tears in every kiss. He longed to kiss her lips but a sense of propriety held him back. He had no idea what was happeneing to her or to him but he felt himself overwhelmed by the waves of emotion that seemed to engulf them both. Just lying next to her he couldn't hold back the effect she had on him, far less trust himself to lie with her inside his bed. Instead he kept the duvet between them and with her arms holding him and her face so soft against his, he surrendered to the relief that came unaided, whilst the soft cotton of the duvet smothered the hope of love and life that flowed forth from him to her. He felt as though he had disintegrated into a million fragments, and all the time her hand stroked his hair fondly like a mother.

Much much later, when the sun warmed the room through the drawn curtains Milana whispered 'Thank you' to him.

'What for?'

'You could have done what you liked with me, I would have let you, but you didn't.'

'I love you but you don't belong to me, I know that. It would be like stealing.'

'Who from JC? Who would you be stealing from?'

'From you. You want to give yourself to me but you can't.'

'Love is an act of will,' said Milana with sudden strength. She meant that she would learn to love him, and JC understood. 'But Malala you can't deny a truth once it exists.'

'What truth?'

'What you told me days ago by the river. Your heart is somewhere else.'

'Then give me time.'

'I don't want you to be obliged to love me. Love should be a spontaneous combustion. It should flare up from within you, setting you on fire, lighting up your world.'

'A poet and an idealist.' She smiled at him weakly. 'And if you discovered such love, JC, inside you and then learnt that it was impossible?'

'Nothing is impossible.'

'Wrong then? '

'How could love like that be wrong?'

'If you loved your own sister it could.'

'Oh Malala your own sister doesn't do that for you,' he rolled over. 'Not in a million years.'

'Well what if you didn't know she was your sister, and after she'd woken every fibre of your being, someone told you.'

JC turned and looked at her.

'Gees, Malala, that would be the cruellest trick of fate.' The way he said 'Gees' reminded her of Ricci and the tears pricked her eyes again.

Time passed in silence and JC rarely left her side that day. Eventually he raised his head on his elbow and looked at her. She was turned away from him, curled up under the duvet and every now and then her body gave a tiny shudder as a silent sob wrenched out of her.

'Malala,' he whispered, 'I don't pretend to understand what's happening in your life. It sounds very painful and complicated and I know nothing gives me the right to pry, except love of you. But whatever is going on, I know one thing for sure. You shouldn't be alone. You shouldn't stay in that shack any more. Please will you stay with me, here? No conditions, no obligations. You gave me back my life, let me at least offer you a room and a shoulder to cry on. Please. Do it as a favour to me.'

'My heart is all drained out,' she whispered back as though she felt that only love could repay his kindness.

'For heaven's sake don't try to love me, Malala. That's not why I'm asking. It feels so good to love you and you need me now. Your trust in me is all the payment I need.'

Chapter Eleven

Santiago strolled through the double doors of Heathrow Airport. An elegant girl in a fur hat that covered her pretty blonde hair separated herself from the crowds and raced into his arms.

'I've missed you,' she said looking up at his dizzingly attractive, suntanned face.

He ruffled the fur on the hat. 'Hey. You shouldn't have come, Lizzy.'

'Why not?'

'It's far too early in the morning for you!' Santiago put his arm around her and pulled his suitcase behind. She noted he took his arm away to check his pocket, but he didn't put it back around her waist. A slight tension clouded his usual nonchalant charm.

'Tired?'

'Very.' He brushed her cheek gently. 'I won't be very good company,' he smiled apologetically. She took hold of his arm affectionately.

'So you didn't stay for your big Opening Night, I thought you would have been tempted.'

'You know I hate those society dos,' he said brushing off the subject.

'Well I thought maybe your mother would force you.'

He raised an amused eyebrow at Lizzy. She gave a little shrug, 'You never know.' And secretly she wondered if only his mother had more sway over him maybe she'd stand a chance too.

'I thought you could come back to my place today and we can drive to Cambridge tomorrow. That way we can stop off for lunch at my parents'.'

'Lizzy,' he stopped, concerned, 'I must go back to my digs now. I've got a load of unfinished reading.'

'Oh, come on. You'll be far too jet lagged to do any sensible work. What's in a day or so?' She touched the beaded bracelet round his wrist. 'What's this? The new Cartier man bracelet?' Santiago looked momentarily confused. She wished suddenly she hadn't asked, but struggled to understand why it mattered. It felt like an icy breeze had blown between them.

Lizzy's BMW soft-top sped along the M4 towards Draycott Avenue. The sun, pale and feeble, rose above the bare branches of trees shedding no warmth at all. Lizzy glanced at Santiago every now and again. He had reclined in the passenger seat and shut his eyes. His long legs showed off Argentinian leather boots similar to those that had first attracted her attention when they had planted themselves in front of her as she searched for a lost earring at a Cirencester Park polo match. He had still been holding the cup given to the winning team as her gaze travelled up the boots, the white trousers, to the broad shoulders clad in the team shirt and finally the perfect teeth smiling down at her. A wry 'Can I help you?' had accompanied the stunning smile in an almost perfect English accent, but with sufficient trace of Spanish to make her so forward as to say, as she had lifted herself up off the ground, 'I don't think it matters anymore.'

He'd raised one eyebrow.

'Doesn't matter?'

'No. The earring I dropped. You don't mind me in one earring do you?' Her boldness had astounded her, but the thrill that accompanied the rush of blood had made it worth it.

'You look perfect. Now I see more of you, much better.'

That's how playfully it had begun. He a Cambridge undergraduate from Chile, invited to play polo at Cirencester, she a graduate from Bristol, about to start a design course in London. A week later she invited him to stay with her parents, Lord and Lady Bertie in Godmanchester. For fun he had sketched their labrador as a present. For Christmas, he had sketched the house and had it framed for them and for Lizzy's twenty-second birthday, he had presented her with a small oil portrait of herself that went up in the drawing room where it was much admired.

'Does he make you happy, Lizzy?' Lord Bertie, her father had asked of her on Santiago's last visit, between drives during a pheasant shoot.

'Insanely happy, Daddy.'

'Then marry the boy.'

'It's not up to me. Besides he's hardly thinking of settling down.'

'Rubbish girl. It's always up to the woman. I'd never be married to your mother if she hadn't set her mind on me. Lassoo the boy, my dear, before someone else does.'

'You do like him then, Daddy?' she'd asked, immensely gratified that her father should approve of her foreign boyfriend.

'As a matter of fact I do. His father was a fine chap, Hidalgo. Used to stay at Boodles on trips to England. Played polo with the royals a couple of times; a fine, generous man. Horribly murdered years ago in his own home by some ghastly servant boy. This Santiago's a clever chap too, and you won't be short of a penny or too, his father left him the Hidalgo fortune.'

Lizzy Bertie knew that to try to lassoo Santiago Hidalgo would be as silly as trying to catch a panther on the run. At best she might tame him, if she let him be himself and didn't ask too many questions and made him laugh. But there were times when she could not reach him. Lizzy glanced at him now; just having him in the car next to her made her feel triumphant. She could count on one hand the times he had made love to her. No one had ever made love to her like he did. Maybe it was feeling this enigmatic creature surrender to love-making with such intensity that galvanised her senses. Once she had whispered, 'I love you,' to him and he had stopped, and with extraordinary tenderness had touched her face and held her hand but the passion had ebbed away like a tide. She had cried that night, after he had left, not quite sure why, but in time she recognised that she must have startled him from a dream to which she was a stranger and his honesty had got the better of him.

As she drove, she placed her hand on his lap. He took it. She squeezed but he did not squeeze back.

'Did you manage to sleep on the plane?'

'Not a wink.'

He let go of her hand so gradually that she wondered if he had fallen asleep.

'Lizzy why are you so kind to me?' he murmured suddenly. Lizzy glanced at him unsure of how to respond. His mood was different, something had changed in him. She saw his eyes were still closed. It was not tension between them exactly that made her feel slightly awkward, but rather an unaccustomed intensity that seemed to emanate from him.

'You make me sound like a carer.'

'Maybe I need a carer.' She saw a familiar grin spread over his features, at odds with the sadness in his tone.

'Don't be silly, Santiago.' She paused. 'You need a lover.'

'Love is too complicated.'

'No. Love is very easy, you either feel it or you don't.' She wished immediately she could take that back.

He opened his eyes, looked ahead at the traffic and closed them again.

'What's the difference between love and attraction, then?'

'Oh, come on!'

'Just answer the question, if you can that is,' he replied, almost playfully.

'I don't know. Attraction is just like a tickle under your nose. You have to pay attention to it, but it may pass,' she stated matter of factly.

'And love?'

She thought for a moment and then she laughed, 'OK I'll tell you what love is. Love is when something is torn out of you and if the person goes away they take a piece of you away with them and if they don't come back with it you feel maybe you'll die or lose a bit of yourself forever.'

'Whoa! Where's that come from?'

'You. Last year, after the Grosvenor ball, when you felt so sick because you'd mixed all those drinks.' She glanced at him.

'My God,' he sat up and pulled his fingers through his hair. 'Did I say that? How do you remember these things?'

'I wrote it in my diary' she admitted sheepishly. She could feel him thinking. They hit traffic on the Cromwell Road. Lizzy shot him a glance. He caught her eye.

'Have you ever felt that, Lizzy?'

'What?

'Come on, you heard.'

'I thought you were tired.'

'I'm knackered.'

'Can't this wait.'

'It's a simple question.'

'I don't want to do this now, Santiago. I can't think straight.'

'I don't want you to think, I want you to feel the answer.'

'I don't know.'

She felt his hand gently laid on her arm.

'It's OK. I just asked you a question about yourself.' Was he teasing? She could never quite tell.

'I hate those kind of questions.'

He smiled and took away his hand. The sudden tension in her chest spread to her stomach. They turned into Draycott Avenue. Lizzy parked and pulled up the handbrake.

'God, you just pull me inside out sometimes, Santiago.' She crossed her arms over the steering wheel and rested her head on them.

'I want us to be honest, Lizzy.'

'Aren't we always.'

'No. We play games and understand the rules. Wouldn't you say?'

'Gosh.'

'Hey, I'm no good at this either. But I reckon you're braver than I am.'

'And you,' she murmured into the sleeve of her coat, 'will you be honest with me then?'

'Yes. I'll give it my best shot.'

'When you're with me...' she began, her voice slightly muffled. She felt the urge to mock and belittle, her classic defence to block out truth and feeling. 'I can't do this,' she concluded weakly.

'I'm just asking what you feel, Lizzy.' Frustration stung her eyes. She didn't want emotion to make her vulnerable, she'd fought it so much. Now he was opening a dangerous door and she knew he offered no guarantee of safety on the other side. She looked away at the blocks of elegant red brick buildings, so fixed and imperious; an unbroken, unshakeable, definitive line of solid brick.

'You've never taken a piece of me from me,' she said suddenly. 'You've never taken anything from me. I wish you had, then a little bit of me might actually belong with you. If that's what you mean.' Lizzy sighed, and turned to look at him. 'What's all this about Santiago. You've changed suddenly.'

'No, I'm just grappling with my demons.'

'You know, that first time I asked you to make love to me, Santiago, I thought it might bring you closer to me, but it doesn't work that way. Sex won't bring a man any closer.'

She saw the corner of his lip twitch to a smile, 'I think you'll find it will,' he corrected her playfully.'

'Ok yes, some men, but not you. I've learnt that with you. It just made it more clear to me that I couldn't reach…' she paused looking for the exact words; 'the place in your heart that I wanted to curl up in,' she finished sadly.

'You mean sex won't make them love you more,' he suggested.

'I mean it didn't make you love me any more.' She felt a lump rise from her stomach to her throat.

Santiago seemed to be listening to her as though every word she said mattered desperately to him and yet she felt his thoughts were far away.

Lizzy burst into tears.

'Hey, Lizzy.' He leant over to her putting his arms round her. 'Whoa, what's the matter?'

'It's just I know what's happening.' She tried to smile and wipe away the tears but they just came faster. 'I feel you're very far away and I've lost you. I don't feel I've lost a piece of me forever. I've just lost you; the man I want to be loved by more than anything else in the world right now. But you've never loved me like that, and somehow you've managed to stop me falling for you like that. I cheapened it all by seducing you as best I could. It's like I stole something that wasn't really meant for me. I've thought that so many times and not wanted to face it.' Tears rolled down her face.

'Lizzy, you've never cheapened anything. Being with you was wonderful, the best thing that could have happened to me. You're warm and intuitive and you're kind and funny. It's just there's so much darkness inside me Lizzy that I try to steer away from. You've brought so much light and happiness into my life. Don't say you've lost me,' he said hugging her with real feeling. 'You've never tied me down. I feel free with you. I feel so much for you Lizzy, I find it so hard to distinguish what these feelings are. There are so many ways we can love.'

'No. You feel intensely grateful. I know the difference, Santiago.'

'Have I been that selfish, Lizzy?' He pulled away enough to take her face and cup it gently in his hands. 'It's the last thing I want to be. None of this is fair to you, Lizzy.'

'We make our bed, we lie in it,' she answered stoically, smiling through her tears.

He shook his head.

'Don't you dare feel sorry for me now, Santiago,' she said with unexpected vehemence. She took his hands from her face. Why was life like that, he wondered. This was so easy, so potentially perfect, why did his heart pull him back to a wasteland of river and an almost impossible hope. Part of him longed to lean over and kiss Lizzy and make love to her as though by doing so he could kick start a stalled hope and forget the agony of longing that pulled him back thousands of miles to an implausible love. Her eyes darted over his face studying the shadows that crossed there.

'Talk to me, come on, Santiago. I deserve that much surely.'

'Oh God, Lizzy you deserve that and much more.' He pulled his fingers through his hair and looked at her lovely earnest face, still streaked with tears.

'I spent a whole night awake in Chile, staring up at that southern sky with its endless stars that make you feel so tiny and insignificant and I thought about what I was doing and I knew I wasn't being fair to either of us. Sometimes you do need another person to talk to, to get a perspective on yourself. The problem is I've never let anyone close, not really.'

'Couldn't you talk to your mother?'

Santiago laughed. 'My mother, Lizzy, is like a scorpion, passionate and with a sting in her tail. She doesn't know how to love, only how to control. She's the last person I'd open my heart to. When I look for love it is as far from her world as possible.'

'When I met her, she seemed so gracious, so warm, and she loves you so much. You were so sweet to her.'

'A bit of sweetness to counter a lot of bitterness.'

'I wasn't very intuitive there then.'

'That just means there were no cracks in our performance.' He smiled.

'Gosh. I see. What about Isabel, do you confide in her?'

'Isabel is part of my mother's world and, for all her sweet letters, I've told you I don't love Isabel. I've never done or said anything to suggest I love her. I think I held her hand once on a walk, now everyone wants to believe she's my girlfriend.'

'Why don't you stop them?'

'I've told her I'm a lost cause. If she doesn't get that, more words will just complicate things.'

Lizzy sighed. 'Women love lost causes.'

'The point is Lizzy,' he said gently stroking her hair as she rested her head on his shoulder. 'I think you have actually found a place in my heart to curl up in, because when I was out there alone that night that's where I found you, unexpectedly. Though, maybe not quite in the way you might have hoped.' He brushed her nose affectionately with his finger.

'I get it,' she whispered. She felt him kiss her head and a kind of calm stilled the tension in her heart.

'So who taught you what love is? Like that, like you

279

described it?' She looked up at him. Santiago met her gaze and raised an eyebrow.

'Don't evade the question. Someone must have done, and it obviously wasn't your mother.'

Lizzy touched the bracelet on his wrist.

'The girl that gave you this?'

'Maybe,' he smiled knowing she was drawing him into an intimacy never broached before.

'How long have you known her?'

He shook his head and sighed resignedly.

'Three years.'

'Oh God, all the time you knew me?'

'No, before that. I was seventeen, nearly eighteen. She was barely fourteen back then, Lizzy. I saw her for one brief spring. I never slept with her. I only kissed her once.'

'But you wanted to?'

'I was seventeen, eighteen.' As though that explained the obvious.

'And now did you sleep with her?'

He shook his head.

'Why not?'

He smiled and shrugged. He seemed so young suddenly that Lizzy felt infinitely older, almost jaded.

'Fourteen, God that's young.'

'She's almost eighteen now,' he reminded her

'And you saw her?'

'For a moment.'

'And you still… I mean you both still feel the same after all that time. You could tell that?'

'Lizzy, don't…' But she didn't let him finish. She put her finger to his mouth.

'Let me ask, or these questions will plague me. Don't you see? You could have slept with her, but you didn't? Why?'

Feeling himself torn by the honesty she seemed to want to drag out of him, he whispered, 'I'd have missed my plane.' A fleeting look of wistfulness suggested he was telling the truth.

'My God, Santiago. All this time, the dashing polo player, so strong and aloof, with every girl in sight swooning over him, has been in love with… I mean a fourteen-year-old girl won your heart.'

'She's not fourteen anymore, Lizzy.'

'Why did you fall in love with her? What was it about her?' asked Lizzy watching how Santiago's face so quickly creased into that familiar smile behind which he hid his real emotions.

'I don't know.'

'You won't hurt me by telling me.'

The smile faded and his eyes rested on her gravely. He put his hand momentarily over hers, and looked out thoughtfully at the line of red brick mansion blocks.

'Please tell me about her,' Lizzy whispered, 'I can take it.'

'I don't know,' he sighed still looking away and leant his head back against the head rest.

'Believe me, Santiago, it would really help me to know about her. I know it sounds masochistic to you, but don't try to understand it. You said you never could get your head around women. So just talk to me.'

'Maybe she had a belief I lost a long time ago,' he said quietly. Lizzy waited very still, not wanting to interrupt the flow of feeling she could sense washing over him.

'She feels with her heart. Most people say they do but they mostly feel with their head, their reason and their prejudices. She works through her senses, she's naturally wise. There's a kind of fluidity about her.' He closed his eyes. 'It's like she can pour herself into you and all the absences inside you are filled by her energy, her sense of wonder. She's a completely free spirit. Maybe all shantytown girls are like that but she's the only one I know. Sometimes I feel it can't be real, it can't last; this feeling. It's too pure, too…' He opened his eyes suddenly and their blueness seemed brighter than ever.

'She sort of unfroze my soul when I barely knew I had one.'

'What did you do for her?' asked Lizzy softly.

Santiago looked taken aback.

'You may be really selfish,' she teased, 'but you must have done something for her or you wouldn't be so fused together after three years apart.'

'I suppose I unleashed her talent,' he said after giving it some thought. 'All that energy, the essence of her was waiting to be expressed, she has real talent. Now maybe everyone will see what I saw in her, through her art, then the world will fall in love with her, and I'll lose her.'

His unexpected albeit reluctant intimacy took Lizzy's breath away. His voice melted into her like a balm. This was the Santiago she had searched for, hidden until now. It was as though the veil of melancholy that had shrouded his heart had been lifted and she saw it beating for the first time with all the vigour and passion she had longed to awaken in him. She knew that for him to open up to her was the closest to his love she would ever come and she had the presence of mind to treasure the moment.

'Go on,' she whispered.

Santiago took Lizzy's hand covering it in both his, as though to protect her from what he was saying and yet recognising in himself the longing to confide.

'I find myself thinking about her suddenly. It's just like a random heartbeat that I feel unexpectedly that tells me she's still alive in me.' He met Lizzy's eyes, 'I tried so hard to forget her.'

'You wanted to forget her when you were with me.'

'Of course I did. I wanted to be able to give you myself, but I couldn't. That's why I had to ask you, what I asked you just now. I never wanted to take from you what I couldn't give back.' His look seemed to search for a much deeper understanding of the why's and wherefore's of love.

'Well you didn't take anything I didn't want to give,' she whispered, 'but I couldn't give what you needed, I realised that.' He turned her hand over in his and, thoughtful, he traced the lines of her palm with his finger. 'You won't ever know what you've meant to me during these years, you kind of saved me, Lizzy.'

'I didn't think you needed saving,' Lizzy declared, 'but glad to oblige.' She added with a sudden flippancy, 'Now just tell me more about this girl, and how she managed to get such a foothold in that icy heart of yours.'

He laughed, 'Icy?'

'Frozen then. Your word not mine.'

'She gave me a new perspective on everything and somehow that helped...' but he didn't finish his sentence. Heavy clouds were gathering in the darkening sky. They both surveyed them.

'Free you? From the nightmares you painted last year?' suggested Lizzy tentatively, glancing at him out of the corner of her eye. His face was in profile and in the gathering shadows it seemed the roughness of his dark unshaved appearance gave him a rugged strength. For a moment he seemed a stranger who had lived and seen a world irreconcilable to her own. He turned and caught her looking.

'No. Not those, but maybe to face them.' He paused, 'And that's a very small snout to be ferreting in so deep,' he added playfully brushing her nose.

'What are you going to do. I mean with her?' Lizzy persisted quite undeterred.

'Well, let's see.' He raked his fingers through his thick mane of hair. 'I'm going to finish my degree and I'm going to find her and take her away from Chile, all that prejudice and prying, and marry her and have a thousand babies with her.' There was a quizzical half laughing expression in his eyes. Lizzy stared at him speechless. Was he teasing again? He raised an eyebrow, a smile spreading over his face. 'I've never really had a family.' He pulled his fingers through his hair again and looked at her slightly abashed, 'I've said it,' he laughed, 'I haven't told a living soul but you, Lizzy. Do you know what a relief it is to say it, to tell you all this. To allow myself to think this crazy stuff at all?'

Lizzy couldn't help laughing at the way he seemed so surprised at his own confession.

'You've let me in, Santiago. At last! I feel almost triumphant, though I'm insanely jealous,' she teased, with a little wistful smile. 'You won't shy away from me now just because you've opened up to me.'

'How could I? You've liberated me. This is true friendship, Lizzy.' A few random flakes of snow began to fall. He took in her sweet face, her lively eyes and how they seemed riveted on him and wondered how the thought of Milana could have such a hold over him. And then to break the gravity of the moment, he added, 'You want to be Godmother to my first child, I understand, I'll consider it.'

'Santiago, you're impossible.' she threw her furry hat at him and opened the door to get out.

He grabbed her wrist. 'Hey, are we really OK here. I mean, here.' He indicated his heart. She bravely met his candid eyes. The snow was falling in great flurries now. It settled on her coat and her arm as he held her.

'Let me down gently, Santiago, I still need your company. I need time to grow into our friendship.' Turning over her hand in his, he bent his head and kissed its open palm.

Chapter Twelve

A stone hit the car windscreen and, like ice cracking, the glass shattered into a million pieces.

JC swore as he swerved on Kennedy Avenue and skidded to a halt. Milana had covered her face with her arm. On the overpass, kids raced out of sight. They'd scored a direct hit. 'Bloody slum kids. They could have killed us!' he added wrenching open the car door. Milana bristled momentarily. JC looked back at her instantly apologetic.

'You're right, shantytown oiks, I saw them,' she sighed, 'don't apologise.'

JC paced up and down on the grassy verge, mobile phone pressed to his ear, his mouth opening and closing but inaudible over the traffic. From inside the car, Milana watched him and thought of fish in aquariums moving their mouths, staring out at an unfamiliar world. She looked out of the jagged hole in the windscreen through which the heat of the day was penetrating the still air conditioned interior. The Andes mountains towered snow-capped and imperious in the midday haze. She reached out to feel the thickness of the broken pane and she studied the glass where it had held together and caved in like a concave puzzle of infinite broken lines.

Milana opened the car door and called to JC, who stood, his cheek muscles twitching with tension, punching numbers into his mobile.

'This is amazing, JC! You can almost peel it away from the frame like a fragmented carpet of glass.' She picked up a few stray pieces. 'They're like little diamonds.'

'They'll be bloodied diamonds if you start messing about

with them. My God! What a mess!' he added noting for the first time where the glass had sprayed into the car. He passed his hand over his face as if to check there wasn't any embedded there.

'We were lucky you know,' she murmured as she pulled at the bits of glass still stuck to the window frame. She glanced up and noticed JC's infuriated look.

'Blood rubies! Just think how pretty…' she added teasingly.

'Great! We nearly get killed by falling rocks and you think of jewellery making. Let's just grab a cab and get the Automobile Club to sort out this mess. We can't drive the car like this.'

'Wait JC, I've got an idea.' Milana walked round to the back of the car and took out an old plastic bag which she started filling with bits of glass.

'Malala, I'm not going to stand here while you clear this up. They've got ways of vacuuming it.'

Milana glanced at him. 'I'm not clearing it up. I'm collecting it.'

'Whatever,' JC covered his eyes, a smile spreading suddenly across his face as he realised how carefree she was of any concern for possessions. He laughed out loud. 'Is this what I'm in for, hanging around with you? You're going to start bringing home bits of broken glass? Next it'll be banana peels and soon I'll be living at a dump site.'

Milana straightened up, delighted with her pickings. 'I guess we all try to recreate home wherever we are. You should have thought of that before you asked me to stay.'

'I'd rather have you make my home a regular dump than live alone in pristine splendour,' he replied looking at her fondly.

'I'll do my best,' she said collecting all the bits she could lay her hands on.

JC had spent each day of the last week convincing Milana that she should stay one more day with him. Finally, last night, they had shared a bottle of wine and he had dared to ask her straight out if she would stay for a few weeks, until the summer was over. To his surprise she hadn't balked at the idea. Her first question had been:

'What about your friends, won't they talk? You know how people are.'

'They're all away for the summer.'

'Why didn't you go away with them?'

'I had other plans, remember.'

'You planned to die?'

'Well, not exactly die, but just do my own thing and then I thought why not die after all, who would care? Loneliness is awful, Malala. I'd like it if you stayed. I don't go back to university till March.'

'And then what?'

'I don't know. I'll go to class and come back each evening and you can paint all day. Who cares? We can do whatever we like.'

'Nilda left me some money when she died. You saw where I buried it by the crosses on the riverbank. I'll need it.'

'Is that a yes?'

Milana shrugged.

'Malala, I have money, enough for both of us.'

'But I want to use my own.'

'Have it your own way. I'll get it for you but I can always lend you anything you need.'

'I want you to be my friend not my keeper.' JC read the pain and sadness in her still. It was the fly in the perfect ointment of their togetherness. She reached for his hand on the table.

'I do want to stay here with you. I want to try,' she looked away awkwardly, 'you must give me time.'

JC's love was like the kiss of life. She felt it even if she couldn't return it. All her hopes, every dream that she had nurtured, lay shattered. Her love for Santiago, all the more powerful for having been sustained spiritually for so long, had fed her strength as intangibly as oxygen breathed life daily through her lungs. Denied it, she felt as though she were gasping for air, holding on to JC for saftey.

'I can't go back to the river or the shack, I can't face any of it. I feel so weak still. I need you now, JC,' she whispered, 'but

I'm afraid. If I get strong again. If I get over all this, and I leave you, you won't die on me, will you?'

'I promise I won't die on you,' JC said soothingly as he got up, averting her scrutiny.

JC didn't pry into what had happened to cause her so much distress. The less he knew the happier he felt. All he wanted was to live the present with her. To have her near, to enjoy her company. But all the time he noticed she was apprehensive, like a bird that doesn't want its wings touched for fear they may be clipped.

'I'm going to make candle holders,' Milana declared opening the bag and looking at all the little bits of glass she'd collected.

'What?' JC looked up from yet another number he was punching into his mobile phone, 'Candle holders out of that shattered windscreen?' He shook his head in mock despair. Clutching her bag of glass Milana sat on the grass and watched the traffic. The stone breaking the windscreen into smithereens had somehow released the pressure of anguish inside her. All the way towards the river she had felt a ribbon of oppression tightening in her heart as she realised she should never have agreed to go back to the shack with JC to fetch her belongings. Rashly she had decided it might purge the memory but that was wishful thinking.

JC walked up.

'We have to wait for the police, I can't drive the car like this.' He sat down beside her.

'I was wrong to come with you today,' she admitted.

He looked at her earnestly. 'Why?'

She longed to peel her love from Santiago like a transfer and smooth it onto gentle, loving JC.

'I wish the riverbank was something you could shatter like glass, like one of those globes, you know with snowflakes that you shake and they fall on a little scene trapped inside the glass, and if you drop it, it cracks and all the water flows out and the snowflakes are just bits of plastic.'

JC picked up her hand and played with her fingers, touching each tip in turn.

'That woman Iris,' he said quietly, 'I don't want you to see her again.'

'What? Why?'

'I think she has a hold over you. I don't know. It's not good that's all.'

'It's not like that. I know she's a bit of a witch, I always thought she was a real witch actually. You know she's from Vichuquen, but it's not that. That's not why I feel as I do about the shack and the river… it's just that…'

'What is it?'

'Iris told me something, or rather it was something I overheard, about my past, a long time ago, that's the only real hold she has over me.'

Despite a longing to disbelieve the story Iris had told three years back it made even more sense now. It explained why she and Santiago had been so inexplicably drawn to each other. Something greater than chance, blood itself, had pulled them fatally together. *There is no such thing as coincidence*, the words rang out in her ears. The story was more believable than ever. The knowledge she had acquired from overhearing it made it her responsibility to put an end to her relationship with Santiago that now had no future because of the prior one that already existed.

'Why do you have to speak to me in riddles Malala?'

'Sometimes that's all we have JC. There aren't any explanations for why shit happens.'

'Can't you just forget about Iris and her stupid stories and all the weirdness.'

'JC, Iris is not relevant anymore, it's just I have to give something up because it's the right thing to do, but I'm afraid I won't be able to and it scares me.'

'What, like drugs?'

She laughed, 'No, but yes, rather like that.'

'Oh, well, that's OK then.'

'How is it OK?'

'Well this can't be about Santiago because you can hardly be hooked on him.'

'And why not?' she asked feigning to tease him.

'Because you have to be with someone to be hooked on them?'

'Maybe, but do you think love stops when you don't see someone? I love God and I can't see him.'

'So this is about Santiago?' JC looked crestfallen.

'JC, I'm just saying...'

Even the mention of Santiago's name shifted the equilibrium within her and set her pulse racing. She wanted to hear his name again and again. She longed to ask JC everything he knew about Santiago, to the most insignificant detail. Was it so terrible to love a half-brother? The thought crept stealthily up on her, and once again she crushed it down. The image of the knife flicked in her face and the man tearing the medal from her so that it rolled into the gutter now made miserable, unequivocal sense.

'Let's not do this to each other,' JC said moodily.

'Let's not talk about Iris, or the river anymore,' countered Milana.

'You never need to go back there. I hope the shack gets blown away in the wind. Start again Malala, you and me – no baggage,' he said hopefully.

Milana pulled over the bag of broken glass.

'My new beginning.' She smiled, showing him the little fragments within, 'You'll see, I'll make something of it.'

It wasn't quite what he'd meant but he squeezed her hand and leant over to kiss her cheek. Despite a few false starts he felt there was hope for them together and his mood lifted like a morning mist pierced by the sun.

JC's mobile rang, he fumbled to answer it as he lifted himself off the grass and walked a few feet away. The sun caught his hair forming a halo around him as it had the first day she had met him. Milana thought of the fragments of glass and china she had collected from the mud of the riverbank. She was seventeen now, and still, all she had in the world seemed to be a bag of broken glass. She leant back on the grass while JC described their location to the operator, and stared at the luminous sky that stretched like a blank blue canvas above her and wondered how the stars still shone there in a darker place beyond.

Chapter Thirteen

The summer was all but over, heralding the start of the new academic year.

Outside the window of JC's flat, the caki fruit hung on the trees as rich and ripe as fat tomatoes. Humming birds hovered sucking out the sweet nectar. The one thousand *peso* note Santiago had left outside the shack remained folded within easy reach, under the mattress of Milana's bed where her fingers could search it out at night. Its message; the Cambridge address, so hurriedly and hopefully written on it, unheeded by her. Still she tried to limit the times she looked at it.

The door slammed shut behind JC. She knew he would be gone for hours. The clock on her bedside table showed the time and date: 9.30am, Friday March 6th. The sun's rays coming up over the mountains streamed in through the narrow loggia windows and lit her bedroom. Milana fingered the thick petals of the red hibiscus flower she held, studying how magnificently they had unfurled from the great trumpet in the centre. Stroking the petals against her cheek she thought of what had just happened. Her hand travelled over her stomach pensively tracing the ghost of a path. She tossed the flower onto the bed and watched it turn on itself and come to rest like a patch of blood on the whiteness of the bed linen.

The room was tiny, no doubt meant for a maid but she had finally given JC the ultimatum that she must sleep here or leave. The first two nights in the flat with him had been too gruelling. JC had insisted she slept in his bed and he had placed himself on a makeshift mattress on the far side of the room, by the window. She had woken the first night to find him propped up on one elbow, wide awake and staring at her.

'I still can't sleep,' he had admitted meekly, 'you go back to sleep I'm just an incurable insomniac.'

The next night she had woken again to find him in the same state of wakefulness. Concerned, she had slipped out of bed and suggested that, if he let her sleep on the mattress, he might get some sleep back in his own bed.

'This just isn't fair on you, JC, I can't do this.' She had repeated, standing over him with her arms folded refusing to get back into bed. 'I'm taking that little bedroom behind the kitchen, and that's that.'

'Please don't,' he'd said grasping her arm. 'I love to look at you,' he added awkwardly.

'God JC, that's just weird. You can't look at me while I sleep.' But she was touched by his honesty.

'I can't sleep with you in the room.' He shrugged, 'But it's so much better than sleeping with you in the other room.'

It had made her laugh, them standing there in the middle of the night in such a peculiar predicament. But sense had prevailed and she had made the move to the little box room in which she felt happy and safe. It opened onto a loggia where she had placed the easel and canvas he had bought her. She was working on an abstract painting inspired by the many fragments she had collected, past and present. Meanwhile she had devised a way of colouring and varnishing broken glass from windscreens onto cheap wooden photo frames and simple candle holders so that it reflected the light like little diamonds. So the weeks passed. While JC cycled and swam and played tennis at the Golf Club, she painted and varnished and invented more unusual decorations. She was enterprising and persuasive and unusually articulate, and when JC introduced her to the marketing director of the shop House and Ideas, by chance over a drink, the woman was taken by her original creative vision and a deal was struck. She had a buyer for what JC termed her 'crazy creations'.

Milana stepped out into the loggia knowing she needed to finish varnishing the candle holders she had made in order to box them up and deliver them to House and Ideas in time for their sale on Monday. She took a moment to cast her eye over the unfinished painting on the easel and found herself reliving the events of the past hour, as though she needed to fix it in her heart like a foundation on which she could build something that would bring peace to her restless soul.

'What will you call it?' JC had asked walking breezily into the kitchen in search of breakfast and tilting his head this way and that to get a perspective on the picture. It depicted pieces of multicoloured glass flowing through an hour glass that itself was distorted by the glass of a window through which it was being viewed.

'Lifetimes of glass? Glass Lives?'

'Mmm, shouldn't you be varnishing those candle holders in the other room.'

'Yep,' she said unconcerned, and stood back from the easel. 'But this cries out for my attention. Like a baby wailing and my paintbrush is the pacifier.'

'OK, weird, but I know what it feels like.'

'What?'

'Wailing for your attention.'

'Careful!' She poked her paintbrush in his direction, 'Want a mouthful of bristles?'

She looked back at the painting.

'You know my whole life could be measured out in bits of glass. The only thing is, I wish I didn't always pick my stuff out of dumps, you should see the car dump I had to go to yesterday to get the last supply of broken glass.'

As she chattered, Milana pulled off an apron that covered her little T-shirt and shorts, and draped it over the back of a chair.

'Aren't you going to have breakfast?' She moved about the room, barefoot and bare legged, unaware of the gracefulness of her movements as she slipped between the easel and the chair and around the little table that all fitted into the tiny loggia.

'Later, I'll grab a coffee and a croissant. Tell me about the dump you went to yesterday.'

He watched her, enjoying the lithe quickness of her movements.

'I asked the *taxi collectivo* to wait at the dump seeing as I kind of know him now, besides he didn't have any passengers. But guess what? While he was waiting, listening to the radio, his taxi got that close to being airlifted and crushed to pulp by the great claw cruncher. Poor bloke opened the door and ran out screaming, that's when the guy driving the machine figured it wasn't scrap metal!' She glanced back at JC from the sink where she was washing paintbrushes.

'I joked he could have ended up as a candle holder but I know that's the last time he's going to wait there for me. I hate going to that dump because they've got Alsatians and they're not always chained up. They're aggressive those blokes, I hate their type.' They reminded her of the *micreros* Letty used to be so friendly with. JC listened, leaning on the lintel of the door, feeling the happiness of sharing his life with her.

'I hope you don't go dressed like that?' he quipped.

'They don't give a rat's ass what you're wearing, JC.'

'I'll go with you next time.'

She glanced at him and smiled. 'Hey, no special favours OK?'

'I don't know what I'd do without you here, Malala,' he sighed. She carried on moving between the loggia and the kitchen, passing him once and again, as he stood there, with his hands in his pockets following her moves like a hopeful dog.

'You might go and breathe some fresh air instead of all the varnish fumes round here, they're probably messing with your head,' she retorted.

'No, I mean it.' He grabbed her arm and pulled her back as she passed. 'For the first time in my life I'm happy, really happy. I never thought I'd be happy, ever.'

'Me too.' She looked up at his kind face and felt a sudden rush of gratefulness.

'I've invited some friends over, we always meet at the Golf

Club and as you never come along, I've told them to come over. They want to meet you.'

'Whoa, I'm not an exhibit,' she said releasing herself from his gentle grip.

'Yeah but you're not a figment of my imagination either, are you?' He swept back her hair and let it drape itself over the back of his hand. 'Because I think they think you are.' He lifted her hair and let it fall over her shoulders in its tangled profusion.

'OK, let them come, they can get high on the fumes. I have to varnish all day.'

'Really? I'm going cycling with a friend, we're going up the Manquehue Hill, don't you want to come?'

She laughed. 'You know I can't ride a bike silly.'

He stared after her, wondering at the simple things she had never done and the complex things she achieved with such ease.

'I won't be back till nearly sundown.'

'OK I'll make pizza,' she said covering the last of the paints.

'Malala,' he said, folding his arms and following her with his eyes, 'do you find a flower on your pillow every night?'

'Yes.' She thought of the stunning splash of colour it made on her white pillow each evening.

'You've never mentioned it. Do you know what it means?' his voice was suddenly huskier than before, like it came from some forbidden place. She turned then and felt for the first time a wrench in her gut, the first frisson of a tension somewhere deep, like the awareness of a life within responding to him that surprised and pleased her.

'Yes,' she said bravely and felt the colour rise to her cheeks. He looked so surprised that she laughed, 'Don't you?'

His face creased into a boyish smile, 'Not really,' but he took a step closer. 'Maybe you could return the favour.'

'Really?' she said standing her ground, 'What with?'

He moved a little closer, astounded by what he could hardly believe was happening, 'Something better, more surprising.'

'Than a flower?' Her lip curled very slowly upwards, but she stayed stock still, 'A little pile of varnished glass perhaps?' She felt as though blood were flowing to forgotten parts of her being and she was afraid to move in case the tingling feeling stopped and left her bereft of the joy of feeling again.

'I was thinking of something softer, warmer,' he was standing now so close that she could feel the warmth of his body through her T-shirt, the touch of his jeans against her bare legs. She could see him breathing and the fibres of his shirt lifting to the pounding of his heart and she felt a corresponding thrill that sent a quiver of emotion like a shudder. He reached out and placed his finger across her lips. She closed her eyes.

'Open them,' he said, 'look at me. Is this for real?'

'Don't ask,' she whispered.

Milana felt JC's lips against her forehead. His hands rested on her shoulders pressing her skin and then slid gently all the way round and down her spine to the small of her back where, very slowly they pressed her towards him so that she felt him stiffen against her pelvis. He knew she could feel him and he watched her as though seeking her consent and she looked at him, blankly, without thought or expression, feeling him hard against her and wondering if the tension that she felt was his or hers. She became aware of her hands placed on his hips. She eased them slowly towards his back, feeling how her fingers travelled over the cotton of his shirt. She pressed him to her and felt him catch his breath, once and then again. She turned her face resting it against his shirt, but the pounding in his chest resounded in her head and she glanced up at him. His impassioned eyes rested on her. He was breathing in great gulps of air, his mouth was slightly open and she saw the look of a boy caught in the thrall of an experience that overpowered everything but the physical. His shoulders lifted slightly with every intake of breath and yet he barely moved against her. Her hands travelled back over his chest and up to his face, that, perplexed by so much sensation seemed to have forgotten to respond. She put her hands over his cheeks and smiled at him and he smiled, a quivering almost impossible smile. Tentatively his lips came over hers, a little awkwardly hardly daring to take possession of her mouth. She let him kiss her, slowly exploring the territory, wary and desperate at the same time. He kissed her deeper and then a shudder travelled the length of his body and she felt his sudden exhalation like a guttural sigh of release as he came.

JC hugged Milana and buried his face in her hair and for a moment she wondered if he was crying. But when he lifted his head she realised he was laughing.

'I'm sorry that was too unexpected, beyond my control.'

'Hey, don't explain.'

'I can't hold back where you're concerned.' He looked at her apologetically. 'Will you ever want me to be with you again at this rate?'

'You haven't been with me, you just kissed me,' she corrected gently, 'the rest was your bonus.' His face both contrite and radiant creased back into a smile.

'You make me feel like I've never slept with a woman.' He adjusted his jeans and glanced up at her with the face of a naughty schoolboy, 'What a mess.' He grinned almost triumphantly.

'And here I was thinking I would make you feel like an old pro.' She stepped back and smoothed her T-shirt and realised he hadn't even lifted it, his hands hadn't even touched the skin beneath.

He flicked his blonde hair back with a quick gesture and passed his hand over his face, suddenly abashed. 'Gees, how can you sweat when you're barely moving.'

'Your heart was struggling so hard to pump blood to the rest of your body, I thought you'd pass out,' said Milana with a wry smile.

'Thank you,' he whispered, 'for not making me feel like a complete idiot.' And suddenly he looked so vulnerable and so hopelessly enamoured that her heart grew a little wary of its new found happiness.

'Tell me I'll get another chance, just to be that close again, tell me I didn't blow it.'

Milana kissed him quickly on the cheek, 'You didn't blow anything, JC. You're the most lovely man and I'm so grateful to you.'

'I don't want you to be grateful, Malala.'

'I know, give me time, OK, just give me time. Now go climb Manqueheue.'

She heard the shower turned on and wondered what it would be like to walk in and let the water flow over them both, and cry and make love and mix tears and water and sadness and love in the hope of making a potent love cocktail to forget the pain that lurked in the dark recesses of her heart. What harm could it do either of them? She wrestled with the longing to be loved. She hesitated on the verge of something new, and then thought better of it and went back to smooth the duvet in her bedroom. She was holding the hibiscus flower when he looked in, his hair wet and slicked back and a mischievous smile on his face.

'Now I don't want to go. How about I stay and play?'

'Get on with you,' she laughed.

'I can't wait until this evening?'

'Don't hold your breath.'

'I've been holding my breath all this time, you just released it didn't you notice?'

And with a smile that lit her aching heart he left her.

It was past four on that same Friday afternoon and Milana had gone to the corner shop to buy cheese and ham to make the pizza and she still had a lot of work to do on her glass. She hadn't even started varnishing yet. As she stepped out of the lift on the sixth floor with her bag of groceries Milana noticed a lady in a light linen jacket and pretty matching shoes standing by the door to JC's flat. Her hair was pinned up showing an attractively long neck. For an instant Milana thought it might be JC's mother, whom she had only seen in photos, but as the lady turned, Milana's eyes widened in astonishment.

'*Señora* Lisa.'

'Don't worry,' Lisa lifted a hand. 'I haven't come to take you back south,' she replied smiling. 'I've just come to see you, Milana. I didn't mean to shock you,' she added noticing the sudden pallor that served to accentuate the dark circles around Milana's eyes.

Milana rummaged in her bag for the keys trying to overcome her confusion. The awareness that she'd been found in some wrongdoing assailed her. *I'm caught*, screamed her mind, as she turned the key in the lock. Weeks back she had come to the capital to make something of herself; she had set out from the south, strong and independent and full of hope. Now she was no better than a leech, a parasite on JC's love and wealth. It was like a ray of searing lucidity had suddenly pierced the veneer of her new life to expose its truth.

'Come in,' she smiled weakly, 'I'm sorry about the mess.' Her panic striken mind was working on overdrive. She tried to combat her feeling of vulnerability by filling in the silences. 'I've got a contract with House and Ideas, you know, the shop.' She went to leave the groceries in the kitchen while she continued speaking, 'I'm making them another hundred candle holders and I haven't even started varnishing them.'

'May I see?' asked Lisa with undisguised curiosity.

They were standing in the sitting-room of JC's flat. Originally this L-shaped room had been designed to serve as a sitting and dining space, but the smaller part of the L had been partitioned off with a bamboo screen behind which Milana now showed *Señora* Lisa her large pine work-table purchased by JC from a downtown furniture warehouse. It was almost completely covered with the candle holders, leaving only a little free space for her to varnish and paint.

'May I?' asked Lisa reaching for one of them.

'They're quite sharp. They still need to be varnished. That's what gels them together and makes them softer to touch. I tint the varnish to make the colours they want.'

'They are really beautiful, Milana, what a brilliant idea. They look as if they've been covered in little jewels,' she held one up to the light. 'Look how the glass refracts the light. How ingenious you are.'

'They want me to do a whole line in this, candlesticks, frames even trays. Sorry it's all such a mess,' she added uncomfortably.

'You've done well for yourself. If you carry on like this you'll be able to afford a place of your own,' suggested Lisa, putting down the glass. Milana shrank back a little. 'You'd like that wouldn't you?'

But Milana found herself at a sudden loss for words.

'Did Doris send you?'

'No one sent me Milana. I'm so glad to see all the work you're doing.' She took up another candle holder and ran her finger over the sharp glass.

'Juan Carlos goes back to university next week you know. Law is a tough degree to take. It needs a lot of focus.' Lisa looked back at Milana.

She watched Milana's face crease with anguish and confusion.

'Please, *Señora* Lisa, someone must have sent you here. How do you know JC? Please tell me what's going on.' A sudden burst of frustration thrust her out of her awkwardness.

'Why can't we be left alone? He might not even be here if it weren't for me. Why do people have to interfere?' She didn't care suddenly, now that she'd been discovered. Defiance like adrenalin pumped through her.

'What do you mean, Milana, "He wouldn't be here"? Where would he have gone? Was he going to drop out of university?'

Milana looked at her despairingly, for an instant she understood why JC had wanted to die, to run away from them all, the eyes that pried and judged and demanded explanations. Defying her own better judgement that would have cautioned and advised reserve, Milana blurted out the truth she felt they deserved to know.

'He was going to drop out of life. Die! That's what! Because people wouldn't leave him alone. He's so funny and kind and clever and nobody cared about how he felt. He's done me so much good too. He's so generous. He took me in. He cares about everyone. Look at all I've achieved because of him.'

Lisa paused only a moment to digest the bombshell.

'You'd have achieved it without him. You're very capable, Milana. Very talented,' she said quietly.

'I couldn't have done it all alone,' Milana's voice rose and the distress on her face was palpable. '*Señora* Lisa please tell me why you're here. I don't understand.'

'Why was Juan Carlos going to die? What do you mean, Milana?'

'I didn't mean anything. I'm upset and confused, *Señora* Lisa. You're upsetting me.'

Lisa approached Milana and put her hands on the girl's shoulders. They were cool and firm to the bare skin beneath the thin straps of her T-shirt, and strangely comforting.

'I don't mean to upset you.'

'How did you find me?' Milana stood her ground, boldness turning her cheeks pink.

'You and Juan Carlos made a fine couple at the Hidalgo and Garcia Art Exhibition a couple of months back. You'll soon realise, Milana, that there's not much one can do in certain circles without people finding out.'

'That exhibition? I never saw you there.'

'Your photograph was in Cosas; you with Juan Carlos and Grazia Menendes, in the society magazine.'

'I was in that?' Milana looked incredulous.

'If you go to those society events, you'll find yourself quickly in print.'

'I didn't do anything wrong.' She shrank away as she thought back to that fateful night.

'No, but I do have Juan Carlos' interests at heart as well as your own.'

'Why? What do you know about JC? What do you want with him?'

'He's my godson, Milana.'

'Oh God!' Milana turned her face away, but Lisa saw the frustration and despair.

'Milana, you are very young, but you're intelligent and sensitive. Can I talk to you openly?'

'Just tell me you want me to get out. Just like last time. What's the point of pretending, It's like every time I get lucky. It's all spoilt.

'By me?'

'I don't know.' Milana's green eyes sparkled with vexation, 'I feel like I'm living in a fishbowl. There's no freedom anywhere.'

'I haven't seen you for over three years, Milana. I had no idea you were back from the south or indeed where you were until I saw your picture with Juan Carlos. Then I put two and two together, and realised it was you he'd been living with these last weeks. You can imagine my surprise. I think life is like a tapestry and if you live long enough you see how the many threads have a way of coming together, not to trap you Milana, but to weave beautiful designs if you let them.'

'We just want to be left alone.'

'Life doesn't leave us alone, Milana. You must know that by now.'

'We're harming no one.'

'You live together and that's not good for either of you, not for his studies or for your reputation or your independence.'

'You mean his reputation. I bet his father's happy now I've sorted his son's gay reputation out, I bet he likes me living here, I'm better than some paid for whore,' she said too bitterly to notice the effect her words had on Lisa.

'As for me, I don't have a reputation, *Señora* Lisa. We're not big on reputation in the shantytown.'

Lisa saw the misery on Milana's face, telling a story that Lisa was only beginning to grasp the measure of. She took a step closer, not quite knowing how to comfort, not this time. 'Don't do yourself down,' she whispered gently. 'You have a future ahead of you, you must concentrate on. If you knew that I had been looking for you for some time, nothing to do with Juan Carlos, would you believe it? All the times I heard about Juan Carlos's new girlfriend I was looking for Milana, the girl who disappeared from Panguipulli. I just never put the two together, until I saw that photograph a couple of weeks ago at the hairdresser.'

'I never asked to be looked for,' Milana almost snapped back. 'Why should you care where I went. I'm doing OK. I don't need your help *Señora* Lisa, and nobody gave JC any help when he desperately needed it, so how come they care now? His parents don't deserve him.'

Lisa was silent and thoughtful.

'I'm going to the kitchen to put the groceries away,' said Milana somewhat fiercely. Lisa stayed where she was. A short while later Milana appeared with a cup of lemon tea and handed it to her. Lisa's look of surprise was genuine as was the look of gratitude. Milana remained standing, watching her take a little sip.

'Tell me his parents don't want me in his life. Tell me I've done my bit and that now it's inconvenient to have me around. That's what you want to say. I bet they're thinking I may ask for money because I'm from the shantytown and no better than a tart, or worse still, he might just fall in love with me and chuck Law to have babies with me. That's it isn't it?'

'I said you were intelligent and sensitive. You make them nervous.' Lisa spoke nearly in a whisper.

'I'm only seventeen and I'm a nobody. How can I make them nervous?'

Lisa turned swiftly, deadly serious, 'Oh so easily, Milana. They don't know you. They don't know what makes you tick. Tell me Juan Carlos hasn't fallen for you and offered you everything?'

'He has. But I wouldn't take it. I won't take a thing from him,' replied Milana heatedly.

'And do they know that?' Lisa pointed out.

Milana sighed. 'He's set me up here, the table, the easle, but I'll pay him back for all that with my earnings. Sometimes he gives me presents, very nice ones, but that's all. I try to pay for as much stuff as I can with my own money. I don't want to scrounge off him. He's my friend, *Señora* Lisa. My freedom and my friendship with him depend on our being equal in that way.'

'You are so like your mother Milana. She had such integrity.'

'Integrity?'

'Honesty to yourself, Milana. You have conviction and principles that you stand by. That's a rare quality,' she said, shifting position as she set down her tea cup. 'You don't love

Juan Carlos do you?' Lisa paused, as though to give the question time to penetrate. 'He's very much in love with you. He told me, though then I didn't know it was you he was talking of. He relies on you utterly, emotionally.' Her glance swept up to her and her knowing eyes seemed to pin Milana to the spot, albeit gently, 'How do you think he'll cope when you leave him? And you will leave one day. You know that as well as I do.'

'Why?' Milana looked astounded. 'How can you know that?'

'Because you have a gift. It's why I was looking for you. If you want to follow that talent, you'll go far. I have it on good authority.' She smiled enigmatically. 'Meanwhile you're like a life-support machine for him. You need to fade gently out of his life so that he can pick himself up again. Your leaving later will be like turning off his oxygen supply when he no longer remembers how to breathe for himself.'

Milana looked away awkwardly.

'You know we are just friends. You know I don't sleep with him?'

'He told me himself. But one day, any day, you may feel sorry for him and let him in when you don't really mean to, and then it will be much more difficult for both of you.'

Shame and guilt filled the silence. Milana knew she had this very morning. For the first time she had physically allowed herself to use JC's love to push out a prior one, hoping that by letting him close like that she might force her feelings to pay him the attention she believed he deserved. She knew tonight would have been a turning point. Now, suddenly, it felt as if some unseen hand had guided *Señora* Lisa here just in the nick of time. It made Milana wonder that her mother might be watching her.

'Why were you looking for me, *Señora* Lisa?' Milana asked at last. Lisa put down her tea and turned to her gravely.

'Do you know the work of the painter Matias Vidal?'

'Of course, everyone does. He painted that metro station. JC took me to see it. I even shook his hand but he wouldn't remember me.'

'Well, Matias Vidal saw your work in the church in

Panguipulli. He's an eccentric that's for sure but he has an eye for raw talent and discovering young potential. He was in Panguipulli, quite by chance, and talked to Father Juan about the paintings in his church. Father Juan told him all about you and how you had come down from the shantytown of San Damian. Matias came to me to ask where he could find you, knowing my connection to San Damian. I've been making enquiries for some time but only Doris could tell me she had seen you once in the graveyard.' Lisa paused and gave Milana a quizzical look, 'Try to imagine my impression when I opened Cosas magazine at the hairdresser and discovered my own godson had been enjoying your company all along. He calls you Malala that's why I never suspected. He says he met you down south, gave you a lift when your car broke down. He told me your parents died in a car accident and you lived with an aunt near Pucon.' She smiled seeing Milana' surprise. 'Frankly Milana, I don't know how you do it, but I have never forgotten how you managed to persuade Victoria Winters to give you English lessons at my house when you were thirteen.' Milana wasn't sure if the faint amusement in her voice was mocking, teasing or disapproving.

'I was fourteen,' she corrected.

'Don't you see Milana, your drive, your enterprise, your irrepressible creativity, it's a gift too. You'll go far, Milana, so choose your path carefully.'

'What would *Don* Matias want with me?' Milana enquired hesitantly.

'He wants to meet you, teach you, if you get along.' Milana's eyes grew wide and her cheeks flushed. Lisa felt a warm rush of pleasure at her reaction.

'You could arrange that, for me?' she asked incredulously.

'It was his suggestion. He obviously thinks you are very talented. He launched Hernan Garcia's career and he's launched other young unknowns, call it his hobby. You've caught his eye that's all I can say.' Lisa smiled fondly at her. 'I could take you to his studio. It's not far.'

'Now?'

Lisa cast her eye towards the lines of candleholders and then at her watch. 'You seem to have your hands full but...'

'You really mean, now?' Milana interrupted.

'This was why I came in the first place, not to lecture you about Juan Carlos. Although I want you to think deeply and honestly about that too.'

'I was so rude. I'm sorry.'

'There's no easy way to say those things. But they needed to be said too.'

Milana nodded, pensive and confused.

'I've said my bit, Milana,' she added seeing the concern that furrowed her brow.

'Give it time to sink in. I'm not asking for immediate solutions. What I say with relevance to JC should stay between us, just as what you have told me will remain with me. You will only help him if the decision to leave comes from you and he must understand and feel it to be honest and true. I trust you, Milana. You will do the right thing at the right time. Anyway,' she went on changing to a brighter tone, 'Matias said I should bring you over if I found you in, so he is expecting us if you want. And if I were you I would strike while the iron's hot, before he finds another project to enthuse over. This could be your Godsend and your answer to everything.'

'Oh I do want, and I know how special this is, believe me.' Her excitement spilled over filling Lisa's heart with hope.

As they waited for the lift together, Milana felt Lisa's eyes on her. She looked up.

'I was so angry before, *Señora* Lisa, I had no right to…'

'That's forgotten already,' she said shaking her head, but Milana sensed her disquiet.

'*Señora* Lisa, what I said about JC. I really shouldn't have. I was upset.'

'But it was true?'

'That's how I found him, on the riverbank, drunk and asleep with a shotgun by him, everything else is what he told me. How could anyone as special as JC is, be made to feel so worthless by his own dad?'

Lisa shook her head and looked away from her, communing with unspoken thoughts.

Matias Vidal's studio turned out to be in an elegant high-ceilinged house with French windows and balconies, tucked between a teashop and a drycleaner's. Lisa rang the doorbell which was eventually answered by an old maid who shuffled along in a pair of surprisingly smart velvet slippers. She led them through a long, marble hall and up two flights of stairs and knocked on a door.

'Come,' said a deep, resonant voice. The door opened on a room of large proportions, basking in natural sunlight. Some years previous, *Don* Matias had lifted the roof off the house and replaced most of it with a glass dome, and it was under this dome that they now stood.

'So you've brought her!' His hair was long to his collar and swept back from his face revealing a remarkably smooth brow. His pale, honey coloured eyes were so bright and the skin around his eyes so free of wrinkles that, on closer inspection Milana realised that if it were not for his silver beard he might have looked a good deal younger than his fifty-six years. He was tall and slim with elegant tapered fingers. He wore a silk tartan scarf over an old shirt and a very misshapen, threadbare tweed jacket. His trousers were unusually well cut in comparison and gave an unexpectedly jaunty look to his peculiar but not unattractive quixotic appearance.

'This is Milana, Matias,' Lisa announced by way of introduction 'She was so eager, that we came immediately.'

Matias took a step forwards, grabbed Milana's hand enthusiastically and shook it.

'Now, let's see, Milana, what can I possibly teach you? You already paint walls beautifully,' he said dropping her hand just as suddenly and turning away with a mischievous expression.

'Oh but you can teach me so much,' Milana took a step forwards. 'I've only learnt how to make paints and egg tempera and use varnish, I don't know enough about oils and I need to learn so much about texture and perspectives and...'

He turned back smiling, 'I'm teasing you Milana.'

'Oh. I'm sorry.'

'No, on the contrary I want to hear what you want to learn, but you have an excellent sense of perspective.'

'I just guess, but I don't know much. There are so many rules, Leonardo da Vinci....'

'Leonardo?' echoed *Don* Matias, he glanced at Lisa. 'Yes, he could teach us both a thing or two.'

Milana looked down, suddenly abashed.

'What do you think, Milana, would you be willing to work hard? That church you painted! You have oodles of talent! We must dig deeper now to release the creative juices.' He rubbed his hands together and then suddenly released them, fingers outspread making them look like two wings parting slowly. Milana laughed at the impression, he looked like *Don* Quixote turned magician.

'Milana, it is our responsibility to nurture God's gifts. If you can bring canvas, you can use the paints here. By and by you can get your own paints. That's if you're willing to give it all you've got.' He wagged a long, elegant, paint-covered finger at her.

She raised her eyes and met his scrutiny.

'*Don* Matias, I can't believe my luck. I'll work so hard. I'm so grateful.' Again Matias exchanged an amused look with Lisa, the girl's enthusiasm was delightful.

'Don't think it's all charity,' he said walking away to get a cloth, 'if you're a success, I make money too, out of launching you.' He rubbed the paint off his hands. 'In time you may have an exhibition, if you've got the stamina and the focus for the workload it involves. If it's a success it will make us both money. What do you say? We artists have to live. I launched Hernan Garcia, now he's painting his little heart out in New York.'

Milana just shrugged helplessly, 'I'll try, *Don* Matias.'

'No pressure, the art will speak for itself; already has, my dear, to me, or you wouldn't be here.'

'Thank you.' She looked from one to the other, unsure of what to say. Lisa smiled.

'Don't worry Milana, you'll get used to *Don* Matias, in time.' She laughed.

'Tell me, my dear,' Matias said folding himself into an armchair and surveying her suddenly anew. 'Your painting in the church in Panguipulli has noticeable echoes of Santiago Hidalgo's painting, at least the work he did three years ago, before he was sent off to study economics in England. Crazy! Such talent, wasted on finance.' He placed the tips of his fingers together making a steeple and tilted his head expectantly. The mention of Santiago sent a bolt of electricity through her. The colour rose to her cheeks.

'I...' she hesitated, 'the church he painted was close to the *poblacion* where I lived, I went in there quite a lot.'

'Did you meet him?' inquired Don Matias casually.

'Sort of.' She paused, again, searching for a suitable answer, 'Atilio, the caretaker, let me into the church and I watched...' she trailed off.

'That would explain it.' He seemed to exhale himself right out of the chair. He sauntered over to the door.

'There is very much of his feeling in your work. I wondered if he had been your earliest teacher.'

'In a way, I suppose, he was.'

'Very good. When do we begin, young lady?'

Lisa told Matias about the candle holders and the work for House and Ideas.

He looked impressed. 'So, you're becoming quite the little business woman.'

'But that's not art, *Don* Matias, that just gets me by.'

'Good for you. Artists need to have their wits about them.' He swung the door wide open. 'How about Monday?'

'Really? So soon?' She could barely contain her excitement.

'Arrive at ten or thereabouts. I am always in the studio on Monday. We shall start on oils.'

He thrust his hand out by way of farewell and she noticed him wink at Lisa.

'Shall I bring a canvas, I know where to buy it?' she offered a little breathlessly

'Good girl. But I shall have a canvas waiting for you, this time.'

All night, after the pizza evening with JC's friends, Milana worked on varnishing her candle holders. When in the early morning JC came to find her he saw her fast asleep amidst the empty pots of varnish. Her head resting on the table, her hair trailing down in a mass of waves. He came over and touched it and the curls quivered and stilled. He thought of the morning before and it seemed he had imagined it because he felt her once again so distant as though her dreams were taking her far away to a place he could not reach.

Chapter Fourteen

Rain poured relentlessly from low rumbling clouds. Streets turned into rivers and cars were left stranded in flooded underpasses all the way up and down Kennedy Avenue. The Mapocho River swelled until the lunchtime news was filled with fears of it bursting its banks. Sandbags were piled up in strategic places and men on street corners charged a few *pesos* to ferry people across on bicycles from one pavement to another to avoid the waves of water that rushed over saturated gutters.

'I still wish you wouldn't do this,' said JC as he piled yet another cardboard box into his car.

'Not the best day for a move, I guess.' Milana was as soaked as he was. 'At least it's not cold.'

'I wasn't referring to the rain,' he grimaced, sweeping his wet hair off his face.

'It's better for us both, JC, before I take over completely.'

'I wish you would.' Water trickled down his face.

'One day you'd have come home to find your whole flat glassed up and varnished, one great big candle holder,' she joked.

'I shall always hold a candle to you.' He looked at her gravely.

'In this weather it would go out rather fast,' she replied, grinning.

JC sighed and adjusted the boxes to enable the boot to close.

The past weeks had flown by. Milana worked on her increasingly successful creations for House and Ideas and JC had returned to university, radiating a new spirit of happiness and confidence that in turn made him more attractive so friends sought out his company. Milana encouraged him to go out as much as possible while she stayed behind in the flat, gluing, constructing, painting and varnishing. He respected the fact that she shied away from meeting his friends, not realising that by never allowing him to make her a part of his social life, she also ensured that he would miss her less when she left. She knew she was just passing through, and like it or not, she should not pretend to herself or to him that this was home. She saved up every penny she made from her work with House and Ideas and lived each day as a bonus trying not to think about where she would go if she was forced to leave. Meanwhile, just knowing Milana was there and would still be there on his return, bending over her work, glowing under the lamplight, her cheeks flushed by her efforts, brought JC a kind of peace he had never known, and emboldened him.

But in the midday hours, when the sun was strongest and the light at its brightest, it was usually in *Don* Matias' studio that Milana could be found painting under his glass domed roof. When she had arrived there, for that first Monday morning lesson, armed with nothing but raw talent and enthusiasm, Matias had observed her with amusement as she surveyed, in dismay, the table he had set up for her. On it he had placed a carafe of wine, a bowl of lemons and a thick crusty slab of white bread. Her look had said it all.

'I don't really like painting this kind of thing,' she'd admitted, her eyes glinting with a touch of fire that revealed the 'passionate, driven nature of the beast' as Matias had described it later to Lisa.

'I know, my dear. It's a Still Life,' he had replied with a mischievous smile. 'You have painted with your imagination until now, boldly and magnificently. You have painted from your inside out. Now you must paint from the outside in, how else are you to learn my dear.' And he had rubbed his hands together gleefully as he realised the challenge before him.

Her stubbornness delighted him, for it meant he could shape and guide her all he wanted but her own strength and vision would drive itself though; her style would remain individual, original and again he sniffed the sweet scent of future success.

For Milana, Matias turned out to be one of those teachers whose inspiration overcomes all the challenges he sets and who wins the love and respect of his students in equal measure. In no time, Milana learnt the secret of all painting was light. She learnt to achieve the transparacy of glass and the diaphanous quality of silk, draped over all manner of objects. She worked on the textures of skin; apple skin, lemon skin, furry peaches. Light was her master and guide, how it was absorbed or reflected, the subtle ways it shaped every form.

'You understand, my dear, once you can paint what you see, your vision can speak through your art. Instead of just drawing people into your imagination, you hold the power to literally draw them out and open their eyes to the world, a fresh new world, pulsating with possibility that they have never seen.' And with that Matias introduced his first live models for her to work on. The young students came and sat for her of an afternoon and Milana learnt to translate 'truth' into oil. 'The truth cannot be captured in a photograph my dear, it is the spirit of the sitter you must capture. The secret lies in the lights and shadows of his face.'

Lisa came often, dropping in for cups of coffee, watching the dedication and devotion with which Milana embraced every aspect of her work. Rarely did she break off her concentration; her capacity for total absorption was remarkable. Watching her at work, Lisa understood that JC might well love this girl, but she saw too that Milana's sights were set on horizons as yet unseen, and it eased her mind.

If Milana mentioned Lisa at all to JC it was only ever in relation to her lessons with Matias. Nevertheless Milana had, over the weeks following Lisa's visit to the flat, gently distanced herself from JC, not emotionally, for they continued to have long conversations about life and ideas, but physically. She was careful never to draw on his love or his closeness but rather to find solace in her painting. And to some measure it did assuage the inner solitude and the empty place within her that yearned for an impossible love. The strokes of her paintbrush became bolder and more defined and their strength was not lost on Matias.

It was Matias who persuaded Lisa not to meddle, and to leave the young be and let them gradually take their own way. And take it she will,' he had added with a knowing raise of his remarkable eyebrow.

'My dear, she has a path to follow and it is not with JC. If you force them apart they will only hanker after what was lost, blaming others for their sadness and creating unrealistic aspirations of love from a far more banal truth.'

'Which is what?' Lisa enquired with a wry smile.

'That they needed each other for a brief time. They held hands to get over a rough patch, they helped each other over one of life's little hurdles,' he went on waving his hand to indicate the nature of these inevitable humps and hillocks of life, 'and hey presto they will arrive at new pastures, the hands will slip apart and they will skip off on their way. You'll see my dear. JC is in love with Milana's energy. She has been giving him it intravenously for the past months as he lives and breathes her drive and optimism, soon even he will have had his fill and it will all be fine.' He patted Lisa's hand and chuckled to himself. 'Relax Lisa, you can't control any of it, so just relax and enjoy. What a find! What a remarkable find, my dear.'

It was in fact Matias who, one wintry day, drew Lisa's attention to the old building around the corner and in his languid, throw away manner, had suggested maybe the little flat that had just come up for rent there, with its high ceilings and bright light windows, would like Milana as a tenant.

'You know this means the parting of the ways, don't you?' JC gave the boxes one final push and straightened up.

'What do you mean?'

He closed the boot of the car.

'It's amazing how you came here with nothing and now all these boxes. I can barely get everything in.'

315

Milana put a hand on his arm. 'What do you mean, "parting of the ways"?'

JC smiled wistfully at her for the first time that day.

'Get in the car, will you.' The rain cascaded down the windscreen in bucketfuls. 'I'm just being realistic. My Malala's gone. I can't call you that anymore, it's like holding on to the past, and I have to let that go. Your life caught up with you, Milana.' For the first time he called her by her name. 'It had to happen sooner or later. You've got a regular business going, and an exhibition to prepare for one day soon.'

'Not yet. Not till the end of the year, and not unless I get my act together and paint till I drop.'

'It's the beginning of the rest of your life, and I've got my exams, and, well… are we ever going to be together again? Like we were?'

Milana didn't answer.

'It won't ever come back. Time passes and we never get it back. I'm just nostalgic, that's all. Look at this weather, it makes it a million times more depressing.'

'Don't you like it, just a teensy bit? It's such dramatic weather.'

'No, I don't like it. Not one incey wincey bit.'

'You know, JC,' said Milana thoughtfully, 'life is all about living through stages. You get opportunities, you take them, you move on. If we don't we're in danger of holding up our future. You can't hold onto anything in life. You have to go with the flow. But the flow can bring things back to us, like friendships that last forever,' she smiled.

'I know. It still hurts though, when the flow's going in the opposite direction, if you get my drift.' He was trying hard to be brave. 'I'm not sure we're going to get anywhere in this flow,' he added looking out of the car window at the rivers of water that flooded all the gutters.

'Oh but we must! It's all packed up now. What's that?' Milana pointed to the unfamiliar box on the back seat.

'That's paint, my kind of paint. I'm going to paint that dreadful grey off your new place, if it's the last thing I do.'

'Thank God! I hate painting ceilings.'

JC smirked. 'You'd never have made the grade with Michelangelo.' But he felt like he wanted the river to swallow him up.

The building she was moving into, like many others in Santiago, was built in the 1940s in the French style and was only a few blocks away from *Don* Matias' studio in Providencia. Its cellars had been converted into parking spaces so they were able to load all the boxes into the rickety old lift without getting soaked any further. Together, they piled her belongings into Milana's newly rented two room apartment. One room was large and light: it was to be Milana's studio, sitting room and eating room. The other was smaller and more dingy, and here she put the camp-bed *Señora* Lisa had given her.

'You can't sleep on that thing for long. You'll do your back in,' cautioned JC. Milana laughed.

'If you saw the things I've slept on in my life, this bed is sheer luxury. In fact this whole place is sheer luxury. And I'm actually able to rent this with my own money and just a loan from *Señora* Lisa that I shall pay back after my exhibition. No one rents flats where I come from JC. I should be living in a wooden box with a window and a door in a shantytown, not in a flat in fancy Providencia.'

'Hardly fancy.'

'Well it is to me. This is, in fact, the most extraordinarily weirdly wonderful thing that could ever happen to me.'

'What? Renting a dilapidated grey-walled flat in Providencia?'

'Yes.'

'And how can that be weird, let alone wonderful?'

'Because the likes of me would never do the likes of this and that makes it an adventure beyond my wildest dreams.'

'Not true, you always dream wild dreams. This one seems to fit the tamer variety.'

'JC you don't know what this means for me, I'm over the moon.'

'OK, I get it, you're pretty excited.' *More than when you moved in with me.*

'You bet I am,' and she squealed with delight as she threw some old sheets onto the bed.

JC could not have felt more devastated at the prospect of losing his flat-mate of the last few wonderful months. He watched her busily opening boxes. He understood that her happiness was such that she could not begin to perceive his desolation or, possibly, it occurred to him, she chose not to. He stood, thoughtful and gloomy, like a child deprived. After a while observing her, growing more morose as she ignored him, he suddenly stepped forwards out of the shadows and remarked, 'All this hype wouldn't have anything to do with some news I've heard would it?'

'What news JC?' she turned, her face so bright with joy and anticipation that he fell silent.

'What is it?'

'Nothing, not relevant.' He was overcome by his selfishness in her hour of happiness.

'But you said?'

'Are you going to paint this place now or later?' he asked in an effort to change the subject.

'You said YOU were going to paint it,' she said giving him a winning smile.

'Oh, so I did,' he answered dismally, strolling around with his hands in his pockets.

Milana was watching him closely.

'What news, JC? Don't keep things from me, remember, we promised each other.' For a few moments he stayed silent considering his reply.

'Santiago's back. He's just graduated.'

The blood rose to her face and an instant knot formed in the pit of her stomach. She bent over a box and pulled out the contents, desperate to disguise her feelings.

'How do you know?'

'I saw Iris.'

She raised her eyes; 'Iris. You saw Iris? Where?'

JC turned back to face her. 'I didn't want to tell you. But I can't keep it to myself,' he looked at her with a pained apologetic expression.

'Milana, I went back to the shack and I took that picture of Atilio that you painted. You didn't want it and I wanted to have it in my flat. Is that OK?'

'Of course it's OK but I would have painted you another. What do you want Atilio on your wall for?'

'I went to the shantytown. I walked along the alleys. I tried to find the house where you said you'd lived. But there's nothing on that corner. I was standing there when someone called me. I was so surprised. Who there could know me? It was that witch Iris, I'd have known her anywhere. She was visiting Doris that you've told me about. Doris was ill, nothing serious though. She told me Santiago was coming back for the winter. You know how it's summer there and they've all finished the academic year, so he's finished his degree. He's due back anytime now. And I wondered, well, I just wondered.'

'You wondered if I'd heard and I was happy because of him?' JC was shocked to see how completely the joy had drained out of her until her face had become a kind of death mask.

'JC,' she began, straightening from the position on the floor, 'Santiago is not for me. Maybe you'll never understand, but just accept it.' Even the voice was dull, as though muffled by a death mask. JC had the urge to shake her, like one might a favoured toy that had run out of batteries.

'I would understand if you explained,' he exclaimed, exasperated. 'I've never understood. I guess, while you were with me, I didn't want to think about it. I was so glad he was in England and you were free to be with me.'

'I don't know if I'll ever be free.' Milana sat down on the bed amidst the clothes and sheets and blankets. Slowly, dejectedly she started folding items.

'His coming back doesn't make me happy, it wraps ribbons around my heart. I wish you hadn't told me,' she said softly as though addressing the clothes.

'I couldn't keep it from you, Milana. I'd have felt I was lying. I can't keep anything from you. I don't understand why you won't confide in me.'

'There's nothing to confide, only idle gossip. It's relevant to me, only me, and that's it.' Milana stood up and walked over to where JC stood propped up against the window frame. She looked him in the eye. 'I can't see him, JC, and the greatest favour you can do me, and him, JC, is not tell Santiago where I am.'

'But Milana, I know you love him. Now that you're leaving me it's easier to face it, it almost helps to know he has the prior claim so I never stood a chance.'

'What I feel doesn't matter and I don't want to explain any of this, I don't want to think about it. Just don't tell him. No one else knows about our connection. No one else will tell him where I am. *Don* Matias won't and *Señora* Lisa won't. They want me to concentrate on my painting for the exhibition. You're the only one who could tell him.' JC shook his head uncomprehendingly. 'I don't want to be with him anymore. Isn't that enough for you? JC promise me, please.'

'OK, OK. I promise. But I don't understand and he won't understand.'

'We just have to accept some things.'

'*He* won't, Milana. Santiago won't just accept.'

'But you do promise?'

'Yes, I promise. But it makes me bitter.' He turned away. 'It's crazy! I was so jealous of him. Now you tell me to promise to keep your whereabouts secret from him. Gees man.' He faced her suddenly impassioned. 'It's dishonest. You've never been dishonest. It's playing with emotions. But I'll promise, just because, as you said, love is an act of will. I'll trust you on this. But that's it. I don't agree with it and it makes me angry.'

'Angry?' Milana repeated taken aback.

'Yes, angry.'

'Why should you be angry?'

'Because I love you but you don't love me because you love Santiago. Now you won't even tell him where you are. I saw that painting he drew of you. Did you see any others like it? No. He could have any girl but he comes to you in the middle of the night and leaves you a note saying "write to me". I guessed that medal you wear every day belongs to him, I guessed it when I saw how you scrambled after it when it flew into the gutter that time; you don't care about possessions but by God you cared about that. And I know you kept that note under your mattress, where you can touch it as you fall asleep, because just once I came to look at you as you slept and it was on the floor, and the next day I found it neatly tucked in there, just within reach. I never wanted to say anything because I wanted you to forget him.

'You gave me hope, but I knew these things about you and they made me wary. Even that time you let me kiss you, I was wary. Despite everything, I do have an instinct for self-preservation.' He breathed in deeply, 'If you're going to hide from him why do you wear his medal, or fondle notes he's written on. Why do you lead him or yourself on just to tease like that. I don't get it.' He flicked back his hair impatiently, 'So if you think I can believe you when you say you don't want to be with him, well I can't. It's a lie. I just can't understand why you should lie to yourself and to him and to me. You're just going to give yourself up to your art in your grey walls and not let anyone get a look in? Is that it? You fill everyone with hope then you snatch it away. Why don't you just go and bury yourself in some convent?'

Milana looked at him in horror. She had never witnessed such a bitter explosion from him. His face was livid and his lips drawn and there was no mistaking the level of his condemnation of her.

'I'll never understand this,' he said as he looked at her, deeply wounded. 'There are some things that deserve an explanation for those who care for you and love you, to understand them in context.'

'What about trust?' Milana suggested quietly.

'What about trust? This isn't about trust, it's about powerful emotions. You're playing a very dangerous game if you think you can make your own decisions independent of everyone elses when it comes to love and loss.'

'Santiago's got a girlfriend anyway,' she said suddenly, feeling her eyes sting with tears of impotence and frustration. 'You heard Grazia that evening. The evening from hell,' she added bitterly

'You believe that? No. You don't fool me. Don't play with me too. Just one thing, Milana, don't hurt Santiago. He's too good to hurt.' Her name sounded cold and distant on his lips.

The silence hung between them like a sudden void. Neither moved. They didn't look at each other. Eventually it was Milana who spoke first and very softly.

'Is this about him or you, JC?'

'I'm going. I'll get over it! And keep away from that witch Iris, she'll only bring you trouble.' He opened the door and walked out slamming it behind him. Moments later she heard his footsteps echoing away from her.

Chapter Fifteen

The pilot's voice came over the tannoy.

'On the right of the aircraft you will see the Aconcagua mountain, the highest peak of the Andes, second only to Everest.'

Santiago leant his head against the little oval window and stared out. The mountains seemed so close that one could almost reach out and touch them as they spread out as far as the eye could see like waves of stiff meringue. The snow lay rippled to the patterns of the wind, dazzling in the sun.

'Breathtaking,' sighed the English lady next to him.

The plane began the steep descent into Pudahuel, Chile's International Airport. As they neared the capital Santiago saw fields of green had been transformed into lakes; roads reflected the trees in the still waters that submerged them and farmlands looked like paddy fields.

'Isn't it pretty; the sun reflected in all those little lakes,' murmured the lady beside him. Santiago glanced at her. Was there any point telling her that these little lakes she delighted in were the flood devastation played out over the countryside that would bring so much hardship? Everything was a matter of perception.

'Santiago!' He heard a yell as the automatic doors of the customs area closed behind him and he was delivered into the huge waiting throng. Juan Pablo and Diego came up on either side of him.

'Hey,' he cried embracing them, surprised and grateful, 'I didn't think you knew. I'm a day late.'

'We knew. Look at you!' JP grabbed his bag. 'You're so tanned! Is that English sun capable of such a thing?'

'I left England at its best this time,' and there was almost a hint of wistfulness, 'but hey, look at you, Diego, brown as a biscuit, you ski bum,' he joked, 'can't keep away from the slopes can you? At least you'll have powder snow all season at this rate.'

'You come to Chile at its worst,' murmured Diego somberly, thrusting his hands into the pocket of his jeans, as if embarrassed to think his skiing might benefit from this disaster.

'I saw. It looked bad from the plane.'

'It just got worse.'

'I brought the Jeep,' JP said, looking back at them over his shoulder. 'I didn't think anything else would get through. The Mapocho River broke its banks.'

'What do you mean?'

'I mean it broke its banks, Vitacura is flooded,' he explained. 'The water crashed through all the houses near the river. You should have seen it this morning, contents of homes just being swept down the river.'

'It's total devastation,' Diego shook his head.

'What about the shantytown by the river?'

'God help them,' said Diego slipping into the back seat of the Jeep. 'The army have come in to help clear up the mess and they're building up the banks as best they can. There are sandbags everywhere. It's like a bloody war zone.'

The palm trees along the central reservation of the highway from the airport stood tall and elegant. Further along they were replaced by lush pepper trees, but beyond the road, the fields lay sodden under muddy brown water. Beneath the water lay the rotting produce that just a week ago had displayed growing green leaves to the sun.

'We're so vulnerable to nature,' mused Santiago surveying everything in quiet concern.

'And we never learn. The banks of the Mapocho nearly broke two years ago, remember? They build new fountains in every plaza, but they don't spend money on the real problems until it's too late.' Diego leant back and stretched his arms along the back seat.

'We live for the moment. It's part of the national character, you can't change that. You should see how planned and lacking in spontaneity everything is in England,' sighed Santiago. They passed a horse drawn cart, piled high with damp wood and bits and pieces salvaged from the river.

'Yeah well England doesn't get eruptions or earthquakes that shake you down every ten years or floods like these, or tidal waves… you can't plan in a country like this, it's a losing battle.' JP veered to avoid a huge puddle.

'Hey Santiago,' Diego leant forwards suddenly, his elbows resting on the two front seats, 'you've finished your degree, man! You're done!'

Santiago turned and gave him a broad grin. 'God what a slog. But I'm almost sad not to be going back.'

'Did you have a real send off?'

Santiago passed back his iPhone. 'Just scroll down the photos.'

Diego whistled, 'Who's the doll in the centre with her arms round you.'

'That's Lizzy. She's the best friend I have out there.'

'Friend?'

'Yup, friend.'

'OK, anything you say!'

The tumultuous waters of the Mapocho swirled beneath them as they took the overpass.

'You wouldn't think this river had the nerve to do so much damage. It's almost a trickle in summer,' Santiago leaned out looking back at the rushing waters.

There were road blocks up stream to their left on nearly every street.

'We'll have to take Kennedy. At least that's passable.'

The six lane highway sparkled in the sun. The Andes towered above the capital.

'Not a whiff of smog, look at that,' admired JP. The rains had cleared the heavy winter air and crystallised everything into perfect focus.

'You can see La Parva and Farillones.' The ski resorts were visible as tiny dots on the sheer white of the mountains.

'Now this *is* breathtaking,' sighed Santiago laying his head back against the seat and staring ahead.

'You should have been here two weeks ago; the smog was so thick it was at emergency level,' sighed Diego. 'One problem sorted by a bigger one!'

The new clock tower of the Lider supermarket came into view, Santiago turned suddenly to Juan Pablo, 'Do you think we could check out the shantytown, JP?'

'The boy's got a conscience,' JP grinned.

'Comes from living in the lap of luxury at Cambridge for three years,' teased Diego, but the memory of the last night they'd been together, six months ago, flashed into his mind, the night they'd waited drinking beers at the Polo Club with the other guys while Santiago took his car on some garbled pretext no one could quite understand. Then he'd returned, barely an hour later, breathless, elated, his eyes sparkling. Santiago never said where he'd been. He hadn't spoken all the way to the airport. They'd guessed maybe he'd been with a girl, but none of them knew, for sure. Why the secrecy, they'd asked themselves afterwards. Diego passed his hand thoughtfully over his mouth as if to wipe away the questions he longed to ask.

They turned down one of the side roads in the direction of the river. There were no police blocks here, it wasn't deemed necessary. These were roads that ran through the shantytown and ended in the river. As they came to the network of alleys, JP stopped the Jeep. 'I can't go any further.'

Santiago jumped out, 'I'll just take a quick look.'

'OK. We'll stay with the car, or all your stuff will be looted. Remember, you're not in England now.' JP lit a cigarette and stood with his back against the Jeep.

Santiago ran towards the riverbank, but even before he got there, the water surged around his feet. The banks had collapsed in a heap of mud, tearing homes away from their neighbours, pulling asunder the makeshift walls and corrugated roofs. Trucks and cars were hurled over each other and dashed against the sides like so many broken toys. Where the waters, in their unstoppable journey, could not flow fast enough they had torn out the bridge under which he had first met Milana, and passed over the top of it, ripping it from its foundations. Now it stood, barely clinging to the bank, its irons snapped like bones.

Women and children looked on as Santiago stared in horror at the devastation. Their hollow eyes showed the dismay of the past night. All their worldly possessions lay around them, drying in the winter sun like broken soldiers on a battlefield. Here and there little swirls of water, like cunning snakes trickled from the corners of ruined homes to slither back to source.

Santaigo turned back to the car. His face grave and rigid, in the effort to cover his emotion.

'Look, let's cross to the other side here, where we can, and go as far as the next bridge, past the church,' he pointed upstream.

'Oh the church is fine. Your murals will live as long as Giotto's. It's higher ground there. Thank God or all the graves would be washed out and we'd have bodies down the river and then the whole water supply would be contaminated.'

'Yeah, OK Diego.' JP scowled at him in the rear view mirror. 'Nice homecoming! You sure you want to go there?'

'Humor me, JP.'

'You mean Old Man River's bridge?'

'Carerra's shack, remember? Where he lived out all those years,' mused Diego.

'Yes, said Santiago, subsiding into his seat, 'that's exactly where I mean.'

'It's a pretty weird city tour you want, my friend.'

Santiago stared silently ahead. JP glanced curiously at Diego in his rear view mirror and Diego shrugged. As they crossed the bridge Santiago stared downstream.

'My God! God…' was all he could say as he shook his head in dismay. They turned right, bordering the river along a little-used slip road. The wheels of the Jeep became completely submerged.

'I may not be able to go much further,' said JP, spotting a tree fallen across the road a hundred yards further on, mud and water swirling around it. Santiago wrenched open the Jeep door.

'Isn't that where the old shack was? You'd think there never had been a bank there at all. It's all gone, the whole lot. Awesome isn't it?' mused Diego coming up beside him. 'Just think, thirty years or whatever Old Man River lived there. Then he dies and the river carries off his home. Makes you wonder.' He glanced at Santiago who stood with his hand on the back of his neck staring at the angry waters that swirled about the bank where the shack used to be.

JP came up and slung his arm round Santiago. 'Hey man, what's up? You look like you've seen a ghost.' JP glanced at Diego, a kind of realisation dawning between them. They moved back towards the Jeep while Santiago took a few steps closer to the river, and stared into its heaving mass. Whole trees lay tossed there this way and that, as the waters flipped and hurled them; pieces of broken furniture littered the mud pools that were all that was left of the bank. Everything had been ripped to shreds by the raging waters; the debris of so many homes swept along with the carcasses of old trucks and cars, by the unstoppable current. It was a grim scene.

'Why would you do this?' Santiago wanted to cry out to the river. 'What have you done with her? Where will I find her now?' But the river roared on, implacable, remorseless and triumphant.

PART 3

Chapter One

'Three miles along the main road to Lake Rapel you'll see a junction and a green sign to Alhue. There's an old hut with clay pots all around it and in front of it a small blue bench. You can't miss it. Ask the bus driver to drop you off there. The man that sells the pots has a brother-in-law who runs the local *taxi collectivo*. He'll drop you off at the house. He might charge $3000 but don't let him go higher. It should take you about thirty minutes along the dirt track.'

Milana curled *Don* Matias' scribbled note around her index finger. The silence and the emptiness of the barren landscape unsettled her. A lizard darted under her bag seeking refuge in its shade. The evening sun hung low and crimson on the horizon. Time appeared suspended with it. Shading her eyes she stared self-consciously along the dusty road that snaked into the unfamiliar distance.

When Lisa had turned up unexpectedly at Milana's newly rented flat she had found her unaccustomedly despondent amidst the blank canvases that leant expectantly against the walls.

'I think Milana should go away somewhere to paint for a while, Matias,' Lisa had insisted, dropping by his house on her way back home. 'It would do her good and make the break from JC easier.'

'She's doing fine. We must resist the impulse to meddle,' Matias had retorted from the top of the step-ladder where he was painting red and black hearts onto a vast canvas.

'She needs a clean break, believe me. I thought of my house

in Zapallar,' Lisa persisted. 'My housekeeper there would be company for her. What do you think?'

'No, no. Dear Lisa, Zapallar is far too manicured for her with its pretty fishing boats and tidy bay.' He stopped painting and considered for a moment. 'I want her to go back to her roots, you know; the desolation of the dump where she lived, the faces of the women in the shantytown. I need the spirit of her past to haunt those pictures. That's what will strike a chord in the exhibition.'

'With all the flooding, she can't possibly paint in the shantytown, Matias, really!'

He sighed in response to her exasperation. Pursing his lips, he frowned and standing above her like a quixotic statue on his ladder, he opened and closed his long fingers as if grasping the air for a solution.

'Matias,' she started, 'what about the old house in Alhue where I grew up? My parents' old house that your son Gonzalo bought off my uncle, that's certainly a "place of spirits" if ever there was one.'

'Brilliant! Bravo, Lisa! That's it exactly.' He thrust his fist triumphantly into the air and immediately continued dabbing red paint. 'If she can't get the spirit of that place seeping into her canvases, no one can.' He laughed mischievously.

'But your son and his wife, wouldn't they mind?'

'Gonzalo? He'll be delighted. Always has waifs and strays hanging about, will do anything for the arts. The house is rampant with children and they have a new baby. They can use Milana's help.' Matias climbed down off the ladder and leaving the paint brush he was using in an empty pickle jar, he sauntered to the phone.

'What are you doing?' asked Lisa.

'Calling them at once. No point wasting time.

'Gonzalo?' his voice boomed out. 'How are you keeping? Good, good, I've got a real treasure for you that I picked up. Call it a present for the wife. No… no… nothing like that. It's a girl…Milana…. talented artist, baby-sitter, helper, carer, you name it! Got an exhibition in a few months, a big one. She's destined to take the art world by storm. Mark my words boy! And she needs to paint somewhere remote. I thought she could get board and lodging with you in return for helping... Get her to do a sketch of the house, before the place falls to ruin... ha ha.' Matias looked over to Lisa with a broad grin and gave her the thumbs up.

'Oh yes, very presentable, really quite a looker... Where?... Oh... Lisa brought her round...' Matias raised his eyebrows and glanced at Lisa covering the receiver he added, 'Thinks I'd waste my time with some thieving waif... No she's not a waif, Gonzalo, she's been sharing a flat with Juan Carlos Miranda... That's right, yes, the same... No, it's nothing like that. They're just friends. She's a very decent girl, I tell you, good head on her shoulders... Good, good... It's settled then. What? Oh, Stella will love her... great manners, well spoken, clean, lovely girl, real treasure. The children will be devastated when she leaves, got a real way with her...Her age? Hmm... fifteen?' Lisa gesticulated urgently that it was more than that. 'Seventeen! That's it... No not a child at all, very mature, in fact she may even be eighteen, could even be older. Very capable; got a little business going supplying the House and Ideas... You'll be over the moon... Yes, of course she's quite a find... Didn't I tell you so. Really boy! You must trust me on these things... Yes, yes, marvellous... whenever... I'll let you know, sooner rather than later... Bless you boy! Keep well! Get that vineyard going... No, I can't bring her myself... I'll send her on the bus and she can get a taxi collectivo to the house... Tootle pip.'

Don Matias put the phone down. Lisa was laughing.

'It's all sorted,' he clapped his hands together. 'Why on earth didn't we think of it sooner? Just what was needed. And so easy. Just a phone call you see. Marvellous thing the telephone,' he added gratified.

'Well, Gonzalo didn't get a chance to disagree.'

'Why disagree? It's an excellent idea. Just have to shove it forwards. They're very lucky to have her.' Matias rubbed his hands together in their customary woollen gloves with the cut-off fingers, 'Gonzalo will be telling Stella she's getting a nice girlfriend of Juan Carlos Miranda to stay. Stella's such a snob, she'll love it.' Matias turned to Lisa, 'No telling her where we found her, you hear. Stella's a bit touchy. She'll be our mystery girl.'

Delighted he climbed back on his ladder and continued to paint hearts draped out of black coffins.

'Very effective,' said Lisa looking at his work thoughtfully.

After a few moments Matias stopped dabbing paint.

'What's on your mind, Lisa? I can almost hear you thinking.'

Lisa laughed nervously, 'It's silly, I was just wondering how Stella is liking it down there? I mean, it's been nearly a year hasn't it? The place was left pretty desolate by my Uncle Gustav. He rather let it go to ruin when his wife became ill. Is Stella coping? I always thought it was quite a daunting project for her to take on.'

'Plenty to do to it, plenty to keep her busy, and keep her mind off the spirits,' Matias chuckled.

'What do you mean?'

Matias put down the paintbrush and clambered down the ladder. He disappeared momentarily onto the landing. 'Clara, Clarita!' he boomed down the stairs. From the bowels of the house the maid's answering echo was just audible. 'Do you think we could have some tea up here, Clarita?'

'Come. Sit down, Lisa. I've been meaning to ask you, Stella wants to write a book about the myths and legends of the place. You must have a few stories of your own?'

'Oh, I don't know. I really should go, Matias. You're right in the middle of painting.'

'Nonsense. Don't go all coy on me now. You're always in far too much of a hurry. Sit down and have some tea. I'm supporting Stella on this writing lark. There must be some tidbits of information you can give me to whet her appetite and set her off.'

Lisa shook her head, 'I left a long time ago, Matias. I didn't really spend any of my adult life there, I don't remember much.'

'Come now, Lisa. I can't believe that. The house is rife with haunting and history. There's nothing more fun than dipping into the history of a place. Between you and me, Stella's not awfully good at this painting lark. In fact she's quite dreadful, much better switch to the pen.'

Matias folded his tall frame into a baronial armchair in the corner of the room leaving the red velvet chaise-longe, occasionally used by his life models, to Lisa.

Lisa sighed. 'What I remember best is the temple up on the hill. That was my favourite place, and the rose garden. Every time I found a pretty piece of jewellery left about, I'd bury it in the rose garden and put a circle of pebbles around it.' She laughed. 'Why on earth I did that, who knows? But I loved thinking of it as my secret treasure garden. My dear mother was so unbothered about jewellery she never noticed any went missing. I wonder if Stella will find any of it.'

Matias leant back and laced his slender fingers together, 'Your mother, Mercedes,' he drew out the name, 'what an extraordinary woman she was; ethereal almost. I remember meeting her, such a far-away look. People said she was crazed by the house, that the spirits drove her insane. I don't believe it for a moment, Lisa. Do you?' He gave her a long, penetrating look.

'I don't know. I never really knew what to think. It was a solitary place that's for sure. There was always an atmosphere about it that encouraged fantasy and strangeness. I suppose my father rather left her to herself too much.'

'I was a little boy when I met her. She gave me a blue crystal rosary that sparkled. I loved it. She told me to pray for the dead, that they came to visit her and needed lots of our prayers. As you can imagine, I never forgot that.'

Lisa laughed, 'Oh, Matias, have you ever done as she told?'

'Well, I prefer to busy myself with the living,' he shrugged. 'Maybe once or twice for good measure. Enough of my prayer life, ah ha! Here's Clarita with more material sustenance.'

Clarita shuffled across the wooden floor with single-minded determination to reach the coffee table. On it she placed a tray with a silver teapot and two bone china cups, a silver jug of milk and a plate of French wafer biscuits. Matias got up and fetched the sugar from a cupboard on the far side of the room.

'Can't expect the old dear to remember everything,' he chuckled, 'I'm wondering, Lisa, do you think we should tell Milana about the place? It might grab her. Inspire her creative juices. I was thinking particularly of the big house.'

'But there's nothing left of the old house except the long drive. I don't think Milana would get much inspiration from that.'

'I was thinking more of the legend. There were so many fires in that house but, in the end it took an earthquake to bring it down didn't it?' He glanced at her wryly.

Lisa couldn't help smiling. 'Fishing, fishing, Matias.' She shook her head at him. 'You know how I hate those devilish stories yet you insist on bringing them up. You're impossible, Matias.'

'How else can I get Stella to turn her hand to writing instead of painting? I have to feed her the thrill of the place.'

'I'm sure the locals…'

'The locals don't talk. They're scared of even mentioning names for fear of some kind of evil curse. Good heavens, Lisa, you should know.'

'It's true. They don't talk about any of it, except in half whispers.'

'Come on Lisa. What was all that stuff about fires breaking out suddenly, and the devil's curse on his own birthplace? Stella has no strange feelings whatsoever about the place. Except she's noticed that library books are sometimes found taken off their shelves and left open about the place, when no one purports to have touched them.'

'That used to happen when I was a child. That was Waldemar Castello's library. My grandfather kept it exactly as it was and so did my father. Gonzalo and Stella just inherited it intact.'

'And there's another thing. One of the rooms overlooking the rose garden suddenly locks itself. Stella has told the cook and the maids not to lock it but apparently they exchange sly looks and say nothing. I believe it's a guest room.'

'That was my bedroom, Matias. It only locked itself once

when I lived there. I remember my mother came to the room and tried to open it, but,' she shrugged and trailed off.

'You were in the room?'

'Yes. She said she called to me,' a faint pink blush tinged her cheeks suddenly, 'I think I must have been dreaming, or deeply asleep. I never heard her.'

'Did anything happen to you?'

'I wouldn't know. Maybe I was possessed,' she teased Matias. But he looked back at her puzzled.

'There's more to you than meets the eye. I've always known it. You are a dark horse, Lisa, that bolted its haunted stable for a good reason and never went back.'

'Really Matias, I am quite as bright as one of your painted hearts. Nothing dark about me at all,' she assured, looking at him with her melting eyes.

He whisked the plate away as she leant over to pick out another biscuit. 'Not another wafer until I get a story out of you,' he chuckled.

Lisa took a sip of tea and eyed him over the rim of the cup.

'Very well, but I'm like the locals, I don't like dredging up the story. It's like turning the soil and releasing the moisture. You know, like the mists of time rising from the earth and enveloping the present.' She raised her eyebrows at him. 'It's unsettling.'

Matias put the plate down, and rubbed his hands together. 'Ah ha. The lady speaks. It's remarkable how a good cup of tea loosens the tongue.'

Matias' enthusiasm was irresistible.

'All I know,' said Lisa, 'was that some couple of hundred years ago the great house was built by one of my ancestors, Casimiro Delafont Castello. He bought an old mansion and shipped it over from England, stone by stone. "Netherleigh". The name was carved over the arched entrance. They say there was some curse on it even then, but by bringing it to a new land the curse would be broken.' Lisa shrugged. 'You know I don't believe all this stuff.'

Matias leant forwards. 'This is excellent, just what I wanted to hear.'

'I'm sure you've heard it before, Matias.'

'Of course, but never took it in, not really. Now that Stella and Gonzalo are there, we've got to milk it all. Besides, I didn't tell you, they're thinking of getting the vineyard going commercially. Think how this will help the marketing. Go on, go on,' he added, impatient for more.

'As far as I know, Casimiro installed his mistress Romany there. That's why he built the house in such a godforsaken place, so his wife, Genevieve, would never come. I am told he would arrive in a carriage with four black horses, or riding his distinctive black stallion, sometimes just for a night and be gone by morning. They liked to say he made a pact with the devil and that's what had made him such a rich man. We don't know where he found the woman he installed there. Rumour had it, he brought her from England on the ship with the house, a wild gypsy woman, hence her name. She gave birth to a son in the great bedroom at Netherleigh, tended by the local women. The story goes that the night she gave birth, they took the baby away to a wet nurse but at dawn local people were alerted by flames coming from the huge windows of the master bedroom. By the time they reached the room, her bed had been burnt to a cinder. They never found any trace of her body. It was assumed the fire had consumed her, but not a bone or a tooth was found. As a result there was no official burial. What fuelled local gossip was that the fire stayed in the bedroom, it never spread to the adjoining rooms. Ever since there has been talk of "the spirit of evil" that is loose in Alhue.

'Casimiro continued to visit the house, drawn, it was surmised, by her roaming spirit. He kept the baby boy at Netherleigh. He called him Waldemar and had him brought up by a succession of English governesses. Waldemar grew up and married one of his governesses and had a daughter and a son by her. They continued to live at Netherleigh until once again, fire enveloped the bedroom and this time destroyed half the house. Waldemar, his wife and daughter were burnt in the blaze that spared the youngest son. By this time Casimiro was an old man. He left the capital and retired to Netherleigh with his young grandson and his servants. Many say that the fact he went to live at Netherleigh after the two fires had caused so much tragedy, showed his total disregard of any curse and fuelled suspicions of a pact with the devil. Casimiro was one hundred and six years old when he died. All I know is that neither Casimiro or his grandson, who was named after him, ever rebuilt the burnt wing of the house that had claimed four lives.

'The story goes that when old Casimiro died, young Casimiro, whom they called Castello, took over the house. He fell in love with a local girl, Rosa, and asked her to marry him. Rosa was deeply in love with him but she remained afraid of the curse on the house and refused him. So, he built the house where I grew up on the ruins of an old colonial house in the grounds, restoring the colonnades around its ancient garden and called it "Jardin de Rosa". He built it for her, with a rose garden to the east and a chapel to the west and vineyards all around and a library in which he placed his late father, Waldemar's, collection of poetry and romance. Then, once again he asked her to marry him. But she was still afraid of the locals who insisted he was the spirit of the devil, come to seduce her, all because his father had been born of "a whore, now burnt and unburied".

'If you look above the great wooden door of my old room, carved into the lintel you can read the name "Rosa". Castello, ever hopeful, told Rosa he would wait for her for as long as it took. Meanwhile he lived in the remains of the great house, Netherleigh, saying he would never live in Jardin de Rosas, until she came and lived there with him.

'Castello would ride away for weeks at the time and then return unexpectedly, always alone, and spend days at Netherleigh, before riding off again. A couple looked after Jardin de Rosas, and it was their daughter, a maid at Netherleigh, who would often spy Rosa walking in the rose garden at twilight or early in the morning when the master was away. She would see Rosa look in through the window of the room with her name carved over the door. On one particular night, the young maid left the window of the room open and hid to watch what Rosa would do. Rosa came as usual to walk and when she found the window open she ran and hid. Slowly she emerged, and gingerly, like a wary animal, she climbed in and she lay on the velvet bed. From then on, every night when the master was away, the young maid left the window open, and each night Rosa would come. The young maid befriended Rosa who confided that she loved Castello but feared her brothers would kill Castello rather than let her near him.

'One day, on one of Castello's visits, the young maid came upon him sitting in the rose garden all alone. And before you think I'm making this up, let me tell you I was told all this by that young maid's granddaughter who was our old cook. Apparently Castello was a rather beautiful and melancholy youth and very kindly and she couldn't resist confiding in him; she told him how she left the window open and how Rosa came at night and slept in the bed when he was away. She became his go between and with her help he secretly came to Rosa while she slept and made love to her and every night after that, visiting more and more often. For nearly a year they lived like this, until a trip took him away to Europe for several weeks. Before he returned Rosa was discovered by her brothers hanging from an old tree in the vineyard. She was dead and several months pregnant. They say the child was still alive inside her when they buried her, and that no one dared touch it, or save it for fear of perpetuating the Netherleigh curse.

'History doesn't relate whether she had been betrayed or discovered and turned out of the house by her terrified parents, or whether she had been taunted for carrying the devil's child, whichever way it seems she was driven to suicide. The night Castello returned, he learned what had happened and the following morning he too was found dead, in the chapel he had built. He'd shot himself. His own servants took him away and burnt his body and threw the ashes in the river as he was the last of that blood line. They wanted to be well and truly rid of him and the curse. The locals came together after that and pulled down the chapel because, they believed, he had defiled it with his suicide but more than that they feared his spirit might remain there. A year later, what was left of the great house came down in an earthquake, not the 1965 one, but further back the 1906 one that was even more devastating.

'Remarkably, Jardin de Rosas remained standing but empty for a long time, until my grandfather inherited it from some aunt, of tenuous parentage. Anyway, he renamed it "Place of the Spirits". That was probably a bit of a tease to the locals but I know he considered the name Jardin the Rosa pretentious and unfitting. My father farmed the land and restored the vineyard. As for Alhue, it was there long before my ancestor built his supposedly cursed house. Even then, I believe they called it "the devil's birthplace". So I don't think it needed a mansion from England to wake old legends. They were there waiting to be resurrected in the collective unconscious of the locals themselves.'

'What a superb story, Lisa. My blood curdles, just to hear you tell it so sweetly.'

'You are incorrigible Matias,' Lisa took a biscuit, 'And I don't think that story should be told to the more susceptible.'

'Stella will revel in it,' Matias declared delighted.

'I'd rather you didn't tell Milana all of this, Matias. She's closer to myths and legends than the rest of us. It's in her blood, her culture.'

'Oh she'll find out about it all the same. She will talk to the cook and the gardener. She will loosen their tongues. You can be sure of it.'

'They take fantasy too far sometimes,' Lisa paused.

'How so?' He coaxed, waving the plate of wafers under her nose.

'Well.' Lisa gave a little laugh, 'There is a story that the young Castello haunts Rosa's room. He only comes to young girls.' She raised an amused eyebrow.

'What? A rampant ghost?'

'Lovelorn,' she corrected wryly.

'He comes to sleep with them? Now, let's see, would that be a confessable sin or a spiritual perk?'

Lisa laughed again and shrugged. 'They never wanted to let on much about that because I was young and they thought I would be terrified. But I'm told that kind of haunting is not to be confused with the much older legend that predates Netherleigh, that the devil comes to circle the souls of the dying, and for every soul that escapes him, he takes vengeance on a virgin or a wife, taking one's innocence or another's fidelity.'

'I see,' said Matias stroking his chin. 'And you're telling me all this excitement ocurrs in the guest room they'll probably put Milana in,' he mused. 'How splendid.' He chuckled like a naughty schoolboy, 'And what a superb story for Stella to get her teeth into. Would you mind, my dear, if she writes about it?'

'Why not give it an airing?' She took a last sip of cold tea.

'What became of the young maid that befriended poor Rosa?'

'She lived to a ripe old age. She waited many years before telling her story about the open window, but I believe it was true.'

'Weren't you afraid, Lisa? In that old house?'

'It didn't feel old. Netherleigh was old, but not Jardin de Rosas. It was just home to me.'

'But your mother felt things there, everyone knew that.'

'Whatever my mother heard or saw, I have no idea. She never told me anything that made any sense to me. I know the house passed on to my Uncle Gustav after my father's death but I don't know what caused *Don* Gustav's wife's illness while they lived there. All I can think is that the place is desolate, and there is a great deal for an active imagination to feed on.'

'How splendidly thrilling! I'm rather partial to legends myself.' He paused and eyeing her puckishly, added, 'Come now, did Castello's ghost ever visit the young and beautiful Lisa?'

'Maybe,' she intimated unexpectedly, rising from her chair. Matias opened his eyes in surprise.

'Matias. You have no shame. You deserved that.'

Matias rose too, unfolding himself out of the chair to his full height.

'Intriguing, intriguing. Dear Lisa, you have come up trumps.'

'Just do me a favour. Let them believe it came from the dark recesses of your memory, Matias. Don't say it came from me.'

'Where did you say the house was?' Milana had asked Lisa when she dropped in on her the following day, to tell her the news.

'Alhue.'

'Alhue,' Milana echoed, her eyes sparkling with interest.

'Do you know the place?'

'I've heard of it. My mother...' Milana hesitated and changed tack, 'Thank you so much for all this. You are so kind to me, *Señora* Lisa.'

'It was *Don* Matias who organised it, Milana.'

'When can I go?'

'In a couple of weeks or so.'

'Do you think they would like me to take them some candle holders or something?'

Lisa smiled at her naive charm. 'Maybe sketch the house for them while you are there. I think *Don* Matias would like that.' She turned to go, then hesitated.

'I was born in that house. I had the best and the saddest times of my life in it.'

Milana's eyes opened wide. 'You never said you came from there.'

Lisa felt compelled suddenly to tell her about the place. By sending Milana there, something of her past was being released, like perfume or music.

'The house has been in our family a long time. It was built in the grounds of a much larger house. When my father died his brother *Don* Gustavo Guerrero took it over, but he spent so much time here in the capital with his wife after she became ill, that it rather went to ruin. A part of the house fell down in the 1985 earthquake, and was never rebuilt. *Don* Matias's son bought it for a song.' Lisa sounded a little wistful. She glanced at Milana and to her surprise, finding the girl's gaze curiously riveted on her waiting for her to continue, clammed up suddenly.

'Life moves on,' she said with a self-conscious shrug, something long buried, now released and reawakened, was stirring within her.

'Is it very big? Will I get lost in it?'

'It's not big like the great house "Netherleigh" was. There's only the drive to that house left now; the place is a ruin.'

'Did it burn down?' Milana pressed her.

'No,' she sighed, feeling herself drawn back through the door of memories Matias had opened. 'It was an earthquake that brought it down a hundred years ago. Netherleigh was magnificent and full of ancient furniture that was looted by gypsies after the quake. Some say it took an earthquake to rid the place of the curse of the devil. It's old folk lore that my ancestor who built it had made a pact with the devil.'

'With the devil?' Milana's eyes were round as saucers.

'Yes, you know like Faust who sold his soul to the devil. They say his papers used to spontaneously combust on his desk.' Her eyes brightened suddenly as though lit by those same flames.

'Did you ever meet him?' whispered Milana, drawing her knees up to her chin and wrapping her arms around them.

Lisa chuckled, 'The devil or my ancestor? I may be old, Milana, but that was more than a century before I was born. I'm hardly that ancient.' Lisa's laughter tinkled like the clinking of cut glass. 'But the locals are full of superstition, they whisper that his ghost rides when there is to be a death and the devil rides with him to claim the souls of the dying or maybe he is the devil, I forget which,' she finished with a wry smile.

Milana cocked her head curiously, 'Are you trying to frighten me, *Señora* Lisa?'

'No! Goodness no, dear! I'm trying to breathe history into the place for you. You see it's brimming with mystery and strange myths. My grandfather renamed the house "Place of the Spirits". It was called "Jardin de Rosa", and it was built as a gift of love for a girl called Rosa, who never became mistress of it. Both she and her lover died young and very tragically, like Romeo and Juliet. Folklore and myths are in your blue-print, in your collective unconscious as Matias would say, he wants the magic of the place to seep into your paintings, Milana.'

Milana sprang up eagerly as Lisa rose to leave.

'What are they like, *Don* Matias' family?'

'Oh, let's see. Gonzalo is a self-styled farmer-come-recluse who lives out his days in far-flung wildernesses and hasn't quite won over his wife to his peculiar ways. Stella craves more company. She's an artist, like you, only she specialises in pictures of androgynous figures drawn in such proximity as to form patterns of colour and waves. Quite effective, but Matias doesn't like them much,' she added confidentially. 'They have three children and a baby. The baby has a nurse from those parts, but they need all the help they can get with the children, so you could be a great bonus to them.'

'I'd like that. Do they know about me?'

'Know what about you, Milana?'

'Well, I'm, I mean will they put me with the servants? I just want to know my place, that's all…' she trailed off.

'Forget your place, Milana. Just live and breathe your art. Don't carry any baggage from your past, dear. Let who you are speak for itself. OK?'

'I'll try. Were you ever haunted there, *Señora* Lisa?'

'Ghosts are just shadows like myths and legends are just stories, Milana. They can inspire us but they can't hurt us.'

'Can't they?' whispered Milana staring intently back at her.

Chapter Two

The page of instructions from *Don* Matias was beginning to tear along the folds. Milana sat on the blue wooden bench with her bag at her feet watching the sun sink towards the horizon as she waited. Beside her, three clay pots were arranged in order of size. A grubby white flag attached to a stick indicated that there was fresh bread for sale in the little hut behind her where dusty toiletries displayed ancient price tags alongside recyclable bottles of Fanta and Coca Cola. Dust eddied around her, lifted by sudden gusts of wind, like a fine gauze it settled on everything so that nothing appeared perfectly focussed. To either side of her the long empty road stretched into the ether.

Eventually a car appeared out of the dust, sporting a huge sign on the roof on which several names of places were written. It swerved to a stop lifting clouds of dust and narrowly missing the clay pots.

'Alhue?' enquired Milana of the small, sinewy man inside. He nodded, spat on the ground and, with a practised flick of his wrist from where he sat, opened the back door for her to get in. His eyes stared at her in the wide rear-view mirror that reduced her to a miniature while expanding his own line of vision. He set off at speed. A woman with dyed hair through which the roots showed black, sat in the front. She had a basket covered with a white cloth on her lap over which her hands were crossed. The inside of the taxi smelt of cheap air freshener. The back seat had lost its springs and in places the foam stuffing showed through. Every bump on the dirt track shook the taxi so that it rattled and groaned. The driver stared through the windscreen, chewing a toothpick that he shifted methodically from one side of his mouth to the other.

A few kilometres ahead, they came across a broken-down fiat on the side of the road. Two men waved them down with frantic arm gestures.

'Blasted car's packed up on us,' said one of them peering in through the window. He stared at Milana and the woman in turn and then addressed the driver with an aggressive 'Hey *Hombre, vamos a Tierra Dulce.*' The driver spat again. He flicked the back door open like one whose only action in life was to open and close the door of his taxi and to drive on. Milana thought of the old ferryman in the novel by Herman Hesse, endlessly ferrying people across the river, ageless and silent. She moved into the corner of the taxi and stuffed her bag on the floor by her feet, but the two men were having none of it. They came at her from both doors, thrusting themselves into the back seat, on either side of her slim frame. One pushed her out of her corner with a toothy smile, and the other wedged her into the middle and shoved her bag into the space between the two front seats. The larger of the two men stretched his arm along the back of the seat so that her hair brushed against his hand. She had the sensation his fingers toyed with it. Their legs were fast up against hers, thick and muscular under their filthy jeans. The stocky one rested his hand on his thigh, millimetres from her leg. His fingernails were long and packed with black filth. He wore a tight gold ring with a stone in the centre. His fingers strayed closer brushing the side of her leg with studied indifference. She could smell their thoughts like a bad odour.

The woman in the front looked at them in the wide rear-view mirror. Milana caught her eye for a moment. The light was failing fast. The heat from the men's bodies penetrated slowly and uncomfortably. She stared ahead between the two front seats at the desolate countryside; no houses, no living soul just a dirt track winding endlessly through the valley towards the mountains. Behind them, a cloud of dust lifted by the tyres blotted out the road. The driver took the occasional bend at a devil-may-care speed. Shades of darkness came in waves, imperceptible yet swift, until there was only the pool of light made by the headlamps and beyond that, pitch black.

Suddenly the shape of a woman was picked up by the headlamps. The taxi screeched to a halt. The woman's face was covered against the dust by a black shawl. She approached the car. The driver rolled down his window and said something to the faceless traveller, then he leaned across the woman in the front and flicked open the door. A blast of cold penetrated the stuffy interior. The woman shifted herself up onto the handbrake to make space for the stranger. 'She might be the devil herself,' whispered the man with the gold ring, of the newcomer, his exhalation uncomfortably close to Milana.

'Or his mother,' laughed his friend relishing his proximity to her as he leaned forward in response, breathing warm garlic and cigarettes into her face. They leant back again their shoulders pinning her back into the lumpy seat.

Milana stared out into the blackness while the car rocked and shuddered on its way. The man on her left took a cigarette from behind his ear. The man on her right flicked open a lighter and reached across. The flame danced unsteadily. He turned his face towards her, she could see the pores and the scars on his skin. He winked at her and she caught the glint of the flame in his eye. He made to return the lighter to his pocket but his hand lingered there near her thigh, exploring the possibilities. The driver took another bend with devlish abandon flinging them all to the left. When she settled again she discovered the man's hand was underneath her, squirming at its own proximity to forbidden pleasures. A sudden wave of nausea mounted from her stomach to her throat. All the memories of El Negro seemed to want to spew themselves out and, with them, the awakened rage. Meanwhile the man's smirking face leaned against the glass looking out at nothing. The driver pressed and released the accelerator relentlessly as though it were a game. Milana breathed in and out deeply through clenched teeth, concentrating furiously on the darkness while the heat of the hand beneath her buttocks penetrated through her skin. She scanned the blackness for some point of light, some sign of human habitation so that she could hurl herself out. Suddenly she knew she could hold out no longer. Thrusting herself free of the shoulders that wedged her in, she gripped the seat in front and turned towards her assailant, her hand about to fly at him. The driver fixed his eyes on her, riveted by the drama unfolding in his back seat, just as the blinding lights of another car appeared suddenly infront of them. The sound of screeching brakes tore through the air like an animal's cry. Then there was motion, uncontrolled and brutal, like her venom released…then there was stillness.

Milana moved her head a fraction. Her fingers wriggled between cotton sheets and curled around the side of a wide bed, cold as a tomb. She passed her tongue over her parched lips and felt the pull of pain at the corner of her mouth where it touched a crust of dried blood. Her breath, trapped by the sheet, spread warmth about her face and re-entered her lungs. She began gradually to stretch her legs which until now had been huddled up, her knees almost touching her chest. Her feet ventured into parts of the bed where icy dampness had not yet been warmed. Pain jabbed through her like cold prods to full consciousness. She opened her eyes.

Dust glittered in thin shafts of sunlight that penetrated through the slats of ancient shutters and reflected on the tall bronze bedstead, stained with age to a dull gold. A grim ancestral face stared out of an ancient frame as dull and darkened as the picture. Only the glow of the painted skin and the eyes gave it any light at all; eyes that looked down at Milana impassively.

She remembered the taxi, the dust, the long road, then, with a jolt, she recalled the sensation of a hand lodged under her, its fingers eager to penetrate her intimacy, and the blinding lights of a sudden car. There was no venom in her now, it lay strewn over the dusty road mingling with escaped petrol. Could she have made it happen? A streak of guilt like the cold brush of metal brought her to sudden wakefulness.

Who had folded her clothes so neatly on the crimson velvet of the divan? Who had placed her boots, cleaned and dusted, by the bed and left her bag by the chest of drawers? Milana lifted herself slowly out of the bed and let her feet touch the rough weave of an old rug. There was a samovar close by, with the remains of burnt out embers. Someone had pushed a note under the door, a clean white folded rectangle waiting to be noticed. Blood rushed to her head and made her momentarily dizzy as she stood up. She reached out for it and unfolded the paper but the writing was unreadable in the semi darkness.

Little spasms of pain shot through her body as she moved to the window. Half kneeling on a flaking window seat she pulled at an old window latch. The frame shuddered but remained firmly stuck. Cold swept across the floor and circled her bare feet. She placed herself by a crack of light to read the note.

> 'Dearest Milana, rest all you need. We all look forward to seeing you when you wake up, and Matias has rung to check on you. We told him you were sleeping.
> Ask anyone for whatever you need. I will be back later.
> Welcome to our home.
> Stella.'

Milana began, hurriedly, to throw on her clothes, ignoring the soreness of her limbs. Pain spiralled up suddenly through the back of her head. She touched her neck. A small amount of blood smeared the palm of her hand. Tangles of dried-in blood nestled under her mane of thick dark-gold tresses. She looked at herself in the pitted mirror of an ancient wardrobe. Large green eyes stared back at themselves. She touched her bruised face as though it were a stranger's, with her nail she tore off the annoying crust at the corner of her mouth. It left a tiny raw spot, she felt for it with her tongue; it stung. A large fluffy towel lay folded on a chair close to the door. She picked it up and felt its softness. She put it to her face and smelt the scent of roses.

Her hands, like her face, were dry and dusty. She wanted to find a place to clean up before someone found her and drew her into the world that lay beyond the semi darkness. She hesitated, listening for sounds. Cautiously she pulled open the heavy bedroom door and stepped out into a bright winter's day. The air had an icy chill but where the sun shone it warmed. She found herself standing in the centre portion of a long colonnade, like a cloister. Thin wooden pillars ran along three sides of a garden. Behind her, the walls of adobe were painted a faded rusty pink and punctuated at intervals by high carved wooden doors like the one from which she had just emerged, above which some ancient craftsman had engraved the name *Rosa*. The garden in the centre was large and, given the twisted thickness of the vines that wrapped themselves around the trees, it had been there a long time. The gallery in which she stood, enfolded this garden like arms jealously hiding its enchantment from the outside world.

There was a primitive earth hut in the centre of this little sanctuary that appeared held together by the intertwining branches of the surrounding trees and flowering creepers. It dated back to an earlier age when all such houses had a refuge from earthquakes in their inner courtyard. The trees here had grown tall and sunlight pierced through their lofty canopies forming pillars of light, spectral and incandescent. Red petals from a huge camelia tree carpeted the ground while palm trees with colossal trunks like sombre elephants' feet towered between the shiny mandarin trees. Pots of red geraniums stood at regular intervals between weathered urns that trailed cascades of bourganvillea.

An old man was bending over a pile of what seemed to be long sticks. He was a few steps away, but he had not noticed her. Milana could hear his litany of complaints as he staked them into the ground. She realised they were torches that he was planting around the perimeter. He moved on, stopping at intervals, muttering and cursing all the while. He seemed oblivious to her presence or to the hens that pecked about his shoes or the small grey kitten that rushed out to climb the torches. Milana watched, fascinated, until the noise of footsteps nearby attracted the old man's attention and broke the spell.

Reluctant to be discovered just yet Milana drew back quickly, through a door that stood ajar a little further down from her own. Above her head she noticed that the roof in this derelict room had caved in leaving a jagged frame for the deep blue sky beyond. Tentatively making her way over fallen debris she approached the French window in the far wall; no shutters concealed the view of the rose garden beyond. Its glass panes were cracked and broken and in places all the glass had fallen out. Milana stepped through the broken window, as though she were Alice stepping through the looking-glass.

Chapter Three

A veranda bordered this wing of the house. Pretty mosaics criss-crossed its sun-bleached tiles beyond which flower beds of winter roses clustered round a stone sundial. A woman in a white nurse's uniform sat on a wicker sofa knitting a red mantle. Two hens circled a navy blue polka dot pram close by. Milana tiptoed closer. The nurse seemed to be sleeping, her head slightly bowed over her work. As Milana bent towards the pram, she glanced guiltily toward the nurse and only then realised that she had been fooled by the way the sun glanced off the lenses of the woman's steel rimmed glasses: the nurse was watching her intently.

'You slept well then,' she murmured, her eyes moving over Milana with unflinching intensity.

'Yes thank you.'

The nurse took up her knitting. Milana watched the bony brown fingers flicking the wool and twisting it this way and that as she weaved a complicated design. She glanced at the tight dark curls clustered about the woman's head and the curve of her finely drawn lips that smiled knowingly to themselves.

'Someone must have put me to bed, and tidied my clothes. Maybe it was *Señora* Stella? ' ventured Milana.

The nurse sat bolt upright, impassive and composed, with her knees discreetly covered by the hem of her white pinafore over which the mantle she was knitting cascaded like a red waterfall.

'That would have been me,' she said softly.

'Oh. Thank you.' Milana felt herself unnerved. 'I don't really know what happened last night, I'm a bit lost really.'

'You're fine. That's all that matters. That taxi could have got you all killed, driving like a maniac, sending the car spinning out of control. But he didn't so don't fret about it child,' and her eyes lifted and rested on Milana. There was an imperturbability about the nurse that Milana dared not trespass by asking any more questions. Instinctively she wanted to dilute the power this woman seemed to hold over her by concealing her desire for information about last night.

A sudden cry broke the silence that until now had been made up of a hundred tiny sounds – the clicking of the knitting needles, the twittering of birds, the cluck of a hen, the distant bark of a dog. The cry was followed by a crescendo of complaint from the waking baby. The nurse put down her knitting and lifting the baby out of the pram whispered to it softly in its ear. As though she were pouring in some bewitching balm, his little round face relaxed and his pouting mouth began to suck an imaginary dummy as she rocked him to and fro purring her peculiar lullaby. Milana watched his eyelids flutter and close. The nurse bent over and laid her little charge to rest again in the pram. Then she walked away without a word.

Milana stayed by the pram, as if glued there by some will other than her own, staring at the garish knitting left behind on the wicker bench, amidst the soft pastels of the faded cushions. After a few moments the nurse returned. She walked with a slow dignified step. Unusually prominent cheek bones pushed through her sun-browned skin. Her belt was too tightly drawn about her waist, cutting into her ample figure, but her legs were surprisingly thin and shapely in their tawny stockings. She wore simple black shoes with an inch of heel that gave certain elegance to her uniform.

Resuming her seat, the nurse placed her knitting on her lap and turned to Milana indicating for her to approach. Milana stepped forwards tentatively. The nurse reached out her bony brown fingers with long tapered nails and taking Milana's hand she deposited something small and unfamiliar into her palm before gently closing her fingers around it. Milana stayed stock still, feeling the jagged edges of some cold uneven object digging into her skin. The nurse held her gaze as though she were weaving some tenuous thread of understanding between them.

'They'll bring you luck,' she smiled, satisfied, 'think of it as a welcome gift.' Turning back to her knitting she added, 'You should open the shutters to your room, or the sun won't have a chance to warm it before night comes again.' Then, almost as an afterthought, she continued, 'That was some way to arrive! I had to sponge you down like a baby. You were that grimy and bloodied, moaning and thrashing about the whole time like you was wishing you'd been left for dead on that there road for "El Negro" to get you.'

'El Negro? I said that?' Milana found herself wringing her hands.

'I'm not here to pry, *Señorita* Milana,' said the nurse watching her closely now, 'but I doubt El Negro, whoever he is will find you in this godforsaken spot, if that's any comfort. Still, this ain't no refuge for the fainthearted, if that's what you're after.'

'How do you mean?' Milana leaned in.

'I mean this is a place of spirits.' The nurse took off her glasses and rubbed them against her skirt. She looked up then and her eyes were dark and penetrating. 'You can't hide from the spirit world, it knows your secrets and pulls them out of you.' She replaced her glasses. '*I* came back to make my peace,' she murmured. 'And *you…*' she seemed to change her mind suddenly and follow a different, less ominous tack, 'You're probably hungry, girl, you'll find Matilda, the cook, in the kitchen.'

A dog bounded past them barking wildly and the baby, startled from sleep, started screaming. The nurse lifted herself up to take the baby but this time, like a bird suddenly released, Milana sprang away as though if she dawdled she might become imprisoned again by those spellbinding eyes.

She walked in the opposite direction to which she had come. Leaving the rose garden and circling the house Milana passed wrought iron lanterns hung on iron posts between ancient pines. She stopped at the foot of stone steps that led up to what appeared to be the main entrance. A massive oak door stood open to a drafty hall and beyond it, through a further arch, the inner garden she'd first emerged from, with its lofty palms and bourganvillea, was just visible. She felt the object she carried digging into the softness of her palm. Still oddly wary of it, she kept it hidden in her hand. The distant sound of a car approaching diverted her attention. Behind her, across swathes of young vineyards she glimpsed the cloud of dust lifted by its tyres. Turning back she walked quickly up the steps and through the hallway into the cloister and the sudden stillness of the ancient inner sanctuary.

There was no one about now. A long wooden table had been set up under an arbour of vine leaves at the far corner of this garden. In the foreground, so that it would be seen from the entrance of the house, someone had built an untidy bonfire. The torches were all in place around the perimeter of the cloister. Milana looked around her to make sure she was quite alone before she opened her tightly closed fist and looked inside; opalescent diamond-shaped crystals in little clusters reflected rainbows of colour. She held the delicate pair of earrings up and watched them sparkle in the sunlight. Snatched memories came back to her – of tinsel, scintillating in the glow of Christmas lights, of tiny foil wrapped Easter eggs dropped in the dust by a child with overfilled pockets, glittering in the April sun. A surge of excitement stirred her senses.

The car she had heard moments before, drew up outside. Dogs barked. Milana heard voices from the kitchen and the sound of running feet.

'Where's Gonzalo?' A woman's voice called out from the forecourt. It echoed though the hallway.

'He's not come back yet, *Señora*,' someone replied.

'But I saw the Jeep in the garage?' The voice sounded tense and irritated.

'*Don* Gustavo Guerrero is with him.' That was *Señora* Lisa's uncle, Milana remembered, the one who had sold this place to Gonzalo.

'They've taken the horses, Madam. They said they would be back for the evening party,' cried another woman whose footsteps now approached, 'Don Gonzalo said he had some things he needed to show Don Gustavo, said it would be easier to do it today.'

There was an exclamation of exasperation. 'I can never rely on him, damn it.' A car door slammed. There were sounds of things being shunted and lifted, and then a change of tone, quick and excited. 'Are the torches up?'

The voices came nearer.

Milana shrank back. Already she must have put them to trouble. They would be relieved to know that she was out of the way, not lurking about in the corridors. She darted towards her room only to be faced by the series of identical huge wooden doors that stood proudly along the south east side of the cloister. She could hear impatience and agitation mixed in that voice that she had no doubt belonged to the mistress of the house, Stella.

Milana tried one door but it held fast. The footsteps were already in the hallway so she swung round to face them rather than be spotted skulking away. But the footsteps had turned briskly into a room where they were muffled by carpet. Milana tried the next door down that opened to reveal a dark room lined in books, huge and lofty as her own. Gingerly she crossed to the tall window on the opposite side, afraid that her presence might disturb the quiet aura. She stepped up onto a low window seat and turning the brass oval handle she pushed open the windows and found herself peering acrosss the verandah into the rose garden again. All the rooms along the south east wing, she realised, looked out onto this garden beyond which hills rose out of barren land. The nurse and the pram had disappeared. Climbing through the window and closing it as best she could, she ran lightly along the veranda until she reached the shuttered window she thought might correspond to her room.

Breathless, Milana gripped the wooden slats and wrenched them back. The shutters flew open. She reeled, just managing to keep her balance. A shaft of light pierced the darkness within, through the half drawn lace drapes. Milana leant her forehead against the window and cupping her hands around her eyes to shield them from reflections she pressed against the cold glass pane. She could not believe what she witnessed. The room was writhing as though convulsed by some feverish activity. The air itself seemed to oscillate visibly. Everything she looked at through the glass pane was deformed into a child's nightmare; every solid outline was in flux. Every palpable thing was volatile, strained and twisted by a kind of invisible violence. Even though she was standing outside, Milana felt agitation quiver through her. It was as if every atom and molecule within every solid thing inside that room had suddenly taken on a life of its own. If a place or thing could be possessed, she thought, this surely must be how it would appear.

It lasted no more than a moment, then the violence drained away. Pockets of stillness spread about the room. The air grew quiet and invisible once more, and there was peace. Milana saw the room she had slept in recover its composure; the faded watercolours and crimson divan, the large bronze bed, all quiet, inert. The old ancestral portrait stared back at her, the expression serene and benign. In their restfulness these objects all proclaimed their innocence of what had been. She might have imagined it all as a wild unreasonable fantasy brought on as an after effect of the accident, or some hallucinogenic drug administered intravenously by the creepy nurse. Nothing was changed, except for a perception of evil that left her chilled to the bone.

'I saw it too,' said a small voice behind her. Milana turned abruptly. A child was standing in her shadow cuddling a small grey kitten.

'What did you see?' Milana asked, crouching down to be level with the child's pale face. She shook her head and started to cry into the manky fur of her kitten.

'Don't cry,' Milana encouraged softly. 'We don't have to tell anyone.' The child looked up with dark, woebegone eyes. 'I've seen it before, only they don't believe me.' She lifted her sleeve revealing a big dark bruise on her arm.

'They pinch me and tell me not to tell fibs.'

'Who?'

'Matilda, the cook and Jose the gardener.'

'That's because they're afraid. I'm not. I won't do anything to you. Tell me what you see?' Milana urged her tenderly, her eyes darting anxiously over the child's troubled face.

She shook her head. 'I don't know.'

'When have you seen it before?'

'Yesterday night when *Don* Gustavo was sitting smoking a cigar. He used to live here, you know, but something happened to his wife. That's what cook said.'

'Did *Don* Gustavo see anything?'

She shook her head again.

'Is it good or bad, what you see?'

She shook her head again and her eyes grew wider, 'I don't know.'

'Shall we turn it into a fun picture?'

'I love pictures,' said the girl with sudden pleasure.

'Let's go back to my room the other way, that'll give the room time to rest.' The girl giggled. Milana took the hand she proffered and together they climbed back over the debris of the room with no ceiling and found Milana's room through the door that only a moment ago had held fast when she tried it. Lodged at the bottom of Milana's bag there was a sketch book. She pulled it out along with a little pencil case from which she took a pencil and a fine-point pen; she handed the girl a sheet of paper. The little girl put the kitten down on the bed and took the paper and pencil with a look of bemused interest.

'Can I draw anything?'

'Anything at all, that's what's such fun. You can make it all up if you want.'

'Will you draw too?' Milana nodded, already she had put pen to paper and in quick, vibrant strokes had produced an image of the room as they had seen it. The little girl forgot to draw as she watched in fascination how lines became objects that seemed to come alive on the paper so you wanted to untwist and reshape them. The little girl started to laugh, 'Oh, it's so funny. Look, the mirror's all fat and thin, like it's a person.'

'What's your name?' whispered Milana to the little girl.

'Consuelo,' she said with laughing eyes.

'Let's call this Consuelo's Dream.' In a beautiful script she wrote 'Consuelo's Dream' under the picture.

'It's wonderful,' sighed Consuelo contentedly. 'Now they'll believe me won't they?'

A shadow fell across the floor.

'Mummy!' The child ran up to the glamorous woman framed in the window and unhooked the latch with practised ease.

'Milana, I see you've met Consuelo, I'm Stella,' she said stepping into the room over the low window sill to embrace her warmly. Milana stood up to greet her hostess, 'Oh thank you for having me,' she stammered rather foolishly. Then quickly recovering her composure she added, 'I must have put you to so much trouble last night.'

'Nonsense,' Stella tossed her hair back. 'That awful accident. You look recovered, thank goodness. What a terrible fright. You poor girl.' She spoke in a flurry of staccato sentences, her gaze travelling quickly over Milana as if to assure herself she was still in one piece.

'It's all a haze, really, like I dreamt it,' Milana confided.

'Oh that's so much better isn't it. Dreams are so quickly forgotten.' Stella seemed mightily relieved. 'But are you sure you're alright? The nurse looked after you, you know. She's a funny old stick. Said you were sleeping like a baby when she came to find me last night. Nothing at all for me to do, so I left you to sleep.'

Stella touched Milana's arm as though to verify her presence. Then she gave a little laugh.

'You look well, so well,' she exclaimed appreciatively. 'Your paints and canvases all arrived safely yesterday, you know. You must ask Matilda for them.' She gave Milana a gloriously reassuring smile.

'We're having a little gypsy party tonight.' She winked at her daughter who looked back gleefully showing her perfect rows of baby teeth.

'Do you think you'll be up to it, Milana? Oh but of course you will, the young are always up for everything.' There was a momentary silence, as though Milana were allowing the silken stream of words to settle before attempting a contribution.

'I didn't bring many clothes.'

'Oh don't worry about that.' And she went on in the same breath, 'Gonzalo's gone off and left everything to me. He doesn't much like parties. You do, don't you?' For a brief instant Stella cocked her head to one side in a childish fashion. 'You are an artist like me. I'm glad you've come. Isn't it a lovely idea, a gypsy party?' Her enthusiasm was at once comforting and unsettling, 'We'll have torches and a bonfire and a barbeque, all kinds of meats and marshmallows.' Milana's heart skipped a beat as she recalled the only other time she had eaten marshmallows. 'I'll lend you my red and black skirt with petticoats if you like,' she went on, 'and I've got necklaces you can borrow. I do want you to enjoy yourself.' In a softer, almost intimate voice she added hurriedly, 'Our man Pedro brought you in, he won't say anything about the accident. I expect nurse knows. She knows everything. But they're funny round here you know, they don't like to talk about some stuff incase it tempts evil,' her eyes sparkled. 'You know Alhue means devil's birthplace. Well they're very touchy about it.' Then, almost furtively she asked, 'I suppose you don't remember what happened?'

Milana shook her head. A flat pause followed and she felt momentarily drab and jaded trapped in Stella's web of gleaming hair and streaming words, like a hapless victim.

'Nothing at all?' Stella probed.

'Only that I was in a taxi, and it stopped for two tourists and then for a lady in a black shawl and… I can't remember anything else,' she added quickly.

'Mmm,' Stella looked thoughtful.

'Didn't anyone see what happened?' suggested Milana.

'No one tells me anything, least of all the nurse who usually knows the most. She just didn't want me fussing I suppose. I'd love to know what goes on under those steel rim lenses of hers. I'm sure she's a witch,' she mouthed 'witch', so that Consuelo who was playing with her kitten wouldn't hear. 'But as long as she doesn't turn Gonzalo into a toad or feed beetles to the baby, she'll do.' Stella laughed merrily.

Milana was reminded of her own thoughts about Iris. She liked Stella's confiding manner and her spontaneity and the inquisitive childlike side that, she percieved, longed to be included.

'You mustn't let her frighten you. She's brimming with superstition but she does make me laugh sometimes and she gets the baby to fall asleep every time. I was worried she gave him stuff but I've watched her. She just whispers to him and he's blissfully asleep in no time.'

'Maybe that's how she got me to sleep last night.' Stella looked confused then realising what Milana meant she laughed. They both laughed.

'You've got some little cuts there,' Stella reached out and gently swept a lock of hair off Milana's forehead. 'Does it hurt?'

Milana shook her head. 'I've seen her, dressed in white, knitting, out there, on the wicker bench.'

'That would be her. Did she talk to you?'

'Not much,' said Milana, and she thought of the earrings now in her pocket but kept silent. And then suddenly Stella was back on the accident, drawing a little closer so her perfume, intense as flowering magnolia, filtered into the conversation. 'Old Pedro is a real character. Sinewy like a tight knot and quick as lightning on a horse. Seems he passed the accident, last night. Guessed it was you. We were expecting you, you see. Crafty so and so, he took you in round the back and gave you over to the nurse and she only came to get me once you were asleep. So I never saw you. I should be cross really but there's no point. He won't speak, anyway. Never does. No one tells me anything.' She looked momentarily put out.

'*Señora* Stella…'

'Stella, please, just Stella. *Señora* makes me feel so old.'

'You're not old, Mummy,' Consuelo looked at her mother adoringly before continuing her game of waving her pigtail at the kitten.

'Did the nurse tidy all my things too?'

'Yes. She's very professional in her work but she goes about it silently like she's engaged in some covert operation. I don't like to interfere. I think she enjoys appearing like a ghost out of nowhere. You never hear her approach. Gonzalo loves her. He says she's an angel in white, perfect to have around because you never know she's there. I think it's all a bit creepy but, so what. You can't get much help in these parts.'

The scent of magnolias was making Milana giddy.

'We've got quite a few people coming, tonight,' Stella added, moving away to take a quick look at herself in the full length mirror. 'There are a couple of girls from the village helping out and stable hands too. I've been out all morning. No one does anything unless I'm home. Come with me?' she turned on her heel towards the door, 'No one's expected before nine tonight so we've still got plenty of time. I'll show you round. That's if you're up to it?'

They left Consuelo to play with the kitten on the bed.

'I feel I've lost touch with everyone now that I live out in the sticks,' Stella sighed and snatched a look at Milana as they went along the inner corridor towards the reception rooms. 'You're quite pale dear,' she added as they turned through the hallway and then onto an ancient and worn Aubusson carpet that covered a vast expanse of room. Again she stretched out her hand to touch Milana's skin. Her fingers felt cool. Milana found her both irresistibly alluring and disconcertingly intimate in unexpected moments.

'I can't tell you how glad I am you've come.' She spoke breathlessly as she bustled about adjusting tables and armchairs. Pulling a great linen tablecloth out of the dresser she laid it over a vast walnut table at the far end of the room. She disappeared down two steps and through a little stone archway into the kitchen, to re-emerge moments later with two spectacular silver candelabra complete with ivory-coloured candles.

'We haven't been here long.' she explained, 'This isn't really my taste, all this,' she swept her hand around the room. 'But we bought it as it was, including every last bit of furniture, from Gustavo. You'll meet him later. He's out riding with my husband. Gonzalo thinks it suits the place. You're the artist, what do you think?'

'I think it's splendid,' Milana offered. Her head was beginning to ache.

'What will you paint? The nurse?' she teased, 'The gardens? The hills? It's so exciting to have a painter come and get inspiration here. One day you'll be terribly famous. Matias has a good eye for talent, like a hawk for its prey you know.' She glanced up from where she was rearranging a huge vase of mimosa on the sideboard.

Milana laughed, embarrassed, and looked at the mimosa. For a moment she felt a twinge of sadness in her heart as she remembered the mimosa tree under which her mother parked her white metal cart.

'I'm deadly serious. You will be famous. Besides I can feel it in you, you know how one can sniff out winners and losers. You've got a zing to you, you're going places,' and then suddenly changing tack again she added, 'I'd like to be remembered in a picture… maybe one that could hang on these walls; "The lady of the house reclining on a chaise longue" she drawled theatrically, 'before the children turn my hair grey.' Leaving the flowers she reclined attractively for Milana on the old velvet sofa. Milana laughed, enchanted by her uninhibitedness. 'Or you could paint the children, of course.'

'Where are the children?' asked Milana, hoping for some brief respite. She liked Stella but she needed to get away. She wasn't strong enough yet for this unstoppable whirl of conversation.

'Oh they're about. Antonio, he's almost seven, is playing in the pantry and Francisca, she's nearly five, she'll be in the stables or feeding the hens with cook somewhere. You met Consuelo, she's eight, she loves painting, but now she never leaves that kitten alone, that's why it looks so straggly.' She bounced out of the chaise longue and nearly skipped across the room. 'We've got three enormous tortas for tonight, they're made locally in the village; one of *lucuma*, another of nuts and *dulce de leche* and the inevitable black forest gateaux, and tons of little sweets and canapés. I haven't done this for so long. Isn't it exciting? This house was made to be full of people. It's so desolate otherwise.' As she moved she brushed her hair out of her eyes and flicked the loose curls behind her ears; she was restless, ebullient.

'Does your husband make wine here or does he farm?' enquired Milana politely. For a moment Stella smiled back blankly, as though Gonzalo were someone who had slipped her mind yet in another instant, she was talking about Gonzalo and his many projects and his vineyards. Milana got the impression that Stella had been starved of conversation the way she talked now, but then she wasn't sure; she still didn't know how people in these circles behaved. Maybe it was normal for women to chatter endlessly in this nervous fashion before a party. Maybe it was what one did in polite society to make people feel at ease.

As Milana listened, she watched Stella making minute adjustments to the room, snatching nervous glances at everything followed by quick charming smiles at Milana, and glimpses of herself in the mirror. There was a flurry of motion in the way in which she addressed details; a kind of feverish anxiety that everything should be just perfect. As she watched her, so charming, so irreproachable in her kindness and cheerfulness, Milana glimpsed something irresolute and a little rash about her manner, that intrigued.

Chapter Four

Shadows spread like tides of darkness under the dusky lilac sky. Milana turned on the light by the dresser. On her bed she found several long, colourful skirts and a couple of gypsy blouses with an abundance of frills. She guessed Stella had left them there after tea. Milana tried each one on, carefully studying the effect in the mirror, finally deciding on a black top, low cut and trimmed with lace and a very full red and black skirt. Delighted she twirled about the room imagining herself as Stella, exuding elegance and excitement.

In the dim light of the room Milana made herself up, concealing the traces of her bruises as best she could. From the dresser she picked up the earrings. Why had the nurse given them to her she wondered? Did it relate to some superstition about giving a stranger a gift to heal past ills? Superstitions excused the strangest forms of behaviour. She remembered seeing Iris cutting Letty's hair after El Negro left, sitting in the back yard in a pool of moonlight. Iris would know why she had been given the earrings. Iris would say; 'Oh that's simple, she's casting out the evil you're bringing to the house from your accident by welcoming you with a gift,' or some such explanation of the type she'd heard in the past.

Milana clipped on the earrings in front of the mirror. They accentuated her slender neck with their alluring delicacy. She felt a frisson of pleasure and twirled again to watch how the skirt lifted and undulated about her willowy figure. She was eager now to meet these people that would suddenly materialise out of the desolate countryside and relieved that tonight this remote house would be full of guests. The words of *Don* Matias rang in her ears; 'You must look ahead now, Milana. You have everything before you. You must go forwards with courage and grasp the opportunities life is giving you.' But all the same Milana found herself haunted by thoughts and feelings that whispered to her from the shadows of the past.

Love, she thought, in an effort of will, as she gazed at herself in the ancient glass, comes when you least expect it. Now, she teased herself, there was a real possibility that she was sent here to meet someone. She encouraged this fancy as she danced about the room enjoying the flowing skirt. She would beguile and bewitch; the girl in the mirror was hardly recognisable to her; maybe that too was due to Stella's peculiar influence on her. She swirled round and round in an attempt to confound the suppressed longings. Eventually she fell onto the bed dizzy and light-headed.

There was a soft knock on her door.

'I came to tie this for you, if you want,' the nurse held out the red head scarf and looked her up and down critically. Then she came up close to Milana.

'Look,' she produced a tiny square photograph from her pocket, showing it to Milana with a confiding smile. Milana saw a picture of a fine looking woman of about thirty, with glamorous hair, wrapped in a fur collared coat.

'That was me once,' the nurse took the photograph back and slid it into her pocket. She seemed to want to communicate something, but Milana couldn't quite understand what. She sat on her bed while the nurse wound the scarf about her head, her hands expertly shaping the turban so that the ends weren't left loose. When she finished, she stayed contemplating Milana and shook her head gravely.

'Maybe you should leave here.' She paused and shook her head slightly as if to dislodge the suggestion from her mind. 'You will not leave of course,' she opened the door to go and looked back, her strange luminous eyes holding Milana's for a disquieting moment.

'Do you believe in destiny?' she asked Milana pointedly.

'I think I do. Don't most people?'

'Humph.' She shrugged and seemed to look suddenly disinterested. 'Don't be fooled, life has many destinies, but only one exit.'

There were twenty, perhaps even thirty guests. Milana couldn't count them because they were never still. They moved between the rooms, eating and drinking, admiring each other and the ancient tapestries, the collections of guns and the crystal chandeliers that had survived countless earthquakes. One had his face painted black like a ruffian, others had extravagant gold streaks on their cheeks or eyelids shaded in blues and greens, pinks and purples. Their mouths contorted in endless chatter. They all seemed to smoke and the smoke lingered above their heads like long attenuated fingers of blue.

Milana was introduced to them as 'Our little protégé, soon to become great and famous.' She caught herself reflected in mirrors and windows and fancied she saw a stranger, not her at all. Who was she now? The gypsy? The painter? The protégé? She smiled at the guests from behind her party mask. All the time she looked over her shoulder in case there was someone in the shadows, someone she hadn't met yet who was meant for her.

'What are you thinking, Milana?' A little voice reached her from the step on which Consuelo sat looking up at the stars.

'Oh my. You surprised me. How come you're not in bed like your brother and sister?'

'I'm old enough.'

'You're only eight and it's very late.'

'I'm allowed. What were you thinking?' she insisted. 'You looked very sad. This is my first party,' Consuelo declared proudly. 'Don't they all look magical?'

'It's my first party too, Consuelo.'

'But you're much older than me,' the child protested.

'I know, but I've never been to parties.'

'Don't you like them? Is that Mummy's dress? Don't you have a party dress?'

Milana shook her head.

'Are you poor?' Consuelo smiled up at her.

Milana sat down beside her and huddled close stroking the kitten on her lap.

'Yes, I grew up by a dump where people left all their rubbish. But I had my own store of treasures.'

Consuelo's eyes grew bright. 'Treasures?'

'Yes, coloured stones and fragments of china and beautiful bits of painted glass. They were like all the colours here tonight and I would put them together to make pictures.'

'Are you sad because you lost them?'

'No.'

'Are you sad because you love someone?'

Milana put her arm round Consuelo and smiled. 'That's a funny thing to say.'

'People are always sad when they love someone.'

'Why, Consuelo? Love makes one so happy.'

'Really? I love my kitten.'

'Doesn't that make you happy.'

'Only when he's with me, but when I go to bed they won't let me have him in bed and I'm afraid a big owl or an eagle will come and take him in its claws, like they do the mice in the fields.'

'Oh I'm sure he'll be safe.'

'Don't you want to go and join the party?'

'I like sitting here with you, Consuelo.'

'I'm glad you came. Mummy and Daddy said you'd be nice, but nurse said it was the seventh day of the seventh month of the seventh year or something and that meant it was a bad day to come.' Then she leaned into Milana and added, 'I don't like nurse very much, Mummy thinks she's a witch.'

From the kitchen porch, the old cook, Matilda, watched the pig turning on the spit, its carcass stretched across the flames like some sacrificial offering. Guests milled about seeking warmth. The night was cold but clear. Torches blazed dimming the distant stars with their brightness. The servants were restless at the absence of *Don* Gonzalo, *'El Patron'* and Milana, passing near, sensed their concern. From the far end of the kitchen they searched the drive for a sign of him or *Don* Gustavo, who had ridden out with him earlier.

'They should have been here hours ago,' said the cook, her deep voice at odds with her diminutive frame. Jose, the gardener, grunted and took another swig of wine at the kitchen table. The nurse sat near the open fire over which a kettle steamed, knitting a long red sleeve,

'It's an evil night out there.'

'There's the chill of the grave about it,' said the gardener brightening.

'There's the truth,' said the cook. 'If ever there was a night not to ride abroad, it'd be tonight.' Her tiny black eyes reflected the flames.

'And there's *El Patron*, out in it like a child to the slaughter. He don't know nothing about this place, but *Don* Gustavo, he should know better,' added Pedro, the man who Stella said had brought Milana to the house last night. He had come in from the stables to warm himself in the kitchen. 'No point waiting out there for them,' he muttered rubbing his hands before breaking off a piece of bread from the loaf on the table.

'Nothing's right tonight,' frowned the nurse. 'The baby wouldn't drink its milk, and there's no moon.'

'But there's stars and bright too,' murmured Jose.

'When the moon won't show her face, it's a rare night,' breathed the nurse.

'And the Misses is come over all strange, not like herself at all,' said the cook

'He's abroad, I'm sure of it,' said the nurse, laying down her knitting. 'It's him, the Old Gentleman.'

'Shut up, old woman. You'll make me quake in my boots,' said the cook.

'Here, warm your bones with wine and you'll be forgetting,' Jose lifted his glass to her.

Milana strolled away along the open colonnade of the quadrangle, where her eye fell across the door to her own bedroom. A faint light glowed from under it. She was sure she had left no light on in her room. As she approached the light faded. A voice behind her called her name. She turned. There was no one about. A few steps away the flames from a torch licked the air hungrily. She heard it again, her name, like a rustle in the leaves. Milana walked rapidly, her footsteps echoing on the tiles. Sounds of laughter and shouts and conversation, disjointed and meaningless came on sudden breezes and echoed about the slender wooden pillars. She ran on, away from the whispers of the leaves and the flickering of the flames, and her foolish imaginings, across the entrance hall and into the quiet of the deserted forecourt.

Cars and Jeeps were parked between the trees. As she passed she felt their still warm motors breathe heat into the chill night air. Under the trees little wrought-iron lanterns, robed in a soft light that pooled about them, stood sentinel like gracious visitors from a magic world. She found herself wandering without purpose, not wanting to return to the party, wondering where Gonzalo might be and preoccupied by his absence as though it were somehow significant. A feeling possessed her that he was the missing piece to the puzzle that confused her. If he came back everything would return to normal; without him here nothing was centred. His house was like a boat without an anchor, spinning in the wind.

Her footsteps took her eventually towards the rose garden where she had first seen the nurse. The veranda was bathed in a faint opalescent light, turning it into an ethereal place of ghostly shadows under the great expanse of sky that shimmered with all the stars of the southern hemisphere. Gradually she became aware of a coloured light that penetrated this argental magic. Milana stepped up onto the verandah drawn by the strange glow. It came, she realised, from her unshuttered window. This time she had no difficulty taking in the weird vision that met her eyes. As before, the room had become a lurid, senseless living thing, pulsating with intense motion and violent garish colour. Milana did not move. She dared not even shut the shutters for fear that if she touched anything, she might be hurt or damaged by the energy that seemed to flow up to the very window. She felt like a trespasser on some forbidden show, like a child glimpsing some deranged scene of adult sex. She experienced a violence of emotions that riveted her to the spot; of shame and guilt and a loss of innocence. Between herself and that strange place where she must spend the night, there was a cold pane of glass, in which her face reflected the contorted horror of what she saw.

Then, with the same imperceptible speed that dusk chases away the brightness of day, the vision began to drain of colour, until Milana found herself staring at the dark, becalmed room into which a faint diaphanous light trickled from the starry sky. She closed the shutters and turned her back to them. She rested motionless against the flaking wooden slats wondering if it was something in her drink or in the cakes that was playing havoc with her mind. A cat mewed beside her, it was like the cry of a baby. Milana opened her eyes as though from a trance. She tore herself away from the window and ran from the shadow-filled rose garden. Its pale, passive existence seemed to jeer at the turmoil within her.

Chapter Five

A hand gripped Milana's arm as she passed through the hallway. She looked down and saw bony fingers and red-painted nails belonging to a small lady of uncertain age.

'You are Mercedes? You must be! Come to life tonight. My dear, who are you? Her daughter? No, that would be Lisa. You're not Lisa, but her grandaughter, maybe? The generations pass me by. I knew Mercedes before she died, I knew her when she lived here. Before Gustavo bought the place, and before he sold it on to Gonzalo. So much sadness in your eyes, so much loss. You're so like her my dear I just had to stop to look at you.'

Milana smiled graciously at the lady not knowing how to respond. The bonfire, recently lit, played shadows across the hallway.

'What do you think of this place, my dear?' she went on, not waiting for an answer, her eyes dwelling joyfully on the fine familiar features of the beautiful girl before her.

'I think it's rather frightening, actually.'

The lady still had her by the arm, her beady eyes peered into Milana's. Suddenly her face creased into a smile that turned to laughter, 'Mercedes too was sensitive to "vibes", my dear, it must be in you. She would never have come to this place but they made her, and it made her ill. She only had God to console her when Lisa ran away.' The old woman caught the flickering shadows on the wall and stared at them momentarily. 'I believe it made Gustavo's wife ill too. Mercedes would have said it was haunted, yet she stayed here and died here and was buried here. But you don't believe in such things as hauntings, do you?'

373

'I don't know,' Milana answered thoughtfully, wondering if the woman was mad or unusually sane. 'Perhaps I do.'

'I do too,' said the lady, her eyes bright as a forest animal. 'Oh my dear, there's so much life that the naked eye cannot see,' she whispered, glancing about her, as though searching for one of these phantasmagorical characters.

'Gustavo's here tonight, I'm told. I hoped to see him. But I'm too old for parties. It's way past my bedtime. Besides,' she leant towards Milana and rolled her eyes, 'it's one of those nights, you know, when they say the devil rides.'

'Do you believe in the devil then, Madam?' asked Milana, suddenly emboldened.

The woman crossed herself, 'Bless my soul dear girl, I have seen him.'

'Seen him?'

She raised her eyebrows and pressed her hands together.

'He comes in thoughts and in dreams. He turns himself into what he will. Never underestimate the evil one. I saw him as a black hound circling an old chapel on our *Fundo* once. We had no dog, and the blessed sacrament was in the chapel. Mercedes was with me. We were childhood friends then. When we were children she used to hug herself like this,' the woman clasped her thin arms around herself, 'And she'd say, "I'm getting funny feelings".'

For a moment, she became lost in a private world of memories. Milana stood a little apart, observing her curiously, listening for clues to riddles that she didn't understand. The lady gazed back wistfully at Milana, 'I wish you were her, come back. What one wouldn't give at my age, for a taste of the past, but you bring it back, it's in your eyes, and your hands.' She smiled taking Milana's hand and turning it over, 'So small, like Mercedes." She sighed and glanced out through the great front door. 'You know what they say? Alhue, it means birthplace of the devil. You can believe it can't you?' She stared into the darkness beyond the forecourt. 'It's a desolate spot if ever I saw one. But Gonzalo likes it. I wonder where he is, dear boy? He's my great nephew, you know. I don't often see him. You'd think he'd bother to show up for his own party wouldn't you?' The old lady breathed in deeply. 'Hasn't Stella done a lovely job? So artistic. You know she's writing a novel. Must be perfect here, lost to the world. I wonder where she is.'

'Come on Blanca, time we were going,' Blanca's husband joined them bringing with him a black shawl that he put over her shoulders. They swept away together towards the cars, the lady turning to give Milana a little wave, but Milana wasn't looking. She was standing on the black and white tiles against the faded yellow walls of the hallway facing the other way watching the bonfire. It whined and spat like a dying creature, as the flames licked the damp winter wood. Tiny red hot splinters shot through the air and died into the darkness. The heat came in sudden waves struggling against the chill night. It was only gradually that Milana became aware of a noise, a sound so integrated into the din of conversation that only little by little did she distinguish it as the roar of the flames like hundreds of hungry beasts ravaging the chopped up trunks of ancient trees.

A stranger stood apart from the rest, staring into the fire. She couldn't tell how long he'd stood there or when he had come. He was strangely compelling. His tall svelte figure was silhouetted against the light. Despite the heat, he did not turn away from the fire and seemed lost in its contemplation. A large black dog with a pointed nose and slightly bowed legs nuzzled him. His hand touched the animal distractedly, reaching into the short glossy coat and ruffling the fur. The dog stayed swaying under the strong caress. The man crouched down beside the dog. He bent his head as if to look the dog in the eye but at the last moment he turned it slowly so that first his angular profile was visible against the flames, then his shadowed eyes lifted and met hers. Inexplicably embarrassed, as though the man had seen her in the privacy of nakedness Milana took three steps back and turned away, shaken. When she looked back, he was gone.

Confused, Milana took the path that led her back past the kitchen. She peered in. '*Don* Gonzalo?' she asked, 'has he come home?' They looked at her, their old faces full of suspicion, and shook their heads. She ran on then through the kitchen gardens at the side of the house. Pulling the turban off her head she shook her hair down, as though that might release the strange heat inside her. The wind lifted the ends of her hair. It made the grass shiver and young shoots tremble. A twig cracked; the yellow eyes of a cat stared out of the night. Suddenly the wild whinny of a horse somewhere near made her jump. A slight glance over her shoulder brought with it the sudden terror of autosuggestion.

Breathless, she reached the forecourt again. A car was pulling out. The sound of the motor revving and the sudden glare of the headlamps chased away the shadows in her mind and gave relief. She ran on towards the hall, and met Stella coming from the far side of the house, from the direction of the rose garden, stepping lightly, moving rapidly. There was a devilish abandon about her that made Milana stop and stare. Stella glided past, her mouth a little open, her eyes wide and fixed. She left a cold fragrant breeze behind her.

'Stella,' Milana called. She ran after her and bumped into the nurse.

'I'm sorry,' stammered Milana.

'Don't fret girl. It's the spirits of the place. It's the night of the spirits. They are all around us, calling to us. They'll be gone by morning. Here come,' she took her to the door of a room off the kitchen and disappearing inside she returned with a cup of something warm. Milana looked at the water, it had leaves of something floating in it. She glanced at the nurse.

'Drink it. It'll help you sleep,' she soothed. Trustingly Milana drank it. The sugar disguised the faint taste of something bitter.

Milana stood in front of the ancient mirror, alone in her room. The light from two appliqués fell obliquely on her. Her hands undid the buttons of her blouse, and slipped it off her shoulders. They unzipped the skirt so that it fell to the ground. They released the clasp of her bra and let it fall off her shoulders and slip down her arms. She stepped out of the skirt and placed a hand on her flat stomach, while with the other hand she followed the curve of her waist and down along her hips to her thighs. All the while she watched her hand in the mirror as though it were another hand, not hers, learning her body, caressing it. She kept looking, fascinated by herself as though she were a stranger she was studying, capturing the first glimpse of the integrate, mature woman in her, the first awakening of something akin to experience but that seemed to come from within. The cold hardly touched her. She didn't care that there was no lock on the door, that any guest might walk in on her and surprise her in this weird ritual of the senses. She seemed to stand there in her nakedness provoking the elements to reach out and touch her. The room no longer filled her with fear. She felt at one with it as it accommodated her movements and sheltered her nakedness. She sat on the bed and pulled off her boots. She felt the satin of the quilt smooth and cold against her skin. She lay back on it and closed her eyes and there he was again, silhouetted against the flames.

Her body shuddered, as though an icy breeze passed over it. She opened her eyes.

He was there, at the foot of the bed, as though he had been there all the while, watching her, waiting. The light in the room seemed to have faded as though the very blackness of his clothes absorbed it. He lifted his hand in a gesture at once gentle and authoritative as though he were claiming her for himself. He put his finger to his lips to silence her unasked questions whilst his eyes penetrated her, holding every nerve ending to ransom. She closed her eyes, feeling her body wracked by overwhelming desire. He knelt beside her spreading his hands over her. His lips brushed her neck under the mass of curls, then touched hers briefly, moving on, racing over her body, awakening it, tantalising her until she could hardly breathe.

His mouth crushed on hers, cool against her flaming lips until there was no space, no air between his exhalation and her inhalation. She felt she was reaching out to find something that was just a moment away, on the threshold of fulfilment. He drew back again and waited until her body shuddered, aching for him. Then he fell on her, like a hungry animal, taking her into him as though he were drinking her soul, thrusting into her as though he wanted to destroy her. Like two creatures in a struggle to the death they writhed and moved against each other as if each tried to rob from the other the most supreme self-gratification. She craved from him the consummation of a promise, abandoning herself to him in an endless realisation of desire that was forever just out of reach. Even as it gripped her body, even as her back arched up to him in a final climax she felt there was something still eluding, still kept from her, something that would be the culmination of everything, of all her being, her purpose, if she could just reach out and possess it. All the while strange lurid images rolled through her mind, like snapshots of the past; the filthy hands that had defiled her reaching out to her like charred ineffectual bones from a roaring fire.

The morning light bathed the room. Milana woke from a deep sleep and spread her hand across the sheets. Strange memories drifted through her mind like disjointed images from a half remembered film. She felt different. She crushed the pillow to her naked body feeling its coldness real and comforting and sensual. What had happened? She spied the glass on the dresser. Had her dreams been caused by the bittersweet drink the nurse had given her. The pillow grew warm against her skin and she pulled it closer, overcome with melancholy as though in some way she had been violated, and something had been stolen, something hers and only hers that she had no wish to give. Somewhere deep down lurked frustration and emptiness, the perception of shame and the feeling of having been seduced and betrayed.

She pulled on some clothes, and, taking the bath towel in her arms, she opened the door and slipped quietly along the empty corridor to a bathroom. She let the warm water run down her back and over the tiny cuts and bruises from the night of the accident and watched it swirl away. Shampoo trickled over her temples. She massaged her hair and watched the foam fall in dollops. She lifted her face to the water and felt it rain on her eyes, her mouth, her cheeks, like so many tears flooding down over her, purging her of so much lost innocence. She felt like a woman who had known many lovers, experienced, almost satiated, and yet dissatisfied. She was gripped by an inexplicable sadness and despondency as though now nothing else was worth waiting for, all other men would bore and aggravate.

The love-making, dreamed or real, had been compelling yet destructive, evil and corrupting; it sought to suck the very soul from her and leave nothing. Whilst true love was generous and fulfilling, rewarding and creative, this love awakened every sense whilst mocking the creature it seduced. It was as cold as the reflection in a glass is to the real thing. It promised everything and gave nothing. Only the memory of Santiago could purge what she felt, but that memory lay suppressed, unspoken and feared.

She emerged at last into the silence. The house seemed to have caught its breath as though it knew her guilty secret. The pale sun filtered through the high clouds and slanting across the inner courtyard fell on her face. The smell of eucalyptus filled the air chasing away the smoke of last night. Milana stepped quietly into the hallway, not wanting her footsteps to intrude on the silent household. She noticed shadows moving in the strangely lit dining-room. Curiosity drew her. The door was ajar, gently she pushed it open.

The room was dark and the shutters drawn. It took a while for her eyes to adjust. Four candles stood squarely about the four corners of the dining-room table on which, last night, she had seen cakes on silver salvers. Now upon it lay a man, his hands folded on his chest, a rosary between his fingers. Gradually she noticed people; quiet shadowy figures in the half light murmuring the Hail Mary over and over like when Letty had died.

Stella rose from amongst them. She came to Milana slowly like a spectre. The candlelight fell on her red eyes. Her face dampened by distress rested for a moment against Milana's cheek.

'Death is so terrible,' she whispered. She took Milana by the hand to where the body lay. Milana saw a stranger, a silver haired man past sixty, with a kind face. His eyes were closed with two coins resting on the lids and around his jaw they had tied a white handkerchief as though the man had tooth ache when he died. His lips were closed and there seemed to be just a hint of a smile on them. There was dust in his hair and, one side of his face was scratched and torn.

'I hardly knew him,' Stella gave a tiny wistful smile and turned away. 'How terrible to come back only to die here like this, so horribly.' She laid one hand on Milana's arm and looked back at the body. A man approached them from the shadows, tall and thin, in riding boots. His shirt was bloodied down one side where he had held the face of the dead man to him. *He's like Don Matias*, thought Milana, as she looked up at Gonzalo's pleasant, honest face. He wasted no time on pleasantries or introductions, but emanated warmth.

'Don't stay in here, Milana,' he whispered kindly, 'go and get some breakfast. They've left some in the study.' He placed his hand reassuringly on his wife's shoulder, 'Stella will come presently.' Stella kissed Milana on the cheek and rejoined the others.

Milana sat alone at a small table in the room they called the study. The walls were hung with rifles. The sun did not reach this room till late afternoon. It was grim and chilly. The nurse passed by with the child in her arms. She stopped and looked in, her eyes hard as steel pierced through Milana's guilty conscience, 'I'm sorry,' Milana said quietly, 'I can't seem to find the earrings you leant me, they must have fallen.'

'I know,' she looked at Milana as though she knew far more than that, 'I found them.'

A young maid brought steaming hot milk for Milana's coffee and then knelt by the grate and put a match to the logs that were piled up in readiness. A flame spread through a cluster of twigs and balls of paper and licked at the edge of a log before bursting up around the dry bark. The maid drew back. Milana reached out to her as she passed.

'Who is the man lying in there?' she asked softly, glancing in the direction of the dining room. The maid looked blankly at Milana.

'The man lying dead on the dining-room table, who is he?' She couldn't be sure, after all.

The maid looked at her incredulously. 'Why that's *El Patron* Miss.'

'But *Don* Gonzalo is *El Patron* here.'

'I mean *Don* Gustavo Guerrero, Miss. He was *El Patron* here, before,' she said it as though she felt his place had been usurped and he was still the rightful master.

'What happened to him?' Milana persevered, determined to draw her out.

The maid met her questioning with an implacable stare, then, unexpectedly she chose to confide. 'They brought him in in the small hours. They couldn't stop the horse, crazed it was. Crazed! *Don* Gonzalo shot it,' she whispered.

'Is there anything the matter?' The nurse was standing in the doorway, without the baby now. Her arms were folded across her starched white uniform. The young maid slipped out of the room.

'Why did he die?' Milana asked, 'What happened?'

'*Don* Gonzalo,' the nurse replied, 'bought this place from *Don* Gustavo who inherited it from *Doña* Mercedes and her husband, but it only brought him unhappiness. He shouldn't have come back. But it's the spirits, they pull you back, won't leave you be. They were riding around the *fundo,* checking the new vineyards, but it was one of those rare nights, sends the horses into frenzies. They should have come home before nightfall. *Don* Gustavo had been dragged for miles when he was found.' She fell silent, her face pale, her eyes burning as she stared at the fire. Milana followed the line of her vision; in the flames, for a fleeting instant, it seemed she saw the face of a man. Milana approached the fire, and knelt by it as though she might put her hand in it to search out something lost.

'You see it too,' said the nurse, in a soft matter of fact tone. Milana didn't answer. 'They say he dwells in the heart of fire and if you look long enough his face will appear trapped in the flames.'

'What? What do you see?' murmured Milana the heat burning her cheeks.

'Can't you see him? He comes to lure the soul of the dying. *Don* Gonzalo was a good man. He lost that soul to God, so he must find his comfort elsewhere.' The nurse eyed her knowingly, nodding sagely, as Milana covered her face with her hands to shield it from the flames.

Chapter Six

'These are the most powerful paintings I have seen in years.' *Don* Matias turned to Lisa, triumphantly. 'It seems we were right, Lisa, my dear. The girl has found inspiration of the most impressive sort here. Look at this one, the way the face emerges from the fire, and this other, the head bent over the flames; such intensity!'

'I like this one,' Lisa pointed to the child with the kitten, sitting on stone steps in a pool of moonlight. *Don* Matias turned to where Milana sat beside Consuelo with Consuelo's little sister on her lap. 'This is magnificent work, Milana.'

Gonzalo approached and placed his big hand on Matias' shoulder.

'Father, you have found an unsung genius,' he smiled at Milana. 'She will make us all famous in her paintings. Look, Consuelo,' he turned towards his little daughter, 'here you are centre stage, and that little grey kitten too.' Gonzalo picked out another painting. 'Look at Stella, Father. Lying like a Madame on the red sofa. What a grand old pose.'

Stella peered up from her flower arranging on the far side of the drawing room.

'It's perfect, Milana, I shall hang it in here in a splendid frame and in centuries to come they'll say, "Who is she, that distinguished lady painted by Milana Romero?"' Milana smiled and looked down at the kitten she was stroking.

'This place will have fallen to ruin like the rest of us by then and they'll be no one left to care,' laughed Gonzalo.

'Spoil sport.' Stella came over. 'Now where's my favourite?' she looked over the paintings.

'Where is it, Milana? You've hidden it,' she teased.

'Which one?'

'The one of Consuelo dressed as a gypsy girl, where is it?'

'It's in my room, I put it up over the fireplace as you suggested. Shall I get it?'

'Yes. It's so lovely. Do you mind?'

Milana returned carrying the small rectangular canvas. It was painted in oils in bold strokes of colour but the face was delicate, full of lights, breathing the spirit of Consuelo.

'Look how perfectly she's caught the sense of wonder in her eyes, and those little rosebud lips,' Stella crooned. 'And the way the light reflects off the crystal earings onto her skin, making it look so soft, translucent; it's sheer perfection.'

'Oh!' Lisa let out a slight cry of recognition. 'Those earrings,' she turned to Consuelo. 'Where did you find them?'

Consuelo pointed to Milana. 'They're hers.'

Lisa looked at Milana, puzzled, then she peered again at the picture. The cook came in, a streak of flour across her nose. 'Will you be wanting the *pisco sours* in here, *Señora* Stella?'

'That would be perfect,' Stella smiled distractedly.

'I must just go and freshen up before the aperitif. I feel covered in dust from that awful dirt road,' Lisa rose and left the room but she hesitated in the hall and instead of going straight to her room, walked back out into the forecourt and then stole quickly round the side to where the rose garden stretched beyond the terraces. She stopped here and looked about. Very slowly, almost gingerly, she walked up to the grey stone sundial, her fingers playing over the cold stone and the aged bronze dial. She moved on, pausing to smell a late flowering winter rose. She touched the slender pillars that supported the roof of the veranda, and trailed her fingers over the wicker bench and the cushions as though she recognised the old, worn fabric. She peered in through the panes of one un-shuttered window.

'That's the room I sleep in *Señora* Lisa,' said Milana in a quiet voice behind her.

Lisa looked about her as if wary of prying eyes but she was not startled; it was almost as though she were expecting Milana.

'*Señora* Lisa, those earrings, they were given to me by the nurse.'

'The nurse? I have not met her yet. I have barely arrived, Milana, but my dear, I don't need explanations, I wasn't saying...'

'Oh I know you would never accuse me of stealing. I have been so trusted and welcomed here. I am so happy now and grateful.'

'Now? Were you not happy at first?'

'I had some strange experiences that confused me, but I know it's just this place.

'It must have been very shocking, the accident and then my poor Uncle Gustavo's death. But I heard from Stella that you are both good friends and that reassured me. It is really magnificent painting that you have done here, Milana. Very powerful.'

'It's this place. I feel a connection with it. I don't want to leave yet, *Señora* Lisa.'

'Oh my,' Lisa smiled shaking her head, 'Matias and I have not come to take you home, be assured of that. In two months you have produced so much work, what might you do in two more? We are greedy to see!' and she laughed. 'Matias came to see Gonzalo. *Don* Gustavo's death was a great shock to Gonzalo, from which I fear he has still not recovered. He feels himself responsible in some way.'

'What happened, *Señora* Lisa? I don't really know. I haven't dared ask anyone but the nurse and her explanations are always kind of spooky.'

'There's nothing he could have done. *Don* Gustavo's horse bolted and though, eventually, Gonzalo found the horse, half crazed by something, it took them hours to find Gustavo in the dark. If it weren't for all the silliness round here there would have been more men out looking and they would have found him sooner and it might have made the difference.' She lost her pensive look and focused back on Milana. 'My dear girl! I have not stopped thinking of you, your accident and then this terrible tragedy happening within twenty-four hours of your arrival. I can't imagine how you must have felt'

'Oh the accident, I don't remember what happened, so there's no need to feel sorry for me,' Milana smiled, 'I woke up in a lovely soft bed and I was here. Anyway, like Stella says, my paintings are my catharsis for everything.' Lisa smiled back and patted Milana's hand affectionately.

'Matias persuaded me to come today. I have not seen this place since, well, many, many years. Now, with my Uncle Gustavo's death, here of all places, I felt I should come. And I wanted to see you, Milana, and find out face to face how you were getting on.'

'The nurse says I should have died in that accident, but I was lucky, and that *Don* Gustavo died instead, because it was the seventh day of the seventh month of the seventh year.' Milana left out the other bit about the devil seeking out a virgin in place of the lost soul.'

Lisa laughed, 'There they go again. They'll be telling you about the devil coming to dinner next and how he makes love to virgins who have lost their true love.' Something in the way Milana stared at her made Lisa hesitate, and the corners of her mouth twitched and she burst out laughing, 'I see they have already. That's it, you've captured it all in your paintings. Oh Milana, you are so sensitive, you grasp everything. Are you really not afraid of this place?' She became suddenly serious. 'My aunt was.'

'I've seen him, *Señora* Lisa.'

'Who?'

'The devil. It must have been him. There was no one else it could have been. Oh I have to tell you. I feel so guilty, that terrible strange night. It was so powerful. I think Stella has seen him too.'

'Don't dwell on it, Milana. Never dwell on these things. Give it all to your art and let it flow out of you. Hauntings are only possible if we allow them, they are our deepest sensibilities played like musical strings by the insinuations of shadows.'

'Oh but he came to me at night. I felt him. He was so real.'

'I always say we are haunted by our senses. They are so powerful, they recreate sensations we long for, people we have lost, loves that we desire…it is part of our humanity to be slaves to our senses, even in our dreams. Our subconscious is so cunning, Milana dear, and we are such a mystery to ourselves.' She paused, 'I see a theme to your paintings, Milana. And I don't think it's the devil.' A smile played on her lips but Milana had lowered her eyes.

'The nurse is so creepy, she looks at me as though she could read my thoughts. Stella thinks she's a witch.'

'Nonsense, don't let these superstitions mess with your mind, Milana. The imagination is a powerful drug and guilt is the plaything of the devil.' Then she whispered confidentially, 'I must meet this strange nurse.'

'*Señora* Lisa, those earrings you recognised, I don't know why the nurse gave them to me, almost as soon as she saw me. She said they'd bring me luck. Are they yours, from before? When you lived here? I can give them back to you, I'm a little scared of them actually. I don't like the way she gave them to me. It was spooky.'

'They look like one's that belonged to my mother, that I used to play with as I child. I used to bury all sorts of things under the rosebushes there.'

'What was your mother's name, *Señora* Lisa?'

'Mercedes.'

Milana remembered the old lady at the party, her bony hand gripping her arm and her beady eyes darting over her face.

'*Señora* Lisa, do I look like her?' Lisa considered for a moment,

'I suppose you do a bit around the eyes.'

'Do I really?' Milana faced her eagerly. 'Isn't that strange, that I should look like her?'

'In all the millions of human beings God creates there must be similarities.'

'On the night of the party a woman stopped me as I walked through the hall. She said she had been friends with *Señora* Mercedes as a child. She thought I was her daughter or granddaughter.'

'Oh my, she said a lot,' Lisa walked slowly away from Milana so she could not see her face only her hands resting on the stone sundial and the gold of her rings glinting in the sun. 'Maybe you were wearing her earrings?'

'Yes I was.'

'Maybe the lady was a little loopy,' she smiled as she turned, 'What else did she say?'

'She said *Señora* Mercedes should never have come to this house, that it had made her ill. Is that true?'

'Maybe,' Lisa looked towards the hills. 'You have to be strong to survive it.'

'You survived it,' said Milana smiling.

'Not really. I succumbed…' she trailed off, the blood drained from her face and she stood motionless. Milana followed her gaze to where the nurse sat on one of the wicker benches further along the terrace. Beside her, in the pram, the baby slept. She had placed herself down, silent as a secret, the only movement came from the sharp short clipping of her knitting needles. The nurse lifted her gaze. On a sudden intake of breath Lisa's hand rose to her mouth and Milana saw the look that passed between the two women.

'I'll join you in the drawing room, Milana,' she said moving off with a quick light step. The nurse looked to her knitting again. Only her needles betrayed any agitation as they clicked this way and that weaving a long red sleeve.

Matias reclined into a large Victorian armchair and busied himself with lighting the Cuban cigar that Gonzalo had offered him.

'Dreadful habit,' he muttered. 'Can't resist though after such a splendid lunch. Best reason to visit my son, apart from setting eyes on his lovely wife, are the cigars and that excellent pear liquer. Come Milana,' Matias addressed her warmly. 'No doubt you know where it's hidden, procure some for me, my dear.'

Milana turned to Stella. 'I'll get it, if you like.' And she disappeared on her errand.

'Where does Milana paint? I see no signs of easel or paints anywhere,' Matias remarked as she returned, bearing a bottle of the liquer and four miniature glasses.

'That's the best part, Father, she paints in the stables.'

Milana set down the tray and filled the glasses, watching how the sun reflected through the cut glass into the golden liquid.

'Really?'

'Yes, says the light is perfect, doesn't care about the cold; really quite remarkable.'

'You don't happen to have a handsome stable boy do you, Gonzalo?' inquired Matias winking mischievously at her.

'Oh no, Matias,' said Stella, 'a stable boy wouldn't do for our Milana. Come, this is the mystery man she has her heart set on.' Stella picked out the painting of a man, silhouetted against a raging bonfire, in dusty riding boots, a bloodied shirt and a whip held behind his back; the clothes might have been Gonzalo's but the face was not.

'By God! That's... no... let me see again. Yes! The young rascal. My dear, it's Santiago Hidalgos' face. I'd know it anywhere, he spent half his young life messing around in my studio, picked up everything I could teach him by the time he was sixteen without my barely knowing it. The boy was a natural.' He sighed. 'Do look. See the eyes, Lisa. She has caught that perplexed intense look of his, and the sensuality in the mouth.' Matias looked thoughtfully at the painting, he was surprised he hadn't noticed the similarity before.

'Just look at his black hair, his stance, it's unmistakeable. Milana, I had no idea you knew him so well,' Matias turned to where Milana had been standing.

But Milana had left.

'Look now, Father, you've gone and embarrassed her,' sighed Gonzalo from where he half lay stretched out on the sofa.

'Mere artist's model would be a bit of a come-down for Santiago,' Stella giggled.

Matias roared with laughter.

'There are no come-downs for that boy. He's in New York as we speak. There's no stopping Santiago, his art wells up from within, ready made, like those geysers in the Atacama. What confounds me,' he said twisting about in his chair, 'is where on

389

earth she got the model for him, the girl doesn't know him, barely met him some years back. You haven't been hiding him here have you?'

'Father, you are so stubborn, leave her alone, poor girl. It isn't Santiago at all. You're just too full of the boy.'

'Oh fiddlesticks.' He rose and studied each painting in turn.

'You philistines can't even see what you're looking at. Behold the same face in all its guises,' he said pointing to the pictures displayed along the wall and on top of the sofa.

'They're all very handsome,' admitted Stella.

'Come on, Lisa. Don't you think it's fascinating? I mean it's his face, give or take a bit, in all the paintings. How would she have come to know him so well? They could not stand further apart in the social spectrum.'

Lisa smiled and offered no comment.

'I tell you the boy is her muse. What a story there is in that.'

'I shouldn't think anyone else will pick it up,' said Stella.

'They would if I pointed it out. What titilation it would cause; such publicity for the exhibition.'

'You will do nothing of the kind, Father. Indeed I shall never release her or the paintings back to you if you do.' Gonzalo crossed his arms and winked at Stella.

'Oh we are protective of her.' Matias turned towards his son with a half amused look.

'She's been through a lot with us,' said Stella defensively.

'So she has, so she has. Still, let me have some fun. Give us some more of this pear aqua vitae, it quite blows one's insides away. Where are you off to, Lisa? You can't just beetle off like that,' he admonished, 'not without some of this pear fire-juice.'

Lisa laughed, 'I thought I'd sneak off to have a siesta. Any complaints?'

'Fair enough. You should try this stuff, though, Lisa. It would set you alight.'

'I don't know that I want to be set alight,' she replied with good humour.

Slowly Lisa opened the tall oak door. The room was in semi-darkness. Only a shaft of sunlight fell across the bed where Milana lay face down.

'This used to be my room,' murmured Lisa, looking about her, 'it hasn't changed much. Only it was fresher and brighter. I was fresher and brighter too, then.'

'Oh, *Señora* Lisa,' Milana looked up.

'Don't let Matias get to you my dear. He's a terrible tease.'

She came over to where Milana lay.

'They are the most exceptional paintings, Milana. You've captured the magic of this place, its very essence. He's so thrilled, that's all.'

'I'm going to burn every single picture of him. I never want to see his face in my paintings again.'

'Santiago?' Lisa asked tentatively.

'I didn't see it! I never saw I was painting him,' she admitted, too humiliated to dissemble.

'Maybe that's why the paintings are so good. You paint from within, you can't help it, it's what gives your paintings their remarkable virtuosity, your talent passes the border controls of your hard exterior, unchecked.'

'My hard exterior?'

Lisa sat on the bed beside her. 'In time we develop a system of barriers and controls for everything we feel, what we say and do. That's why we often lose our spontaneity as we grow older. You're still free of all that, and your painting shows it. If you love this boy, however it is you met him, then let yourself love him. There is no harm in loving.'

'You were so against me and JC. Why is Santiago different?' Milana turned on her with sudden vehemence.

'Oh, Milana. JC is young and impressionable. He's not a very strong character. He has a long way to go to mature and become his own man. He needs to focus on his studies and give himself time. Santiago, on the other hand, has always been fiercely independent. His paintings show a maturity way beyond his young age. You and he share a passion for something over and above each other. In my view, real, lasting love is not found in two people who simply contemplate each other with devotion, but rather those that can walk together in the same direction, seeking something greater than themselves that they both understand and share, and maybe see a glimpse of, in each other.'

'You mean you're not even going to ask me how I know him, or where I met him?'

'Why should I? It's obvious you know him and I can guess you must have met him when he was painting the old Hidalgo chapel. You implied as much to Matias the first time I took you to see him. There's no harm in love born from inspiration, Milana. Those who inspire our greatest works carry our love to the grave, in some way or other.'

'You don't understand,' she said turning away, 'I've tried to block him out but he's still there in my painting.' Tears sprang from her eyes.

'Does he love you, Milana?'

Milana nodded. Lisa looked bemused. 'He's been away for years, in England and now in New York. You mystify me, Milana, and intrigue me. But I believe you. Does anybody else know about this?'

'No. It's over. It should never have existed. It was all a horrible mistake.' She folded her arms over her stomach, and bent her head, 'I can't face him.'

'You're not pregnant are you, Milana?'

'No, nothing like that,' she looked at Lisa in horror. 'God, he doesn't owe me a thing.'

Lisa put a cool hand to Milana's face and wiped away the tears that streaked down her cheeks. 'Don't fret so. It's just you feel exposed. It'll pass.'

Lisa tried to understand what it was that she felt drawn to say to Milana, it was as though the girl was reaching out to her and she felt compelled to answer.

'I want to take you for a walk,' she said suddenly. 'I want to show you something.'

'But I've been crying.'

'No one will see where I'm going to take you. We'll step out of the window.'

Lisa pulled open the window and the sun flooded in.

'No one will miss us. Come.' She stepped through the open window and held out her hand to Milana.

Chapter Seven

Milana let Lisa guide her through the gardens and away from the house until they were walking briskly uphill through heather and flowering gorse, past wild mimosa and slender eucalyptus. Lisa was fast and surprisingly agile, turning this way and that to avoid thorns and brambles. Suddenly she came to an abrupt halt. A wild horse, nostrils flaring stood yards away; so sudden and so splendid, close up, that Milana fancied it was a unicorn from one of the magic tales she used to read. It waited calm and inert, flies circling its right ear, eyes locked on them. Slowly it lowered its head towards a small pink wild flower before turning unexpectedly and galloping away, its hooves thundering over the dry earth. Lisa flashed Milana a smile. 'That was a rare gift.' She moved on faster stepping effortlessly along the stony path that appeared and disappeared under the overgrown vegetation as it climbed more steeply.

'I used to come here all the time as a child,' said Lisa stopping briefly to look about her. The sky was a deep blue and below them, the house with all its patios and gardens already appeared small as a doll's house.

'My parents once owned all the land for miles around here and the best place to see the lay of it all was from the top of this hill. My father had a temple built for my mother on the spot, a beautiful old folly like those you find in Europe. But my mother rarely came here. Hardly anyone came here but me.' Lisa swept her hair off her face and lifting it off her neck, let the breeze cool her. Milana came and stood beside her surveying the mellow colours of the afternoon.

'As a child, I pretended I was a princess in my castle on this hill, and as I grew older, I would play-act my fantasies with the whole world at my feet or so it seemed. I lived very sheltered from the real world.' Milana noticed a rueful shadow pass over her animated expression.

'Didn't you go to school?'

'No, I had a sort of governess from England who taught me English and maths and French. I fed off novels; romances and mysteries. Luckily for me Miss Jane had a limp and never climbed this far so this was my secret haven.'

'Didn't you ever see any other children?'

'During the holidays we sometimes had the company of cousins. But when my parents travelled to Europe they always left me here with Miss Jane. I didn't mind, I didn't really think I was missing anything,' she laughed, 'my fantasies absorbed me into their own magical world.'

The white horse appeared out of nowhere again and bent its neck to sniff the heather. It was so close they could see its muscles twitch. It looked at them, unafraid, and stayed a while, then slowly it moved away. 'He's checking on us,' Lisa laughed.

'Wow!' said Milana. 'He's so tame.'

They started walking again in silence. Traces of cloud like attenuated fingers reached out across the sky behind the silver spec of a distant aeroplane. Lisa pointed up to it;

'Look how the plume floats, merges, spreads and finally disappears into the blue, that's how I feel about the past. It has been consumed by time, just like the tracks of that plane.'

'But the plane is where it is because of the route it took. That can never be erased.'

Lisa glanced at Milana with a certain pride. 'You're a remarkable child, Milana.'

'I'm not a child, anymore.'

'Oh, I know.' Lisa's eyes met hers.

'Please tell me about your mother, *Señora* Lisa. The old lady that said I looked like her told me she could sense things. Did she see things, here?'

Lisa walked silently on. Milana felt herself shrinking under the brilliant sky, embarrassed by her own forthrightness. Lisa glanced back at her.

'I want to tell you, Milana, it's just a very long time since I thought about it all.' She picked her way more slowly now over the ever steepening path.

'My mother, Mercedes, was a deeply religious woman. She would spend hours in the rose garden with her rosary saying her beads. She wasn't strict or harsh or judgemental, she was simply consumed with such a love of God that nothing else got a look in, and in this solitary place, nothing distracted her from her contemplations. I used to wonder why she never became a nun. She fell between two worlds here. She was neither part of the disciplines and rigours of community life, as she would have been if she was a nun, nor was she accountable to the rigours and demands of society as she would have been had she lived and entertained like any other hostesses in Santiago. It was I think too solitary an existence. My mother had a natural docility of nature but she was left too much alone, without the comfort of rules and order and a role in life. Do you understand what I mean?'

'I think so.'

'My father would ride off to manage the *fundo*; his vineyards and his tenants, and return late at night only to leave early the next morning. In truth I think he was too independent for marriage. Meanwhile, my mother seemed to live in another world. Honestly to hear her…' Lisa sighed, 'She talked to me sometimes about what people had said or asked of her, but they weren't living people, you understand.' She glanced at Milana with a touch of humour in her eyes. 'She would explain they were souls from purgatory that visited her and asked for her help. I never saw them though. My own dreams were of a more romantic nature.' Lisa laughed and stopped to brush her hair off her face and tie it back with a black velvet ribbon from her pocket.

'My dreams tend to end up in pieces,' sighed Milana.

'Dreams don't shatter, Milana, they are like the clouds that form and separate and reform again, different, new. You must have faith in them.'

'I don't know what I have faith in anymore. Even my painting betrays me.'

'Because it traces your feelings into your pictures? That's not betrayal, it's just the truth. We can't escape what we feel, we must face it. In the very centre of that journey we are set free. I've made mistakes that I'm ashamed of and yet all the pain and the shame has made me what I am today. Like you said about the plane, I'm here because of the route I took. I am stronger and wiser and love better for it, so I am deeply grateful life has brought me to this moment. There were many times I was so full of regrets that I wished I was dead.' Her eyes sought out Milana's, gentle and impassioned at the same time, 'My husband Victor taught me that to be cured of all the bad in your life, you must take responsibility for the choices you made however bad they were, face them and then bow your head and in humility and recognition of your faults surrender them to God. They are the past, and life flows on. It has no time for guilt or self-pity.' She paused and sighed and eyed Milana with a smile, 'It was also at those lowest points of my life that something stirred in my soul. In the anguish and pain; one tiny part of me, deep down, seemed to rejoice and say, I can feel, yes, I'm alive, I have a heart and a soul too. So I am grateful for that too.' She reached out and touched Milana, resting her hand on her arm. 'Pain sharpens our senses, it can become a magnificent creative force in us and it is a bridge to our soul.' She paused as if, with that small gesture she were trying to connect their two worlds.

'Look, Milana.'

They were standing on a small ledge into which a few steps had been cut, providing a route up to the folly built by Lisa's father. Far below, the dirt track became a brown ribbon winding this way and that. The landscape, barren and breathtaking, spread to the distant horizon like some primeval earth mass, shot through with rich mineral colours, creased into hills and mountains by the great thrust of volcanic activity, watered by the lakes and rivers that collected in its valleys. Here and there, splashes of green like the random colourings of a child, showed the areas tamed by man, cultivated and nurtured to produce the famous wines of the area.

Milana inhaled as though she were breathing in a whole

emancipating vision of creation. She followed Lisa up the three steps to where eight slender columns enclosed a hemispherical dome.

'Oh! It's beautiful,' she exclaimed, walking around the little temple, trailing her hand over each carved column feeling the stone warmed by the sun.

'This is where Heathcliffe would have brought his Cathy,' she murmured and added, turning towards Lisa, emboldened, 'Did you ever bring anyone here?'

Lisa patted the stone bench on which she sat. Milana came and joined her.

'I remember when they brought this bench up here, in three pieces; the gardener's son, the stable hand, and a few of the boys that came to work in the fields. It was a very hot day. The grass was brittle and with each step they took, clouds of dust lifted scattering little green lizards. They stripped off their shirts and left them like discarded sails on gorse bushes half way up the hill.' Lisa leant back resting her palms on the bench, her elegant neck stretched to the sun whilst her hair danced in the breeze. 'I was fourteen when I became aware of boys,' she smiled. 'I would watch them, wondering. Did they think the things I'd read in novels?' She glanced at Milana who was listening intently, the point of her shoe worrying at a little pebble caught in the dust beneath their feet.

'My mother never checked which books I took out of my father's library. I adored *Wuthering Heights* best of all.' She smiled. 'I read Garcia Marquez, D.H. Lawrence, Hardy, Flaubert, Dumas, Daphne Du Maurier; I was drunk on romance. But there was no one in my life on whom to focus any of these romantic fantasies. Besides, no one matched my idea of perfection, certainly not among the stable boys or the farm workers. Then, one day, my father brought a chap down from Santiago. He was Carlos, a distant cousin and his father had been to school with mine. He came to learn about the wine business and he was to spend the summer with us. He was just eighteen.

'The first time I saw him I was in the stables getting my horse saddled. Carlos galloped in, shouting to the stable boy that he was horribly late. He leapt off my father's horse and as he passed the reigns to the lad he said "I owe you one," and he high-fived him. I'd never seen anyone treat the stable boys so nicely. Then he turned and saw me. He had a streak of mud across his nose and down his cheek and there was mud on his clothes and his forehead. He just said "Hi" and grinned at me briefly. He put his hand up to his face to pull the hair from his eyes and smeared even more mud over it before he raced out. He'd hardly noticed me, but inside I'd just melted.

'"He's been riding down the river again," muttered the stable boy, "My dad says he'll break the horse's legs doing that, but I think he's cool."

'I thought so too. I began to search out his company. Mostly he was out in the vineyards but he ate his meals with me and mother. My father on the other hand often had meals in his offices in the vineyard, joining us for coffee on occasions. My mother thought this cousin Carlos was charming, she didn't really think of his effect on me, she was simply pleased that I had company and encouraged me to spend time with him.

'Like you, I collected bits and pieces: jewellery that I loved to take apart and remake and flowers which I pressed and stored in an old sea-chest that I kept up here. I brought him here to show him.' She laughed. 'He was the first boy I ever really knew. We came here often. He was so easy going, I'd tell him my thoughts and the plots from the stories I read and he would listen and tease and laugh and sometimes grow serious and look at me more deeply, and I'd melt again inside. He smoked up here and taught me to blow smoke rings at the sky. Suddenly I didn't need novels. This was it, unfolding before me. I began to note how he looked at me, how he brushed past me or touched my hand or held my gaze a moment longer than expected. Sometimes when we ran up this hill he would catch my hand and nearly pull me all the way up, then he would lie with his hands behind his head and tell me this was heaven.

'For my sixteenth birthday he bought me a huge bunch of white roses from town and presented me with them in front of my parents. They thought he was splendidly gallant. Truth was they hardly took any notice of us together. My father was delighted he worked so well in the vineyards and had a mind for business. He would offer him a cigar and invite him to talk with him sitting on the veranda. He was impressed that the boy had won a scholarship to Harvard, the top American university. He called him Charlie though his name was Carlos and I could tell how much my father enjoyed his witty company. I, on the other hand, was never more than a charming doll to my father, to be enjoyed for brief periods. It never occurred to him that I was an un-erupted volcano of thoughts and feelings and desires or that this young man might actually take a real interest in me.

'That night of my sixteenth birthday I kept my shutters open and saw him climb the hill alone. It was a beautiful clear night and there was a full moon. I followed him. He was here where we are now, standing above me as I climbed the last steps. I had raced so fast that I could barely breathe, my heart was pounding like it might just jump out of my chest and I was laughing. I felt so free. He took me in his arms and kissed me. Not gently, but like Heathcliff; he was hungry and I felt I was breathing in his soul and it was all the air I'd ever need. He took me to a patch of soft grass where I could see the moon playing hide and seek between the columns of the temple. He lay me down.

' "I want to be loved," I said. I didn't really think, it was just what I wanted with all the passion of an overly romantic sixteen year old.'

' "You're very young," he whispered.

' "So are you," I said. I was determined I must seize the moment or die an old maid.' She laughed.

' "What if you have a baby?" he asked me.

' "Oh I won't, don't worry about that." I was so naïve Milana. I led him to believe that it was not possible that I should have a child. If I had created him myself to feed all my fantasies, I could have done no better. He lay down beside me and whispered, "I must be the luckiest man in the world. I will love you as no one will ever love you," and he loved me true to his promise. It was the single most beautiful experience of my life. I surrendered everything to him, in total innocence. No one had ever taught me a single fact of life, but love needs no teaching.

'He left two days later and went to America. It was only three months later that I discovered that I was expecting his baby.' Milana gasped and glanced at Lisa.

'What naivety! I can hardly believe it now! But I was so happy, Milana, I actually couldn't understand why my mother broke down and cried when I told her. She must have told my father but he never spoke about it to me.

'Later my mother explained everything would be all right and necessary arrangements would be made. Meanwhile the cook secretly suggested to me that I should have an abortion. She told me she knew how and no one would know about it. I would just appear to lose the baby. I didn't even know what an abortion was. It wasn't in any of my novels and it was not something Miss Jane, my governess, had instructed me in,' Lisa added with humour. 'But the cook filled me in pretty promptly. I was horrified. Nothing would induce me to kill the baby I treasured almost as much as the memory of the father.

'When I was about seven months pregnant I was sent to live with a midwife a few kilometres away. Her name was Carmen and she had a daughter Esperanza, who had had a child. The idea was that I should have my baby there and that Esperanza would become its wet-nurse while I would return home absolved of all responsibility. I went along with the plan. I knew no better. Secretly I actually looked forward to staying with these people in their funny little house made entirely of wood and white tiles. I barely asked for explanations; this was my novel, writing itself. In my short life this was the most exciting thing that had happened to me.

'I spent nearly two months in this strange house with all its peculiar inhabitants. I had never seen so many people live under one small roof. There were cousins and aunts and uncles and children. Some lived at the back of the house, others at the top, others had the run of the front room. There were foam mattresses on the floor where there weren't enough beds. I had the only tiny but perfectly contained bedroom to the front of the house, but I lived in the kitchen. I made friends with Esperanza's younger sister, Irene, who talked incessantly of running off to the city but complained that she had no money. I knew I could get some money and so we planned that as soon as I had my baby we would run off together to find adventure.

'It never occurred to me to stay and look after the baby because from the first my mother had explained that the baby would be taken care of by Esperanza and her mother and that that was best. It all seemed so simple. None of those novels I read dwelt on looking after babies. Babies didn't seem to register in the grand scheme of romantic novels, they just grew up behind the scenes. I was so far removed from reality at that age that I lost all sense of responsibility. I gladly imagined I could surrender motherhood to virtual strangers.

'In all the time I was in that house my parents never came to see me once. Miss Jane came to keep up my English lessons while I stayed, quite voluntarily, waiting for the baby to be born. When the time came, Carmen looked after me and Esperanza assisted. No sooner born, the baby was whisked away from me and I was delivered back to my parents.

'I yearned for my baby but seeing my parents so happy and relieved and the status quo so well preserved, I chose to believe, in the way only a child can, that everything was fine. Still, I grew restless at home. Without knowing it having a child had opened me to a whole new dimension of feeling. Physically I yearned for the baby and for Carlos. I felt the searing anguish of loss without quite understanding it. I never adjusted to the solitude of home again. I had experienced people and raw human emotions all around me in that small house; shouting, crying, laughing, fighting and making up. Life at home seemed interminably and intolerably dull, even worse, it did not feel like my home, not anymore. I realise I also felt the pull of a maternal instinct that I never allowed myself to recognise as such. Finally, I asked my parents for money on the pretext of paying back the family's many kindnesses to me. That very day Irene and I escaped to the capital on the back of a truck.

'We ended up on the outskirts of the city sleeping in shanties belonging to Irene's friends or relations, I lived off their charity. Can you believe it. The poor are, I discovered, far more generous than the wealthy. My family looked for me in all the wrong places. Then one day in a shopping-mall a cousin spotted me. We had a coffee and spent the day together. I never told her where I was living. We met the next week and she invited me to Zapallar for the summer. From there I never looked back. My parents were so relieved to have found me again that they happily sent money to fund my studies in Santiago and organised for me to live with an old and very respectable aunt. I was in the real world at last, and I began to grow up.'

'But what about Carlos?'

She met Milana's intense clear gaze.

'Five years later, I saw Carlos again; I was working in the university hospital, downtown, and studying to become a theatre nurse. I was walking to the corner cafe when we saw each other. He stopped dead in the street. We just stared at each other for a moment in utter disbelief. He came forwards first. He took my hand and asked me how I was. I could have told him about the baby then, but I froze. "She's married, or engaged, or embarrassed by my attentions; she doesn't want me to talk to her now, that's the past, leave it be…" I watched those thoughts go through his head as clearly as if they'd been written on his forehead and I let him think them.

'You see, a sudden awareness of my short-comings told me I didn't deserve him, Milana. It's hard to understand now but I allowed guilt to overwhelm me. I had abandoned his child, the child he never suspected existed. I knew instinctively that he would have embraced it, cared for it, loved it and I felt I had done a terrible thing. I deserved to be punished for being such a selfish and worthless mother. As I looked into his eyes that day I knew it was my responsibility and mine alone to have taken care of her, because I had made my choice the night I lay with him and he had warned me.' Lisa paused and took a deep breath, 'If ever a moment can mature you, that moment was it. I stood face to face with the enormity of it all, our love, the child, motherhood, responsibility and future. In forsaking the child I had forsaken our love. I had no right to it. I had walked away from the only responsibility life had ever trusted me with. So I let him walk away from me. Although in truth it was I, wearing a false smile, who took my leave.

'I looked back once, then I turned the corner. He was standing on the street watching after me, not moving. I could have changed my life forever at that moment, Milana. But an overwhelming guilt and the fact that I couldn't forgive myself stopped me from taking that one opportunity of being with the man I loved. I had the choice of telling him what I had done and facing his judgement or letting him walk away. I chose the easier path, although it broke my heart.'

'But the baby? What happened to your baby?'

'I came back here to look for my baby. It's as though all the longing I had for her father was suddenly transferred to the child. But five years is a long time. I found the house where Esperanza lived, that was easy. But there was no sign of Esperanza. No one would tell me where she was. No one would tell me about my child. It was as though a veil had been drawn over it all. I was distraught. My parents were kind and welcomed me. They were happy to hear of my progress but when I begged them to tell me where the child was, it was as if they had not heard me.

'The cook told me that she thought Esperanza had gone to the city, but even she did not mention the child. I looked for Esperanza everywhere, in all the shantytowns where she might have known people. I asked the names of all the new comers. I knew where Irene lived though I had not seen her for about four years. I went to see her. She helped me look, but everywhere we drew a blank.'

Lisa paused and let her hand cover Milana's for a moment. 'You must be tired of listening,' she suggested kindly, 'and your hands are cold.'

'Oh no, I'm not cold, it's just my heart's beating so fast with your story the blood doesn't reach. Please don't stop.' Lisa continued with a smile.

'I met my husband Victor when I was at my lowest ebb. He

found me crying into my coffee in the university canteen where I was attending a lecture. He was a young lawyer lecturing at the university. He sat beside me and whispered. "If you hit a dead end, don't be afraid to turn back and try another way." I was so surprised I just stared at him and said, "How?"

'"We could start with dinner."

'He was funny and kind and I felt safe with him. He had started a system of legal aid as a university student and now his practice helped those less fortunate who could not afford lawyer's fees. He had got a name for himself, he was frequently interviewed and invited to lecture in other South American countries that wanted to learn his methods. I admired him immensely.

'When he asked me to marry him a year later, I felt I had to tell him about my past. But as I was about to launch into my big confession, he just raised his hand and said, "What's past is past, I take you as I find you. I love you for who you are and all that brought you to where you stand today, there is nothing to excuse and nothing to explain." That's when I really began to love Victor. He put my mind at rest and I understood he didn't need to know. We had four children, all grown up now.

'A few years later I met Carlos again. Like me, he was married by then. It was Victor who, quite innocently, introduced us at a party. It turned out he and Victor were friends and associates. It was such a strange evening. That night I felt if I didn't tell Victor about Carlos I would be betraying trust. When we got home I started to tell him but he sat down beside me and said; "He's already told me everything. He congratulated me on being a very lucky man. Is there anything you need to add?" I just shook my head, "Any confusion in there?" he indicated my heart. And I just shook my head. Why should I complicate things explaining about the baby I had given up. I loved Victor and that was that.

'I was to meet Carlos many times after that at various events, but I was never alone with him, I never entered into a real conversation, because I knew I would feel guilty that I was concealing a truth he deserved to know and I never wanted to tell him about the baby, and for his part he was careful never to betray Victor's trust. As for our love, we both honourably drew a veil over it. It was as though we carefully and eventually, expertly, averted our eyes from what was there, unresolved in the room with us every time we met.'

'You never found your baby?'

'I searched and searched.'

'Now I understand!' exclaimed Milana suddenly, the light finally dawning.

'Oh *Señora* Lisa, that's why you came to the shantytown, that's how you came to know us. You helped everyone, because really you longed to find and help your lost child. You must have suffered so much thinking about her, but no one really thought about helping you.'

'Why should they? They didn't know.'

'But,' persisted Milana.

Lisa put her hands on hers, gently, 'Wait, let me explain, there's more.

'One day, after we had been married a few years a young man came to see my husband. He knocked very late at night. I was called to the door and saw him in a terrible state, he had blood across his shirt which was torn, and cuts on him as though he'd run through glass. He was breathless and desperate but he was also polite and considerate as he begged to see Victor, apologising all the time for his state and the hour and the inconvenience. He explained he had been a junior in my husband's legal practice until he had taken the job of gardener in Carlos' house. Victor heard the commotion and came to see what was happening. As soon as he saw him he told him to come in. "Don't worry," he whispered to me, "I'll take care of this, Lisa, I know this man. His name is Ricardo Romero."'

Milana looked wide-eyed at Lisa, stunned by the unexpected revelation. Lisa put her finger up to her lips to indicate quiet and continued. 'My husband was shut in his study with this man for hours and when Victor came out, he locked the study door so as not to allow anyone in. He had told Ricardo to rest on the sofa and get some sleep.

'He took me aside, and told me the story of how Ricardo had been in love with a girl called Letty who had worked as a maid in Carlos' house. He explained the events of that night; how Carlos' wife, Grazia had entered the house in a fury, how she made them go to the study where they had seen Carlos talking with Letty, the maid. He told how Grazia had pushed Ricardo towards her husband and challenged them to fight him. Ricardo had stumbled and fallen on Carlos, and as he struggled to get up, he saw Grazia lift a lamp and throw it at her husband. It killed him.' Lisa paused and breathed in deeply as though mustering strength before continuing.

'Unthinkingly, Ricardo had then picked up the lamp and thrown it out of the window. My husband was very factual. He explained to me that Ricardo's story held together however he questioned him. Ricardo had come to him for help because he knew that the *Señora* would accuse him of the murder and that, in effect, no one actually saw her take the lamp. It would be his word against hers. Ricardo told Victor that Letty was pregnant, so he did not know what would happen to her. He also explained that Letty was being blackmailed by some unpleasant character she knew, in order to extract money from Carlos. She had gone to *Don* Carlos's study that night, on Ricardo's suggestion, to show him the blackmailer's note and ask what she should do. Ricardo explained he had never believed that Letty had slept with *Don* Carlos, but so much had happened that night, that he did not know what to believe.

'We spoke for a long time together that night, my husband and I. I learnt that Ricardo Romero had sought Victor's help once before, when he had asked him how he could get his girlfriend Letty away from the bad people that were using her. It was Carlos who had helped. For my husband to take on Ricardo's case and defend him now against Carlos' widow would destroy the Hidalgo family. They had a son after all.' Lisa paused and looked at Milana, 'Santiago.' Milana felt the muscles of her stomach tighten.

'Victor felt that to bring the case to court in Ricardo's defence would be horrifically damaging for young Santiago. If

Victor won the case for Ricardo, Santiago's mother could be jailed for life. On the other hand even if Ricardo were spared jail, no one would employ him after that, at least not till the whole case was forgotten and such a high profile case is never quite forgotten. And if Victor lost the case, highly possible given Ricardo's fingerprints on the murder weapon, then Ricardo would be jailed for life and the Hidalgo family would have been destroyed anyway.

'My husband made a decision and told Ricardo he would protect him all the way, but he must give himself up. He told him which police commissar to go to, where Victor had influence, and under which court he would appear. He said he would see to it that he was sent to Collina Jail, and he would arrange for his escape. He told him he would have to lie low for some years, or make a new life in Argentina. He would help him with references and connections there, and at least he would be a free man. It was the the only way to minimize the damage to everyone.'

Milana's eyes grew larger and larger.

'Your husband is the one who got him out?' she trailed off, speechless.

'After the trial Victor told me he had promised Ricardo he would see that Letty was okay. So I wasn't looking for my baby anymore when I met you, I was on a mission to find Letty and help her.'

There was a long pause. The breeze circled them as if trying to listen to their thoughts before drifting away.

'So *Don* Victor, I mean your husband, still never new about that baby? And *Don* Carlos died without knowing.'

Lisa took a deep breath and exhaled slowly.

'That night, when I learn't Carlos had died, the floodgates of all the past guilt just opened up. I told him everything and Victor listened not because he needed to know, but because he understood I needed to confess and put it all to rest. But yes, Carlos died never knowing he had had a daughter.'

Milana was very quiet suddenly.

'Hey,' she whispered in concern, seeing Milana's eyes glistening with unshed tears.

'So she really was a prostitute wasn't she?' breathed Milana.

'Oh,' Lisa looked at Milana's pained expression and understanding suddenly placed her hand over where Milana's lay folded on her lap.

'Letty was the most dignified woman I ever met, Milana. That awful gang forced her to work for them. She met Ricardo when he was a part-time waiter and an office junior in Victor's office. He fell in love with Letty and, desperately worried about her predicament, he went to my husband for help. She was young and vulnerable and beautiful and when by chance my husband was dining with Carlos at the restaurant where Ricardo was waiting tables, he introduced her to them and Carlos was moved to help. He persuaded his wife to interview her, saying she came with excellent references from Victor. He did not realise that these men she worked for, often followed her and took photographs of all her "clients" in order to blackmail the wealthiest of them. They saw Letty with Carlos Hidalgo several times and knowing him to be an influential politician photographed them as cleverly as they could, so that their innocent meetings would look clandestine and be seen in a more sordid light. Carlos had acted on impulse, without thinking of the dangers. But then he always was an idealist. My husband Victor and I, knowing Carlos ourselves, chose to believe Ricardo's version of the story. It all added up. Your mother, Milana, was loved and admired.'

So Iris had told the truth, Milana thought to herself, remembering what she had heard those three years back.

'How did he get out of prison?'

'It's rather macabre but he got out in a coffin.'

Just as Iris had said. There seemed to be no loophole for hope.

'Ricardo went to Argentina but he lay low in Chile for a couple of years. He came to see Letty several times. She conceived Ricardo and Juanito during those visits and was faithful to him, but eventually she heard no more from him.'

'Is he dead?'

Lisa made a little helpless gesture, 'Who knows? Letty was

so strong, Milana. She had lived through abuse and loss, fear and pain and total abandonment and she never lost her integrity or her dignity.'

'She tried to kill herself once,' whispered Milana, lowering her eyes to the ground.

Lisa looked surprised. 'Did she tell you that?'

Milana nodded. 'She said you were her angel.'

Lisa hesitated. In her mind, she wrestled with the truth. Was it not Milana's right to know everything about herself and her mother? What good had it done her, Lisa, to live always sheltered from the truth. So she continued.

'That was how I found Letty the first time. She had cut her veins, in the hope that she and her baby would die. I found her unconscious on the floor of her shanty.'

'Was I that baby?'

'Yes. Letty thought she couldn't bring a child into the world to suffer as she had done. She was alone and deeply damaged by her experiences. I took her home with me. She stayed for two weeks, until she was strong enough to go back, I begged her to stay longer but she said it wouldn't be right. But for me, Milana, it was the best thing I'd done in my life. A sort of making up with God for abandoning my own child.'

Lisa looked away to conceal her emotion. She felt a hand touch hers and Milana's small voice whisper, 'So you saved my life.' Lisa fought to control her tears.

'It was lucky that I came then, but it was Ricardo, through Victor, who sent me looking. He really loved Letty.'

'Was Ricardo my father?' Milana's heart was pounding. Lisa let the question hang for a moment; how could anyone be sure who Milana's father was? She imagined all the men Letty might have been forced to lie with. She struggled to know how best to answer.

'He's the one who really saved your life.'

'But don't you know, for sure?'

'How can one know for sure after what that poor girl was put through. He loved and cared for all of you. He sent money when he could, but he had to remain in hiding from the police.'

'So you don't know if he was my father?' Milana's face showed such disappointment and anguish that Lisa put her arm round the girl and pulled her to her.

Milana tried a different tack; 'Did Letty love Carlos Hidalgo?'

'She owed so much to him. He was there in her hour of need. He freed her from the vicious circle she was in.'

Do you think she slept with him, was I his baby? But she couldn't bring herself to ask it, it seemed so impertinent.

'You really knew Santiago's father then.'

'Yes.' She looked thoughtfully into the middle distance. 'I knew him.'

'Didn't it hurt you terribly when you heard he had been killed like that. I don't mean the guilt part, I mean the fact that you'd loved him so much and now he was dead.'

'Later, yes. Not then. You see sometimes we instinctively suspend belief and have to let truth in slowly in order to grasp what it really means to us.'

'And those bad guys just let Letty go, the ones who were blackmailing her?'

'Victor knew who they were,' Lisa said drawing herself back from some faraway place. 'He saw to it that *El Paco* and his gang ended up behind bars.

'Did he? Did your husband do that?' Milana stared in disbelief, 'Wasn't he afraid they'd get to him?'

'People who take advantage of other's weaknesses are cowards themselves. When you stand up to them they crumble. What scum they were! They would have destroyed Letty given half a chance. How many girls did they use and cast off, pregnant or forced into back street abortions that killed them in the end. I've seen so much pain and sorrow and self-destruction, Milana. I sometimes think it's to make up for so many years of innocence, when I lived in my fairytale castle up here on the hill.'

'I thought you were so fine and elegant that you'd never seen anything bad,' whispered Milana looking down at where Lisa's hand still rested on hers.

'My mother always used to say we mustn't see bad things but I saw so much misery when I left this place that, one day, I walked into a church and knelt down before a statue of Our Lady and I suppose I had a sort of religious experience; I said, "My mother prayed that I might grow up pure and gracious like you, not seeing the bad things of life, so why is it you want me to see all this horror?" You know what Our Lady answered in my heart, Milana? She said, "I see it every day. I want to share it with you." I learnt compassion then, Milana, my heart burst with love. I wanted to help the whole world. Then I thought of my little daughter abandoned somewhere, and her father, dead, and I realised, if I just help in my own limited way, in my small patch of life, God will help where I cannot reach, and that's the pact I made with Him. It brought a measure of peace.'

For a long time they sat silent, side by side, thinking. The breezes blew about them and the shadows grew a little longer, but neither felt the need to move.

'My mum never had a chance in life,' Milana said suddenly. 'What opportunity was ever there for my mum to seize?'

'Oh but there was. Look how she brought you up Milana. Look at yourself. You are splendid because she taught you integrity and self-belief; she inspired you to dream and to laugh in the face of adversity.'

'But I've had so many good things happen to me, so many chances, for all the ones she never had.'

'Maybe that's her legacy to you, a legacy of very great love.'

'And you, *Señora* Lisa. You never found Esperanza? Wasn't that her name, the woman who looked after your baby? She would know what happened to her, wouldn't she? You have to find her, *Señora* Lisa?

Lisa rose from the stone seat on which they had been sitting.

'Let's go down again, the light is fading and we will be missed. I used to run down this slope as a child. Run with me, Milana.'

Together they ran down the hillside, almost stumbling, steadying themselves as they raced all the way down.

'I haven't done that since I was sixteen,' Lisa was breathless. She swept her lovely hair back into its velvet ribbon.

'I feel I still have so much to ask you,' said Milana wistfully not wanting their moment together to end.

Lisa smiled, and on a sudden impulse she kissed her cheek. 'Don't worry, there'll be time for all that later. Now, quick, it's nearly tea time and we must freshen up.'

'But you didn't answer me. Did you ever find Esperanza?'

Lisa looked at Milana and taking her hand she turned her gently.

'Look over there,' she whispered, her heart beating faster beneath her pale blue cashmere sweater. Milana saw the nurse walking away from them towards the forecourt pushing the baby's navy blue polka dot pram.

'That is Esperanza, Milana. The woman I have looked for, for so long. I'm sure of it.'

Chapter Eight

Yelps of delight came from the small hut that nestled between the palms and bougainvilleas and flowering winter veronicas. Inside the hut, Stella's three children were holding an imaginary tea party whilst Esperanza the nurse sat on a bench knitting under the shade of a mandarin tree. Although she donned the regulation white uniform worn by all privately hired maternity nurses in Chile, her elaborate gold earrings and her painted nails betrayed a more wayward lifestyle. She looked up and saw Lisa. She rose then and putting her knitting down on the bench, she folded her arms over her ample bosom. There was something mildly threatening in her manner, or was it defensive? Either way she stood straight as a rod watching Lisa approach.

For one long awkward moment the two women stood facing each other while the volume of things unsaid took time to settle.

'So you found her,' Esperanza said, her head high and her eyes boring into Lisa.

'Found her?'

'Found the child.'

'How could I Esperanza? I have searched high and low for you. I had no hope of finding her without you.'

'Well, I've been here these few years past.'

'I came back to look for you but you'd gone and taken her with you, no one knew where,' said Lisa accusingly.

'I had your parents' blessing. They thought it best,' the nurse retaliated.

'What? To take her away from here?'

'Yes, further away. So there'd be no problems later. People talk.'

'You did a good job of hiding her, and yourself. I searched everywhere, Esperanza.' Lisa's usual gentleness had an unaccustomed steely edge.

'My life weren't about to stop on account of your baby, *Señora* Lisa. I went into service. The family took me to Europe and then to Japan, they was diplomats. Then to Buenos Aires.'

'So you dumped my baby and went away.' Pain and anguish narrowed her eyes.

'Your parents knew. I did nothing wrong. *I* didn't run away,' she added pointedly.

'Esperanza, where did you leave her?' she almost shouted it.

'It doesn't matter now. Why bother yourself?'

Lisa clasped her arm, 'Doesn't matter? How can you say that?'

'The child was five or six, I took her to a home down south, to a woman whose son had committed suicide. She was beside herself. Her husband suggested it would calm her nerves to have a child to look after. I don't know the ins and outs, but I left her with them in Osorno. They had a little wooden house by the lake overlooking the volcano.'

Hope switched on like a light in Lisa's face, and the stiffness in her dissolved like ice melting. Esperanza drew her shoulders back and smiled at her naivety, 'Don't bother yourself with them. They are both dead no doubt. The girl grew up, flew the coup. Is that so strange?'

'You mean you know what became of her?' Lisa felt a tightening inside her, as anticipation threaded itself through every fibre.

'She was a wild one she was. Got herself stowed away on some fancy boat going across the San Rafael Lake. Befriended some of the staff and got into bad company. Then she got taken back to Osorno by the authorities seeing as she was a minor. But her new friends, they came looking for her. Pretty thing like her with no attachments, perfect for their racket.'

'How do you know this?'

'My Ma got wind of it. The old couple wanted to see her again afore they died, so they called up my old Ma and she learned the story. It was quite a thing what she did, stowing away. Twelve, thirteen she was and easy on the eye, that's how come she attracted their attention. Two men and a woman, came to call on the old couple, said they needed her for waitressing and a bit of filming in the city. They said she'd be one of Paco's girls and never want for nothing. They told the old people to sign the papers and gave them money.'

Lisa listened in horror.

'My God they let her go? Just like that with perfect strangers.'

'*Señora* Lisa, they was humble country peasants what did they know? You and I have lived. We've seen the world, we know things, but what would they know? What would those good country people know about the ways of the world, about what goes on? It's nobody's fault. Don't go blaming no one for it, *Señora* Lisa. She had spirit, always had spirit.'

'What happened then?'

'I only know what my old Ma told me and she's dead now, died of pneumonia last year. She never heard of the girl again. One of Paco's girls that's what they called her. It weren't too good to be one of Paco's girls, as I hear it. But I was off living abroad. I had my own life.'

Lisa sat down abruptly on the bench outside the hut.

'*Señora* Lisa, you alright. You look deathly pale.' Esperanza was struck by a sudden compassion for this woman who had previously epitomised a class of careless advantaged offspring whose mistakes others were paid to take care of.

'You mustn't go worrying yourself. It's water under the bridge, it's the ebb and flow of life. No one can stop it. There's nothing you could have done.' Lisa didn't look up, her voice was strained. 'Why did you give my mother's earrings to Milana?'

'Oh them.' She straightened. 'They belonged to your baby, they did. Just before I took her away to Osorno, I brought her here, see, to pick up money for my expenses, what your mother was paying me. Your mother she didn't want to see the child, so I left her in the rose garden while we talked.' Tears rolled down Lisa's cheeks as she listened.

'When I got her from the rose garden and took her home, she had them earrings in her hand; didn't want to let them go. She said how she'd uncovered them in the earth and I figured they were kind of hers, by right, you know. When I took her south, she took them and wouldn't let them out of her sight. When she got to Osorno she was that taken with the lake, she left them on the sand to go and play. I picked them up and told her I'd keep them safe in my pocket.

'A bit later the old couple took me to the bus and as it was pulling out she remembered the earrings, and she ran. Oh how that kid ran after the bus yelling for those earrings. What could I do? They weren't going to stop the bus on account of her. So I kept the earrings and well, I'll say it honest, it haunted me a while. Then I forgot and I thought I'd lost them. But then about three years ago I found them, I was that sad to see them. I remembered her running after the bus and I wished I could give them back. Then I get this job here, like life going full circle. I brought them with me and thought I'll bury them in the sand where she found them. But I couldn't bring myself to. Then this girl comes, on the seventh of the seventh, you know. They brought her in unconscious, covered in blood and dust, no hospital to take her to. I thought she was dead. I bathed her eyes and her face, all bloodied. I knew it was her. She'd come back. So soon as she finds me next day, I get the earrings and I put them in her hand, just like that.'

'Oh Esperanza, you did care too,' Lisa covered her face with her hands and with the cuffs of her cashmere jumper tried to wipe away the tears, 'but it's not her, I wish it were but she never could be...'

'*Señora*, it's not her, it's not Pamela I'm meaning, it's her child. That girl, Milana, she's just like her; them eyes, and the hands, them tiny wrists, and that hair, every colour it is, reds and golds and browns, I never seen hair like that, before Pamela that is. It's her child, sure as I'm Esperanza. When I gave her them earrings in my head I said, "Here, Pamela, I should never have taken them from you, you had nothing to remember your mother by." And I gave them to the girl to make amends to her mother.'

Lisa shook her head over and over murmuring, 'Esperanza, you can't know it's her.'

'Did you know Milana's mother then, *Señora* Lisa?' Esperanza fixed her with a penetrating look.

'I did. She'd suffered so much,' Lisa looked up at the nurse in her pristine starched white uniform. 'Milana's mother was abused as a girl and ran away. I heard she was one of Paco's girls too.' Even as she uttered the words she knew the truth and she realised that in some way she had known it always. Lisa bent her head down and sobbed as though her heart would break. Esperanza leant towards her and placed a hand on her shoulder. Then she sat down beside her, watching in bewildered fascination the gut wrenching pain that seemed to be pooling in desolation beside her.

'You've had a good life, *Señora*, don't go beating yourself up, it weren't all you fault.'

'She was just a girl, barely eighteen,' sobbed Lisa, 'she'd slit her wrists when I found her. I'd given up looking for my baby by then. I went to see this poor young mother, as a favour to a friend. Poor girl, with her big frightened eyes. I was drawn to her, it never occurred to me who she might be. I thought if I cared for her, somewhere someone might do the same for my child.' Lisa rocked herself to and fro as though to ease the pain inside, 'I never let the pieces of the puzzle come together. I'd searched so long for her and when I gave up and tried instead to do something useful for someone else, that's when God gave her back to me. I could have done so much for her, so much more.' She wiped her face but the tears came faster. She lifted her eyes and saw Esperanza's face seemed to reflect her own sadness.

'Her name was Letty,' whispered Lisa.

'That's right, that's what they called Pamela, them people down in Osorno, they called her Letty.'

'Oh Letty, Letty, you were my daughter, all along and I never knew.' Lisa uttered each word like a prayer. Her whole body shuddered with the emotion that convulsed it. 'God sent me to her just in time to save them.'

Lisa looked at Esperanza, a kind of imploring sadness in her eyes. Esperanza, not understanding it was too late, touched Lisa's hand and in a vain effort to comfort, delivered the harshest blow:

'Now, *Señora,* after so much heartache. She'll have your love and protection.'

There was a sharp cry from inside the hut as the children's games degenerated into hair pulling and throwing of objects,

'She spilt all the water on purpose,' screamed little Antonio.

'He took my cup, I didn't spill it, I wanted to give it to Antonio,' cried the even smaller Fran. The wails rose louder as Esperanza extracted them one by one disentangling them one from the other, and marched them to the kitchen, leaving Lisa alone on the stone bench.

'What does abused mean?' Consuelo asked the cook after Esperanza had left the kitchen. The cook stopped kneading the bread and passed her wrist over her forehead.

'What's that then?'

'What does "abused" mean?'

'And why would you be wanting to know that young lady?'

'Oh, because the nice lady said that a little girl was abused so she ran away.'

The cook raised her eyebrows, 'Well, well, well, who's been picking up fag ends as usual. And get that cat off the table. Go on run along and don't you be picking up big words like that.'

The door opened slowly and Consuelo crept into Milana's room holding her grey kitten. She came over to where Milana sat on the window ledge.

'What are you looking at, Milana?'

'I'm looking up at the hill.'

'Have you been to the house there?'

'To the temple? Yes. It's beautiful.'

'What are you thinking?'

'I'm thinking about my mother and her life. What about you, Consuelo?'

'I've found a name for my cat, I'm going to call it Messy because its fur's always messy.'

'That's because you cuddle it so much.'

'I just ran away from the kitchen because Esperanza is really cross because Antonio and Fran got into a fight and Fran pulled out a chunk of Antonio's hair and everybody's cross with me.'

'And what did you do?'

'I didn't do anything, I was just standing by the door of the hut. I didn't say anything, I didn't even see them, I was just listening.'

'Oh, what were you listening to?'

Consuelo climbed up beside Milana. Her eyes grew wider. 'That nice Lisa lady was sitting on the stone bench and,' she whispered, 'she was crying. I kept peeking from behind the door. Esperanza, was standing up and she wasn't crying at all, only she looked a bit sad, but only a bit.'

'Did you hear what they were saying?'

'Oh yes, I heard every bit except when Antonio started screaming and then Esperanza came in.'

'Well, what did you hear?'

'I can't remember now.' Consuelo stroked the kitten and seemed to try hard to recall the conversation.

'They talked about you, I think, and some earrings that were buried. Esperanza said she gave them to you.' There was a long pause. Milana waited for more.

'What does "abused" mean?'

'I think it means when you're treated badly.'

'Well someone was treated badly so she ran away. Was your mother treated badly? Is that why you were thinking about her?'

Milana leant closer to the little girl. 'What else did they say?'

'Oh, just before Antonio started to cry the pretty lady really started crying. She cried like grown-ups cry, all silent and their cheeks get all wet and she said, "Letty, Letty you were my daughter." Consuelo rocked back and forth and screwed up her face and tried to say it exactly as she had heard it. Then she gave Milana a sort of disapproving look.

'Are you sure?'

'Yes, she kept repeating it. How can someone be your daughter and you don't know? Don't they come out of your tummy? You'd know then, wouldn't you? Messy, even you would know if something came out of your tummy. It's a bit silly not to know, isn't it?'

But Milana had stopped listening. Her skin had turned to goosebumps. Inside her she felt like something had exploded and a million fragments were falling all around her, and it was the most wonderful sensation in the world; all the collages of her life falling like missing pieces into the perfect puzzle of her existence. She stood in the centre of the room her hands over her cheeks, a smile spreading over all her features.

'I knew it, I felt it, Consuelo, here,' and she pressed the pit of her stomach, 'where one knows the weirdest things.'

'What, Milana, what did you know?'

'That I belonged, really belonged.'

'Where, where do you belong?'

'Here, for a start, and out there, up that hill. I belong in that temple that is so beautiful and forgotten, and in this bedroom. Oh Consuelo, I belong to something beautiful.'

'But I belong here too,' said Consuelo a little concerned.

'That's OK, everyone should belong. Oh Consuelo, I'm so happy I could die.'

'Are you happy because of what I told you?'

'Yes, yes, because of what you told me.'

'Oh,' Consuelo beamed. Then she frowned, 'But, no one else is happy and I can't remember it very well... I'm not sure...'

'Oh but I am, little Consuelo. I'm very sure,' cried Milana throwing her arms around the little girl, kitten and all.

Chapter Nine

'To think I bring Lisa all the way down here and she gets a migraine. I haven't laid eyes on her since she scuttled off after lunch yesterday.' *Don* Matias was standing by the fireplace where a huge fire was roaring, a drink attached firmly to his right hand.

'We'll all get a migraine, Father, if you insist on playing Puccini so loud. Do you think we can turn the volume down now?'

The cook interrupted them from the doorway, 'There's a gentleman in the forecourt, *Señora* Stella, says he's just passing. He's wanting to know if you or *Don* Gonzalo are at home.'

'Just passing? No one just passes round here,' said Stella glancing curiously at her husband.

'Maybe he's selling something?' suggested *Don* Matias, 'I could do with some of those lovely rustic pots you've got outside, truly splendid.'

Intrigued, Stella followed the cook out into the hall and down the steps, where a man stood looking out across the landscape. Hearing her approach, he turned and stepped forwards. He was fine featured with dark, intelligent eyes and greying hair that, though receding a little from his temples, still grew as a fine mane to where it touched the upturned collar of his brown bomber jacket.

'Ah Stella. You may not remember me, I'm Victor Cornejo, Lisa's husband.'

'Oh, *Don* Victor,' Stella kissed him warmly on the cheek.

'Please, just Victor.' He smiled. 'This is an awful imposition but I couldn't resist stopping.'

'We were just saying how could anyone just be passing here?'

'I was passing overhead, shall we say?' He pointed to the clouds and laughed at her surprise, 'Keeping my hours up. I have so little time to fly my little plane these days, and I thought I might as well fly in this direction.'

'Oh my, how thrilling. Where did you land?' she asked with a hint of concern for the recently planted young vines.

'The old drive to the big house, just over there. It makes a perfect landing-strip.'

'Well I never. *Don* Matias insisted on playing a Puccini opera so loud we obviously never heard you. Oh! What a shame to have missed the excitement,' Stella exclaimed leading him towards the assembled company.

'Gonzalo can you believe it, it's Victor, and he's just landed his plane on the drive to the old house.'

'Well done old man,' said *Don* Matias stepping forwards and embracing his friend. 'That old ruin has come in handy at last!' *Don* Matias turned to the others, 'Now here is a man who so misses his wife that he flies over for lunch to be with her. This is truly heart-warming. You timed it to perfection, Victor.' Victor took Matias' tease in his stride.

'You haven't come to deprive me of your lovely wife's company on the way home have you?'

'Wouldn't dream of it old man. She hates flying.'

'I'm afraid Lisa has a migraine,' said Gonzalo shaking Victor's hand. 'We would love it if you would take her place at lunch as she can't be persuaded to join us.'

'I couldn't think of anything nicer. I do feel it's an awful imposition, but, it really was a spur of the moment decision, and when I saw the drive beckoning, well I couldn't resist.' Stella took his jacket, 'Maybe I should check on Lisa before tucking into her rations of Sunday lunch,' he added with a gallant smile.

'The surprise might just blow the migraine away,' chuckled *Don* Matias. 'Milana, why don't you show Victor the way?'

'So you are Milana,' said Victor turning to her as they left the room together.

'Matias and Lisa are full of praise for you.' He met her eyes with genuine regard. 'Will you guide me through this labyrinth of corridors?' he said looking about him and indicating her to lead the way.

Milana smiled shyly trying to hide her enormous interest in him.

'Has Lisa been feeling unwell since yesterday?' enquired Victor confidentially.

'Yesterday afternoon.' The blood rushed to her cheeks and she lowered her face. Milana had not had a chance to see Lisa since their walk. She had retired to her room immediately after tea.

'Mmm. Coming back here after all these years, it's obviously had an effect. She grew up here you know.'

'Yes,' said Milana. 'She told me.' She kept her head down.

'It's a strange place, so desolate.'

'Here's her room, *Don* Victor.' *Will she tell him about me now*?

'Thank you, Milana. Maybe you'd like to come and take a look at my plane later? I don't suppose you've ever been up in a little plane have you?'

'No,' said Milana, smiling at the improbability.

'Well I think we might work it into the afternoon, if you'd like that?'

'Wow! Could I really?' she felt drawn to his gaze.

'Good, I'll take that as a yes,' he whispered, as he reached for the door of Lisa's room.

Milana watched him tip toe in.

Everyone but Lisa went up the drive to see Victor's plane: Stella, Gonzalo and the another couple who Milana learnt were English and had come to sample Chilean wines with a view to importing them for their chain of restaurants. The children came too; their excitement was palpable as they watched Milana seated behind Victor take off in a cloud of a dust. The little plane sailed through the blue sky like a toy, delighting them all as it disappeared behind the hill and re-appeared moments later on the other side, engine rumbling, wings dazzling in the sun.

As they walked back afterwards, Victor fell into step alongside Milana and gradually they fell behind the others.

'I hope you didn't get too cold up there.'

'That didn't matter. It was so much fun. Thank you, *Don* Victor.' She exuded such enthusiasm that he glanced at her and smiled.

'Milana, Lisa has told me that you have spoken at length.'

'Oh yes, we have.' Her heart was beating so fast she feared he'd notice.

'She told me you spoke about Ricardo Romero as well, and you were very anxious to know if he was your father.'

'I was, I mean, I am. I…' She stumbled over words in her confusion. Noticing that she hovered on the brink of a shared confidence Victor remained silent, walking slowly.

'I know *Señora* Lisa doesn't know for sure but what I was wondering…' she paused. *Don* Victor inclined his head towards her very slightly to encourage her. 'I felt I couldn't ask her, but, I've heard things said and I just needed to know. I mean you knew *Don* Carlos Hidalgo. Do you think he was my father?' she blurted out at last.

'Milana,' Victor stopped briefly and pursed his lips thoughtfully, looking her squarely in the eye. 'Carlos Hidalgo could not have children when you were conceived. He contracted TB at twenty-one which left him unable to father children. So unless you were conceived before he was twenty-one, which clearly you weren't, the answer is no.'

Milana stared at him, whilst the significance of what she had just heard penetrated her ears.

'But, he has a son,' she stammered. Her eyes darted over his face as she scrambled to grasp his meaning. Letty, she realised would have been conceived before that, when Carlos was eighteen, but Santiago would have been conceived much later.

'Then Santiago is not his son either?' she ventured slowly. Victor waited for the party ahead to turn out of sight before continuing.

'Milana,' Victor took a deep breath and let his gaze rest on her. 'You're very quick.' He smiled at her. 'My career has been made up of looking at people and judging if they can be trusted. A great deal can be achieved on trust. I stubbornly cling to the belief that you can trust where thousands wouldn't dare. Believe it or not, I have rarely been let down.'

'You want to be able to trust me?' inquired Milana in a small voice.

Victor looked at her and nodded. He had often felt that there might come a time when Santiago's well being, his balance of mind, would have to be put above the jealous fears of the mother; where to keep a secret was to harbour a lie that could potentially stand in the way of Santiago's happiness. Many times he had spoken of it to Lisa, and now, he concluded, such a time had arrived.

'I'm going to trust you with a secret, Milana. There is no other way of assuring you that Carlos Hidalgo is not your father than by telling you he could not conceive and that in turn reflects upon his son. Santiago, as you so quickly noted, is not his son. This is why you must know the full secret, and it is a secret. Probably the most jealously guarded secret I have come across in my legal career. Half truths are dangerous. They can unravel at any moment, whereas whole truths can be safeguarded more responsibly. That is what I am going to trust you with, the whole truth. For Santiago's sake I believe you need to know this and, frankly, the way you have conducted your relationship with Juan Carlos Miranda has shown you to be a girl of integrity.

'Carlos Hidalgo's wife, Grazia, desperately wanted a child, so Carlos took in Santiago as his own. This happened while they were living in America. Santiago's real mother was, I believe, European and of aristocratic birth and his father was studying Medicine at Harvard. Carlos knew him well. You see Milana, there comes a time in our lives when we all search out our past for clues to our identities. As we get older it becomes more important to us. I suspect one day Santiago too may find out the truth and want to know who his real parents were. The point is that no one here in Chile knows about the adoption and Grazia Menendes chose to keep it that way, for the sake of the child and to hide the identity of his real parents from the scandal that might have ensued. And, more importantly, because she wanted him to belong to her completely.

'Grazia swore those of us who had been involved in all the legality of the adoption to absolute secrecy. But I swear my oaths to God alone. Besides the others were all Americans. I was the only Chilean lawyer present, and the only one who has seen Santiago grow up and who feels a sense of responsibility to him. Santiago knows nothing of this. In telling you about Carlos Hidalgo I have placed the boy's secret in your hands and I ask you not to divulge it to a soul. No one but myself here could prove its veracity anyway, and without proof no one would believe it. Grazia was very thorough about that, but I hope I have set your mind at rest.' He smiled kindly at her, with eyes full of understanding. 'Santiago is not and could never be your brother, which is, I take it, what you were afraid of.'

Milana's hand flew to her mouth in a spasm of surprise. Spontaneously and unashamedly tears welled up and spilled down her cheeks. She could neither move nor speak for a moment but when she did, it was to embrace *Don* Victor.

'You cannot know how happy you have made me.' She drew away from him and added, 'You have no idea what this means to me. I will never, never betray your trust, I promise you.' He turned towards her and placed his hands on her shoulders.

'You mean a great deal to Lisa, my girl, more than you can know.' The way he looked at her carried a significance that went beyond that of two strangers sharing a confidence. And suddenly she realised he knew, knew everything that had passed between her and Lisa, knew even what Consuelo had overheard, and that was why he trusted her. This was not a man from whom to keep secrets; Lisa had told him everything. As they stood together on the dusty track, Milana sensed, in the silence of what remained unsaid, the strength of feeling that bound them.

By the time dusk fell that night and *Don* Victor stood on the steps of the forecourt waving goodbye, Lisa was well again.

'I wish I had that effect on my wife,' said *Don* Matias, who for years had been estranged from his second wife. Everyone laughed.

'Are you sure we can't persuade you to stay, Victor?' repeated Stella as they kissed goodbye.

'No, I must keep vaguely within my schedule. I still have a great deal to do before Monday. This has been a most welcome Sunday afternoon.' As he turned to leave he looked back. Lisa followed his gaze to where Milana stood apart from the others with the children and with a quickened heartbeat she let herself dwell on the girl in the light of what she now knew.

After supper that evening, Milana retired to her room. It had been impossible to catch Lisa on her own. Now Milana heard a soft knock. Lisa put her head around the door.

'Matias and I leave tomorrow first thing, Milana, may I come in a minute.'

Milana sat cross-legged on the bed. As Lisa sat down beside her Milana sensed immediately a tension she had never felt before.

'I have had so much on my mind, Milana dear.' Lisa passed her hands over her face and rested her fingers over her lips. 'My migraine was no more than the marathon of thoughts that I've been going through.' She had that look of someone concentrating on some distant sound. 'As usual Victor's invaluable input has given me clarity and peace.' Her eyes rested on Milana and Milana felt their depth and sincerity penetrate all her defences.

'How much truth can a girl take in one weekend?' said Lisa quietly, and her face a little pale and drawn but infinitely lovely, questioned her silently

'The whole truth. Isn't that the best way?' Milana shrugged.

'Milana, I'm your grandmother. I didn't realise it until yesterday after our walk.' She held Milana's gaze. 'You knew?'

'Consuelo overheard something and told me.'

'Ah, from the mouths of babes…' she smiled sadly.

Her fingers laced together as, utterly composed as though she had rehearsed the moment many times, she stared down at her hands.

'Your mother, Letty, was the child they took away from me and gave to Esperanza the nurse. Esperanza took Letty down south and from there Letty ran off and stowed away, then she was effectively kidnapped and taken to the city. That's where Ricardo met her and fell in love with her. Then Carlos, without ever knowing the truth of who she was, how could he imagine she could be his own daughter, met her through Victor and helped her to get away from those awful people by giving her a position in his house as his wife's maid.'

Lisa passed her hands over her mouth as though in disbelief, 'Oh what instinct leads us to do extraordinary things in those circumstances.' She looked at Milana, with bewildered questioning eyes, 'It seems to me our hearts can speak a language that, by-passing reason, leads us to do what we must despite ourselves.' She shook her head in wonder. 'The rest is the history I spoke of to you yesterday.'

Even though Milana knew already, because of what Consuelo had overheard, tears poured down her cheeks. Lisa did not move, she just kept Milana's hand in hers and let the girl release the torrent of emotion. When finally the tears subsided, Lisa peered behind the veil of auburn hair that covered Milana's face and whispered, 'Is it that bad?'

Milana subsided into fits of giggles.

'Oh I can't stop laughing,' she cried.

'It's the emotion, darling. The release of so much tension. It makes you laugh or cry, till you don't know which is which. Believe me I know.'

Milana took a deep gulp of air and got up to get a tissue from the dressing table.

'Did my mother never know?'

Lisa shook her head.

'That's so terribly sad. It would have made her so happy.'

Lisa gave a helpless shrug. 'Who are we to judge God's timing? We can't know what intricate tapestry He's creating out of our life, how each strand has its perfect place and its particular patch to weave. We mess it up so often with our desire to control everything.'

'That means the boy you followed up to the temple on your sixteenth birthday, was my grandfather.' She paused, glowing with happiness; 'Did he really love you as no one else ever would?'

Lisa smiled. 'Yes. Victor is a prize among husbands but truth is you are never loved the same way twice, and there is very much love in God's world and infinite variations of it.'

'To think he imagined all his life he couldn't have children and he never knew he'd fathered one already,' Milana countered perplexed.

Lisa looked astonished, 'Milana how on earth do you know that?'

'*Don* Victor told me. He said he couldn't be my father because he couldn't have fathered a child with Letty because he couldn't have children after he was twenty-one.'

'Victor said that? So he told you everything.' Milana nodded.

'I didn't think he would.' Lisa paused, thoughtfully, 'I believe that is a confidence he would only pass on to a next of kin.' She paused to let the significance of what she said sink in. 'It's true of course, the TB Carlos contracted at twenty-one made him infertile but when I met him, remember, he was eighteen.'

'That means the only child he ever had was my mother.'

'As far as I know,' said Lisa, 'though sometimes fertility can return. But you are Ricardo's daughter. I know that for sure now.'

'How?'

'Victor was Grazia's lawyer remember. He was privy to a lot of confidential information. He knew she'd had a paternity test done on you after you were born, just to make sure. He never told me though until today.'

Somewhere an owl hooted.

'So *Don* Carlos never knew he had a daughter with you. And yet he died with Letty right there in the room with him. She watched her father die and never knew. And he was helping her even though he didn't know who she really was.' She looked rather helplessly at Lisa.

'You see how God weaves the tapestry of our lives,' sighed

Lisa, 'He put me beside Letty to save her life and yours. He put Carlos beside Letty when she most needed a father to save her from a hellish life. God never abandoned her. That's what I meant about the language of the heart that by-passes reason. Now you can understand why I got a migraine. My brain simply couldn't stretch to take it all in. As it is I'm only just beginning to figure it all out. I prayed so hard for her all my adult life, only God could have worked it out so we, her real parents, helped her without ever even realising it. How blindly we can travel through life.'

'All this time I thought I was Carlos Hidalgo's daughter and that…would have made Santiago and me, well, half brother and sister.' And Milana explained the story Iris had told.

'Victor suspected as much,' Lisa sighed, 'but I never for a moment imagined… What you must have gone through.' She lifted her hand to Milana's cheek and lovingly brought it to rest under her chin. 'Now I understand all the repressed fire in your paintings better than ever.' She smiled. 'How clever Victor was to choose you, of all people, to confide Santiago's secret. You are self-posessed and fiercely independent but you have courage and integrity; an honesty that penetrates deep. Given the trauma in Santiago's childhood, Victor has always felt someone other than just us should know that Santiago was adopted. In this case, to know might, Victor feels, release him of a great burden one day. If we were to die, there would be no one but Grazia to tell him the truth about himself. Victor feels we don't have the right to hide such truths, but while she lives he will respect Grazia's wishes, with this one caveat, you are, after all, our next of kin now.'

They stayed talking for a long time after that and when eventually Lisa looked at her watch it was past midnight. The room had grown chilly. Milana walked over to the window. The shutters, usually closed by the maid, had been left open. The full moon was high beyond the hill. She stood with her back to the room, her forehead resting against the cold pane of glass, her eyes staring into the opalescent light that bathed the silent rose garden.

'I long to see him.' She pressed her palms down on the cold of the window pane. 'How will I find him?'

'He's in New York now but he'll come back, just give it time. He'll be back in a few months.'

'Months? She turned abruptly. 'But I don't want him to think that I don't love him.'

'It won't harm him.'

'But what if, what if…?

'What if what?'

'I don't know.'

'Milana you're so young, you have so much time…'

'Sometimes we run out of time,' she said miserably.

Milana turned and saw the effect her words had and wished she had not said it.

Chapter Ten

There was a bitter wind and the ground sparkled with frost in Central Park as Lizzy pulled her scarf tighter round her.

'I shouldn't have made you walk. You're freezing,' said Santiago putting his arm around the shoulders of her suede coat. 'Thank God you came, Lizzy. Christmas alone is the worst.'

'You're terrible at keeping in touch, Santiago.'

'I know. I'm sorry. I should have rung sooner, but everything moved on so fast. Out of the blue, I got this fabulous invitation from The Rosenberg Gallery to do a joint exhibition with Hernan Garcia, after they saw the one in Chile. So I rented a studio here, near Hernan's. No family, no obligations, peace! I kind of lost myself in painting.'

'Peace? In New York?'

'It's all relative, Lizzy.' They walked through Central Park in silence, their breath clouding against the cold night air.

'What about Milana and all the babies?'

'You remember that?'

'How could I forget it?'

Santiago laughed, but the sharp intake of freezing air that followed gave him a sudden fit of coughing.

'God, that's an awful cough.'

'I'm fine.'

'You're the one who shouldn't be walking around in this freeze.'

'It's OK. I'm pumped high on antibiotics.'

'You should be in bed.'

'Really?' He raised a playful eyebrow.

'You look a bit red-eyed to me,' she said ignoring the effect he had on her.

'That's the cold, silly.' He pulled her tighter and covered his mouth with a scarf. 'Don't tell me you came all this way to mother me, Lizzy.'

'So what happened with Milana. Aren't I allowed to know?'

'Nothing.'

'Nothing?'

'She told JC she didn't want to see me. Couldn't even tell me to my face.'

'Who's JC?'

'A guy a couple of years below me in school. There's nothing between them.'

'How do you know?'

'The way he talks about her, like he doesn't get her either.'

'You can't leave it there.'

'What else could I do?' he said suddenly angry. 'Nobody would tell me where she was. Even my old mentor *Don* Matias the painter wouldn't tell me. It all sounded like a big conspiracy. It's all bloody lies and gossip and conventionality out there. I'm so fed up with it, it stifles me.'

Lizzy stopped walking,

'It's that bad?' She realigned her soft cashmere hat so it covered her ears. 'Remember what you said? How you felt about her?'

'Well maybe I've grown up.' Santiago stood in front of her, playing with a stray strand of her hair, twirling it between his gloved fingers.

'Don't be cynical, Santiago. You've been through shit so you just closed off to everything but your painting. You guys are so dumb; you just believe what we tell you and slink off. Think how complicated women can be…'

'And how come you're so uncomplicated then, Lizzy?'

'That's just it. There's not enough mystery to me. Let's face it, she's the one you're in love with, not me.'

'Not any more, Lizzy.'

'Well it lasted a long time. All the way through university, remember.'

'I was just holding on to a fantasy.' His eyes travelled over her face, resting on her lips and she read his intention.

'Come on. It's too cold to stop walking.' He put his arm around her.

Lizzy relished the tightness with which he held her as they walked. Old emotions threatened to rip through the flimsy façade of friendship that she had built around the attraction she felt for Santiago. She was determined not to damage the one thing she held dear; the trust of this complex and independent man whom she adored. His closeness under the circumstances was both welcome and unbearable.

'Is this your way of forgetting her?' she said feeling the old chemistry taking hold of her. Santiago stopped under a lamppost, he turned her towards him.

'Lizzy, I'm over her.'

'Why can't I believe that?'

'I can't think. Maybe you just don't want to kiss me because I've got a bad cold.' He smiled, his face so close to hers that she felt a shiver down her spine.

'Santiago, a cold would never stop me kissing you, but I have met someone,' she lied, on a sudden impulse.

'You have?' He looked surprised.

'Didn't you ever think I would?' she grinned. He was suddenly so serious and taken aback that something moved her to come a little closer. She still longed to do what he had never allowed ever since that day in the car. Now here she was, under a lamppost in New York, far away from everyone else she knew, with Santiago looking so suddenly mournful, his lips so close to hers. Her resolve failed her; she tiptoed, reached up and kissed his lips. He grabbed her then, so tight, his lips against hers.

'God I need this,' he whispered in her ear, 'I daren't kiss you as I want to, Lizzy, because I'll give you this cold and that's the last thing I want.'

'I don't care.' She kissed him deeply. He responded by kissing her hungrily back. When they stopped she could still feel his kiss electrifying her. He embraced her.

'I have no right to do that now. You've met someone else. It's not fair on him.' A familiar mischievous smile spread over his face, 'Yet here we are in this most romantic setting.'

'Except of course that you have a lousy cold.'

'Yeah well, apart from that. It's not really fair is it?'

'Santiago I've wanted to do this for so long. Don't you think I'd better get you out of my system once and for all?'

'You might get me into your system instead,' he teased.

'That's a risk we have to take.' She glanced at him, 'Would you like that, though?'

Santiago took hold of her hand. They started walking in silence.

'I don't know, Lizzy.' He squeezed her hand. 'I've been very lonely, but then the more depressed I am, the better I paint.'

'You, depressed?'

'Depressed, lonely, sad, I don't know; melancholia, nostalgia, all those self-indulgent emotions that young artists thrive on.'

'Are you teasing me?'

'No, Lizzy, I'm baring my soul to you.'

'Why can I never be sure whether you're taking the mickey or not?'

'I am being serious. I did want to kiss you. I've wanted to kiss you since I picked you up from the airport today, but I don't know what it means. I'm being as honest as I can be. Men, Lizzy, are so different to women. We just feel something in the moment and act on it, without really working out what it means. Like kissing you, just because you're lovely and you care and I'm so grateful that you're here and I need you desperately right now because I feel my world is about to implode. I feel safer from myself with you here kissing me.'

'Was it disappointing?'

'God no, Lizzy,' he stopped and hugged her. 'You are so adorable. How could you disappoint?'

'I'd like it to go on, Santiago. We can have a week, just a week together, for old time's sake. Out of all time and space. Would that do your depression any good?'

'You would offer yourself to me for a week to cure my depression?'

'There you go again, teasing.'

'No, Lizzy. I'm gobsmacked. How could you do that, no

strings attached, and then go back to him, whoever this poor chap is?'

'Are you saying it's wrong?'

'No, no, I'd never dream of judging it like that. It's just how can you separate your feelings like that? I thought women couldn't do that. I thought that was what men did.'

'I can try.'

'Lizzy, there's nothing I would want more than to spend a week with you, like that.'

Santiago rubbed his eyes. 'God everything is so blurred I wish I felt better. I can't believe this is happening, and my brains are cooking. Maybe you're making them cook, maybe I'm on fire for you,' but Santiago wasn't laughing. Lizzy glimpsed beyond the face and its infinite appeal for her, and saw the strain there. She took off her gloves and touched his forehead.

'Oh God, Santiago, you're burning up.'

'I'll be fine. Let's walk a little more. The Metro Club is just round the corner. They know me there.' He held her hand but it felt as though he were gripping her for support.

'I really think I should get you home.' But he ignored her and putting his arm around her, carried on walking.

'Nothing a bite to eat won't fix. Come on. It's your first night in New York.' But she could feel him leaning in on her, a little more with each step.

The entrance to the Metro Club was discreet and elegant. A liveried doorman opened the door for them. Santiago released Lizzy from his embrace and stood aside for her to enter. Then, overtaking her, he nodded for her to follow him as he headed for the bar while taking his scarf off.

'Hugo, a whisky and soda and a glass of champagne for the lady.'

'Santiago, don't drink. The antibiotics won't work.'

'Yeah,' he grinned, 'but the whisky will.' He flicked his finger playfully over the end of her nose. 'Relax, Lizzy.'

The whisky started to work and after a couple of sips, Santiago seemed to get a bit better. 'That was quite a nasty turn I had there,' he admitted. 'Don't move. I'll go and throw some water on my face and I'll be fine.' Lizzy's eyes followed him anxiously out of the room.

Lizzy felt that old familiar thrill just to be beside him. As they followed the waiter, into the dimly lit dining room, Santiago took her hand again and squeezed it. With a great deal of ceremony, the waiter seated them both, before placing a napkin on Lizzy's lap and handing her a menu. Santiago flicked quickly through the wine list and closed it.

'We'll have the Montes Alpha, white. Lizzy only drinks white wine.'

She smiled. He still remembered. Together, they studied the menu. She felt his ankle under the table and taking off her shoe she stroked his leg. She felt him tense and sensed the effect she was having. His deep blue eyes seemed to glisten as they looked at her but she could not make out the look. It was direct yet far away. She touched his hand and found it freezing. 'Santiago are you sure you're all right?'

Seconds later Santiago let go of the leather bound menu which fell with a thump to the floor. He held his head in his hands and gave a very low moan. He tried to smile, but it wasn't a smile, more of a grimace of pain.

It all happened in slow motion. First his elbows that were resting on the table slipped so that his full weight fell forwards crashing onto the table. Then his whole body fell sideways off the chair taking with it the tablecloth, the orchid, the candle, the glasses and the cutlery as he slumped down onto the carpet, his arm outstretched, his face turned up to reveal a deathly pallor. A lady screamed. Lizzy stood up, her hand over her mouth as she watched helplessly his total collapse.

Chapter Eleven

Lizzy took the lift up to the fifteenth floor. She hesitated, trying to remember which way to go. Hours before she had stood here with Santiago. Now loneliness enveloped her as she walked into his dark apartment. Turning on the lights she went straight to the bedroom. She was grateful for the cream walls and the reds and yellows of the Moroccan rugs that littered the floor, they gave the apartment a bright warm feel. Santiago's bed was large with a thick fur rug thrown over the duvet. Tired and emotionally exhausted she climbed onto the bed and despite herself, fell into a deep and dreamless sleep.

Lizzy was woken abruptly by a loud buzzing noise. It took her a while to figure out that the telephone on the bedside table was ringing. Warily she picked up the receiver.

'Hey man! Rise and shine.' Whoever it was spoke English with a strong Spanish accent.

'Hello?' said Lizzy.

'You're not Santiago. Who are you?' countered a rather disgruntled voice on the other end. 'Can you put him on?'

'No, I can't, he's not here. Who is this please?'

'It's Hernan. When will he be back?' The voice was impatient and urgent.

'Hernan Garcia, the painter?'

'Yes. Who are you?'

'Lizzy.'

'Lizzy, the English girl? Well, what have you done with Santiago?'

'Santiago collapsed last night, Hernan, in the Metro Club. They took him to hospital.' Her voice shook a little.

'Gees man! What's wrong with him?'

'He's in intensive care. They think it's meningitis.'

'What?' She could hear his breathing. 'Don't move, I'm coming over.'

'Where?'

'I'm coming over to you. Just stay there.' He paused. 'Are you OK?'

'I don't know. I fell asleep. It was so late.'

'Don't do anything. I'll be there in ten.'

Lizzy found her suitcase where Santiago had left it on a low chest by the window, and took out her wash bag. On the bathroom shelf above the sink, next to the shampoo, she saw the bracelet she remembered. She picked it up and fingered it. The painted beads had been worn to smooth wood in places, dulled since the time she had seen it on his wrist a year ago. He must have worn it every day since then. She crushed it in her palm and felt the beads dig into her skin as she remembered the nurse in the hospital calling her Milana, telling her Santiago was delirious and that he was asking for her. If only the nurse had known her mistake and how little consolation she was giving.

When Lizzy emerged from the shower the doorbell was ringing. Wrapping a towel around herself, she looked through the eye hole. A scruffily dressed young man with a scarf wound several times under his unshaven chin was looking impatiently back at her. He looked like he had just got out of bed himself.

'Who is it?' she called out just to be sure.

'Hernan.'

As she opened the door a take away coffee was thrust into her hand.

'I've got croissants in here but you'd better not take the bag or that might fall off.' He eyed the towel she was wearing.

'Hi,' he said giving her a little wave. Walking past her, he went straight to the kitchen and opened the fridge. Lizzy pulled on her jeans and a sweater and returned to find him seated on a high stool eating breakfast. He had put a croissant on a plate for her.

'Don't mind me,' he said gesturing to her coffee, 'I just had mine. Santiago didn't look too good on Wednesday when he asked me for some antibiotics I'd brought over from Chile and that was two days ago,' he said between mouthfuls. 'How did he collapse?'

'He was burning up, but then he seemed to get better. We were sitting at the Metro Club when he just collapsed onto the floor bringing the entire table with him. It was so awful. He was out, like he was dead. They brought the stretcher right to the table. I went to the hospital with him, the Clare something. I put myself down as next of kin, I didn't know who else…They think it's meningitis.' She paused. 'I came back here…'

Hernan shook his head philosophically.

'You sure you're OK? You can stay with me, but this flat is nicer.' He stuffed the last bit of croissant in his mouth and got up. 'You get that down you. I'm going to find his address book.' He was back before Lizzy had finished. 'Got to get hold of his mother first. Sometimes it pays to be old fashioned,' he added as he flicked through the pages of a little leather-bound book. 'I'm guessing you don't have his phone.'

'Don't you think we should check with the hospital to find out how he is? I mean before we ring her?'

'No time for that. Grazia likes to be in control.' Hernan gave Lizzy a look. 'Grazia Menendes will know what to do. She'll be over here like a shot.'

Hernan held the receiver in one hand as he continued flicking through the pages with the other.

'Hello, Iris, is that you? Is *Señora* Grazia in? It's Hernan from New York. Wake her up, Iris, it's important… For heaven's sake, Iris. Quit stalling. It's about Santiago. He's desperately ill. Get her on the phone… Señora Grazia? Yes. Hello. Yes… He collapsed last night at the Metro Club. He was rushed to hospital, the one closest to the Metro Club, I've forgotten the name… Yes, that's it. They think it might be meningitis. No I haven't seen him… Yes. He was with Lizzy, Lizzy Bertie… No, she'd just arrived… Yes. She's in his flat… No, she's not living with him…. It's just for Christmas.'

Hernan rolled his eyes at Lizzy.

'No, I'm at Santiago's flat now… Yes, I am with Lizzy…' He covered the receiver whispering, 'Spanish Inquisition,' to Lizzy.

'*Señora* Grazia, what do you plan to do about Santiago? Today?… You think you'll get a flight?… OK… Will you be staying at his apartment? I can easily have Lizzy stay with me…' he glanced at Lizzy, appraising her.

'Oh… Yes… Fine. The Waldorf… Yes I will. I'm going to see him now.' Hernan gave Gracia his mobile number.

'Roll on the interrogation!' he exclaimed to Lizzy, replacing the handset. 'I don't look forward to having her around.'

'Is she that awful?'

'No, it's just she can't conceive of anything other than her own way.'

'I think you should call Milana,' said Lizzy suddenly, looking assertively at Hernan as she rolled the beaded bracelet between her fingers.

'Milana? Who's she? What's with that old thing? I've seen him wear it. Did you give it to him?'

Lizzy shook her head, 'Haven't you heard of her?'

'No.' He was flicking through the address book again. 'Who?'

'She's a painter.'

'Well I think we've got enough painters round here. I don't know anything about this Milana girl, but we can't just ring all sorts, it's not a party.'

He picked up the receiver again and started dialling.

'I'm ringing Diego. He's a very old friend of Santiago's.'

'Hey man! Yeah… Look Diego, it's about Santiago… He collapsed last night. He's in intensive care… They think it's meningitis. He was unconscious… I haven't seen him yet. I've just found out myself… He was with Lizzy Bertie… She's just come from England… Yeah… I'm with her now… I've just rung Grazia. She's coming tonight and staying at the Waldorf. Typical! Lizzy's here for a week… Really… would you?… Gees man, there's only us here now… You can stay with me or you could stay here at his… I'm going to the hospital now. I should hear something in an hour or so… Ring my mobile, or I'll text you,' he paused, 'Yes… I guess this is as serious as it gets.'

Lizzy was gesturing to him and mouthing something.

'What?… Hold on…Oh, Lizzy says something about a girl called Milana. Do you know about her? Don't know why it's so important… What?… Is she a friend?'

Hernan looked at Lizzy, 'Diego says she's not a friend he knows. Why is it so important?

'Lizzy says can you find her and tell her what's happened.' Hernan covered the receiver. 'Who the heck is this Milana?

'No, Diego… I don't know…she's a painter. Someone must know her. Ask Grazia?'

'No!' Lizzy gesticulated looking horrified. Hernan grimaced in surprise, 'OK scrub that, Diego. Don't ask Grazia. Just see if someone knows… I don't know man, ask Lizzy yourself when you get here.'

Lizzy bit her lip. How could Santiago have kept his feelings for this girl from his nearest and dearest friends, surely he had told somebody. Should she tell them his best kept secret? Lizzy grabbed the phone from Hernan.

'Diego. Hi! It's Lizzy… I know… I've heard so much about you too… Look Diego, any chance of you getting a phone number for this Milana, this painter? I need it… I can't explain now. Just see if you can, but try to keep it sort of quiet. Maybe try someone called Matias or maybe someone called JC. Maybe they'll know. No, I don't know them, but it's worth a shot.'

As Lizzy put the phone down, Hernan gave her a despairing look.

Once more, he picked up the phone. To the Waldorf this time; 'Booking a room for Mrs Menendes…' The staff gushed over the phone.

'Thank God her usual room is free,' he whispered to Lizzy.

'Right! Now we can go. Ready?' he asked turning towards Lizzy. 'You up to all this?' he added genuinely concerned.

Lizzy nodded and grabbed her bag.

Out on the street, Hernan hailed a cab. Once in the back seat Lizzy breathed a sigh of relief.

'I don't know what I'd have done if you hadn't appeared this morning. Last night I thought the world had come to an end.'

Hernan gave her a quick smile, 'You can count on me from now on. Somehow we'll get through this.'

Together, they walked along antiseptic-smelling corridors painted duck egg blue and on through endless sets of swing doors until they came to a waiting area for the intensive care unit. There was a peculiar hush about the place. A couple of people sat close together on a sofa with glazed expressions as though they'd spent days there. Beside them were several empty cups of coffee. Hernan went up to the reception desk and asked for Santiago Hidalgo. Presently a nurse came and spoke in whispers to Hernan.

'We can't go in,' he explained to Lizzy after the nurse had left. 'We can't do anything. He's in a coma. They're still doing all kinds of tests to see how far the inflammation has spread.'

'A coma!' Lizzy breathed the words out slowly, 'What's the prognosis?'

'Touch and go. It doesn't sound good.'

'Do they think he could die?' she said, her lips quivering as the words formed.

'They told me to inform his relatives. They need someone here capable of making decisions. I told them his mother was coming.'

'Oh God! How could it have come to this?'

'Hey, Lizzy, he's not dead yet. We've got to have faith. We've got to believe he's going to pull through. Look, there's no point sitting here. Let's go somewhere for a coffee.'

'We can't.' She she looked at him despairingly, 'I can't leave here. What if something happens? What if he dies and we're not here?'

Hernan put his arm around her and looked around nervously. He wasn't good in hospitals or with girls crying and he knew he couldn't stay in the waiting area with the two people on the sofa and their anxious eyes staring out at nothing.

'I'll tell the nurse we're going to the café across the road. I'll give her my mobile number, OK? She can ring us if she needs to.'

'I want to see him. I've got to see Santiago. What if they're talking about the wrong guy? I must see him.'

Hernan sat down, resigned, his head in his hands, wishing he'd never given Santaigo the damned antibiotics, or at least forced him to see a doctor. How could a cold get this bad? How could you end up at death's door from one day to the next? When he looked up again Lizzy was nowhere to be seen.

Lizzy looked about her, a stubborn streak asserting itself as she hovered around the swing doors into intensive care weighing up the odds of pushing through, ignoring all the no admittance signs. As she stood there a pretty young black nurse came out and glanced at her. Lizzy caught her eye imploringly. The nurse took a step in Lizzy's direction.

'Are you all right?'

'I came in last night with Santiago Hidalgo. I think you've got him in there. He's got no one but me here in New York. I just travelled all the way from England to see him and got here yesterday and now this. I'm so shocked I can't eat or sleep.' Her lips quivered and she took a deep breath. 'I just need to see him. If I could just see him for an instant. There's no one but me here to look out for him.' The nurse took pity on her.

'Look, I shouldn't do this, but if you come this way, you can put on a gown and see him through the window of his room.'

Lizzy followed the nurse through the swing doors into out-of-bounds territory towards another reception area with desks of panels and buttons and little lights and beepers and a multitude of screens. Two nurses sat in attendance; one busily checking records and papers, the other keeping her eyes on the screens. No one seemed bothered about Lizzy. The intensive care rooms radiated off this central area, each one with a large window through which the patient was clearly visible.

'Over here.' The nurse indicated one of the windows. Lizzy was almost afraid to look. She glanced into the room, allowing her eyes to travel over the white walls and the pale green floor to the great cluster of cables that led to individual monitoring machines and screens showing heart, pulse and breathing rates. There were oxygen tanks by the bed. Her gaze followed the grey leads from the machines to the bed. Only then did she allow herself a proper look at Santiago.

He lay half naked under a simple white cover so that she could see his chest all wired up from the waist up.

'He's less pale than yesterday,' she murmured

'That's the oxygen he's on,' replied the nurse glancing at Lizzy, but Lizzy had eyes only for Santiago. He looked striking lying amidst all the whiteness. His black hair shone in the harsh light. It was hard to believe he could be so desperately ill.

'Is he your boyfriend?' whispered the young nurse.

'Will he make it?' Lizzy asked quietly, not taking her eyes off him for a moment.

'I haven't seen his case notes.'

'Can he hear? Can he see? I mean is he totally in a coma? Won't he wake up?'

'In cases where the brain needs to be saved, the patient can be rendered unconscious to slow down the vital functions. This can help to prevent brain injury.'

'You mean when he comes round he may suffer brain damage?'

'I don't know his particular case.'

'But it's possible?'

'Everything that needs to be done is being done. I think we should go now.' She laid a gentle hand on Lizzy, but Lizzy's focus was riveted on Santiago. He looked as though he'd just closed his eyes to sleep while his strong, handsome presence seemed to mock the clinical paraphenalia around him, yet his eyes might open and never see the way he'd seen before. He might be blind or deaf or brain damaged. She kept looking as the nurse pulled her gently away.

'Well?' asked Hernan

She covered her face and bent her head.

'He just had a cold, a lousy cold and now he's like that. Even if he wakes up, he may be damaged forever.

Chapter Twelve

Little Ines was sitting in the warm summer sun, by the old well, playing with pebbles while hens pecked the dust around her. Milana stopped to watch her for a moment before letting her presence be known. Everything was exactly as Milana had left it, even the old, broken-down pick up truck with the fat tabby perched on the bonnet. Beyond them the Villarica volcano rose in all its snow-capped splendour topped off with a little puff of cloud over its crater just to prove it lived and could breathe fire. As Milana set down her suitcase by the flowering veronicas, Ines glanced up and with a wail of astonished delight came running up to her.

'You came!' she exclaimed flinging herself into Milana's arms. 'You really, really came for Christmas, that's my bestest present. Have you got the bracelet I gave you?'

Milana took Ines's hand and led her to the well and sat with her on the step. She picked up the loose brick under which she had left her letter one year ago and smiled to herself.

'So much has happened in a year,' she sighed, replacing the brick. 'I've really missed you and Panguipulli and the lake.' She stretched out her arms and breathed in deeply, 'The air is so fresh here. Up in the capital smog clings to everything.' And she rested her bright sea green eyes on Ines.

'Where's the bracelet?' the little girl insisted.

Milana looked seriously at her and leaning into her she whispered confidentially, 'I sent it on a very special adventure, to England, and now,' she paused dramatically, 'do you know where it is?' Ines shook her head vehemently, 'It's in New York and do you know what else is in New York?' Ines's eyes were growing wider and wider with excitement; 'Snow, lots of snow, because it's midwinter there and here it's summer. Isn't that amazing? Your bracelet is right in the middle of the snow.'

'How?' asked Ines tilting her head and looking like she smelt a rat somewhere.

'Well I put it on the wrist of someone who very much wanted to wear it.'

'Who?' she said suddenly recovering her enthusiasm. 'Do I know her.' She gave a sudden big bright smile, 'Or is it a him?'

'Uh huh.'

'Was it the man who came here looking for you the day you left?'

Milana opened her eyes wide. 'Who came looking for me here?'

'He did.'

It was *Señora* Lucy who spoke, standing behind them in her apron, looking the same as ever.

Milana jumped up. Oh *Tia* Lucy! It's so good to see you.'

Lucy drew Milana into a vigorous embrace. 'Well you look fine,' she said looking Milana up and down appreciatively. 'Are you painting?'

'I am, *Tia* Lucy. I have a wonderful teacher.'

'Humph,' said Lucy. 'You don't need no teacher and never did.'

'We all need a teacher.' She smiled.

'Well, he came, that young man. I saw it at once.'

'What young man? What did you see at once?'

'That he was the one. And to think he comes looking for you and you'd done a runner, you ungrateful child.' With that, Lucy embraced Milana again and wiped away a tear. Milana received the hug but her thoughts were elsewhere.

'I'm going to get my new rabbit to show you,' cried Ines excitedly and she scampered off across the dusty courtyard.

Lucy let out a chuckle, 'She'll have to catch him first!'

'So you remembered us.'

'Did you get the money I sent?' enquired Milana pulling her mind back to them.

'Oh yes. We got the money. You're a good lass you are. Never forgot us for a moment. Ricci went and bought a suit. He's got a job as an office junior in Pucon with a travel agent there. Got board and lodgings at the bakery; helps them out from crack of dawn, then it's off to work smart as a pin and he sleeps at sundown. He'll make us all proud.'

'But then who helps you out on the farm?'

'Juanito does the work of three. He's a good lad, and strong as an ox. I'm that fond of him, and he's got a girl he has, from the village, a nice lass. Father works up at the Fundo Los Reyes. They've been going steady these last four months, bless them.'

Milana laughed, 'But Juanito's barely fifteen.'

'Well that ain't going to stop him. He always had an eye for the girls. The lass is sixteen,' Lucy chuckled.

'It's good to be back,' sighed Milana, gazing at the familiar scene around her.

'Well, you're quite the lady now, Milana. Look at you! And them fancy clothes.'

'They're not fancy, just jeans.'

'And that fancy belt, all fashionable, like out of a magazine. Don't you go doing anything to your hair now,' she touched Milana's long silky hair. 'Gorgeous as nature made it.'

'You will come to my exhibition won't you?' Milana said as she followed Lucy across the courtyard towards her old room.

'You and Juanito and Ricci. I'll send the money for the bus tickets and you can stay with me. It was going to be in December, but *Don* Matias, my teacher, said it would be better marketed in March.'

'Oh don't make me laugh, Milana,' chuckled Lucy snatching a quick glance at her. 'What's the likes of me going to go messing about in art exhibitions with all those "la di da" types?'

Ines tugged at Milana's sleeve.

'Look, do you like him, he's a bit wild.' The rabbit squirmed on his back.

'Are you going to get married, Milana?' asked Ines stroking the rabbit's ears into submission. 'Then you could have babies.'

'Married? I'm only eighteen!'

'That's old! What about the man with my bracelet?'

449

'Yes,' said Lucy, her hands on her ample hips. 'What about him?'

'Oh, I'm too busy for all that at the moment. He's busy too.'

'Never too busy for love,' chided Lucy. 'Don't you let love pass you by. Love flies to meet you in its own time, if you're too busy, the wind carries it off,' she said as she puffed up the narrow stairs. 'Don't let those uptown kids tell you otherwise, Milana. A good man and kids if you're lucky enough to get them, that's what'll keep you happy, that's what stays, that and love, all the love you've given, never mind fame and money.' And she stood looking down at them from the top step.

'Oh *Tia* Lucy, I know, you're right, but in time.'

'Yeah well look at my boys, them as went up to town, I never see them now. Them as Nora put in that shanty. Ungrateful lot!'

Milana did remember. After all, 'that shanty' had been her home, Letty's home. Lucy had never really taken that in. It was 'her boys' that had burnt it down. It was an accident, so they said, but what did anybody know. Still, Lucy had been kindness itself to Milana. It wasn't her fault if the boys were into drugs and thieving up in the city.

'Come and freshen up. You can share your old bedroom with Ines, she's been that excited. We've gone and killed a pig for Christmas. Juanito will be setting it up soon as he's back from the horses. He'll be that glad to see you girl, and Ricci's coming back for tonight. And get that poor critter off its back, Ines, it ain't right for an animal.'

Meanwhile in the city, JC rang and rang Milana's flat... but there was no answer.

It was Christmas Eve in Panguipulli. The church bells rang for midnight mass. The pews of Father Juan's church were crammed full; young boys and girls stood propped against the walls, girls rested against their boyfriends or held hands, coyly snatching glances at each other. The older womenfolk still wore black lace mantillas, while their men folk donned their Sunday best. The congregation spilled out onto the plaza, some sat on the steps, others chatted only half listening to the gentle cadenzas of Father Juan's sermon over the speakers in the square.

Milana sat near the front with Lucy, Juanito, Ricci and Ines. As she looked at the walls covered in her paintings she felt them at first rebuking her absence. Gradually their startling innocence reawakened the memory of the raw emotions that had possessed her then. She closed her eyes and recalled how the images in her head had so effortlessly shaped themselves onto those walls. How it had seemed as though the warmth of a hand on hers had painted through her; his hand guiding hers all the way, bringing him back to her, bringing her peace. His hand... she dwelt on the longing that imbued her whole being.

'Wake up,' she heard an urgent little whisper in her ear. Ines' warm hand was tucked into her own and her eager eyes were watching her.

'You fell asleep and leaned on me,' she whispered confidentially.

Milana knelt down with the others. As the priest elevated the eucharist a tremendous feeling of love and gratitude came over her. She understood that just as one might want to capture love and keep it in a bottle, she had captured her love for Santiago translating it into painting. Maybe that was the secret to all her success – painting fuelled by unconsummated love. Now that she was free to love him, free to release him back into her life – would she ever need to paint again she wondered? Would she ever be as good? "Pain and suffering fuels great masterpieces because it is when we are most acutely aware of our mortality," Matias had said, "You'll both do better to focus on the work ahead for your exhibitions and wait till Christmas at least. You'll only distract each other to no useful purpose before that." And obediently she had agreed knowing that to try to get in touch with Santiago while he was in New York preparing for his own exhibition was, under the circumstances, out of the question. But she had spoken to JC. Without disclosing any secrets she had explained she now, at last, must face Santiago and what they might still have together.

'Just tell me JC when you know he's back, tell me if you hear anything. I was wrong to hide away from him, I see that now.'

And JC had promised to contact her if he heard anything and he had hugged her and forgiven her the heart ache she had caused him, basking as he always did in her warmth and energy.

Now excitement and apprehension bound themselves more tightly inside her, as Milana considered what she would say to Santiago and how he would take it, while she waited for the moment JC would call her. But above all there was fear; with each passing day the fear grew; would Santiago still love her or would he have buried her too deep to recover.

That night, Milana slept soundly. In her dreams she saw Our Lady as Santiago had painted her, golden rays radiating out and she felt a sense of warmth and infinite tenderness surrounding her heart and a voice like a whisper telling her *go home*. When Milana woke, Ines was sitting on her bed grinning and looking at her.

'You were saying "Why?" a lot in your sleep.' She was dangling a fleshy hibiscus flower in front of the large, overfed, rabbit. 'Why were you saying "why"?'

'I don't know Ines, I don't know.' But the hibiscus flower reminded her of JC and a sudden urgency to speak to him consumed her.

Milana walked along the dusty road to the post office. Ines scampered this way and that, chasing butterflies that rode the wind and circled the dense umbels of the bomarea flowers before settling on the blue clusters of *Madreselva* that grew in wild abandon. The sun warmed the jasmine and the roses causing them to release their heady perfume onto the mellow breezes of high summer while the little town of Pangipulli rested in the embrace of Christmas morning.

Milana rang the bell at the post office and asked the bleary-eyed girl behind the door if she could use the pay phone.

She dialled JC.

The phone rang for ages. There was no answer. She was about to hang up when he picked up.

'Hi,' came the breathless voice.

'JC?'

'Gees, Milana. I just nipped back here to get my sister's Christmas present. We're having a big do at my parents'. Where are you?'

'In Panguipulli.'

'Reception is awful.'

'Happy Christmas, JC.'

'Yes, ditto.'

'JC, is anything the matter?'

There was a pause.

'Milana, it's Santiago. He's very ill in New York.'

Milana was instantly on her feet. She gripped the phone tightly and pressed it to her ear.

'I wasn't sure whether to tell you.' JC's voice crackled over the receiver.

'Tell me what?'

'Everyone's talking about it at the beach. He collapsed in New York. He's at a hospital called The Claremount. I tried to ring you yesterday.'

'The what?'

'The Claremount, in New York.'

'What's wrong?

'He's in a coma. It's meningitis. It's the worst sort. They're saying he might not make it. Grazia flew out days ago. Diego has gone too. Actually I don't know if he's gone yet, Diego Sanchez...'

'Can you give me Diego's number?

'Do you know him?'

'No, just let me have his number.'

'I can give you the number but I'll have to ring you back.'

'Just go and find it, I'll wait. I'm in a phone booth in the post office in Panguipulli.'

'No wonder it's such a bad line, I wish you'd just use a mobile like other people.'

Milana wrote the number on a little scrap of paper provided, with a small blunt pencil.

'Thanks JC.'

'How come you rang me. Who told you?'

'No one. A voice in my head.'

'What are you going to do?'

'I don't know, JC. I don't know.'

'Look, Grazia doesn't like you, Milana. I don't like to say it, but you might as well be warned.'

'I know she doesn't.'

'No, it's more than that. She thinks you've stolen his light. She hates the fact you're going to have an exhibition. She thinks it's because of you Santiago went to live in New York, because you were competing with him. She thinks you stole his ideas, because of the church in Pangipulli. She blames you for pretty much everything including him coming back from England.'

'How could she blame me for that!'

'Santiago had a brilliant job offer there, to work with some Cabinet Minister, and he turned it down. And now she blames you for chasing him away from Chile. She thinks you're out for yourself. I don't know what's got into her but you're like the enemy. I mean there's a lot of venom there. She's got it in for you. She'll try to turn his friends against you, Diego... I mean...'

Milana's heart was racing.

'Forewarned is forearmed,' sighed JC.

'Don't worry, JC. Remember what I said; they can't hurt you unless you let them.' But inside Milana, a voice was screaming: *She destroys lives. She won't rest till she's destroyed me.*

'Be careful. She's not too keen on me, Milana, since we've been close, you and me. She's been spouting off to my mother. Probably hopes it will all get back to you, and you'll run off with your tail between your legs.'

'JC, I'm not about to do that.'

'I thought not! That's why I am worried.'

'JC...'

'Don't explain... Milana. I just hope... Look, sometimes you can hurt someone so bad that they kill the love they had for you. You know? Just don't expect miracles, Milana.'

'I know, JC, if you kill the love inside you, you kill a bit of yourself. I know that now. And that's why you've got to forgive your dad, JC, maybe this Christmas?'

'Yeah, but I'm talking about Santiago. I guess you're right about killing love, look at him now. He never understood the hurt you caused him. Now he may be past forgiving you. You there Milana?' But she could barely answer. 'Just don't get your heart broken all over again. That's all… Hey Malala?…' She heard the nick name he never used now and put the phone down. He sighed and replaced the receiver.

Chapter Thirteen

Milana walked from her bedroom into her workroom. Paintings covered every available wall space, suffusing the room with colour. Only the painting of Consuelo holding her kitten was an oasis of peace and innocence next to the smouldering sensuality shown in the darkly shadowed eyes of her muse, Santiago, who, trapped on canvas, stared down at her as she paced the room.

A suitcase rested against the front door with a borrowed fur-lined raincoat from Lisa draped over it. Milana stared out at the leafy acacia trees. It was hot as an oven outside and she was grateful for the cool interior of her apartment; the thick walls and the cold stone floors through which the heat never quite penetrated. She shut the windows and locked them, turning at the sound of Lisa's short quick steps striking the grey marble corridor outside. Milana hesitated before opening the door, an agony of apprehension threatening to shrink her resolve.

'You're doing the right thing,' whispered Lisa, planting a quick kiss on Milana's cheek. 'Don't doubt it for a moment. Here's your ticket and your passport.' She handed over the documents and waited whilst Milana stowed them carefully in her handbag.

'Now get your things. We must hurry.'

'I can't thank you enough, Lisa.'

'Don't thank me, darling, Victor did it as only he could. It never occurred to me that you didn't have a passport.'

Lisa's Subaru was parked outside in partial shade. Even so, the heat inside was almost unbearable. She turned on the ignition and the air conditioning whirred into action. With time ticking against them they sped towards Pudahuel International airport. Lisa glanced at Milana who sat staring out of the window with a fixed expression.

'Are you all right, Milana?'

'Yes. I'm fine. Just very nervous.'

'You've got nothing to worry about. You're on a direct flight and a taxi will take you straight from JFK to the Claremount. They'll all be there. They're there all day, from what I hear. Everyday.'

'That's what I'm really nervous about. They could all just tell me to get lost.'

'Milana you're not there for them. You're there for Santiago.'

'Yes, I know, but I'm all alone. I don't know any of them. What if he dies?'

'If he dies you'll know you went to him. And he will know it too.'

'How will he know?'

'Because I believe when you die you see everything clearly. Besides if he were to die, you would always regret not having done everything you could. It would haunt you.'

Lisa tapped her fingers on the steering wheel as she waited for the traffic lights to turn. Apprehension translated into restlessness. Lisa knew, were she in Milana's position, she would never have the courage to face the potential wrath of Grazia.

'Do you really think I count at all in this? I feel such an intruder.'

'Love counts. Nothing else really matters in this mixed up world except the love we give,' replied Lisa, expertly threading through the traffic to the next lights. They bordered the river for a while towards downtown with the Andes behind them.

'That woman hates me.'

Lisa took a moment before responding.

'Grazia is a human being. She must be feeling very vulnerable.'

'Well, I'm just a nobody to her.'

Lisa paused and glanced at Milana. 'You know,' she said

457

slowly, wondering at the wisdom of what she was about to say, 'you're not no one to her.'

Milana swallowed nervously, and felt a wave of nausea threaten her composure. Lisa reached out her hand. 'You have to remember eighteen years ago she killed her husband because she thought *he* had conceived you, and she sent your father to prison for her crime. She'll have worked out, by now, who you are, even if she doesn't want to face it.' She glanced at her again. Milana sat pale and tight lipped.

'You are the walking reminder of all her guilt, you think she won't blame you for everything, of course she will, it's easier than blaming herself. Do you understand?'

Milana shook her head with a hollow laugh. 'I could never understand Grazia Menendes. If I thought she was his real mother, I would never make this trip. It's because I know he has no one that I'm going. Still, Grazia may not have a heart, maybe not even a conscience, but that makes her invincible you see, that's why she terrifies me.'

Lisa realised how hard she was clenching the steering wheel and released her grip.

After a while she turned to Milana.

'If you don't want to go, that's fine with me.'

Milana darted a sudden startled look at Lisa.

'What about all the trouble you've been to, the tickets, the passport…'

'You have to be sure you want to go. You have to be sure you wont regret not going, if he…' but she left it unsaid and concentrated on driving. Regret was what had burdened Lisa all her life – Milana must make her own decision.

Milana seemed to be lost in thought for a while and Lisa kept silent as she drove.

'I can't understand how she could love him if she's lied to him all his life.' Milana shook her head bitterly.

'You must understand why she lied, Milana?' Lisa shifted her position. Her back was killing her and tension was gnawing at her shoulders. More and more she wondered if allowing Milana to go to Santiago was like declaring war on Grazia. She wondered if Victor hadn't encouraged it because, deep down he felt the boy needed an ally and maybe his mother needed a worthy adversary. She tried to remind herself that Victor was wise and considerate but still, Lisa couldn't help the growing apprehension she felt.

'Lying doesn't make her a monster. Grazia always had everything she wanted. When she couldn't have a child, well, she couldn't bear it. Then along came Santiago. His real parents needed to cover up their "love child" because one of them was already married. And so they came up with this plan, because it was mutually convenient, Grazia would never need to tell the world this wasn't her child, and in turn, her lie would draw a veil over their mistake forever. She wanted him to be hers, don't you see. She desperately wanted to be his mother. She only did what others have done before her. It's bad, but it's intensely human. She thought she could control fate, but you can't.'

'But she has controlled fate. By lying to him she's taken his chance to find out who he really is. Maybe he'll never know his real parents. She's robbed him of his identity.'

'Are you going to tell him?' Lisa asked quietly, her hands tightening on the steering wheel.

'No, I told Victor. I'll never tell.'

'Milana, there are many adopted children who are never told, do you think they would all feel robbed?'

Milana looked out of the window at the parched fields and dry cracked earth.

'I would. Everyone needs to know where they come from at some point.'

'Well Santiago can't feel robbed of what he doesn't know, he believes he has a family.'

'He has a mother who killed the father he loved. That's not a family. Can you imagine how he must feel? I can't get it out of my mind.'

'We don't know how he feels…'

'He's dying.' Milana's lips quivered. 'He's there dying and everyone he's loved has abandoned him.'

'Nobody's abandoned him.'

Milana turned fiercely, her eyes flashing angrily, 'His real parents abandoned him didn't they, they didn't want *him* they just wanted each other, and his father abandoned him when he died and I abandoned him when he gave me everything.'

A plane's engine roared overhead.

Lisa reached over and squeezed her hand.

'I'm sorry. I don't mean to be angry with you,' sighed Milana.

'I know. You're right to feel angry. You see him as the innocent victim of other people's selfishness,' and with a sudden streak of inspiration Lisa added, 'He's as much a victim as you are.'

'I'm not a victim,' Milana retaliated defiantly.

Lisa flashed her a wry smile, 'And you think he is?'

Milana shook her head.

'Don't underestimate each other's strengths and achievements just because of circumstances.'

'He'd so hate to be thought of as a victim. He hated it once when I suggested he felt sorry for us,' Milana said remembering suddenly the only time she'd seen a flash of real anger.

'You and Santiago have far more in common than you think, that's why I'm here driving you to the airport.'

The highway towards the airport had been planted with palm trees interspersed with bushes of flowering laurel now laden with pink and white blossoms. To the right of them another plane came in low, its silver body dazzling in the sun.

Milana stared straight ahead, silent and pensive. Lisa looked at the clock. They were running late. Milana's passport had only come through at the last minute. There was no time now for procrastination yet she could feel Milana's uncertainty permeating the atmosphere like a fog. For all Victor's encouragement, Lisa felt deeply concerned at the thought of letting her depart on an international flight, on such a difficult mission, confused and uncertain, with no one to support her at the other end.

A large green sign indicated the turn off for the airport.

'Milana is this about you not being sure he cares?'

'That just about nails it.' Milana looked at her helplessly.

There are many leaps of faith you have to make in love. Think about it. Why did you get the call from that girl, what's her name?'

'Lizzy Bertie. She said she thought I should come. She told me she was with him when he collapsed and that he needed me. Oh I've gone over it so many times. Why would she go to such trouble to find me and tell me to come? He must have said something. She didn't say anything else other than, please come if you can, he needs you.'

'And is that why you're going?'

'No, it helps. But... remember in Alhue when I said sometimes we run out of time.'

'Yes, I remember.'

'I don't want to run out of time.' Her eyes welled up. 'I pushed him away when really I loved him so much and, I suppose, somewhere inside I wonder if that's why all this happened.'

Milana wiped away silent tears.

'Santiago made me everything I am now. He opened a door where I could only see a brick wall. All my success is because of what he taught me and I pushed him away, like he meant nothing, when I owe him everything.' She covered her mouth to stop the emotion that gripped her. 'Just because I couldn't bear to tell him to his face what I suspected and because I didn't think I'd be strong enough to resist him.'

Lisa glanced at her and smiled. 'I think you underestimate yourself.'

'No, you don't understand, I knew if I saw him I wouldn't even have cared if we really were brother and sister, what I felt was too strong. I might have even have kept the secret and lied to him and to myself so as to carry on with him.' She paused and looked away, 'I've just realised I'm no better than Grazia Menendes, I'd probably have lied, just like she did, to keep what I wanted.'

A wave of tenderness flooded through Lisa to hear her unexpected compassion.

'But you didn't, you gave him up,' said Lisa gently.

'No, I hid from him. He's a million times more honest and braver than me. I wouldn't even have the courage to go to him now, without you behind me and without that girl's call.' She paused. 'I owe him so much and I owe you so much.'

'You owe me nothing, I'm your grandmother,' Lisa said briskly to stave the emotion that she felt, then more softly, 'but don't go because you owe him, go because you love him. Paying him your dues won't bring him back from the edge of death, but loving him might set you both free.'

'Oh I love him. Everything I've done in a way I've done for him, thinking of him. He might die now thinking I never really cared. He's so ill he might believe Grazia and all those horrible things she's saying about me. I couldn't bear that. The truth is I don't know what I feel anymore, I just know something more than Lizzy Bertie is calling me to him, and if I don't go it will haunt me all my life.'

Lisa smiled and said nothing as she took the slip road marked 'International Airport'.

Milana didn't speak again until Lisa had parked the car in the international departures area.

'I take it you are going then?'

Milana reached over and Lisa gathered her in her arms and wiped her tear-stained face.

When they stepped out of the car, the heat hit like a wall, reflecting off the tarmac. As they walked towards international departures Lisa turned to Milana;

'You know don't you that Santiago came back to Chile after the floods and tried to find you through Father Pancho and then he begged Juan Carlos to tell him where you were and Juan Carlos told him you'd left and he had no idea where you lived now.'

Milana nodded.

'JC told me that. But I didn't expect Santiago to give up so quickly. I guessed I'd underestimated the influence his mother had on him.'

Lisa shook her head. 'Oh but you see he didn't give up; he

went to Matias, by then you were living in Alhue. Matias wouldn't tell him where you were, he told me later that your love life could wait.'

'So *Don* Matias knew all along, he just teased me?'

'He knew after we came back from that visit. Matias isn't interested in people's love lives, only their painting. So every lead left Santiago cold. I can't begin to think of the frustration he must have felt. Finally, Juan Carlos explained that you had told him it was over and it was better he didn't find you. Juan Carlos was terribly upset at having to tell him, but he was so unequivocal that Santiago believed him. That's when Santiago backed off, or, as Juan Carlos says it, "reeled off". He said it was like watching a tide recede so fast you thought there must be a tidal wave coming behind but it never did come. Santiago simply left. He left Chile. Juan Carlos didn't hear from him again. It's a measure of how Santiago felt that he hasn't returned to Chile since then. Grazia doesn't understand and doesn't know who to blame. She feels her boy has turned his back on Chile and suspects it's because of you. And possibly she's right on that. If you deny your feelings... well... maybe, in the end it does weaken you.' Lisa sighed, 'Milana, I know better than most not to underestimate the power of love, at any age.'

Lisa stood outside passport control and hugged Milana one last time:

'If you have any problems, ring me. You're only a plane journey away. I can come if you need me.'

She kissed her cheek. Milana took a deep breath and mustered a small smile.

'I don't feel very brave.'

'You are brave. And remember Milana,' she whispered gravely, 'love doesn't ask to be loved back, it gives freely, like he once gave to you.'

463

Chapter Fourteen

Milana passed through the Baggage Collection and Customs Area and stepped into the bustle of New York's JFK Airport. She looked slim and stylish as she slung her bag over her shoulder and pulled her suitcase behind her. Only the intensity of her eyes might have betrayed the conflicting emotions that battled inside. The overhead lights picked out the golden highlights that the Chilean sun had bleached into her long hair. A crimson polo neck jumper hugged her figure stopping just short of the leather belt JC had given her. Her skinny jeans were tucked into a pair of knee high leather boots. She scanned the sea of faces until finally she saw the sign bearing her name, half-heartedly held up by a man leaning against a pillar, sipping a coffee.

'Milana, Milana, is it you?' A blonde girl wearing a pretty green coat and a multi-coloured woollen scarf, detached herself from the crowd and ran towards her.

'I'm Lizzy Bertie. Thank goodness I found you.'

'You speak such good Spanish.' Milana's relief was palpable.

'Thanks. I learnt at school.'

'How did you find me?'

'Someone rang Diego, a Lisa something or other, and told him your arrival time and that there'd be a driver waiting, so I looked out for the driver and noticed that you picked him out of the crowd. Is it OK if I drive back with you?'

'OK? It's wonderful! I was so scared of arriving alone.'

'I know, New York can be a bit daunting. Have you been here before?'

Milana half smiled, 'No,' she said. 'I haven't.' How could she begin to explain.

'I never thought I'd find your number but Diego managed to get it through *Don* Matias, Santiago's painter friend.'

'How's Santiago?' Lizzy felt herself held suddenly by the intense green eyes that seemed to read far more than she herself intended to reveal. For an instant she experienced the unusual thrill and excitement of being attracted to another human being, like the discovery of a strange new scent. Then the eyes seemed to remember themselves and release her from their piercing scrutiny.

'He's still in a coma. No sign of improvement yet.'

'Can we see him?'

'His mother is allowed to see him. She has two friends who came with her, but they go off together, shopping and stuff, while she just sits with him for hours. She's distraught, it's really sad to see her. She barely eats anything, and she looks so tired.'

They got into the back of the taxi together.

'I saw him too, when he was first in intensive care,' Lizzy went on confidentially, 'They let me see him through a window into his room.' Milana looked at Lizzy, warming to her animated manner, her light blue eyes and the charming way her gums showed above her perfect teeth when she smiled.

'He was lying under a sheet, wired up to so many machines. There were leads attached all over his chest and everything seemed so still and unreal. He'd been walking along the street with me just hours before, he'd...' Lizzy trailed off. 'I'm so glad you came,' she said suddenly to Milana. 'I don't have any friends out here, no girlfriends. Diego is lovely and Hernan Garcia, he's kind of gruff but really great. They've been wonderful, but... I didn't want to go home yet. I didn't want to cop out on him. I only came for a week. I'm supposed to have gone home.'

'You came to stay with him?' inquired Milana.

'Yes, a sort of spur of the moment thing. It seemed such a nice idea to spend Christmas in New York, he's a very dear friend.' Lizzy's expression changed suddenly, 'I didn't think you'd come,' she said, her face serious and her eyes watching Milana.

'Not come? Why?'

'Because Santiago told me you didn't want to be found. You said it was over.'

'He talked about me to you?'

'Of course he did. That's why I rang you.'

'But I had nothing to do with his real life. I was like a hobby or something for him.'

'Is that what you think, Milana, that you were his hobby?'

Milana stared out of the window at the scintillating city. 'He was everything to me but I was fourteen when he met me.' She gave a little shrug, 'Poor, uneducated… a bit like a useless coloured fragment one collects and treasures because it's so surprising to find it in the mud.'

Lizzy grabbed her hand, 'I heard you were better read than most of his friends at that time.'

Milana glanced at Lizzy, 'There was nothing I could give him, believe me.'

'But you brought him joy.'

'What?'

'Joy! Simple as that. It's probably the single most important thing we can be given.'

Lizzy watched Milana tilt her head slightly as though the comment were a thing suspended between them that she must evaluate from various angles.

'Not love?' Milana asked after a few moments.

'When we love we are surprised by joy. It's joy that fills our hearts and tells us we're in love,' said Lizzy simply.

'I'd never thought of it that way.'

'You brought him joy and that's what told him he was in love. Your age didn't come into it. Santiago is a loner. He doesn't believe he can love. He says there's too much baggage from his past, but somehow all that evaporates when he talks of you.'

Milana listened, watching this pretty girl talking in Spanish with a slightly English accent, wondering how Santiago could resist her.

'Goodness, Milana, if you knew the women who have tried to get close to him. He's so attractive to women, they all want to rescue him from his solitude, or his melancholy or his inability to love. The fact is he's simply in love with someone else, you! Until you both face that, he'll never be free.'

'Did you love him?' Milana asked softly.

'I still love him, that's why I sort of understand. I rang you, because I love him. Don't you see?'

Milana turned to face her. 'Just like that? You must have the most generous heart in the world.'

'Literature is full of us,' she grinned. 'It's called unrequited love.'

'He must be nuts not to have fallen head over heels in love with you.'

Lizzy laughed, 'I reckon he is a little nuts but that's part of his charm.'

'Don't you mind?' asked Milana, liking this girl more with every passing moment.

'Strangely, not any more. But I needed to meet you. I understand it better now.'

'What do you understand? I wish I did.'

'There's something about you, a naturalness – it's very compelling. I can't imagine you being anything but who you are. There are no airs or attitudes and no defences about you. You just sort of let life in and contain it.'

'You can see that in twenty minutes?' Milana looked at Lizzy with a feeling of deliverance, 'I wish I did have some defences.'

'What for?'

'To deal with stuff, like…well, like Santiago's mother.'

'Oh.' Milana saw a grin creep over Lizzy's face.

'I shouldn't say this to you but Santiago once said when I asked him about his mother, that when he looked for love it was as far away from her world as possible.' She paused and a look of sadness seemed to turn her eyes watery. 'You should see her now,' she whispered, 'she's totally destroyed.'

The taxi drew up in front of a smart apartment block with a yellow awning and potted shrubs flanking the glass fronted doors. Trees lined the road. Snow heaped on the sides of the pavement glittered in the pale sunlight.

'I thought we'd drop off your suitcase at Santiago's apartment and you can freshen up for a minute before we go to the hospital. I can't say how glad I am to have your company,' she added encouragingly.

Milana looked out of the window at the elegant building. A liveried doorman came towards them. She breathed in deeply and wondered for an instant how she could have come so far out of her comfort zone. She felt like JC had once said about surfing a wave, it's crazy dangerous and you're flying on adrenalin but you have to go with it or go under.

Lizzy led Milana through the brightly lit hospital corridors and into the waiting area. Two women in suede and furs sat deep in conversation, their legs elegantly crossed as they drank coffees from the filter machine in the corner. Beside them several carrier bags emblazoned with designer names disclosed how they had spent their morning.

'They're Grazia's friends. They've probably come to take her to lunch, but she rarely goes with them,' whispered Lizzy to Milana. They looked up as Lizzy passed and smiled distractedly. Lizzy guided Milana towards a pair of swing doors. 'He's through there,' explained Lizzy. 'Diego is usually here but he must have gone out with Hernan. They were here when I left this morning.' At that moment the double doors swung open and Grazia Menendes appeared in a cloud of Chanel perfume. There was no avoiding her. It was a full frontal impact. Milana stared at the woman with a mixture of horror and immense sadness. Her full length mink coat hung off her shoulders. A black silk polo neck jumper, worn over beige slacks accentuated her pallor. There were dark rings under her already dark eyes that gave her face a gaunt look. 'Lizzy,' she acknowledged. Then her eyes rested on Milana, bemused and unsure.

'Grazia, this is Milana Romero.'

Grazia stared at Milana and the look of consternation was gradually replaced by one of disdain. Without a word, she stepped to one side and continued her path towards her friends.

Lizzy watched Grazia greet her friends with stiffness and noted that she said nothing about the encounter for the friends neither looked surprised nor glanced in their direction.

'She's going to ignore you, that's how she's going to deal with you,' Lizzy confided.

Grazia and the two women left, their perfumes mixing and lingering on behind them.

Milana stood pale and trembling in their wake.

'Sit down, here. I'll get you a coffee.' Lizzy led her to an imitation leather sofa.

'If you weren't here I would walk out and go back to Chile,' Milana whispered shakily. 'I really have no right to be here.'

'Santiago needs to see you.'

'But he might never wake up. It's like he's not really here. There's just her.' A shudder of anguish went through Milana.

'Oh Milana. Don't let her intimidate you. You've come all this way. You must be shattered and jet lagged and that'll make you feel vulnerable, that's all. Now focus on Santiago. He's lying a stone's throw away from you as we speak, just through those double doors, the room on the left.'

Milana stared at Lizzy. 'What are you saying?'

Lizzy looked around her, the waiting room was empty. She shrugged.

'It's just an idea, I mean most of the nurses are at lunch. I saw him, after all. There's no harm in trying. It might be your only chance. You know why I've called you here, don't you. It's a very practical reason. It's because of what they say, that patients in comas need something to trigger their return, something,' she smiled, ' or someone, to bring them back from their shadowlands. I really believe you can do that for him.'

Milana's heart was suddenly pounding. Grazia, the women, everything else was forgotten. The faster her heart beat the more she realised the inevitable. Before Lizzy had time to digest the implications of her own impulsive thought, Milana stood up and pushed open the swing doors through which Grazia had emerged only moments earlier. Even if she'd read the stark message 'no admittance' above the door it meant nothing to Milana.

Lizzy glanced at the still steaming coffee sitting on the table where she had placed it for Milana. She felt irresistibly drawn to her frank sincerity and warmth. Although Milana was a little unsure and bewildered by her surroundings, she exuded energy and spirit and she was unafraid, deep down, in the way only those oblivious of rank and status ever can be. Lizzy felt she had brought a rare creature into the city, as alarming and mesmerising and unexpected as walking a leopard through New York.

Despite herself Lizzy smiled; this green-eyed girl, untamed by convention as she was, had a captivating natural grace and dignity that could only further inflame Grazia's resentment. Lizzy watched the doors through which Milana had disappeared, anticipating a commotion at any moment. But Milana did not come back.

A few minutes later, Diego appeared.

'Lizzy! Did you find Milana? What's the matter, wasn't she there?'

'No, she was there, Diego. Now she's here. Just as we arrived Grazia came out through those swing doors and stood right in front of her and ignored her completely. The poor girl was so shaken, she wanted to get the hell out of here. I just wanted to focus her thoughts back on Santiago, so I had this weird idea. I sort of suggested she go in.'

'In where?'

'Into the intensive care unit… to his room.'

'Lizzy you must be nuts! What about Grazia?'

'Grazia left. Like I said. She ignored Milana completely, and she's gone off with her friends. Milana was so upset, I just wanted to distract her.'

'Oh Lord.' Diego looked towards the double doors in disbelief.

'I saw Grazia's friends downstairs but Grazia wasn't with them.' He looked around nervously.

'Oh no! What if she comes back?' Lizzy looked frought.

'Where's Milana now?'

'She's in there. She hasn't come out.'

'But Grazia doesn't let anyone go in.'

'I know.'

'How long has she been there?'

'Ten, fifteen minutes.'

'What's she like?' Diego whispered.

'You feel she's only just tamed. There are undercurrants to her. She's quite riveting. Actually, she's fab, Diego. Really fab.' Diego approached the double doors and opened them slightly. 'I can't see her there,' he said, coming back.

'We'll just have to wait.'

Chapter Fifteen

Two cleaners in green overalls mopped the floor in rhythmic strokes. A nurse busied herself with the monitors. Milana recognised Santiago instantly through one of the windows that looked into the intensive care units. His mane of dark hair against the white pillow was unmistakeable.

'Excuse me,' a nurse appeared suddenly beside her.

'Santiago Hidalgo?' was all Milana could say, whilst her eyes remained riveted on the figure of Santiago lying on the bed. The nurse studied Milana for a moment. She seemed very young for a healer but she exuded a kind of singular and rather commanding energy. The nurse did not understand how this healing worked. To her it was all just wishful thinking, but if it made the relatives feel better, they must allow it. This woman had a far-away look about her, and an unexpected intensity in the way she focussed on the patient through the window that maybe was typical of healers. She hadn't met many after all.

'If you would come this way please,' Milana was asked to wash her hands up to her elbows at a sink and anti bacterial gel was put on. A gown was placed over her clothes.

She didn't speak, she just followed the motions. Then the nurse opened the door of the room in which Santiago lay.

'I'll leave you two alone then.' The nurse watched for a moment through the window intrigued as to what the healer would do. She watched her walk slowly up to within a foot of the bed and stand still. She saw her take another step and kneel by the bedside. She watched her lower her head so her forehead nearly touched the edge of the bed and tentatively reach her hand to where the patient's hand lay flat by his side and place hers over it.

The nurse turned away, perfectly satisfied that some healing ritual was under way. Another nurse passed.

'Is that the healer his mum was talking about?' She nodded towards the room. 'Wasn't she supposed to come with the mother?' enquired this older nurse gruffly.

'I don't know. Anyway, she's doing her stuff.'

The senior nurse glanced into the room, where the woman knelt beside the bed, her hand over the patient's, and walked on.

'Santiago, I'm here,' whispered Milana. She clasped her hand over his so that her fingers were tucked under his palm. An incredible feeling of peace calmed her racing heart.

'I'm here, I know you can hear me, Santiago.'

Milana gazed at the sleeping face; his eyelashes so dark against the unaccustomed pallor of his face, he might have been moulded out of wax, his features smooth, expressionless. He told her nothing, he gave nothing away. She pressed his hand. Only the warmth of his skin told her that he was alive. The endless beeping of the monitors showed his heart and breathing rate, but what of him? Did his soul remain whilst his body was in this death-like sleep? He could have been lying in a coffin he was so far removed from the bustle and cares of the world.

'Come back,' she whispered. 'Come back, Santiago so that I can love you.' As she whispered, two large tears rolled down her cheeks. She caught one on her finger and very gently she left the trace of her tear on his pale chiselled mouth wishing him to taste her, to sense her there, to know her presence. Holding his hand she whispered the rosary as she had that night when he'd come to her. With all her heart she prayed for him to come back. Finally she stood over him and placing her hand on his forehead, moved closer to him until her face was over his. Then, with heart racing, for she barely dared to do it, she placed her lips over his and whispered, 'I love you.' Immediately she drew away lest she should be seen. Then, following some instinct, she rose and left, closing the door carefully behind her.

The nurse was coming towards the room. Milana took off her gown. The nurse took it from her, silently nodding her towards the double doors that led outside.

Grazia Menendez walked into the waiting room deep in conversation with a red head of middle age with a slightly down at heel look and a shaggy fake fur coat over her arm. Diego and Lizzy looked at each other helplessly as Grazia and her companion passed by and walked on through the swing doors. It was only as they got up, panic-stricken at the thought of what would happen next, that they saw Milana, sitting with her head bowed on a sofa at the far end of the waiting room.

'Let's go quickly,' said Lizzy touching Milana's shoulder.

Milana looked up, distracted, deep in thought. She smiled at Lizzy.

'Milana, we must go. By the way, this is Diego.'

Diego touched Milana's elbow, 'I've got your coat. Let's go,' he urged.

Lizzy took her arm. 'We'll come back soon,' she whispered.

Hurriedly, they walked out of the waiting area towards the lifts. They went down in silence and nobody spoke till they were outside in the bracing cold. It was beginning to snow.

'Let's go round the corner, to the little café,' suggested Lizzy promptly.

Diego nodded, pulling up the collar of his coat. He put his arm round Milana, steering her briskly across the street.

The inside of the café was warm, the windows misted up. They walked past the coffee and sandwich counters and sat down at a table.

'What happened in there, Milana? We were so busy watching for Grazia we never noticed you come out.' Lizzy clasped her arm. 'Did you see him?'

Milana's eyes opened wide as if in disbelief.

'I saw him. I held his hand. Maybe he could see me from

somewhere else. It was like he wasn't in his body. He'd gone away.'

Diego leant across the table, 'How the heck did they let you in?'

Milana looked at Diego for the first time, taking in the short curly blonde hair, the bright, kind eyes and the clean cut angular face.

'I think they were expecting someone else.'

'The healer!' said Lizzy raising her eyebrows, 'They thought she was the healer. Oh God.' She covered her mouth and looked at Diego.

'Do you realise what'll happen when Grazia goes in with the healer now and they say she's already been.' His smirk smacked of triumph.

'She'll think we had something to do with it,' said Lizzy looking concerned.

'Us?'

'Of course. She'll think we got Milana in under false pretences.'

'Maybe she'll just think Milana got herself in there,' replied Diego chuckling.

'Tell her it was my fault, I got myself in there,' said Milana quietly.

'You've got to go back, Diego,' urged Lizzy. 'It might look like we're all ganging up against her or something. She's so vulnerable.'

'Come off it,' he said, losing his sense of humour suddenly.

'At least let her blame just me,' persisted Lizzy, 'but not both of us. Santiago needs you there. Go on, Diego, go back before she realises you've left. She's known you for so long, don't abandon her now. It's important.'

'Why's she got to be so bloody controlling.' Diego swigged back the last of his coffee and got up.

Milana caught his hand, 'It's all my fault. But I'm not really sorry.' She gave him an apologetic smile.

'Good to have you on the case.' He squeezed her shoulder and leant closer to Lizzy.

'I go, like a pig to the slaughter,' he whispered giving her a wink and left.

Grazia Menendes stepped out of the lift on the ground floor and spotting Diego waiting, she grabbed him by the arm and moved him away from the lift doors.

'Where is she?' Her dark eyes scrutinized his face, 'Diego? Where is that girl?'

'Who?'

'Don't play helpless with me, Diego. You know perfectly well.'

'Well there's Lizzy and now, Milana, and both of them went home.'

'And you can tell them from me that they won't be setting foot anywhere near Santiago again, I forbid it.' Grazia's voice trembled with rage.

'What? Why?' asked Diego calmly meeting her fury with his gentle eyes.

Her lips tightened together. She was trying to control herself, but she was incandescent. She turned up the corridor. Her fingers pressed painfully into his arm as she pulled him along with her. She backed him against the wall and faced him.

Grazia was a tall woman. With her high heels she was not that far off Diego's six foot two inches. What she did not have in height, she made up for with her black hair piled up on her head held fast by a large bejewelled clasp. Her lips were painted red, her eyes lined in black. To Diego it looked like war paint defining the lines of her rage. She brought her face close to his.

'I'm going to speak to you for a minute. I only have a minute. The healer is with him and I should be upstairs.' Her eyes scanned Diego as though she were seeking a place to deposit her message of umbrage, indignation and hurt.

'I won't have her here. You understand me Diego, I won't. You've been his friend for years. Did he ever mention this girl's name?' Diego sensed her vulnerability and his compassionate heart reached out to her, despite her mask of defiance and strength.

'No,' said Diego truthfully.

Grazia raised her hands in a triumphant gesture of exasperation.

'You see, to his best friend he never mentions her. You think she means anything to him?' It was a rhetorical question addressed to the pale green walls of the corridor.

'This girl may be talented and she may have got everyone worked up because she comes from a shantytown, but she's seeped the life blood out of Santiago. I knew he should never have done that project for the church. He's always been full of idealistic dreams. He has no sense of how the real world works. He'd give his life up if it was asked for a good cause. She has taken his style, his talent and because she's poor it's turned people on. She's driven him out of Chile and away from me. That's how come he's here, dying of some stupid cold that wasn't treated when he could have been home in his bed with no trouble.'

'Grazia you can't blame her for this.'

'Oh I blame her for this and much more. I blame her for destroying his future and now I will blame her for his death.'

Diego put his arm on Grazia.

'Please, Grazia, sit down, please.'

'I won't sit down, Diego. There's nothing I want to hear about her. I've learnt all I need to. She has systematically wheedled her way into the lives of many people, rich people, playing their weaknesses and their guilt. In caring for her they feel they're doing they're bit for the poor. She feeds off their desire to be virtuous. Juan Carlos' parents know all about her; she lived with him and then overnight she dropped him like a hot cake soon as she'd got Matias Vidal interested in her. Now Lisa is falling for her charms. She helped get her a flat in Providencia. You have no idea what she's like. The latest rumours are of how she's established a family connection with Lisa. Matias Vidal is crazy about her, moved her into his son's place in Alhue, if you please. Oh she is the social climber par excellence. I know all about this girl. She's a curse on our family. You have no idea. Her mother destroyed more…' but she stopped herself there, her long fingers with their dark red nails twisted the chain at her throat. 'What a clever, scheming woman like that can do, knows no bounds,' she exclaimed bitterly. A nurse passed noiselessly beside them. Diego remained silent.

'I will never let her near Santiago,' she hissed. 'Not over my dead body.'

'What if he's in love with her?' Diego's question hung unwanted between them and was dismissed with a small grimace. Diego insisted. 'What right do we have to…'

'I have every right,' she growled huskily, 'I know my son, he never thinks ill of anyone. He'll only have compassion for her and she will milk him for it. She will go on milking his talent and his money and his heart, tearing him away from his family and isolating him until she's totally possessed him. Oh I've seen it happen.'

'She's barely eighteen, Grazia,' Diego reminded her.

'Age has nothing to do with it. We are what we are from the cradle. If anything, she gets away with it all, thanks to her age. She's just a girl from the shantytowns trying to make good. One day they'll all wise up to her. But she'll have made it by then and she'll have done it on the back of my son and I'll never forgive her for what that has cost us.'

'I don't think you know her.'

'Do you?' Grazia shouted it at Diego, 'Do you? Or are you just another sucker for her looks and coy ways. Look into her eyes, Diego. I have, and you'll see her strength and determination. You'll see her spirit. She doesn't need anyone to look after her. All she needs is a launching pad and she'll conquer space. She used Santiago and now she dares,' Grazia's voice took on a tremor of fury, 'dares to fly in my face and walk through into his room and see him. Have you dared do that? Or even dear Lizzy?'

Diego looked down awkwardly.

'No you have too much respect for me, and for Santiago, to trespass. She has no thought for any of us, or for the position

478

she puts you into. Have you thought of that? Her selfishness knows no bounds. She is a very dangerous girl.'

'I think she loves him,' whispered Diego. Grazia threw back her head and laughed sarcastically whilst regarding Diego with pity.

'Oh you stupid boys, women deceive you so easily. Love! What does she know of love? She never sought him out in all those years. I tell you, Diego, she seeks him when he's dying, but did you ever hear of her before? No. Not a squeak, because she was playing his game, she was living his art. She didn't want him anywhere near, so that she could shine alone.'

'But Santiago loves her,' said Diego weakly. Grazia was slowly wearing him down. After all, he didn't know Milana at all. He'd only just met her. Why should he fight her battles for her? Grazia had her story all worked out. There was nothing he could say to prove it wrong.

'Santiago loves the idea of her. He loves an underdog. Oh, how she must have looked up to him in awe when they met,' Grazia turned her full force on him. 'She was fourteen when Santiago met her. Fourteen! Don't talk to me about love at fourteen. You think he loved her? Oh get real. You all make me sick.'

Grazia flung herself down on one of the blue plastic chairs.

'I'm surrounded by morons or dreamers. You all live in fairy tales. Why don't you take a look at the real world. Milana is thriving in it while my son is dying. She's taken her lump of flesh and I'm here every day praying and dying inside. Every fibre of my being is willing that boy up there to live. I'd give my life for him. I'm telling you, Diego, never, never let me see her here again. If you respect anything, respect this request from the mother of a dying boy, and see to it. You hear me.'

'What about Lizzy?'

'What about her?' Grazia snapped.

'Don't you want her here again?'

'Lizzy? What's dangerous about Lizzy? For goodness' sake, Diego. I'm not on a crusade here. Who do you think I am? Lizzy's a sweet girl, who's shown me nothing but respect and consideration. What on earth could an English aristocrat like Lady Elizabeth Bertie have to do with a slum child like Milana, even that girl's name is pretentious…' and Grazia turned away exhausted. Diego stood beside her, not sure what to do next. A moment later Grazia got out of the chair and walked away leaving Diego standing alone. But then, on reflection, she turned back and kissed him on the cheek.

'It must be tough for you to see Santiago so ill,' she said. 'You've been a faithful friend, Diego.' He stood quite still imbibing the scent of Chanel as she strode away down the passage.

That night, Milana slept in Santiago's bedroom while Lizzy slept in the guest room and Diego lay on the sofa in the sitting room unable to sleep. He tiptoed to Lizzy's bedroom and knocked softly. There was no answer. He pushed open the door. Lizzy lay fast asleep, her face upwards, her hair spread over the pillow. For a few moments he watched her sleeping. Then, remembering his purpose, he reached out to touch her shoulder. She opened her eyes, startled, and sat up suddenly.

'What's the matter?' she asked anxiously. 'What's happened?'

'Nothing, I just need to talk to you. I have to get this off my chest.'

Lizzy wrapped her thin silk dressing gown around her and got out of bed.

'Come on then, let's go to the kitchen.'

'Grazia is right, Lizzy. She has first call. After all, she's his mother. Milana had no right at all to go and see Santiago without her permission,' Diego passed his hand over his face, 'Oh God, this is so difficult. You see, I kind of see where Grazia's coming from.'

'Oh Diego, of course you do,' sighed Lizzy, getting herself a glass of water. She turned towards him, inclining her head on one side, looking at him thoughtfully. 'But you've only heard her story, Diego. You know nothing about Milana. Besides Diego, it was my idea she go in. She'd never have thought of it herself. She looked so dazed and lost, you should have seen her. It was my call that brought her out here in the first place. And you know Grazia would never have given permission for her to see him.'

'But Lizzy, you don't know Milana either, you've only just met her.'

'Oh but I do. Santiago talked to me about her in England. He could have had any woman there, but no one really got a look in.' At this, Diego raised his eyebrows and Lizzy, with just a hint of heightened colour, continued, 'He committed to no one. If anything it made him infinitely more attractive. I was the one who came closest to him. Of course I was attracted by his looks. Who wouldn't be? But I was attracted even more to his inaccessibility. There he was on his own, desired by all, wanting none. I wanted to know why? I was intrigued by him. "Obsessed" would be the right word. When I discovered her existence I think I became more intrigued than ever. All he wanted was to marry her and have babies with her. This super hero, so mysterious and sought after, just wanted to love so simply. He was haunted by her Diego. He simply couldn't bring himself to love anyone else. I know he tried to forget her, he really tried. I was there, I lived it.'

'How could he love her?' said Diego shaking his head. 'He met her when she was fourteen or something. It's kind of crazy.' But he guessed it was Milana Santiago had meant when he'd spoken to him in Panguipulli, it was all he allowed himself to remember of that strange conversation.

'I think she's special, Diego. Does she strike you as a typical eighteen-year-old even now? And I'll bet she'd lived more, and I mean really lived, in her fourteen years, when he met her, than most of us live in a life time.'

'What if she's using him, Lizzy?'

'How the hell do you use a sick man?'

'I don't know. She's got a major exhibition coming up, her first. It could launch her if she's involved in a scandal or whatever, what's the saying; there's no such thing as bad publicity!'

'You really think Milana took advantage of my call and decided to come here on a marketing ruse. Come off it. I had to persuade her. She's the one who turned Santiago away. She made it impossible for him to find her. She didn't want anything to do with him.'

'So why is she here now?'

'Ultimately because I convinced her to come or she'd never have dared.'

'I don't know, Lizzy, there's some steely determination about her.'

'That's what has made her a survivor. How many shantytown girls do you get to talk to? How come you're talking to this one? Because of her determination, that's why. It's what makes her attractive.' Instinctively, Lizzy put out her hand and touched his. 'Don't let Grazia work her spell on you. Just because Milana is talented that doesn't make her a scheming gold digger.' Diego had to concentrate to figure out what Lizzy had just said, his eyes were riveted to where her hand had touched his.

After a moment he said, 'I don't know about that, I don't like these over-ambitious types.'

Lizzy laughed, 'Oh come on. Then you don't like the modern woman.'

'Maybe not,' said Diego leaning back, 'I like the old fashioned, feminine, kind, gracious, generous woman, not one that's aggressively out for herself.'

'But you do find Milana attractive?'

'What?'

'Oh come on, there's no crime in it, I saw how you looked at her.'

'I find her intriguing, just like you do.'

'It annoys you that you find her attractive and that's why you've sided with Grazia.'

'Lizzy are you mad?'

'No, I'm just perceptive. First of all Milana is beautiful, really beautiful. She's got the face of an angel, like she's lived miles away from any world we know and that's immensely appealing.

Then she's humble. There are no airs about her, she is just herself, and she's not afraid of people, she's just wary of them. Finally, the most attractive trait of all, she's confident, genuinely confident like you rarely see in people. Usually it's their money or their breeding or their clothes that make people confident. With Milana, she just is. She exists for a purpose, whether that purpose is to paint or to love or to bring Santiago back to us… that is what you call her steely determination, but I'd say that is what made Santiago love her. She is the most truthful person I've ever met. I'm not surprised Grazia is terrified of her because Grazia is the least truthful person I've ever met.'

'What?'

'Yes. Underneath her airs and manner and passions, Grazia is a very vulnerable woman and that's why you've allowed her tantrums. You fell for that. You're not a bad guy, Diego,' Lizzy couldn't help a smirk. 'You're really quite compassionate.'

She paused and cocked her head to one side whilst looking at Diego. Just for a moment, their eyes locked.

'Now, I've got to get some sleep. Don't think about Milana then you'll dream about her instead!' She touched him gently on the shoulder as she went, leaving him pensive, the impression of her touch indelibly fixed in his mind.

The next morning, early, Lizzy opened the front door to Diego who was holding two coffees from the corner cafe.

'Milana's still sleeping.'

'OK, I'll have the coffee then.'

He put it down in the kitchen.

'I did,' he said.

'You did what?'

'Like you said, I did dream about her.'

Lizzy laughed.

'That always happens when you suppress a thought that's powerful. You invariably dream about it.'

'Yeah, but I dreamt about you too.'

'You did?'

'Yup.'

'Can I ask in what capacity?'

'You were talking too much and I just leant over and kissed you and you shut up.'

Diego passed her the coffee. Lizzy met his eye.

'It was quite nice,' he added casually

'Only "quite" nice?' Lizzy raised a playful eyebrow, 'And what about Milana?'

'I dreamt we were at Grazia's funeral and Milana was by the coffin. As I came up, she turned to me, tears flooding down her face, and I put my arms around her and she just sobbed and sobbed.'

'I guess that was quite nice too.'

'No, it was quite different, and not as nice.'

Diego met her eyes again. They both looked at each other in silence. It was a significant silence between two people coming to terms with new thoughts and feelings as an unexpected understanding dawns between them.

Chapter Sixteen

Grazia's face was awash with tears.

'He opened his eyes!' she dabbed her face with a lace handkerchief. 'Oh I've prayed so much for this. I knew that healer yesterday would do it. I had so much faith in her. I just never believed that it would be so quick.'

Lizzy and Diego exchanged looks. Lizzy got up and made her way out of the waiting area. Diego followed.

'I'm phoning Milana,' she whispered. 'If anyone brought him back, it was her.'

'We'll work something out,' Diego had said before he and Lizzy left that morning. He had braced himself for tears and outrage from Milana but she had received the news of Grazia's fury with quiet dignity, apologising for putting them through it and letting him know that after flouting the rules as she had the outcome was inevitable.

'Don't worry, Milana,' added Lizzy, embracing her. 'You didn't come all this way for nothing, you'll see.' They left quickly and Milana sensed their awkwardness.

Milana shut herself in the bathroom and turned on the shower. She looked on the bathroom shelf and moved the shaving cream to pick up a bottle of shampoo hidden behind. As she did so, something dropped into the sink. She stared into the white ceramic bowl where the small bead bracelet had made an unsuccessful bid for escape down the plughole. Picking it up she turned it between her fingers; the little bracelet that Ines had given her. The paint had worn off so that the natural wood showed through. How often must he have worn it for the paint to wear off?

Sitting on the carpet in the bedroom an hour later, her hair still damp around her shoulders, Milana unzipped a large leather portfolio that she had found tucked out of sight behind a writing desk. The dust that she unsettled flew into the path of a sunbeam and for a moment she became distracted as she watched the many glittering particles trapped in a sudden upward spiral. The sun-warmed leather released a faint aroma that reminded her of him. She laid it open. It was full of artwork, as might have been expected.

The first picture was an abstract 'study in blues' conjuring up the blues of the blossoming jacaranda tree by the graveyard under which they talked so often that summer. He had said to her once, 'Colour is why I paint.' Santiago could make colour come alive like an emotion. It was followed by a study in reds, then a study in yellows and so on. Big beautiful paintings full of scintillating colour. As with music or smell, the colours stirred vivd memories. She picked up the next and stared at it enthralled. No more than a doodle on a piece of white sketch pad, so few lines but definitely herself. Behind that, there was another drawing, more detailed and larger.

There followed sketch after sketch, all of her, all in pencil, each one more detailed than the previous; as though with each rendering, the memory had come clearer into focus until it was herself, now, perfectly remembered. Each line appeared so fluid it almost moved. The eyes seemed to stare back at her, a blink away from life, the whole face in limbo waiting for a breath, a kiss, to animate it. She laid her hand on the smooth paper as though she were mystically realigning herself to his memory. Then she rose and went to the bed and lay face down on it, to feel his presence, drink him in, but that wasn't enough. Milana went to the cupboard where his jackets hung and buried her face in the fabric to breathe in his smell to bring him alive, here, now. But nothing was enough. Her whole being hungered for his presence.

She lay on his bed remembering the night he had come to her, the night in the shack when she had given him the bracelet she now wore. She recalled his touch, his closeness, his kisses, until her whole being was pulled taut, every nerve strained and the anguish was sweet because she was alive to him, responding to him as though he were there, a promise on the verge of fulfilment.

The phone rang.

'Milana, he's awake. He opened his eyes.'

Milana gasped, 'Thank God.' There was a long pause. 'Have you seen him? Who was with him?'

'Grazia. She said he recognised her.'

'If you see him, tell him I'm here. Tell him, Lizzy.'

'Of course I will. It's only just happened, I must go back now, but I'll ring you, are you OK?'

'Yes.'

'You did this, Milana. You brought him back.'

All day they had waited for a chance to see Santiago, but nobody was allowed in, not even Grazia. Grazia had not moved from the waiting area. Her friends brought her lunch and coffee and tea. Now it was dark outside and it was snowing again. Tomorrow, the doctor had said, would bring them more news and, hopefully, a chance to see him. The staff were urging Grazia to leave and get a good night's rest when a senior nurse approached her. 'He's asked to see you.'

'At last!' Grazia looked triumphant, and followed the nurse through the swing doors.

Santiago opened his eyes. He felt Grazia's hand briefly on his.

'They say you've been here every day?' His voice was husky.

'Why's his voice like that?' Grazia whispered to the nurse who was still standing beside her.

'It's the intubation. It will have irritated his vocal chords for a while that's all.'

'It's been days and days, darling, I was so worried,' whispered Grazia.

She sat on the edge of the chair that had been placed by his bed.

'Could you hear me Santiago, when I talked to you? Were you conscious?'

After a long pause he whispered, 'I was with Father.'

Santiago's eyes were focused on her.

'Are you sure?' she asked weakly. What little colour she had drained.

He closed his eyes as if to verify it in his mind's eye, then his gaze locked onto hers again. He moved his hand to the edge of the bed, extending it towards her. She came closer, pulling the chair up. She put her beautifully manicured hand in his and he closed his fingers over it.

'He said he forgave you.'

Her eyes opened a little wider.

'He said that I was to forgive you too.'

Santiago watched the vein appear on her forehead which displayed her heightened level of emotion. He saw the muscles tighten in her neck imperceptibly lifting the gold choker she wore.

'Forgave me? You, forgive me?' Her voice came out strangled. 'What for?'

Nothing stirred, only the whirr of the monitors.

Santiago watched her. She could not meet his scrutiny and for long silent minutes her eyes remained fixed on where his hand held hers.

'Have you? Forgiven me?' she whispered at last.

'Yes,' he mouthed. Her hand covered her mouth to stop it trembling.

'How did you know? You weren't there?'

'I was,' Santiago spoke slowly, he paused to swallow painfully, 'standing in the doorway all the time.' Santiago closed his eyes.

When, after tremulous moments of silence she could bring herself to lift her eyes to his face she saw his eyes closed and the tracks of his tears. A sudden, desperate sob wrenched through her. Then another. She let go of his hand and bent right down as each uncontrollable spasm shook her to the core. With effort Santiago lifted his hand and placing it on his mother's hair, stroked it, very gently, feeling the sobs heave through her.

After some time, she gradually regained control of herself and whispered, 'You've been so alone.' She put her hand up to Santiago's face. 'My beautiful, beautiful boy, I lost you years ago,' she murmered, leaning over him her face awash with tears.

She stroked his face.

'I was so afraid of losing you, I was so afraid of losing your father; I ended up losing everything.' She bent her head and now her tears fell on him.

Santiago reached his hand up and gently gripped the arm that cradled his face.

'You haven't lost me, Mother,' he whispered slowly. 'You have just won me back.'

Grazia sobbed quietly for a long time, for all the years of pretending, of holding back the truth. Suddenly she pulled herself together and focused on Santiago. His eyes were closed again.

'Do you feel all right, Santiago?' she whispered urgently.

She watched a smile faintly crease his face into the familiar rugged lines around his mouth, 'I feel free.'

Grazia pressed her lips together, her face contorted with pain, 'All these years, you felt trapped by me.' Her hand covered her mouth and she couldn't continue.

'I felt trapped by what I witnessed, I prayed to be healed inside,' he spoke with difficulty pausing yet again for breath, 'Now I've faced it, I can forgive.'

She longed to bury her face in his hair and cradle him to her but she didn't dare. His breathing became slow and even. It seemed that he slept. A nurse appeared at the door and moved away, oblivious of the towering emotions that filled that small room.

Caught between silence and truth she reached out to take his hand, seeking his reassurance, but she stopped herself, afraid of waking him and clasped her hands on her lap. Finally she began to speak, very slowly, head bent, in a whisper, as though she were rehearsing lines to herself.

'All these years you must have carried my guilt. What a terrible burden, I gave you.' She gave a little sniff and fought the uncontrollable quivering of her lips. 'I wanted you to belong to me completely. I guarded you so jealously. But nothing belongs to us completely, I learnt that as I watched you here, nearly die. Our children are a gift, like you were to us. We can't keep them, or tie them down.'

She forgot about the bright lights of the hospital and the whirring of the monitors, she heard only the silence onto which she was impressing her words, as they rose clear and unequivocal from the place she had not dared visit for so long; her conscience.

'You're not like me. You're brave. You could not hurt a soul, Santiago.' Tears fell down her face.

'I didn't want to lose you.'

She took a shaky deep breath and sat staring at her hands on her lap, twisting the large diamond ring on her finger, feeling the pressure of years lifting from her heart as she surrendered to the impulse to confess everything.

'You are my most precious gift and I treasure you with all my heart, but I never gave birth to you.' Her whole body shuddered. 'I watched you grow so talented, so beautiful and so distant and I longed, above all, to feel I had the natural right of a mother over you.' She pressed the lace handkerchief to her nose and mouth.

'All the time, I knew I had given you nothing, not your talent, nor your courage or your faith or your inspiration and most certainly not your goodness, and I have acted as a coward all my life. When I tried to take my own life, it was you, small as you were, who reminded me I had a responsibility to live.' With a deep sigh she looked up at him.

Santiago's eyes were open.

She gave a little gasp.

'You can't be a coward if you love,' he whispered. 'It takes courage.'

For a long time they were both silent. Then, as if he could read her thoughts, he whispered, 'It's OK, Mum, I think I've always known.'

She reached for his hand, 'You were so innocent, Santiago, you came to bring us so much joy and I… I destroyed it all. I ripped that world of childish happiness and wonder from you, as if you were holding a prize and I just tore it from you and watched you look at me from then on, uncomprehending. You couldn't understand that I could bring you so much pain. I understand that now and I would give my life to make it up to you; all that I took away. I have never been anything but pain and sadness to you.'

His deep blue eyes rested on Grazia.

'If I had lost you Santiago without all this left unsaid, my life would have been worthless. Do you know that?'

'So now it's OK if I die,' he coughed and then he was smiling, his old mischievous smile and through her tears, she found she could smile again.

Santiago closed his eyes. A nurse tiptoed in. She looked nervously at Grazia, 'His heart rate is very irregular,' she whispered noting the red swollen eyes of the mother.

'Give me one more minute, please,' answered Grazia. The nurse leaned over Santiago, about to open his eyes and check them when he opened them.

'Just one minute then,' she whispered and left.

'I wish I could do something for you, Santiago, anything to…'

'You *can*.' He paused and swallowed. Grazia saw the words could barely come, so she drew up close. His voice was a mere whisper.

'Milana. Is she here? I…' He brought his hand up to his throat and tried to clear it.

'Lizzy,' his breathing came as a gentle shudder, ' Ask Lizzy…'

Grazia took his hand and pressed it against her mouth, maybe to steady her answer, maybe to drink from his inner strength.

'Lizzy is here,' she said quietly.

He swallowed again and shook his head. 'Tomorrow,' and he closed his eyes.

Grazia stepped out into the cold night and let the wind blow through her hair as though it were blowing out the cobwebs of the past. She was not a woman of prayer, but she did believe in some form of afterlife. Maybe Santiago had wavered on the edge of death, maybe he had truly reached out into the hereafter and found some light and understanding there that had laid to rest all the ghosts of the past and brought him the peace that had escaped his soul for so long. Maybe he really had seen Carlos.

For a long time, Grazia walked. Her suede boots ruined by the snow, but she didn't care. Neither the freezing wind nor the snow that fell like sleet across her path and stung her cheeks, deterred her footsteps. She was too restless to return to her hotel and too elated to sleep. The longing to atone overwhelmed her like a great wave, turning over all the events of the past, dredging up buried memories as she scoured the lies and the pretence of years.

Grazia found herself before the doors of St. John the Divine. On an impulse she climbed the steps and pushed open the door of the great church. The flicker of many votive candles sent shadows playing across the walls. The smell of incense and wood polish mixed with a slightly more sour smell of an unwashed body. Grazia looked down at the pew over which she was standing. A man sat there, his hands folded on his lap; a cigarette, unlit, between his grimy fingers. He looked up at the woman who had blown in on an icy wind.

'You got a light, Miss?'

Grazia looked at him bemused.

'You got a light, Miss?' he repeated politely, his eyes fixed on her.

She peered at him in the half light. 'You're so young. Haven't you got a home?'

'I like it here, it's peaceful. You want to sit down?' And as though that back pew was the only one available in the huge empty church, he moved up to make room for her.

Grazia felt a childish pleasure in being here alone, not having to pretend to be anything at all. She sat down. It seemed somehow impossible to do otherwise. As a fine animal might momentarily sniff a rough mongrel, her mink brushed the edges of his old coat, before slipping off the bench and trailing the cold floor. Her gloved fingers clasped each other for comfort.

'You going to pray then?' he asked, with alarming ingeniousness.

'I…I…' Grazia looked at his hands so still on his lap. She felt inexplicably drawn to this young man.

'Do you pray?' she retorted.

'Yep.'

'What do you say?'

'I say "Hello Jesus, it's Mitch, I've come to see you."'

'Does he ever answer back?'

'He's not very chatty.' The man grinned at her. His teeth were surprisingly white.

'He kind of answered once, though.'

'How could He answer?' she shifted, intrigued.

'I was taken bad in an accident. They said I was for it,' graphically he passed his finger across his throat to indicate what he meant. 'My time was up.'

'But how did He answer you?' Grazia insisted.

'I was in the hospital; all wired up, and maybe I was conscious, maybe I weren't. This guy sits on the end of my bed and says, "Hello Mitch, it's Jesus, I've come to see you." Just like I says it to Him.' He paused as though to savour the memory. 'After that I pulled through. So I come back here every day just to say Hi!'

All the tragedies of her life that had been stacked behind her, fell away as she found herself suddenly humbled. The perception of her own insignificance took shape as a welcome and undeniable fact breaking down the exacting confines of her restless mind. She found herself overcome by the frailty and nobility of mankind.

Grazia reached into her Hermes bag and searched for her wallet. Removing from its silken interior all the hundred dollar bills that nestled there she offered them to him, 'Please take them. You've helped me more than you can know.'

'Oh no. That's what fucked me up see, Miss. Just a light, Miss.'

Grazia left the church lost in thought. When finally a taxi drew up beside her and the driver shouted 'Lady, want a lift?' She took up the offer. She wandered into the hotel bar and sat at a table. The bar was closed but she didn't notice. A young waiter who was clearing up went to her table and asked if he could help. She looked up and ordered a mineral water. He got the water and placed it on her table. There was a brittle fragility about her. He watched her for a while. She didn't drink, she just sat in her fur coat, her hands folded on the table.

Snatched images floated in and out of her mind in slow motion, voices from the past spoke in muted tones. Everything was coming back to her.

It is I who have been in a coma all these years. The thought superimposed itself like a commentary on everything she saw. First she was sitting on a park bench. Carlos Hidalgo so young and immensely attractive, was holding her hand, 'Remember I may never be able to give you children. You must take your time to think about it.' And she was looking at the big diamond solitaire he had given her, resting smugly on her fourth finger. And in her head she thought, *I can't lose him. I love the rock on my finger that shows I belong to him. I never want to take it off*, so she had looked at him and said, 'We can adopt.'

Next, she was standing by the door of the drawing room of their rented house in California. The door was ajar, it was late at night. Inside Carlos was talking to an old college friend. Grazia stayed listening unseen to their conversation.

'I didn't mean it to happen, one thing led to another, we were so intimate once. Don't judge me Carlos, just understand it was a night of laying to rest ghosts of the past but it didn't work out like that.'

Carlos was sighing, 'It never does old friend. We lay down old ghosts and new ones rise up to haunt us.'

Grazia could see the man with his head in his hands. She moved back slightly.

'How can I help?' Carlos said.

'She won't abort and I don't want her to. She was the first girl I ever loved, Carlos, but the timing wasn't right, nothing was right, maybe you remember me saying.' Carlos was nodding.

'It's all so complicated.'

Very slowly, because the solution was only just forming in his mind,' Carlos said 'You want us to adopt your baby?'

There was a long pause. She thought they would be able to hear her heart pounding through the silence. This was the answer to all her misfortunes. She would return home triumphant with a child, no one would ask questions and she need never tell the child that he or she wasn't her own blood baby. That night she lay back on her pillows and smiled. 'My baby.'

She saw herself taking her first steps into the Chilean sunshine; the sound of the plane's engines still whirring and the heat blowing into her face, and in her arms the one-year-old Santiago. Friends waved from the airport building as she crossed the tarmac. They fawned over the beautiful baby. There was no place to ask 'Is it yours?' There never was. The question remained suspended forever somewhere between thought and word.

Then later, the news like a dagger in her side, the test that told Carlos that he didn't have cancer and, moreover he was fertile. The effects of TB had been only temporary. It had been a joyful moment for him and he had come in holding the letter like a reprieve. But for her it was a death sentence; *it is I then who can't have children. It's been me then all along. All those times we've slept together and no children. I'm the faulty one.*' She hadn't spoken of it again and Carlos never mentioned it but it taunted her never allowing her peace; *he loves children and I can't give him one. He'll love me less. He'll want to have one of his own with someone else.*

Her consolation…Santiago. Night after night she cried into his milky warmth as he lay sleeping. She clung to him for strength and hope and belief in herself. His eyes gazing up at her with endless love and devotion were a balm to her fraying nerves, 'I love you Mummy,' he said into her ear at happy moments and when at nights her tears fell on his face, and then the gentle yet random supplication, 'Please don't ever die.'

Then that terrible night coming home a little tipsy and finding the maid, Iris, standing by the gate. The rain pouring down drenching her, her heart sinking, the whole of her drowning as Iris told her that her fears were confirmed; now he would have his child and from a fresh-faced maid. Then the surge of anger gripping her, like a desperate attempt to keep her afloat... walking in and seeing them there, the two of them in the study. Blinded to truth by her worst fears...the death wish had been for herself... *I want to die* her whole being screamed out and went on screaming as she lifted the lamp that was meant to smash her thoughts, deliver her from her anguish but instead, delivered the fatal blow. Nights followed, endless nights of thinking about Letty's child. The child that was also Carlos's. She saw herself standing by the iron bridge, Iris holding the beautiful baby girl as she cut a lock of her hair off and put it in an envelope. Then the day the tests came through; irrevocable proof that the child was not his. He had not been unfaithful. Her anger, her fears; all misplaced, all misguided. Her fears had destroyed everything and all for no reason.

The night she tried to take the pills it was Santiago's cries that brought her to her senses; the night terrors that tortured his little body and sent him rigid, had saved her from herself. She held his hand through them. He justified her existence; he gave meaning to her life. For him, she told herself, she must go on. He was the reason she must live.

There it stopped. Her mind did not dwell on memories of the boy growing up or the nightmares that so often gripped him. Instead it replayed scene after painful scene of her past with Carlos, even as she climbed up to bed, as she undressed and lay between the cold hotel sheets. Each time her conscience became a little more alive to them. Her feelings now, began to relate to her feelings then. She was being pulled back to the yesterday of her life. It was as though her face were being held fast against a mirror of truth, forcing her to look, and look again, and not just look but see, see what happened, why it happened, what she did and why she did it. 'This is real' screamed her conscience, as it became more and more fully awake... this is real, the rest was a lie.

By the time dawn streaked across the New York sky, Grazia had realised that in taking Santiago away from her, albeit briefly while he lay in a coma, life had forced her to face her own wretchedness. Her aching heart had revealed itself to her like a bird fluttering wildly in a trap. The pain had been almost unbearable but now she struggled to free what she knew was real and good.

Grazia watched the sky turn from mauve to lilac and a streak of green, pale and luminous form to the east of the city. The green grew brighter and a stroke of yellow began to spread along the horizon until suddenly the whole sky seemed to blush pink, then orange and finally the tip of the sun, like a great red fireball, nudged its way onto the horizon. She marvelled at all the spectacle and drama that orchestrated together to bring just one day into being. Her spirit was stirred and she longed to embrace this new day, in which for the first time she seemed to be discovering so much beauty and feeling.

Snow heaped on the sides of pavements glittered in the early light. Grazia experienced the first stirrings of the city; yawning cats and early risers from one night stands and those who, like her, had not slept that night. She watched as life seeped into the streets. Tyres slushed through the wet snow. Engines revved and exhaust pipes threw their blue mist in great clouds. The clatter of human beings in motion overtook the city. Grazia stepped into a café across the road from the building where Carlos had bought the apartment when they moved back to Chile. She didn't notice Diego come into the café and order three coffees to take away, and he never saw her because he never looked.

Eventually she saw Lizzy and Diego leave the building together. She watched them hail a cab and get into it. The cab disappeared in the direction of the hospital. Grazia rose from the table, paid and stepped out into the bright cold sunshine.

Chapter Seventeen

Milana sat at the computer and following Diego's instructions, tried to send the email she had written to Lisa but it didn't seem to want to go.

She paused and read through it again.

Dear Lisa,

I did get to see Santiago because they mistook me for some healer Señora Grazia was bringing along. He looked serene and peaceful but far away from us all. I wonder where he's been. I didn't want to leave the room, I didn't want to leave him but I had to. Grazia found out what I'd done and banned me, but, Lisa, guess what? The next day he opened his eyes.

Lizzy will talk to him today and maybe something will happen. I am afraid of Grazia. She's very angry with me. She holds me responsible for everything. I guess I'm the scapegoat, that's what Diego says. She's like a guard. She's there night and day. I don't see how I'll ever get to see him and he's far too weak to stand up to her now.

I watched the sun rise over New York today. It was beautiful, it reminded me of home, I wanted to paint it. I hope Hernan will take me to Santiago's studio today.

I can't help wondering if my visit brought him back (Lizzy says it did) and that was what I was meant to do. I think I should come home now and wait.

Lizzy and Diego are staying an extra week and then Lizzy has decided to travel on to Chile with Diego and maybe visit San Pedro de Atacama! Lizzy is a real friend. I think Lizzy and Diego like each other. Maybe I'm in the way. I think I will come home now.

Thank you for everything. New York is a bit frightening, you know, a bit too big and tall and loud, but the sunrise made it better. It kind of put New York in its place.

    Love

    Milana

Milana pressed the 'send' button, but the message would not go.

The doorbell rang.

'Hernan is that you?' Milana went up to the door. 'Who's there?'

'Milana?'

Milana didn't recognise the voice.

'It's Grazia Menendez.'

Milana remained momentarily paralysed. Grazia Menedez stood there wrapped in her formidable furs. Her face appeared unusually devoid of cosmetic assistance. She looked softer, her lips pale, her eyes kinder; the natural lines around them gave her a gentleness that Milana had not seen before, when mascara and eyeliner had accentuated the feline slant. Grazia wore make-up to guard her against others and prepare her for battle. Without it she was just herself, a face that Milana had never seen before.

'May I come in?' she asked politely. Milana stood aside, holding the door open.

'I take it you're alone.' Grazia turned in the act of taking off her fur hat. Milana stepped forward out of politeness to take the coat and place it on a chair.

'This used to be my apartment you know, I've got little use for it now. I suppose you wonder why I'm here.'

Milana shook her head. Grazia eyed her, 'Come, surely you must wonder?'

'It's not my place to wonder anything. This is your apartment and I have no right to be here.'

Grazia seemed surprised.

'Then why *are* you here, Milana?' she said glancing over her shoulder as she walked towards the kitchen.

'Do you want the truth?' Milana replied following her resolutely into the kitchen.

'The truth would be good,' Grazia looked at her with interest.

'For Santiago.'

'Why would he need you?' She filled the kettle with water, first checking it inside and pouring out the tepid contents. Milana stared at Grazia's fingers curled around the handle of the kettle; her painted nails, her diamond rings.

'Why do you think he never mentioned you to his friends, Milana?'

'Because they would have laughed at him.'

Grazia looked at Milana.

'Why?'

There was something fiercely compelling in her questions. It was like Grazia was throwing bait to catch Milana's thoughts, and like eager fish they were inevitably swimming up to it through the waters of uncertainty.

'Because people laugh at what they don't understand,' Milana shrugged.

'And what is there to understand?' The question from Grazia was real and sincere.

'The longings and the absences in each human being.'

'The absences?'

'We search for what's missing in us, what will make us complete.'

'Santiago felt empty when you met him?'

'I don't know. If he did he wasn't empty at all because he gave me more than I could ever have dreamed of receiving.'

'So you felt empty?'

'I didn't know I did until I saw him. He made me aware of loss; just seeing him made me feel overcome with a feeling of loss.' Milana recalled the day she had seen him and how she had cried and cried as if her heart would break…

'Maybe you felt *his* loss. Maybe it was *his* emptiness that overcame you.'

Milana stared at Grazia. But Grazia wasn't looking at her. She had moved away and was looking towards the skyline out of the window.

'You understand?' Milana whispered. 'Are you telling me you understand?'

'I don't know what I understand but I watched the sunrise this morning. The most spectacular show in the world played out every day and I'd never really seen it. I was humbled. I felt small and very insignificant and I realised that I could only bear it if I let it be.' She turned and looked at Milana. 'I've been through my dark night of the soul. I don't pretend to understand, I don't want to pretend anymore. I hated you. Now I'm trying to reach out to you.' She looked rather magnificent and intimidating.

Milana looked down. She felt Grazia's eyes fix on her.

'Don't you want to know why, Milana?' Milana shook her head.

'I hated you because you filled his loss, his emptiness. What I created in him. He craved a kind of love I couldn't give. You satisfied his yearning. He needed you to survive me. Now he needs you to survive.'

'Santiago doesn't need me to survive,' Milana said quietly. 'Love is a gift from God. It heals us and makes us stronger, it searches out the best in us and challenges us to become our best. My mother used to say you can't feel love unless you embrace life, then life embraces you back and fills your soul with love. Santiago is so honest and real he searched for love and he found it in God and in nature and in his talent.'

Grazia considered for a moment and smiled. 'I think he needed something more tangible than that, Milana, and he found it in you.'

Milana looked up.

'I never want to take him from you, *Señora* Grazia, or hold him back.'

Tears intensified the greenness of Milana's eyes as they pooled and spilled unchecked and it seemed to Grazia that they purged the sadness in her own soul.

'I'm sorry,' Milana added fingering away her tears.

'There is a saying, Milana, that you can only sow love with tears.' She pressed her lips together as though to avoid succumbing to emotion herself, and went on. 'It's true I shunned you, Milana because, amongst other things, you were taking him from me. Now I realise you can't steal what's God given, you can only receive it graciously. I have never known how to do that. I've failed to love well.' Milana looked up at her and met Grazia's pale clear eyes. 'I believe that's why Life nearly took Santiago from me; it gave me a chance to redeem myself.' She pursed her lips thoughtfully.

'We're always only one step away from love,' sighed Milana.

'Can that be right?' Grazia looked perplexed, 'Did your mother say that too?'

Milana nodded. 'She said there's love all around us but we can't see it unless we fly higher.'

'Ah.' Grazia breathed in deeply. 'Fear can glue our wings, Milana, and fear breeds lies. I am not Santiago's real mother, I am his adopted mother.'

There was a long significant pause.

'My mother also said we have only one real mother, Our Lady in Heaven, the other is appointed the honour of caring for us on earth.'

'I like your mother. Now will you come with me to the hospital?'

Milana took a step back.

'He's been through so much. I may just be something that passed for him.'

'Each day passes Milana but we can't live without it.' Grazia reached out and touched her tear stained face. Milana felt her heart swell despite herself.

'You didn't need to come and speak to me like this. You don't owe me anything.'

'On the contrary, Milana, I owe you the happiness of my son. I owe you,' and Milana saw how, overcome suddenly by a grief she struggled to suppress, she covered her mouth and lifted her eyes away and her hand slipped down and rested on Milana's shoulder, as she mouthed the words, 'so much more…'

It was a barely audible whisper of admission from the heart, spoken to one who Grazia believed was ignorant of the magnitude of her crime, and Milana, herself overwhelmed by the magnanimity of love, accepted it gratefully.

Chapter Eighteen

Matias drove like a maniac down the dusty deserted highway. Insects met ignominious deaths smacked against his car windscreen and unsuspecting lizards lay flattened in his wake. He took another bend with relish, speeding into it as though to feel the sideways thrust of the car more vigorously. He glanced at his passenger.

'You doing OK there, Santiago? My driving isn't everyone's cup of tea, I've been told.'

Santiago managed a weak smile. His head ached and each bend made him feel sicker than the last. He wondered how long he could hold out. He'd tried closing his eyes but that made the movement of the car all the more invasive.

'It's probably the excitement,' Matias added airily, 'overcome by the thrill of the chase.'

'Matias, what are you talking about?' Santiago feigned incomprehension.

'Love, my dear boy.' He drew the word out in a way that made Santiago smile despite feeling awful.

'Always knew you had the hots for each other, you and Milana. There's a world of undisclosed emotion that spills over in paint, don't you know. Take that church down south for starters, your spirit in all of it. But her paintings here in Jardin de Rosas, that's its ancient name you know, they blew me away; innocence vying with raw sexuality and you in various guises smouldering away like a swashbuckling Zorro devil.' He laughed out loud. 'Never wanted to admit it to you, my boy, wouldn't have done to go ferreting her out of her hiding place. Marvellous place to paint you see down here, sequestered from the world, it puts you in touch with your inner demons. I'm making it up to you now!' He glanced at Santiago.

'Dear God you look like death, I knew I shouldn't have brought you, damn it, Santiago you're too persuasive for your own good.'

'I'll be fine,' Santiago insisted, 'It's not much longer is it?'

'We're seconds away. Look I haven't told them you're coming, I didn't want any fuss. Gonzalo and Stella will be delighted, always hankering for company, but Milana, well, just take it easy, she's under a lot of pressure to get these final paintings finished for the exhibition next month. Frankly I think it'll do you both good to see each other. Besides you're too weak for any hanky panky, you're still a convalescent, Santiago. Six weeks ago you were on the brink of the grave.'

The car swept up the drive and came to a standstill by a large palm tree.

Santiago ripped open the door and stood against the car taking great gulps of air. It had taken all his willpower not to throw up.

'You walk off that headache, my boy, before you see anyone. Take a seat on those wicker chairs in the rose garden, or watch the sunset. I'll disappear up here and find the family.' And he sauntered off towards the stone steps which he took two by two with the alacrity of a much younger man.

Instead of walking towards the house, Santiago strolled to where young vines were planted in long lines leading to the horizon. Each line end was marked with a red rose bush to act as early warning for mildew. They were laden with full blossoms. He thrust his hands in his pockets and felt the nausea ease. To the right, by a long low building that he took to be the stables, he saw a tap. As he approached, a small grey kitten scampered round the corner and finding a moving object accosted Santiago's leg playing vigorously with the end of his jeans.

Santiago crouched down and stroked the cat before turning on the tap and letting the water spill over his hands. He put his hands to his face feeling the relief of the cool water soaking his skin. He wet his hair and neck and noticed that the cat was playing with the stream of water and becoming thoroughly confused and wet. He turned off the tap and picked it up.

'Who do you belong to?' he said looking into its tiger eyes.

'Me.'

Consuelo had been watching him for a while, too afraid to disturb him but very much wanting to rescue her kitten.

'It's a very pretty cat,' he said handing it back to its young owner. 'What's it's name?'

'My name's Consuelo and he's Messy. Have you come to see Milana?'

'Milana?' he looked so surprised that Consuelo took a step back. But Santiago crouched down quickly and beckoned to her to come closer.

'Do you know where she is? I've really come to surprise her.'

Consuelo's eyes grew rounder.

'She's just round the corner painting. Are you her boyfriend?' Santiago half smiled.

'Well are you?'

'That depends,' he confided, 'if you show me where she is, but very quietly so I can just watch her for a while painting then, when she turns round, you can watch her and tell me how pleased you think she is to see me and then I'll know if she really wants to be my girlfriend.'

'Don't you know if she'll be pleased?' asked Consuelo as she led him around the back of the building.

'One can never be sure with women, what they're thinking. Right, Consuelo?' She glanced up at him self-importantly and he put his finger to his lips, 'Don't let her know we're coming.' Consuelo responded by giving Santiago her most radiant smile.

'Do you want to hold Messy?' she whispered.

'No, Messy might give the game away. You go in and just pretend I'm not here.'

Consuelo skipped into the stable and went to stand beside Milana. She was so breathless and eager that Milana glanced quickly at her.

'Oh dear Messy's all wet,' she declared.

'He took a bath.' Consuelo giggled and after a moment stole a look behind her to where the handsome man stood quietly leaning against the stable wall. He smiled at her and put his finger to his lips to remind her to keep their secret.

'It's a butterfly isn't it?' said Consuelo taking a long, earnest look at the picture Milana was working on.

'A beautiful, beautiful butterfly being born from a rock. Is that how butterflies are born, Milana? Is it?'

Milana couldn't help laughing.

'No, Consuelo, caterpillars turn into butterflies after a long time spent quietly to themselves.'

'So why's this butterfly inside a rock.'

'Well, you see how I've split this rock open, to show, beneath its dull grey surface, all its fabulous veins of colour inside, that you would never usually see. I like to think that all these colours in strange wavy patterns are like its language. If we could read them they would tell us all about this rock, every colour would speak of a different experience that made it up. I've painted this butterfly so that the veins of the rock become the colours of the butterfly. See. They perfectly match up, because I want to say that all things evolve but are connected by the same shared experience of creation. If we could just align them all we would see how they all fitted into one perfect harmony. Do you see?'

Consuelo didn't see at all but she grinned showing a perfect row of baby teeth.

'What's harmony?'

'It's when everything is at peace together and nothing seems out of place,' replied Milana dabbing her brush into various colours to create an altogether new shade.

Consuelo looked over her shoulder again, but Santiago was too absorbed in watching Milana and didn't seem to see her looking so she turned to Milana and confided in a whisper, 'There's a man watching you.'

Milana turned sharply and Consuelo watched as her face registered surprise then a slow blush of happiness and the young man gave a sort of helpless 'I've been caught' look and shrugged.

'I wish Matias wouldn't send you so bloody far away to paint, it's frightfully inconvenient,' he said casually, without moving. His voice sounded so deep and melodious that Consuelo looked at him more closely. He had been rather nonchalantly leaning his arm against a low beam but now she noticed he thrust his hands in his pockets and stood like the boys sometimes did at school when the prettiest girls talked to them.

Consuelo walked over to where he stood, and touched his arm. As he automatically took his hand out of his pocket she put her hand in his and looked up.

'Don't you want to say hello to her properly,' she suggested, while over her head their eyes held each other. Tiptoeing up to get closer to his ear she whispered, 'I think she's really happy to see you. You're not cross with me are you?'

He shook his head and brushed her nose playfully.

'Why should I be cross with you, of all people?' he said tearing his eyes away from Milana to smile at Consuelo.

'Do you want to see where Messy sleeps?' And without waiting for an answer she pulled him away by the hand as though he owed it to her for sharing his secret. He looked over his shoulder, an even broader smile creasing his handsome face.

'Will you be staying for supper?' Milana called after him, preferring to let him go so she could savour the overwhelming feelings he produced in her.

'The whole weekend,' he called back, 'if I play my cards right,' he added indicating his young guide. Milana watched, her heart aching with exquisite anticipation, as Santiago was led up the steps of the house and into the inner courtyard.

'Well I could hardly refuse him the lift, now could I?' Matias was saying over the dinner table. 'But it was against my better judgement.' He waggled a long elegant finger in the direction of Milana and Santiago.

Gonzalo laughed, 'Father you were never such a hard taskmaster to me thank heavens.'

'That, my dear boy, is because you went into business and finance. If we are to rely on the creative juices, on the other

507

hand, these must be nurtured with infinite care and discipline. Young people, well,' he waved his arm about implying a certain degree of frivolity, 'they act as magnets on each other sending all the creative energy that was being expended on some great work in a far less advantageous direction,' and here he pinned Santiago with an accusatory look over his glasses that stood poised on the end of his nose.

'Surely one weekend with her muse won't do any damage?' Stella pointed out sweetly.

'Ah ha, the lady knows how to persuade. There you have it. The muse; resurrected and intact. Milana make the most of him but don't wear him out.' Milana coloured but held his gaze defiantly.

'If Grazia hasn't done that already, who can?' laughed Stella. 'Where did she take you, Santiago, to convalesce? The Carribean? I've forgotten?'

While they spoke the only thing Santiago was really aware of was the way Milana's bare foot played mischievously about his ankle while she helped little Consuelo through the complexities of eating an artichoke. He kept glancing at Milana to see whether she caught his eye but she pretended to be engrossed in her task, thus the pressure she was exerting on him from below appeared so singularly at odds with the reality of what was occurring above table that Santiago found himself more aroused than was comfortable. He raised his eyes to meet Stella's perceptive gaze and with his practiced nonchalance, that easily covered his embarrassment, he described in amusing detail his stay in a converted monastery in Taormina, Sicily, that his mother had taken him to regain his strength.

Finally, with dinner over, and having consumed several pear liquers by the roaring fire, Matias declared that he was escorting Milana to her sleeping quarters.

'All the excitement has made her very tired, we must take care of our budding prodigy who is only next month to emerge from the crysallis of anonymity to take the world by storm. Don't you see? Come my dear.' With a little backward glance of helpless resignation, Milana let herself be swept off.

'He guards her like a hawk,' said Gonzalo turning to Santiago and offering him another drink. 'It must be rather frustrating for you both.' He threw him an amused knowing look. 'I think he fears you might divert all those creative juices she has so successfully channelled into art.'

Santiago laughed and reclined on the sofa, his arms stretched along the back, the ankle of one leg balanced on the knee of the other.

'I'm not sure she's easily diverted. All the same I'm amazed he let me come at all, under the circumstances. We haven't actually seen each other since I was in the hospital in New York.'

Gonzalo took a sip of cognac and swirled the liquid in the glass.

'You've been through it old man.' He glanced at him, 'How are you now, I mean really? Are you quite recovered?'

'Remarkably, yes. It seems I'm pretty lucky to be alive. Meanwhile I haven't been allowed to do anything other than take in the view at various selected destinations. I had to postpone the exhibition in New York. But all things considered, I'm fit as a fiddle.'

'You look well, I must say.'

Stella came up to them and sat on the sofa beside Santiago.

'Did you feel things while you were in a coma, you know, see things, like a parallel world or anything?'

Santiago smiled wryly at her, 'Have you ever been in a coma, Stella?'

'No,' she waved her hand dismissively, 'but I have imagination and I believe we go into the subconscious and have adventures there when the rest of us is held at bay.'

'Maybe I agree with you,' he said meeting her inquisitive eyes with a cryptic look.

'What do you think of our young artist, then?' Stella ventured, realising he would not be drawn on the subject.

'Oh she has potential,' and then playfully he added, 'on many counts.'

509

'Did she bring you back, would you say? That's what I heard. That she brought you out of the coma.'

Santiago drew his fingers through his thick black mane. 'Oh I think Milana might bring any man out of a coma, wouldn't you say?'

'Oh come now,' she persisted, 'but did she do it for you?'

He seemed amused by the question.

'The doctors had been trying to bring me out of an induced coma and I wasn't responding well. Maybe the adventures I was on were far too exciting to abandon,' he jested, 'until I heard from her.' Stella pursed her lips and fixed him with her quiet scrutiny. He grew serious.

'I learnt one thing, Stella from all this, there's not much we're really in control of, be it in our minds or hearts or souls.' He straightened and decided to take his leave.

'You're very kind to have me here for the weekend, I hope Matias won't be disappointed by the results.'

Gonzalo laughed, 'He's probably standing sentry by Milana's door as we speak.'

Santiago raised a quizzical eyebrow at the implication. He put his empty glass on the table and stood up. 'I really wouldn't want Matias to think I'd kept you both up, after his clear instructions to us all,' he quipped. Stella glanced quickly at Gonzalo.

'You remember which room you're in?' Gonzalo said prompted by her look.

'Absolutely. I need no escort, thank you,' he replied with his usual easy grace and left them.

'Don't you think we should have told him which room Milana is in?' whispered Stella.

'Certainly not,' said Gonzalo resting himself back in his chair and stretching his arm out to offer her a sip of his drink. 'It's good this.'

'But don't you think…?'

'Stella, you really have very little faith in the male instinct. Try to remember we were hunters even at our most primitive.'

From the first moment Milana had become aware of Santiago's presence, watching her in the stables, right up to the moment she had left the drawing room with Matias after dinner, she and Santiago had not been alone for a single moment. All through drinks and dinner anticipation had twisted in her stomach like a restless creature. She had feigned indifference while making sure that only he knew where her thoughts lay. The excitement this produced within her was like an electrical current discharging low voltage shocks over and over in a kind of sweet torture until even breathing became something she had to concentrate on to keep it even. Finally Matias had escorted her out and given her a pep talk outside her door.

'My dear girl your hands are freezing, a clear indication that the heart is pumping too fast.' He had smiled disarmingly. 'I couldn't resist bringing Santiago this weekend, I think a snatched meeting might fuel rather than drain all your energies. But remember, Milana, you have a lifetime to love but only one more month to prepare for this exhibition and that requires you not to lose focus. You should sleep and tomorrow you can take a long walk together and discuss matters of the heart under the crisp light of day. Santiago will no doubt have another drink with Gonzalo and retire early. Sleep is essential for the healing process you know. So I wish you goodnight and happy dreams, toodle pip.' And with that he had taken himself off down the corridor, leaving her marooned in her room.

Milana sat on the bed and stared up at the ancestral face that peered palely back at her from the opposite wall. She pulled back the velvet coverlet to reveal sheets that had been delicately embroidered by local nuns. She smoothed her hand over their coolness. The oval mirror in the Victorian wardrobe caught her reflection. The dim light from the lamp on the bedside table glinted off the great bronze bedstead. It too caught her reflection but in miniature, distorting it to fit. The faint ticking of a clock on the chest of drawers marked the time.

There was a muffled knock and before she could answer she saw the bronze door handle turn slowly and the door creak open. Santiago stepped in and closed the door quickly behind him. She stared at the sudden materialisation of her hope. His black hair was longer. It fell in an unruly wave over his forehead and curled over the collar of his shirt. His unshaven angular jaw gave him a rugged manly strength now, while the sudden blueness of his eyes fixed on her, arresting and thrilling. His pale shirt was tucked into worn denim jeans and he wore scuffed leather moccasins. He stood there, without moving, his hand still resting on the door handle behind him, suppressing a smile.

Milana tucked her hands under her thighs self-consciously and whispered, 'It's not bugged, you know?'

He put his finger to his lips and pointed to under the bed and mouthed 'Matias.' And then she watched his face crease into teasing laughter at her horrified reaction.

She got up and walked over to him. Only the tell tale tension in his cheek muscles betrayed his anticipation. She spread her fingers on the cool of his shirt and immediately she felt them grasped in his warm hands. He kissed them.

'My God they're real. I've been living off my imagination for too many weeks!' He pulled her hands around him closing the gap between them.

'You're real.' He buried his face in her neck and the softness of her hair as he enfolded her in his arms so that her warmth penetrated through him. They stood like this in silence each feeling the breathing and the heart beat of the other as though verifying their existence. He lifted his head and touched her face, tracing its outlines as if to assure himself of her identity. His hand travelled over her skin quickening her blood, pulling her taut from within, lifting her stomach and firing desire. Then he kissed her. For whole minutes they remained fused in this interminable embrace, conversing in a language they had dreamt of for so long, barely needing to breathe.

When finally he pulled away and looked at her, she touched her face in an involuntary gesture as it tingled to the touch of the air.

'Too rough?' he questioned, passing his hand over his unshaven face.

'Who cares?' she grinned.

'Instantly remedied. Just wait a moment.'

But she pulled him back, 'Are you crazy, you can't leave me now,' she whispered, adding quickly, 'Matias may lure you away to have more pear liquers.'

He kissed her nose.

'I have to shave because if I don't by the time I'm finished with you you will be a dead giveaway when they see you tomorrow. Either that or you'll have to own up to obsessive compulsive disorder with the facial scrub.'

The minutes that passed served to heighten the anticipation but also allowed them both precious moments to savour it.

'Wow, you look younger suddenly.' She touched the smoothness of his face.

'Don't be fooled,' he said darkly and kissed her again as he did so he laced his fingers through hers and pressed her against the wall. But she moved him towards the bed, until he felt the edge of it against the back of his knees. Only then did he stop.

'No, wait,' he said, 'not like this.' Keeping her hand in his he switched off the light and led her to the window.

'Look.'

The moonlight bathed the rose garden in ethereal splendour turning the roses shades of phosphorescent white and silver. Milana glanced up at him and saw his eyes travel from the stars over her face.

'Let's go for a walk,' she said suddenly.

'My thoughts exactly.' And he unclipped the latch on the window and pulled it open.

'Step this way.' She laughed as he stood up on the sill and proffered a hand to her. The still summer air was warm and scented. They jumped down onto the veranda and hand in hand ran across the rose garden and onto the path beyond where no sleepless wandering eyes would detect them. The moon appeared from behind the house, a huge God-like eye lighting their way.

Together they began to climb the hill that Lisa had taken Milana up months before.

As the path steepened, Santiago stopped and turned to her.

He cupped her face in his hands and kissed her again, as though it were the only way he could express the wonder of the moment.

'Hospital was so cruel, all I wanted was to do this. All those conversations, with you so earnestly leaning towards me,' he laughed, 'I made love to you in my head while you talked, it didn't matter who else was there, I was always making love to you.'

'I know.' She laughed, feeling that fire spark through her again.

He pulled her on upwards, holding her hand all the way, stopping at intervals to kiss her and look at her and sweep the hair from her face. They climbed higher and higher, to where steps had been hewn roughly into the steepest part of the hill, just before it reached a plateau. And then suddenly they came upon it, shimmering in the moonlight; the beautiful folly, eight slender columns supporting the cupola of a perfect classic temple.

'What's this? Did you know it was here?' He stood transfixed by its perfect simplicity. Milana let go of his hand and moved towards it, weaving between the pillars, touching the cool stone until she came back to where he stood. His quizzical look made her stop with a gentle tilt of her head.

'I'm a little in awe of you,' he tapped her nose playfully, 'of us.' Their eyes rested on each other. 'More than I anticipated.'

'Is that good?' She raised a questioning eyebrow.

'You've been in all my dreams since I came out of that coma. Dreams that, well...' he laughed and looked up at the sky, 'let's just say I thought it would be hard for reality to compete with them, but now I see you,' he gave a knowing smile, 'I watched you over dinner, your gestures, your understanding of the nuances of every conversation, the way you tease them all so subtly, your gentle yet steely defiance Milana, it pulls at my heartstrings just as powerfully as your smile or the touch of your skin on mine.'

She put her hand over his lips and traced the outline of his mouth with her fingers. He opened his mouth and bit them gently.

'Do you think this can translate into the vernacular,' he said guardedly.

'Vernacular?'

'I mean the real, the everyday, or is it that we've lived it in our imagination for so long that we've projected every longing, every hope, every desire into each other.'

'You think we'll disappoint? she laughed, 'Don't think.' She felt the grip of his hand tighten on hers.

'Why don't you judge for yourself?' she whispered.

Milana led him to the patch of soft grass that grew in the shade of the folly and she pulled him down beside her.

'Make this real,' she said kneeling beside him. 'Our feelings about each other are floating in space, in our imagination, they're too big to contain like that. Bring them into focus, concentrate them into one act. Don't be afraid, I'm not.'

Santiago lay down on the grass and placed an arm behind his head.

'What could I possibly be afraid of?'

'Love?' She placed her hand on his chest and felt the pounding of his heart. It made her smile. 'Disappointment?' She lay her head beside his and whispered in his ear, 'Chasing away the illusion and holding onto real flesh and blood can be as scary as it is thrilling.'

He pulled her onto him suddenly.

'And where did you learn such experience, my girl?' he whispered,

She gave a little shrug, 'Books?' she suggested. 'Don't you want to make love to me?' she added playfully.

There was no holding back as he gripped her harder than before and kissed her in a way that was startling and breathtaking and overwhelmingly arousing. 'Don't ever doubt it,' he breathed, his hair falling over his forehead, but don't doubt either I can wait if you want me to. You don't have to give me anything you don't want to.'

She looked at him, his face bathed in moonlight, his mouth slightly open not quite smiling and she reached for his belt, and unbuckling it she pulled it off so he could read the nature of her resolve. She raised her arms then and pulled off her dress. He met her gaze with galvanising eyes. In one swift movement he shed his jeans and took her in his arms and she felt the confidence of his embrace. Slowly she undid the buttons of his shirt but before she could finish he had pulled it over his head and flung it to one side. She spread her hands on his chest feeling every ripple of his muscles as her hands travelled over his shoulders and down his arms and to his stomach and down further until she smiled as he drew breath.

'Are you sure?' he whispered to her as he gazed up at her silhouetted against the pale night sky feeling the softness of her hair all around him. Whereas before she had felt the fibres of her body drawn taut and played upon deliciously, now she experienced a stronger craving, frighteningly primitive in its hunger. Kneeling astride him she leant in and kissed him as though she were trying to reach some deeper place that she knew must exist.

His hands swept her hair of her face.

'Is it safe?' even the huskiness of his voice stirred her. She threw her head back.

'Is love ever safe.' She breathed the words as though they too were part of this strange wonderful new sensation she was experiencing.

'Then are you sure you want me like this? With all the risk?'

'You mean with all the possibility. Santiago, I want you and I want whatever this brings? I want no barriers.'

He lifted himself up then tightening his arms around her, feeling her locked around him as though it were the safest feeling he had ever known. He buried himself in the softness of her skin and the silk of her hair and the movement of her against him, surrendering to trust and the overwhelming feeling of belonging. And suddenly he was on top of her gathering her together with such a sure strength that she felt as though she were being knitted together and brought to life as energy and feeling. Then she gave a gasp and stopped and looked at him with large bewildered eyes. Her face in the moonlight appeared sublimely beautiful and more vulnerable than ever in the ethereal glow. She saw his look of love reading her, smiling, his mouth resting on hers as her breathing caught in shudders. Immersed in a sensation of plenitude he had never before imagined, he allowed himself to feel every quiver of her body giving her time, galvanising her from within.

He was gentle, surprising her to new sensations with the unhurried generosity of love, yet the intensity of his lovemaking transcended all her own imagined fantasies. When he stopped, she felt herself resonating to him, awed by the powerful spasms that shuddering through him had trembled through her too and still seemed to reverberate like echoes of fulfilment. He remained unmoving but for his breathing, staring down at the eyes that held him spellbound. A smile of arresting intensity creased his face as she raked her fingers through his hair pulling him closer, her mouth open with astonishment that their combined bodies could experience such a mind blowing consummation that left her overwhelmed and a tiny bit afraid.

He lay with her knowing that for the first time in his life his mind and body and soul had been pulled together into one integrated whole and nothing could ever take away the sense of completeness that seemed to be pulling him fibre by fibre, knitting him together, healing the past, redeeming every hurt. He knew that there was no lovemaking more complete, more spiritually all-encompassing than the one which, celebrating a far deeper love, carries with it the seed of hope for new life. He found himself moved beyond tears, beyond words, to a place where, for the first time, he knew peace.

They remained together on the cool grass resting in the extraordinary intimacy broached and the recognition of something greater than their individual selves.

After a while, held in his arms as she was, Milana smiled to herself.

'What's on your mind?' he whispered.

'We just made it real.'

She felt his arms tighten around her.

Milana drew him closer.

'Why did you hide from me, I never understood?' he ventured softly.

'To be a better painter?' she suggested, but her playful quip could not dispel the pang of concern that shot through her at keeping back truths.

'Liar,' he whispered back. 'Is this where Lisa conceived your mother?'

Milana looked up at him, surprised at his perception. That was a detail she had not divulged during their conversations at his bedside in New York.

'Well, it's a fairly obvious place now that I've been here,' he smiled mischievously. 'She must have told you who he was Milana, this mystery man, who became your mother's father.'

Milana paused weighing up all she had been told by Victor. Santiago felt her shiver and pulled her still closer. How could she tell him it was Carlos Hidalgo, his own father; that would mean explaining everything as Victor had had to explain it to her, and that would be to orphan him at the climax of their lovemaking. So she turned and kissed him.

'Do you know your own grandfather's name on your mother's side, and I mean your birth mother.'

'Touché! That was devious but clever.' He kissed her back and the question was laid to rest unanswered.

Milana knew that despite his mother's confession, that had served to heal and bring them closer, Santiago had chosen to draw a veil over its obvious implications; a veil as impenetrable as it was well guarded.

Later that night as they walked back together through the rose garden, Milana told him the harrowing story of the young Castello and Rosa, his lover. When they reached her window and they crept over the sill into the room, Milana opened the door to show him the name Rosa carved in the lintel above.

'They came to a rather inauspicious end,' said Santiago ushering her back into the bedroom. 'I'm not sure I like that story.' He flung himself down on the bed and spread his hands over the velvet bedspread that was half drawn. 'You don't think this is the same bed still.'

'Quite possibly' said Milana sitting close by. He pulled her down beside him and let his fingers lose themselves in the soft waves of her hair that fell over him.

'You see what happens if you deny love,' he smiled up at her, 'if Rosa hadn't been so frightened of all the gossip and had let him love her freely, they would have lived and filled this house with their love and their children.'

'Hey,' Milana cocked her head, 'are you implying I'm frightened of...'

'Marry me,' he said suddenly, defying her admonishing look. 'Marry me,' he laughed drawing her to him again with the strength of his love.

Chapter Nineteen

One year later

The May sunshine flooded through the ancient stain glass windows of the chapel. The pews were decorated with posies of white roses. On either side of the altar magnificent arrangements of white and yellow flowers cascaded over their marble stands. The church was full to overflowing with friends waiting in the warm sunshine for the bride. It was only a short walk from the big house, along the rhododendron drive, through the azaleas and past the ancient cemetery. Cotton wool clouds like flocks of celestial sheep grazed in the blue sky, playing hide and seek with the sun. The English countryside basked in the dappled light. Santiago stood at the front of the church, very dashing in his morning coat, his black hair striking amidst the pale pastels of the English springtime. He smiled at friends and bowed his acknowledgements, hands clasped firmly behind his back. Beside him Diego, tall and elegant, nervously adjusted his buttonhole before turning to his friend.

'Would you have imagined this in a million years?'

'No,' said Santiago giving him his familiar smile. 'Never.'

'Ready?' said Diego.

'Ready when you are.'

Santiago placed a reassuring hand on his friend's shoulder.

A hushed silence descended on the congregation as the priest appeared at the altar. The organist started to play and Santiago turned to watch the bride enter the church.

Dressed in cream silk with antique lace and the tiara that her grandmother had worn at her own wedding, Lizzy's smile radiated warmth and happiness as she walked down the aisle on the arm of her proud father. She threw Santiago a look of gratefulness that set his heart at peace.

While Lizzy and Diego stood side by side, Santiago's eyes remained for seconds longer on the girl in the cream dress that took her place in the front row. Never had he seen her more radiant or more lovely. His eyes could barely take her in, he needed not seconds but minutes, hours, days to drink in every nuance of her, her face, her hair, the angle of the cream hat that hid her perfect eyebrows, the dress that draped itself so simply and so elegantly over her slim figure. The joy of seeing her sent his heart racing. As he turned to face the altar a smile spread over his features to know that this girl could have such a profound effect on his whole being. As Lizzy and Diego pronounced their marriage vows, Santiago stepped forwards to hand over the wedding rings. While they placed them on each other's fingers and vowed to love and cherish each other until death did them part, he stole a look at Milana. At the very same moment, she glanced at him and smiled. A shiver went through him as he recognised again the feeling that she was somehow crucial to him.

A while later as Milana walked back to the house through the azaleas, surrounded by chatter and questions about Chile, she suddenly felt a hand in hers, pulling her away.

'I've thought of nothing but seeing you again,' Santiago whispered as he led her through a lavender path to a walled garden.

'You certainly know your way around here,' she gasped.

But she had no time to finish, his hands were on her face, his lips pressing down on hers. His kiss was cool like a summer drink. She looked into the startling blueness of his eyes and watched them close as he kissed her longer and deeper. Her arms went around his neck and up to his hair that fell over his forehead in its customary unruly waves. She brought her arms around under his morning coat and over the cool crisp shirt and felt his heart pounding. Then she pulled away from him and watched his smile crease his features as he waited for her, eyes still closed. 'Irrisistable man,' she growled, kissing him again. She wondered if she could ever believe her good fortune that the man before her, the handsome raven-haired god of her dreams, could love her as he did.

'Why wasn't it us?' he whispered urgently. 'Why can't it be us?' he kissed her again, taking her face in his hands once more and drawing her whole body towards him.

'It's not our time yet,' she whispered back.

'I don't know how much longer I can wait,' he sighed, his arms encircling her in an embrace that seemed to crush her right into him.

'You could marry me now and come to New York, I want you as you are, I've wanted you always just as you are.'

'But I want to be a companion to you long after you have given up kissing me.'

'Silly girl, I shall never stop kissing you,' he whispered as he kissed her again, holding her warm, flushed cheeks between both his hands. 'And your natural wisdom will be my truest companion to the grave. I want no more.'

'Then trust me on this,' she said earnestly.

Santiago took her hand, holding it tightly.

'Are you really sure about this? You're not doing this for some other reason? You haven't been talking to Grazia again have you? I'm afraid sometimes, that I'm too far away from you for too long, and people talk and give you the wrong ideas.'

'Oh they talk. But it's not their talk that's made me decide to get myself a proper education, and my English is so much better.'

'I know, I heard,' he kissed her nose playfully.

If I walk up the aisle with you Santiago…'

'No! Wrong word,' he raised his hand.

'When,' her smile dazzled, 'I walk up the aisle with you, there will be no doubt in anyone's mind of the nature of our love. My world and yours will stand together like the pillars of our temple on the hill, that will shelter us from any storm.'

'Your going to university won't make the blindest bit of

difference to our bloody storm shelter. You're a pillar of strength just as you are!' His hands clasped her to him and she felt their warmth, their longing setting her on fire as they moved on over the thin dress. Electricity seemed to flow up and down her spine and come to rest somewhere deep inside her where she ached for him. Milana breathed in deeply, a shiver passing through her. His eyes were on hers. The volume of things unsaid, lay caught in their heartbeat.

'Santiago, I'm barely twenty.'

'Ancient,' he sighed.

'If I married you now, your world and mine would doubt our love, and instead of our two worlds together creating a universe of love for us, they would rise against us and try to separate us just like hens peck each other to death when one dares step out of the pecking order. Believe me Santiago, we don't have to reach out and grab our love, it won't fade. It will grow stronger and we with it. Besides,' she added with sudden mischief, 'you said yourself you'd never painted better in your life.'

'Oh darling, all this two world stuff is poetic nonsense. We're just two people trying to muddle through life, other people don't matter. And of course I've never painted better. Damn it! It's where I channel all my passion. Those paintings are like love letters to you. They're so hot they should sear right through the eye of the viewer.' Then he added gently, 'Even so, I'd rather be with you and let the paintings simmer down.'

'Matias told me my paintings "reach out and grab", she whispered.

Santiago burst out laughing, 'Well I wish you would.'

'What?'

'Reach out and grab, my darling. And never let me go! Damn your blasted education and all those critical old bags back home. They can't touch us.'

'But they can. Believe me I know how destructive people can be. Besides I want to be educated; I want to be able to give back something to the world some day, and especially to our children.' Their look communicated the significance of this last.

Santiago held her head against his shoulder and stroked her hair, 'Oh God, I wish,' he whispered. Moments later he lifted her face to his; 'You are a tall order, Milana Romero, and I love you to bits. I just wish you didn't give so much weight to diplomas.'

'Qualifications are everything in life, if you don't have money and a name that is. I should know.'

'Your paintings are everything Milana. No one can ever take your talent away from you. They're all you need.'

'My five minutes of fame may pass.'

'Well it's lasted over a year already,' he said, kissing her shoulder, then her cheek then her forehead.

'You see Santiago, you are educated. It's all part of who you are. You take it for granted, but I never even finished school. All the reading in the world wouldn't get me a job without at least a school diploma.'

'Oh why can't I convince you that you are perfect as you are,' he hugged her and breathed in her fragrance through the softness of her hair.

'It's so easy, Milana, I have everything we'll ever need.'

'But I have to do this for me, I don't feel I'm complete yet.'

'Which bit is missing?' and he gave her a wry, teasing grin.

She let her head rest back on his shoulder.

'You know,' he touched her face with his fingers, 'your stubbornness and your strength is what I saw in you at fourteen. And I believed in you then. You demand of me the greatest challenge. You ask me to wait, while you turn yourself into an accomplished woman who will need nothing from me,' he paused. 'And the worst of it is I respect you for it more than you can imagine.'

'See,' she nudged him, 'I'm only being true to the me you love.'

Milana stood back from Santiago and faced him squarely. He looked more ravishing than ever. It almost took her breath away, but she was determined on this.

'When I marry you, Santiago Hidalgo, we'll be even. It will be because I can't live without your love. Just that. Not your security, your money, your class or anything else they might invent. I will be free, totally free, to marry you for love.'

'I just hope it doesn't take too long.' He drew her to him and kissed her and brought his hands very slowly and so gently and lightly over her body that they left a shiver of longing where they passed. They stopped on her flat stomach.

'This is where I ache for you, day in day out.'

She put her hands over his, pressing them so that his warmth spread through the dress into her.

'Will you be faithful to me? All those students drooling over you. Can you beat them all off? All of the time?' He eyed her dubiously, bringing his hands up to her face again.

She looked up at his teasing gaze.

'I'm serious though. I'll always come to you by surprise. You'll never know when I'm coming, and when you're done with this lark, I won't wait any longer.'

He kissed her again, long and lingeringly, as if he were committing every instant to memory.

'I also have to wait. It's just as hard on me,' she sighed.

'Hmm,' he said doubtfully. 'I think you're wrong there. You're not a man. You've got no idea what it takes to have to wait for you. It's torture. If I couldn't paint and put the force and energy of what I feel in those vivid strokes of the brush and find some relief I don't know what I'd do. Sometimes I think I can literally reach out and touch my soul, right there on canvas. Even when I think I can have nothing left to give to the canvas, I find there's always more.'

Milana had grown pensive, her mind suddenly drawn on a different tack, one that haunted her however much she tried to ignore it.

'The last time we saw each other, Santiago, you said, "I don't know who I am or where I come from. I don't even know what blood flows through my veins and I may never know," do you remember?'

'Yes. How could I forget?' He pulled his fingers through her hair, feeling its soft silkiness over his skin. 'But don't let's talk about it now, please,' he whispered close to her ear.

She turned her head to look at him, 'Santiago you can't just push it all away, not something so momentous. I mean to suddenly discover the mother you thought you had…'

'Milana, it's not who she is but what she did that I needed to lay to rest. I'm just grateful to have survived, and to have opened up a channel of truth amidst the mire of lies in my life. Let's leave it at that. It has been opened, and at the end of it, if I get there, it might hold answers to questions I don't even want to formulate yet.'

'But Santiago, don't you want to search, know more? You'll never feel complete if you don't…' her green eyes glinted with single minded resolve. But Santiago lifted a hand to stop her, and with a warm and loving smile he admonished her gently.

'That's quite a curse to lay on me.'

'I didn't mean…'

'I know, Milana, but don't make my misfortune your crusade,' he fixed on her with inscrutable intensity. 'That's not an easy journey to embark on. It'll be a lonely and frightening and no one, not even you, can come with me. Do you see that? And, whatever you say, there will be no guarantees at the end.'

Milana took his hand from where it rested on her and kissed it.

'I've been through enough darkness and sufficient revelations for one lifetime.' He brushed her cheek with his finger, very gently. 'Let me savour the open skies and breathe in fresh air, Milana. Don't ask me to look further into the shadowlands of my past. Please, not yet at least. For me it's enough that I'm alive and that I love.'

Milana rested against him. She wanted to confide the secret Victor had told her. And she wanted to tell him it was Carlos that Lisa had loved. Somehow it seemed important to share with him how all the random threads of her life had come together to make something so real and beautiful that she belonged to, that they belonged to, as though that might give him hope for himself. She wanted him to know there was a real story to his past – a secret love between a Harvard doctor and a european aristocrat – yet she recognised she had already invested it with romantic make-believe when the reality might be more sadness and loss he could not yet face. She knew he was asking her to trust his decision.

'You can understand, can't you Milana,' he said, perceiving the nature of her thoughts without knowing the content as he held her close, 'that the present is everything for me, the past doesn't matter, like water under the bridge.'

'You can't ignore your past, it will call to you until you answer,' she whispered.

'I know. But not now, Milana. I can't deal with that now, not yet.'

'But one day you will?'

'Yes, maybe. One day I will. But why does it matter so much to you?'

'Because my past haunted me, until I went out to meet it. Now I know who I am and what I must do and it makes me confident and sure and strong.'

He pulled her face toward him, 'Are you suggesting that I am not confident, sure and strong?' He picked her up in his arms and turned her round and round till, laughing, she begged to be put down.

'Don't doubt me, Milana. I'm stronger than you think. Trust me. We all have our different ways to grapple with life. Don't judge mine.'

For a moment he looked so solemn.

'I'm sorry,' she whispered, 'I had no right.'

'Hey let's not go that far. You have all kinds of rights over me and I concede them all to you. Life is so random,' he smiled down at her, 'it's those benign accidents of life that save one, like meeting you.' But Milana had watched too many sunsets and studied the patterns of nature too closely to believe in benign accidents. To her life wasn't random, it was part of a Creator's master plan.

'Milana, come!'

'Where to?' As he took her hand he picked up her hat from where it lay forgotten on the grass. Laughing, she let herself be pulled on faster through the rhododendrons until they reached a summer house in a clearing bordered by azaleas of every colour. The pretty pavilion was decorated inside like an Indian tent, swathed in fabric that flickered with the reflected light of tiny mirrors while cushions and rugs lay scattered about the floor. Santiago flung her hat on a wicker chest. Milana reached under his morning coat, lifted it off his shoulders and let it slip to the ground. She felt something in the pocket and glanced at him questioningly.

'My best man speech,' he grinned and shrugged.

'Oh,' she gasped, 'won't we be late?'

'Diego asked Lizzy to marry him, right here. He'll know where to find us when he needs us.' Then pulling her towards him, he added, 'Do you think I'm going to miss one second of closeness to you?' His eyes held hers relinquishing all thought of time or responsibility. She plunged her fingers through his hair and pulled his face close, memorising every detail.

'You draw me so perfectly from memory,' she sighed, thinking of the sketches she had seen in his apartment.

'So do you me,' he whispered back.

She still blushed thinking of the fiery canvases she'd painted in Alhue, 'I can only do it when I'm not thinking.'

'But that's so much better,' he said satisfied, a smile spreading over his face as he felt her lips on his forehead, on his eyes and then resting on his mouth for a moment longer than he could bear. He swept his arms around her and turned her so it was he who kissed her with a smouldering passion that at any minute might catch them both alight. Each dared the other closer to the fire, breathing each other in, as though it were essential to their very being, knowing that once the flames had taken they could not be put out.

Voices approached, chatter filled the air.

'Whoa,' Santiago pulled back suddenly. His smile, heightened by intense physical arousal, galvanised her towards him again. But this time he held her back, throwing his head back as he took deep breaths.

'Do you know what I'd be doing to you by now, if I hadn't practised self-control all my life.' She edged closer. 'Back off tigress,' he laughed, his eyes inflamed with desire, 'You've got no idea what I'm capable of.'

Milana laughed back her eyes sparkling.

Rolling away from her, he sat cross-legged watching her with fascination as the sound of chatter came closer. Strangers holding champagne glasses looked in, 'Oops sorry,' and stepped back out, giggling and laughing.

Santiago drew his fingers through his thick dark hair, 'That was a close shave,' his eyes danced over her. 'I have something for you, Milana' he paused, checking his pocket. 'I never gave you the glass I'd painted, that you found on the river, remember? You never asked for it again.'

'I didn't need it after I'd found you. I was going to give it to my mother, like a sort of amulet for hope.' She opened her arms to him.

Santiago stood up and tucked his shirt back into his trousers. Then he approached where she sat, her eyes riveted on him. Crouching down beside her, he placed a little velvet pouch in her hand.

'It's not a ring, Milana, I know that nothing so conventional would appeal to you.'

Tearing her eyes away from him, Milana carefully pulled open the pouch which was made of the finest, softest velvet, monogrammed in gold.

'Oh my!' she gasped, seeing the jewel that fell into her hand. Slowly, she turned it this way and that.

'I've never seen such a gem. Look,' she murmured rising to face the sun. 'It's iridescent like the wings of butterflies, it glows like fire, but in every colour. It's magnificent. What is it?' She looked over to where he stood watching her.

'It's a fire opal. Only the rarest kind show all the colours of the spectrum and that's the one I had to find. I was told Queen Victoria gave this one to her daughter as a symbol of hope, happiness and truth.' He came up behind her, 'You are all those things to me, Milana,' he said, circling her waist with his arms as she held the pendent up to catch the rays. Her head rested back against his shoulder, while she gazed entranced at the rainbow of fire and colour captured inside the smoothness of its surface.

'It's the most magical thing I've ever seen, Santiago. I don't deserve this treasure.'

'The Aztecs and the Mayans used it in mosaics, it's just an upgraded version of your fragments of glass from the riverbank,' he grinned as he thought of his first memory of her, by the water's edge. Turning her face towards him he looked at her with his eyes full of light and warmth; 'You're not the only one who found her treasures on the wasteland. Look what I found there,' and he drew his arms more tightly about her.

He took the pendant from her, astonished by its colour each time he gazed at it.

'If a mere stone can hold so much fire and colour, imagine what the human soul can hold,' he mused as he fastened the platinum clasp around her neck.

'What? What did you say?' She turned back to him, but he stroked her nose playfully,

'There's one more thing,' he whispered, 'in hospital you gave me back the Miraculous Medal I'd given you. Lisa told me that it was just like the one she gave Letty and that you never took it off in all the time we were apart. That's all the more reason for me to keep it now. Besides I need all the graces I can to survive while I'm away from you, Milana. But, I got you this one in Paris, from the actual convent in the Rue du Bac where the apparitions happened.'

He watched the emotions of memories re-lived cross her face like shadows on a landscape as she took the little gold medal from him and studied it front and back.

'This means so much to me, Santiago. I couldn't keep Mum's it felt wrong and I couldn't hold on to yours either. When you were dying it felt so wrong to hold onto it myself. I…'

'Now you have your own, on a bracelet so you can wear it always,' he said fastening it on her wrist. He lifted his eyes and found her watching him closely.

'You make it sound as though we're parting or something.'

'Aren't we, all too soon?'

'How could we? You have me in chains of gold and platinum,' she laughed.

He frowned suddenly.

'Chains?' He raised a quizzical eyebrow. 'Are you suggesting I clip your wings?'

'God no! How can you say that, Santiago? You give me wings.'

'To fly away from me perhaps.' He gave her a reflective smile. She shook her head. How could he ever understand, with his extraordinary success and the brilliant ideas he was constantly developing that it was she who was struggling to keep up, afraid that if she didn't she would remain grounded, unable to fly with him to the heights she could already perceive he was travelling to.

'Hey, don't be sad, not today of all days,' she cajoled, threading her fingers through his and frightened by the chill that came from nowhere like a sudden breeze. 'What about distance and the heart growing fonder and all that.' Milana drew him closer and pulled him down onto the cushions.

'Does your heart still need to grow fonder? Is that what…'

'Stop it.' She kissed him, her face radiant with warmth. 'My love surrounds you, can't you feel it,' she whispered as they lay together in each other's arms wondering at the vein of sorrow that seemed to suddenly pulse between them.

Mine runs deeper. His eyes fixed on the tented ceiling as he wrestled with the knowledge that all too soon he must leave, already gripped by the pain of parting, that threatened to spoil the short time they had together

'Come to Paris with me, Milana. I have to go back there first thing, tomorrow, but we could stay on there and have a week together.'

'Oh Santiago, how can I? I can't just mess up all the plans after all Lizzy's family has done for me.' She sensed his frustration closing in on them.

'You're always with me, in everything I do, even when I study, you're there,' she murmured softly.

'Unfortunately Milana, I need something more concrete than that.' He searched her face for some sign that she felt the same too.

'Then you are destined to set the world on fire,' she said playfully, as Matias used to joke that keeping them apart would inflame their creativity instead, but Santiago did not return her playfulness.

'Will we ever have enough time together?' he sighed, the urgency in his eyes, glazed fleetingly by hopelessness; a sadness she perceived in him that seemed to rise in unguarded moments from a darker place and went far deeper than he ever allowed himself to look, like a bottomless well, with no sense of belonging on which to rest at the end.

She touched his face with her hands.

'Hey, I'm here now, Santiago,' she whispered coaxing him back. 'We have now. Let's not go back yet.' She rested her lips on his as if trying to breathe light into the darkness. 'They can wait. The whole bloody world can wait. This moment is ours.'

He shook his head gently.

Afraid of his thoughts, she brought his face to look at her, her eyes fixed on his;

'Don't you see, Santiago, the language school, the studies – it's because I want to be on a level with you, or at least try. I never want to feel that I pull you back, because I can't speak the language or can't understand stuff. I want to be your partner and your best friend, not just your wife, one day.'

He reached out and touched her face and felt the softness of her skin and saw the purposeful determined brightness in her gaze. A wistful smile creased over his features.

Just love me, that's all – but he knew it was too much to ask.

She searched his eyes, their blueness all the more mesmerising for the circle of golden brown at the centre of them. Bewildered, she watched how they filled with tears she had never seen before, overflowing, streaking his beautiful face whilst his eyes made love to her more completely than touch could ever disclose.